LEGACY
OF THE
MOON

LEGACY
OF THE
MOON

JAMES HEBERGER

CEMETERY DANCE PUBLICATIONS

Baltimore
2024

Cemetery Dance Publications
132B Industry Lane, Unit #7
Forest Hill, MD 21050
www.cemeterydance.com

The characters and events in this book are fictitious.
Any similarity to real persons, living or dead, is coincidental and not intended by the authors.

Trade Paperback Edition

ISBN:
978-1-58767-996-4

Cover Artwork and Design © 2024 by Kealan Patrick Burke
Cover Layout/Interior Design © 2024 by Steven Pajak

Sara took another sip of wine, avoiding the single piece of paper she just set on the cushion next to her. She focused on the candle flame as she set the glass down, pulled her knees to her chest, and wrapped her arms around them. She couldn't allow herself to believe it. If she did, it was a tacit acknowledgement that it was real. Not just the letter, but *his* story as well. Both are impossible.

The more she thought about the entire day and everything that had transpired, the more confused she became. The next session with her patient would be telling and potentially life changing. Tomorrow was going to be one hell of a day.

1

EARLIER THAT DAY

"Again, I'm sorry for your loss. Emily was a fine, upstanding woman. I know this must be hard, especially with... you know."

"Yes, I know," Sara said.

Small towns.

The implication was clear. *Sara's mother was upstanding, unlike her daughter. Her adopted daughter.*

The manager of the America's Best Retirement Home was being as compassionate as expected for someone in her position. That didn't stop her from letting Sara know she was aware of her troubles at work.

Everyone in this town was. Someone committing suicide in that fashion, especially in a small community, was big news. People need someone to blame, and it was clear who the target was. The lawsuit, and the flamboyant attorney who brought it on behalf of the young man's family, didn't help Sara either.

"The staff has cleaned her room and boxed all her personal belongings for you. You will have until the end of the month to remove what you want, or it will be donated."

Sara signed the last form and pushed it across the glossy wooden counter. *Leslie,* according to her nametag, slapped paper with her palm to stop it from shooting onto the floor.

"Is there anything else you need from me?"

"I don't think so," Leslie said as she collected the paperwork, turned them vertical, and tapped them three times on the counter to get them *just right.* "Oh, there's one more thing."

She reached under the counter and grabbed a business card. The effort to make it look like she had trouble finding it didn't go unnoticed.

"Here it is. A lawyer was here yesterday. Asked if we'd give you this card. Said it was important. Hope it's not another lawsuit."

One thing was certain. This woman wholeheartedly hoped it was another lawsuit. The smirk and eyebrows were begging for a slap, but Sara kept her temper.

"Thanks. Or maybe they want to inquire why a healthy sixty-eight-year-old woman, without any known medical conditions, was killed by one of your staff," she said as she put the card in her purse.

"What? I-"

"Don't worry," Sara said, cutting her off. "It's just an accusation. Anyone can make one these days. You don't even need proof. Have a pleasant morning."

Sara walked out before more words were exchanged. The look on Leslie's face provided the smallest hint of pleasure. It was petty, but worth it.

Once Sara got inside her truck, she pulled the card out and looked at it closer. It was from a law firm Sara had never heard of, based out of Ashville.

I hope this isn't another lawsuit either.

Rather than speculate, Sara called the number.

"Hi, this is Sara, you left me a card at my mother's home?"

"Yes. My name is Jonathon Wilkens. My firm is handling Emily's estate."

"What estate? My mother didn't have any assets and she definitely didn't have a lawyer. She lived on Social Security, and between the two of us, we could barely afford the retirement home. This must be some mistake."

"I'm aware, but I assure you, this is no mistake. Emily did have assets, and you are the sole beneficiary. Sorry, but I don't have time to go into the details right now. You'll hear from us soon."

Before Sara could ask another question, he disconnected.

Weird.

2

Sara did her best to clear her mind for the moment, as she still had quite the day ahead of her. She was about to make some serious changes in her life, and soon.

She stopped for coffee before heading to the hospital. When she got to work, she parked, set the cup on the dash, and sat there for a minute. The steam from the coffee created condensation on the inside of the windshield, which she wiped away with her hand. This allowed her to see the sign with her name on it. The personal parking space she once took pride in now just irritated her.

Sara wiped her wet hand on her pants, put the truck in reverse, and began to move. After only a few inches, she stopped and slammed the shifter back into park.

Damn it.

If not for Nancy and her current patient Abigail, she may have never set foot back inside this small-town hospital again. She was leaving, but she couldn't leave like that. She took a deep breath, grabbed her coffee, and went in.

Every decision has consequences. *Going in* was no exception.

3

When Sara walked into the office, she could feel the eyes of her closest friend Nancy follow her in. Sara muttered something close to good morning and shuffled past her. Not to be rude but avoid the welling up of emotions.

"You okay?" Nancy asked as Sara walked past her.

"No, not really," Sara said, trying to avoid eye contact.

Sara bumped into the side of her desk in the cramped space and spilled hot coffee on herself.

"Shit!"

Sara shook the hot coffee from her hand as she dropped into her chair. In frustration, she threw the full coffee into the garbage can, sending little beads of hot liquid up from the small metal can.

Sara put her face in her hands as the silent sobs overtook her. Nancy rushed into her office and rubbed her back like a mother would. This only made it harder for Sara, causing the tears to fall faster.

"It's okay, dear, you let it out," the secretary said. "Don't keep the pain inside."

Sara did just that, and after a few minutes, she wiped her eyes and sat back in her chair.

"Sorry you had to see that," Sara said, grabbing a tissue and dabbing her eyes.

"Don't be silly," Nancy said, "You've had a hell of a week. I'm always here for you, you know that, right?"

That little comment sent a wave of guilt over Sara.

"About that. I may not be here for *you*. I know I told you I planned to make a life here, but…"

"You're leaving?" Nancy asked, leaning back abruptly. "When? Where?"

"I didn't want to say anything until I knew for sure, but after Emily passed, the lawsuit, and dealing with *him*, I just need to go. I'm a terrible friend, I know."

"Stop that. You caught me off guard, that's all. I honestly can't say I'm surprised. That no good son-of-a-possum made me want to quit more times than I can count."

"I can't work with him anymore, I just can't."

"I'm gonna miss you something fierce. Where you off to?"

"New York. I got an offer to join a private practice in Manhattan. I think it's what I need right now. Not to mention their offer was ridiculous."

Nancy nodded with a tight-lipped smile, patted Sara gently on the hand, and went back to work. Nothing else needed to be said. Not now anyways.

Sara turned on her computer, checked some emails, and prepared for the day.

"Any new arrivals?" Sara asked, just above a normal speaking voice.

"Just one."

"Anything out of the ordinary?"

"Well, I guess that depends," Nancy said, which was followed by an unintelligible murmur.

This comment shook Sara from her somber mood and piqued her interest. She walked back out into Nancy's area.

"Okay, what?"

Nancy gave a mock shrug of indifference, which Sara knew as a sign she was dying to tell her something. Sara didn't have to ask again before Nancy lowered her voice and leaned toward her in a conspiratorial fashion.

"Young man, twenties, I think," Nancy began. "The best part is, well, the second-best part, Dr. Kaufland tried talking to him when he came in but didn't get anywhere. A complete snub."

"You mean *he* failed? Oh, I wish I could've seen that. Of all days to be late."

"He didn't report it that way, though. He told me he checked on the patient, found him sleeping, and didn't talk to him. I know damn well he tried for over thirty minutes," Nancy said, grinning. "He said he had some other business to attend to and assigned him to you."

"What's the first best part then?"

Nancy motioned down the hall with her eyes.

"He's the talk of the nurse's station. Can't imagine why."

Sara grabbed her folder from her desk, and when she walked past Nancy again, she muttered, "Small towns."

"Franklin is a medium-size town!" Nancy yelled in mock anger as Sara walked away.

The doctor read the new patient's file as she made her way down the hall. When she arrived at her first stop, she put the file under Abigail's and made her way into the room. She could see the young woman sitting in her chair staring out the window. Sara was making quick progress with Abigail, even though she had only been in her care for a week. It was this development that almost kept Sara from leaving, but she knew there would always be patients in need. She couldn't get emotionally involved.

Sara knocked on the door and walked in. Like many patients in her position, Abigail startled easily. Sara made a point to knock lightly and enter slowly. She was a special case, and Sara loved working with her. Her father had her committed after a failed suicide attempt. Abigail's husband died in a car crash along with their two-year-old daughter Annabelle. Ever since their passing, she had developed psychological symptoms that were a cross between Alzheimer's and manic depression.

"Good morning, Abby. How are we this morning?" Sara asked.

"I haven't heard from my husband, and I'm getting worried. Has he arrived yet?" Abigail asked innocently.

"No," the doctor said as she sat next to Abigail.

"That's okay. I'm sure he'll get here soon. Annabelle has a birthday in a few days, and we need to make plans."

Abby directed her focus outside, where a bird was enjoying the bath in the courtyard.

"I lowered the dosage of the last medication, Abby, and I've added some newer vitamins. It may help with the dizziness you experienced last week. I also have a few more physical exercises for you to try if you're feeling up to it."

"Thank you, doctor. I feel good today. Be sure to tell my husband what room I'm in when he gets here, okay? He is very handsome; you can't miss him."

"I will, Abby. Let the nurse know if you need anything."

Abigail just smiled and nodded.

Sara left her room and made the short walk to the next room down the hall. Her attention was pulled to the sign next to the door.

The name plate read, *John Doe.*

4

The doctor looked through the little square window in the door, and she could only see the back of her patient's head as he lay in bed facing the wall.

You never knew what reaction you would get from a new arrival. Sara walked in slowly, went to the window, and opened the blinds. She made her way to the center of the room and sat down in one of the conversation chairs. Sara sat there in silence, waiting for a response. This was her first test.

The young man rolled over, squinting as his eyes adjusted to the invading light. With a slight sigh of annoyance, he sat up, put his feet on the floor, and focused on his guest. He sat still for a moment before brushing back his collar-length brown hair with his fingers to get a better look at his guest.

As the light reflected off the patient's eyes, the doctor couldn't help but stare at them. She had never seen such a unique shade of blue. *Or were they gray?*

Now I know why Nancy was being coy.

The young man got up, shuffled over to the vacant chair across from the doctor, and sat.

The stature and physical presence of this young man was undeniable. Even through the scrub pants and oversized white T-shirt he was wearing, she could tell he took care of himself. He was not the typical drug addict his file made him out to be.

They both studied each other for a good thirty seconds.

"Who are you?" he finally asked, bordering on the rude side.

"I'm Doctor Sara Richards."

"Are you the one in charge here?"

"Of your care and well-being, yes."

"Why am I here?" he said, taking in his surroundings.

The room was sterile, and aside from the light shade of turquoise paint on the walls and the small plastic plant in the corner, the room was lifeless. No pictures, no carpet, and the only pieces of furniture were the chairs and a bed.

"Didn't the other doctor explain that to you?" Sara asked, wondering if Dr. Kaufland made any real attempt to help this young man.

"Some guy came in here for a few minutes this morning. I thought he was the custodian."

Sara almost let out a laugh but held her composure.

The patient looked around the room as if evaluating everything for the first time.

"Oh, I see. You have me in the crazy house? This is obviously a misunderstanding. Can I get my clothes, so I can get out of here?"

Sara was observing the young man, trying to get an idea of what she was dealing with. She didn't see any obvious track marks on his arms, rotten teeth, or any other sign of the hopelessly addicted. She was serious about her treatment and made every attempt to leave no stone unturned.

"Do you know why you're here?" Sara asked.

"I'm guessing because I passed out before I made it inside the hospital. If you mean Crazyville, then no."

"What were you doing at the hospital?"

"Looking for a job, why?" he said as he crossed his arms and leaned back.

"What kind of job?"

"Anything that was available. I heard the hospital was hiring clerical and management positions, both of which I'm way overqualified for, but in this economy, a job is a job."

"What'd you do before?" Sara pressed.

"I was in the art business," he said without expounding on the answer.

"Like at a museum?"

The young man gave an irritated chuckle as he shook his head.

"No, not *like at a museum*," he said mockingly, as if her statement was insulting. "I was running the European division of one of the largest art dealers in the world. I was on a first-name basis with the presidents of both Christie's and Sotheby's of New York and London."

"Sounds like a very exciting and lucrative job. Why did you leave?"

"Long story."

The doctor thought she should get right to the heart of the issue with this patient. With the change in tone, she could tell beating around the bush wouldn't get her anywhere.

"Why didn't you speak with the other doctor that came to visit you?"

"I told you. He-"

"Yes. But why didn't you ask him what you asked me about getting out of here?" Sara interrupted. "You obviously heard him come in."

This hole in his story was obvious and needed addressing.

A smile creased the face of her new patient. It was thin, but visible.

"You're direct," he said with a knowing look. "I just didn't want to talk to him. I'm guessing you aren't fond of him either."

"Dr. Kaufland can be abrasive at times but..."

"I can tell he disgusts you. Why hide it?"

Either he was just taking a stab in the dark, or this young man had a knack for reading people. She thought it better to move on to another topic.

"Can you tell me what kind of drug or drugs you took just before you arrived at the hospital? This is for your own health and safety as some drugs do not mix."

"Why would you ask me that?" he said, offended by the accusation.

"The file says they found drug paraphernalia near your body. It also says you were uncooperative with the medical staff during the initial screening. This is not true?"

"Do I look like a drug addict?"

Again, a question to answer a question. Classic diversion.

"No, but-"

"Check my blood results. I'm sure that was the first thing they did when I got here."

"I will check them when they come in, but for now I will take you at your word."

Dr. Richards pondered the possibility that this was indeed a mistake, or rush to judgment. He sounded very confident in his delivery. Sara could tell when a patient asks you to check something if they are secretly hoping you don't. There is a completely different delivery.

"Okay, drugs aside, what about the note?"

"What note? Oh, you mean the *personal correspondence* I had on me?"

"Yes. There was a subtle indication you were thinking of taking your own life. Do you want to talk about it?"

"Did you read it?" Jack asked. Then he leaned forward a little, peering at the doctor. "No, you couldn't have."

How could he possibly know this?

"How do you know I haven't?"

"Had you read it, we would be having a completely different conversation."

"What kind of conversation would we be having?"

"Different from this one," he said with a raise of his eyebrows. "Much different."

He gave the doctor an inquisitive look as if trying to figure something out. It was the look you give a stranger when you think you may have seen that person before.

"Why is that?" she asked.

"What do I have to do to get out of here?"

Sara believed this disruption in thought was intentional and not by accident, as it might be with other patients in similar circumstances. She didn't confront him with it but made a mental note.

The more Sara thought about the letter, the more aggravated she became. Outwardly, she controlled her emotions, but inside she was fuming. The on-call social worker failed to make a copy of the supposed *suicide note*, which was protocol, before the police took it as evidence. She did not like having limited information when dealing with a patient. Not only is it bad practice, but it could inhibit the recovery time. Not to mention, if this was all just some weird coincidence and misunderstanding, she did not want to keep someone against their will without cause. Taking someone's freedom is a tremendous responsibility.

"Let me do my job. Once the police petition you, the law requires a seventy-two-hour evaluation," Sara said.

"Seventy-two hours? I'm not suicidal."

"I understand, and you make a persuasive case, but until I am thoroughly convinced you are not a danger to yourself, or others, I can't legally, or in good conscience, let you go. I'm asking for your patience here, please."

He stared at Sara, but there was no malice. He wasn't happy with the situation, but his face read compliance.

"I'm stuck here for three days?" he said as he leaned back in his chair, shaking his head ever so slightly.

"I'm sorry, but yes."

It relieved Sara to see his acceptance, which would make treatment much more possible, if in fact there was something that needed treating. She was still uncertain if this patient needed help, and if not, she would release him early. She would sit on that information for now.

"I think we need to start over. I'm here to help you, not judge you, but for me to do that, I need complete honesty and cooperation. I in turn promise not to lie to you."

"Will this get me outta here faster?"

"It will most certainly keep you from being detained further than necessary," the doctor said, trying to be reassuring without making false promises.

"What do you want to know?"

"Let's start easy. What's your name?"

"Jack."

"Nice to meet you, Jack...?" she pressed, with a slight nod of her head.

"Karness."

Now we're getting somewhere.

"If you do not want to talk about the most recent events, we could talk about whatever you want. I would like to hear about you. What's your story, Jack?"

She said this while giving Jack a reassuring smile to help him relax and open up.

Jack gave a half smile back and a quick snort of laughter.

"What's funny?"

Jack got up and walked to the window, leaving the doctor's question unanswered. He was looking outside, and something appeared to catch his eye. After a few minutes, the doctor broke the silence.

"What is it?"

"Blue jay," he said with a point of his finger. "They're beautiful, aren't they?"

The doctor got up, walked to the window, and stood next to Jack. She looked at the bird and then back to Jack, trying to get a read on him.

Is this young man in need of help, a victim of several unfortunate human errors, or is this something else?

Jack turned his attention to the doctor and gave her his undivided attention. Sara got a nervous feeling in her stomach.

"Do you really want to hear my story doctor, or did you just say that because your doctor manual tells you that if you can't get your patient to talk about their core problems, find some common ground, get them talking, then revisit the issues once you've gained their trust?"

Sara couldn't be sure what book he was referring to, but she was more than certain it was a direct quote from a psych book she read in college. This young man was clearly intelligent, and the usual tactics would be useless as he would see right through them.

"Yes, that's *shrink trick* number one. That doesn't mean I don't want to hear about you."

"I believe you do," Jack said, directing his attention back outside.

Sara waited for a minute or two for anything further, but he remained silent.

"Well?" she asked.

"I'm not sure if that would be a good idea."

That was a strange thing to say, but Sara let it go. She was off to a shaky start and felt like an idiot for her lack of facts to begin with. She knew she couldn't continue right now and get anywhere.

"Get some rest, Jack. I'll come back later, and maybe we can talk then."

Sara gave him a soft smile and then headed for the door. She was hoping for some sort of response, but Jack said nothing. He was very calm and collected for someone in his position.

Sara left the room and went back to her office. She dropped his file on her desk and sat down. After three seconds, she got back up and went out to Nancy's area.

Nancy was eating a donut when Sara sat down across from her. She sat in a swivel chair and moved back and forth like an impatient child fighting boredom.

"What do you think?" Nancy asked, as she chewed on a glazed chocolate.

"Not sure yet. He claims the drug paraphernalia wasn't his and he's not suicidal. Did his blood work make it over here yet?"

"It might've, but you know how long it can take to filter to our section. The data on the medical server doesn't network with our computers yet. Kaufland said he would take care of it, but you know," Nancy said.

"Yeah, he's an incompetent idiot," Sara said without missing a beat.

"What about the suicide note? I heard through the grapevine it was pretty clear what he was thinking."

"He's adamant there was no suicidal content at all, and there was a subtle implication he didn't even write it. Of course, I can't dispute any of it because I never received a copy of the goddamn thing. How is it that the attending psychiatrist does not get a piece of information like that?"

Nancy knew the question was rhetorical and didn't bother to respond.

"I really don't know if this is a huge mistake or not. He's far from the normal patient I'm used to dealing with," Sara said.

"No kidding," Nancy said with a quick whistle.

"You know what I mean, Jezebel."

Nancy giggled like a schoolgirl.

Sara got up and started walking away before stopping and turning around.

"Is the hospital hiring right now?" Sara asked.

"Yeah, a few office positions, I believe."

"Thanks."

Sara headed toward the medical wing and went into the social worker's office. Sara did not get sufficient answers to her questions and gave him a proper ear full.

After the brief conversation, Sara went back to her office. She would rely on her experience and interviewing skills to determine if Jack needed help. With liability these days, she had to be certain. Sending a suicidal subject back on the street without the proper due diligence was a certain lawsuit. As she was well aware.

Dr. Richards had no plans to release him just yet. She told herself it was for his safety, and that was true, but another side of her really wanted to know more about this person. She was about to learn far more than she ever expected, and not just about her patient.

5

I t had been over an hour before Sara returned to her interesting yet evasive patient. She gave a quick rap on the door and walked in.

She found him still standing, looking out the window right where she left him. The staring out the window part was normal, but his calmness wasn't. Pacing back and forth and other overt physical gestures were far more common.

"Hello," Sara said.

Jack didn't respond verbally, but he walked over to his chair and sat. She followed suit and sat across from him, feeling optimistic.

He no longer looked upset. He had a serene look about him and didn't appear the least bit agitated as he had before.

"Are you willing to have a conversation with me?" she asked.

"I've been contemplating that very question."

"And?"

When Jack hesitated, Sara continued.

"Listen Jack, I would like to talk to you, but if you're not up to it, that's okay. Keep in mind, not speaking to me could delay your release exponentially. Is that what you want, to be stuck in this room for days on end?" she said as she looked around, raising her arms, showcasing the miserable surroundings.

Jack looked Sara in the eyes, almost hypnotically, before he spoke.

"You got it all wrong, Doc. My reluctance to speak with you comes from a far different place than you might think. I'm not worried about my *feelings* or *well-being*; it's you I'm thinking about."

This was unexpected. Sara worried she may have missed something in the previous conversation. She leaned back with mild apprehension in her body language.

"What do you mean by that?"

Sara was showing no signs of fear, but the statement troubled her. She knew more than anyone that a patient's demeanor could change in a flash. If this patient became violent, she knew she would be in serious trouble.

"You've heard the phrase: *Some things can't be unseen*?"

"I have."

Jack leaned forward in his chair and spoke the next sentence very matter-of-factly.

"Some *stories* cannot be unheard."

"And yours is such a story?" Sara pressed.

"It is," he said as he took a more relaxed posture.

Sara relaxed some after his explanation. This statement also excited Sara for several reasons simultaneously. Maybe he needed help after all, and this wasn't a mistake. If there's one thing Sara loved, it's a challenge. This patient was far from the norm, and Sara relished the chance to explore him further. He displayed no common signs associated with such patients, which made him a special case. In short, he fascinated her.

"I've heard some horrific, terrifying, and disturbing things in the course of my work, Jack. I'm sure I will be okay to hear what you have to say."

"That's because you have no idea what I'm going to tell you. You're probably expecting some sob story about a terrible childhood, or something of the like. It's most definitely not one of those. You know what they say about truth and fiction."

"I do," the doctor said. "Is your story true?"

"It is, but I'm afraid you may not be so quick to agree," Jack said with a light shrug.

She would never let on, but Sara swelled with anticipation. He had almost convinced her that he was fine and should be released. Now, only a few hours later, he risked whatever progress he may have made. Whatever fantastic story he told could shatter her perception of him entirely and require him to stay for further treatment. So why say anything? He also seemed to be aware of their protocols, which only added to the mystery. Sara got into the field for this very reason. The chess game of it all.

"I don't know what you *think* you know about me, if anything at all, but I'm not your average psychiatrist. The reason I'm good at what I do is because I don't follow the strict guidelines of text and old-school philosophies," Sara said.

"You are anything but average," Jack said.

Sara knew she had a reputation, but the odds of this stranger knowing about it seemed unlikely. Jack's tone also implied it may be something else.

"What makes you say that?"

"I'm... insightful. If I decide to talk to you, would all this stay between us?"

"Of course, the doctor-"

"I know all about the confidential HIPPA laws," Jack said, cutting her off. "I just want to be sure you don't share our little adventure, even the smallest of details, with supervisors, other shrinks, or anyone else who may be confidentially exempt."

Smart indeed.

"You have my word, I promise," she said.

"Once we start this journey, there may be no turning back. Please take my warning seriously as this isn't some ploy storytellers use to raise anticipation and excitement. The risk may be real."

Sara hadn't had such a patient in some time. During her intern phase, she ran into a very convincing dual personality case that involved a murder and a kidnapping. This patient intrigued her even more. She wanted to hear about this young man in the worst way.

Sara leaned back in her chair, got comfortable, turned her hands upward, and then put them down in her lap. Her answer was simple.

Ready and waiting.

"Okay," Jack said. "I will try to keep things in order, but much of what I am going to tell you was told to me second or third-hand, as I was not there. If I seem to wander, be patient, pardon the pun, as I will get us to where we are going. I will make you a promise as well. You will not forget this day."

6

From my earliest memories, it had always been just me and my mom, Patricia. We lived in a middle-class suburb of Detroit for most of my younger years, and my mom had very little help in the way of family. No living grandparents that I was aware of, and my mom had no siblings. I didn't think this was odd until I discovered families were typically much larger.

She worked extremely hard and made countless sacrifices for me. One income and no help with childcare is a tall order for anyone, but she never complained. Things got a little easier for her when Helen came over from Belgium to live with us full-time. My mom told me she was a childhood friend who she had met while on vacation. Helen had always wanted to move to America, so my mom sponsored her.

Her coming to live with us worked out great for everyone. She was an extraordinary woman with a knowledge base that could rival a Harvard professor. I was still young, maybe eight or nine, and she impressed upon me that school was not a place to loathe as I had previously thought.

She specialized in art, and I soaked up everything she taught me. I fell in love with the masters of the Renaissance and even learned to appreciate some of the modern abstract works. If that wasn't enough, she also taught me to speak fluent French and German. She was an outstanding teacher, but she told me I had a knack for languages. It only took me a few years to grasp the bulk of both languages.

Helen passed away before I started high school, and it devastated my mom and me. We were told she died in a car crash the first time she went back home to visit. The details of the crash were sketchy at best, and we never heard exactly what happened. It was hard on my mom, and she never wanted to talk about it.

Shortly after Helen died, my mom met David. He was the perfect man for my mom, and he even treated me like his own son. It was great having that father figure in my life. It was something that I had always wanted.

They got married after a short courtship, and David moved us into an upscale neighborhood in the city of Plymouth. We had a nice house, I went to an excellent school, and for a short time, life was good. It took less than six months before David's true colors came out, and *out* they came.

The abuse started slow, of course, verbal at first, then mental, and before long it turned physical. David was a master manipulator and took advantage of every one of my insecurities and fears. He had groomed me to believe that every beating he gave me was because I deserved it. He was also very careful never to leave visible marks because he knew my mother would never stand for it.

David never abused my mother, it was just me. He was big and had the most intimidating look about him. To a young, skinny kid, he was absolutely frightening, especially when he was angry. He constantly used the threat of kicking me and my mother out on the street if I ever said anything. The last thing I wanted was to see my mom hurt or sad, so I did as I was told, and kept my mouth shut.

In hindsight, I should have told my mother right away, but you have to remember, I was a scared, naïve little kid. I had put up with the abuse for several years, and I believe I was at my breaking point. I was getting older and just about ready to call David's bluff when the weirdest thing happened. The abuse stopped. All of it. The taunting, threats, and especially the assaults, literally ceased overnight.

At the time, I didn't care how or why the change occurred, I was just glad it did. I figured he found God, became older and wiser, or had a near death experience. I didn't know it at the time, but one of my theories was spot on.

You could say the real beginning of my story started in college. They accepted me at Michigan's finest university, thanks to Helen, and the fact I had the proper genetics for memory and common sense. Please don't think of me as a braggart when I say I'm smart. I had been accepted to the top three Ivy League schools but chose to stay in Michigan. I guess I felt the need to be close to my mother, not because I was a momma's boy, though I'm sure I was, but I never fully trusted David.

Before the fall semester of my sophomore year, I felt the need to get out of the dorms. I looked at several rooms with no luck. It was one flop house after another, or far too expensive.

I was about to give up when I saw an ad in the college paper for a room to rent. It was close to campus, which usually meant it was expensive, but this one seemed reasonable.

When I got there, I thought I had the wrong place. The house wasn't small by any means, and given its location, a block from the downtown area, I knew it had to be a mistake. Ann Arbor is nothing if not rustic, and even the run-down, outdated, about-to-be-demolished houses were expensive.

I knocked several times before the door opened. As it did, the occupant stayed partially hidden behind the door. His apprehension and shyness were evident right away. He was about my age and wearing a Star Trek T-shirt that matched the color of his wavy red hair. His heavy-set frame and wire-rimmed glasses accentuated his shyness.

"I was wondering if the room was still available to rent?"

Though hesitant, he invited me in to look around. The place was even nicer on the inside. He had all the cool college amenities, such as an impressive stereo system, a big TV, and some gadgets I had never seen before. The most impressive part was how clean it was. It was not just tidy, but the bleach smelled clean. It looked professionally decorated, aside from the extensive collection of pop culture toys and figurines.

As we toured the house, I remembered where I knew him from. He was in my freshman Statistics class.

"Ted, right? We used to have class together every Wednesday."

He looked a little surprised but then nodded.

"Jack?"

"Yeah. Good memory."

"You helped me with a... situation, once."

Though I had a good memory as well, it wasn't until he said that that I remembered what he was referring to. He had spilled a bottle of water on his lap during class, and it looked like he had wet himself. I had a hooded sweatshirt on, took it off discreetly, and handed it to him. He wore it around his waist until he got home and brought it back the next class. That was the only time we ever spoke.

"Oh, yeah. It's funny, the same thing happened to me at the bar, but I actually did piss myself."

He let out a good laugh.

"You can move in right away. Start paying rent the month after next. Is that okay?" Ted said.

"Really?"

I was taken aback by his offer. Not only did it seem kneejerk, but it was over the top generous.

"Yeah, if you want too, if not I-"

"Deal," I said, cutting him off. "I'll start bringing my things over tomorrow."

As luck would have it, we hit it off right away. I couldn't believe my good fortune. Not only was my room immaculate, it had an attached bathroom. A college luxury few had. I found out much later that Ted came from a very influential and wealthy family. He didn't need to rent his spare room to anyone, as money was never an issue. I think he hoped to find a friend, and he did. My kind gesture went a long way with him, and he paid it back and then some. I was very fortunate.

I moved in the next day, and everything was going as planned. Over the next year, I couldn't have been happier. That was all about to change.

7

A month into my senior year. I invited my mom and David to dinner. Including David surprised my mom, and I think she appreciated it. Though I never told her about our past, she knew I didn't care for him. I made a special effort for my mother's sake and for no other reason.

Plymouth was only about a twenty-minute drive, and my mom needed little reason to come to Ann Arbor. She got to visit me and window shop, two of her favorite things to do, especially in the cool fall weather.

I left the house a little early and had some time to kill before heading to the restaurant. As I walked around daydreaming, I realized my mother's birthday was only a week away. Just as this thought hit me, I walked by a fine art shop called *Piece of History*. I remember it opening my freshman year but had never ventured inside. The store was intimidating as hell, as everything appeared to be very old, and in miraculous condition. Everyone knows that those two things equate to big money.

Now I know why I had never been inside.

I'd been working a part-time job since I arrived at school, but nothing that paid very well. If it wasn't for Ted's generosity, I would've been constantly broke. I cashed my work check earlier, and it was larger than usual because of several hours of overtime I had put in. My mom had sacrificed so much for me, and just once I wanted to get her something nice.

The aroma of fine leather, faint vanilla incense, and wood filled the air. The store even smelled expensive.

As I looked at the magnificent pieces of art, out of the corner of my eye, I saw someone walk out from the backroom.

"Good evening," the man said.

I think I surprised him as he had an odd look on his face. He must not have heard me come in.

"Hi," I said, glancing at him briefly as I looked around.

"Anything I can help you with?"

"I'm not sure. It's my mom's birthday soon, and I have no idea what to get her, but from the look of your store, I'm not sure I came to the right place."

The man stood silent for a few seconds and then stated without a hint of anger or agitation in his voice, "Because she hates art and antiquities, or because you think my inventory is inadequate?"

I realized he misunderstood, and my face flushed.

"No, no. Sorry. That came out wrong. Your pieces are beautiful, amazing actually. I just meant that I believe I'm very much out of my depth. I'm still a poor college student on the brink of financial collapse. The items in here are a little above and beyond if you know what I mean. My mother would love everything in here. I think she actually worked in a place like this once."

The shop owner gave a hint of a smile.

"No one's mother should go without because of money."

I was looking at a tiny lamp on an old oak end table when I saw the price tag hanging from the shade.

$495

"I'm afraid mine might, unless you're having a ninety percent off sale," I said as I looked up at a painting hanging above the end table.

"Boucher?" I said as I glanced over to the man.

"You know your art, my young friend. That was his end table your hand is resting on," he said as if it wasn't a big deal.

I jerked my right hand off the table quicker than if it had been a hot stove. Obvious embarrassment was written all over my face for such a careless act. I knew better.

"Sorry. This was Francois Boucher's table? The table he himself owned? I hate to ask how much that is."

"That one is a little pricey, yes."

The man motioned for me to follow him and then moved over to the glass case near the counter.

"I think we can find something in here that might suit your mother," he said as he unlocked the bottom portion of the case not visible to the public.

He opened the door and pulled out a slender shaped jewelry box and placed it on the counter in front of him.

I stepped up just as he opened it, displaying a beautiful bright silver charm, attached to a thin black leather rope. The craftsmanship was amazing. The entire size of the charm was that of a half dollar coin. I wasn't positive, but it looked to be made of white gold. The color just wasn't right for it to be silver.

Sir, this is extremely nice, and I know my mother would love it, but..."

The man cut me off.

"It's $185. It's been sitting here for months and I'm tired of looking at it."

I looked up from the necklace and straight into the man's eyes, really looking at him for the first time. I was trying to see if he was playing a joke on me. I knew antiques and had a fair knowledge of precious metals as well. It seemed too good to be true. I'm always leery of the *too good to be true*.

The man had an overall striking look about him. He looked to be in his mid-thirties but had a confidence and presence about him that made him appear older.

I looked back at the charm, which was a beautiful full moon with a long stem rose cutting through it diagonally.

"Sold," I said, trying to contain my excitement.

My mom was going to love it. She used to say there's magic in a full moon.

"Great. I can have it wrapped up for you if you like."

"That's okay. The box is fancy enough," I said.

The ornate wood box was layered with purple velvet on all sides and looked handcrafted.

I hadn't expected to spend that much, which now left me broke until payday, but I knew that piece was worth far more than he charged me. I put the box inside the inner pocket of my jacket as he handed me the receipt.

Before I walked out, I turned back toward the man.

"Thanks again, sir. I really appreciate the deal. It wasn't lost on me," I said sincerely.

The owner nodded once, making it almost a bow.

"I can see that. You're welcome young man. I hope your mother has a happy birthday."

Just before I got to the door, I stopped, distracted by another fine piece of furniture.

"Hepplewhite?"

"Indeed."

I thought he was going to say something else, but he remained silent.

I exited the store into the perfect fall evening. It was warm but cool when the breeze blew.

It was a short walk to the restaurant, and I couldn't wait to see my mom's face when I gave her the necklace. She was going to love it.

8

The restaurant was a nice little place not too far from Ann Arbor's city theater. It had that turn-of-the-century vibe to it, and my mom loved the seafood there.

I walked in and found my mom and David already seated near the fireplace. The hostess walked me to their table and when I approached, my mom's smile lit up the room.

"Hey," I said as I approached. "David," I added with a quick nod.

"How's my little goofball?" my mom asked.

"Your goofball is good."

I hugged her and kissed her on the cheek. She had been calling me that since I was an infant. She said I was always trying to make her laugh even before I could talk.

"You guys have a hard time finding a parking spot? The streets looked jammed. There must be a game tonight," I said as I sat down at the table and grabbed a menu.

"We should have met in Plymouth. We had to park on the third level of the parking structure," David said, shaking his head as he motioned for the server. "Next time, I'll make the reservations."

"Stop it, David. It's fine. I like to walk, you know that." She gave David *the look*.

"Sorry about that. If I knew it was going to be so busy..."

"Don't be silly. A little exercise won't kill your mother. Plus, it's beautiful outside."

I wanted to give my mom her present right away, but I thought it would be better to give it to her after dinner, right before we were about to leave. She was going to flip when she saw it.

"I cannot believe my baby is a senior in college," she said with a proud smile. "Any idea what you'll want to do when you graduate?"

"Since I'm majoring in Art History, I'm sure any number of coffee shops in the area would love to get their hands on me. I'm not just talking about the indie shops either. I think some big chains have been scouting me."

My mom laughed out loud, but David remained quiet and rolled his eyes. I could always make my mom laugh, but David was a tougher crowd. He shook his head and studied the menu in silence.

So much for cordial behavior. Bastard.

Mom gave me that sympathetic look and a soft smile I had seen so many times before.

"I'm starving; let's order," I said, trying to curb the awkward silence from David.

After dinner was over, we made our way to the front door when David stopped.

"Just one second. I need to use the restroom," David said as he headed to the rear of the restaurant and out of sight.

My mom and I were alone in the vestibule when I noticed her staring at me.

"Okay. What is it?" I asked.

The seriousness of my mother's face scared me.

"It's nothing, really."

"Are you sure? You have that look. I know that look."

She smiled and touched the side of my face.

"I'm just so proud of you."

"Thanks. You're sure nothing is wrong? You don't have cancer, or something?"

"Nope. Fit as a fiddle," she said.

She looked toward the back of the restaurant, then back to me.

"There is one thing I would like to talk to you about... alone. It's nothing to worry about, I assure you, just something I have been meaning to discuss with you for a while now."

"You're sure everything is fine, though?" I pressed.

"I'm sure. It's nothing like that," she said as she gave me a reassuring smile. "It's about your father."

"What?"

The comment caused me to lose my train of thought. She never brought up anything about my actual father before. She always changed the subject if I even came close to talking about him. I came to believe he was some asshole that left my mom after she got pregnant, and to spare her feelings, I left it alone.

"I've been struggling with this for a while, but now I think it's time we talked about him."

"When? Can I call you tomorrow?" I asked, hoping to get this information as soon as possible.

"I'll call you when David goes to work."

"Looking forward to it," I said, then I grabbed the box from my jacket pocket and pulled it out. "Happy almost birthday."

"Oh, Jack. You didn't have to get me anything," she said, smiling. She loved getting gifts and couldn't hide it.

I watched her face as she opened the box, expecting to see a huge smile, but I couldn't have been more wrong. Her face became solemn and confused.

"Where did you get this?"

Her tone wasn't angry, but it was borderline accusatory. It didn't make any sense.

"Don't you like it?" I asked, taken aback by her demeanor. "I'm sorry, I thought you-"

"No, honey. It's not that..."

She became distracted, looked around the room several times in quick succession, and put the box inside her jacket pocket as if hiding it.

"What is it, you're scaring me?"

"I'm sorry. It's nothing. We'll talk about it tomorrow as well. I'm-."

She was about to say something else when she looked over her shoulder and saw David returning from the restroom. She stopped herself and regained her composure.

"I'll call you tomorrow," she said again, but this time it was just above a whisper.

I knew my mother, and I could tell this was a big deal. Mentioning my real father was a bombshell, but the reaction to the necklace unnerved me.

She gave me a forced smile and long hug before we walked outside.

"Have a safe ride home," I said as I walked in the opposite direction.

I saw her look back one last time, but her face was unreadable. I shook it off as best I could, knowing that I would get the answers to my questions in the morning.

I went home to find an empty house and a note from Ted saying he would be at his parents' for the weekend. My mind was racing as I laid in bed. It took a full hour before I fell asleep.

The vibration of my phone, which I had on silent, woke me out of a dead sleep. I thought it was my mom calling me until I looked at the clock. It was only two-thirty in the morning.

What the hell?

I didn't recognize the number on the caller ID, but I answered anyway.

It was that phone call that changed me forever.

9

"Who was it?" Sara asked.

"It was the police. They called to tell me that my mother had been murdered," Jack said.

"I'm very sorry."

Sara figured this was the first breakthrough. Just getting a patient to talk about an event like this was a positive step toward recovery. The more she could get him to divulge, the better.

"Thank you."

"What happened next?"

"I was picked up by a patrol car and taken to the medical examiner's office to identify my mother; then I was taken to the station to talk about my whereabouts that night. I was cleared after the police were able to retrieve video footage of me walking by a gas station several blocks from the parking garage where they were murdered. They had footage of my mom and David entering the garage and a black van leaving in a hurry a few minutes later."

"So, David was killed as well?" the doctor asked.

"His body was never found. There was a large amount of blood in the driver's seat of the car, as well as the pavement just outside the door, leaving the authorities to believe he was a victim, and not the killer."

"I know this is hard to talk about, but how was your mother killed?"

Sara knew she may be pushing the boundaries, but it needed to be dealt with sooner or later. She watched Jack closely, taking note of any emotions, or lack thereof.

"Well, she didn't die from the several broken bones. I'm guessing those were more for torture than death. It was probably her missing throat that did it, though I'm not a doctor."

There may have been a small indication of sadness in Jack's eyes, but anger was the dominant emotion by far. When Sara saw Jack balling his right fist, she thought she better deescalate things.

"When did this happen?" the doctor asked.

"It's been a few years now," Jack said. "And I've come to terms with it."

"Did the police ever catch the killer?" she asked.

"No, they did not."

Sara gave pause at the way Jack used the word *they*.

"Would you mind if we took a quick break? I need to look in on my other patient and check to make sure we didn't get any new arrivals. Should be less than twenty minutes."

ONCE SARA GOT BACK to her desk, she got onto her computer and searched *Double Homicide in Ann Arbor, Michigan*.

It was the last entry on the fourth page, and she almost missed it. *Parking Structure Massacre* was the headline. Sara read the entire story, and from what she could tell, it was consistent with what Jack had told her. The story also described the horrific scene in detail. It was even worse than she imagined.

The article mentioned the surviving son as Jack, but no last name was listed. Just before Sara was about to exit the page, she noticed something else.

The date.

The murders occurred over twenty years ago.

He must have known I would check.

The doctor could tell from looking at Jack that he could only be in his mid-twenties. Late twenties would be a stretch.

It was not uncommon for her patients to tell lies during the evaluation period and even believe them sometimes. She couldn't explain why, but she didn't expect this behavior from Jack.

"How's it going with our new guest?" Nancy asked when Sara walked out of her office.

"He will not be a dull one, that's for sure," she said, not really looking at Nancy.

"I could have told you that, honey. Now that I think about it, I did tell you that."

Sara smiled. "You did. Any new arrivals?"

"Just a referral from the city. I think it's a work-related competency case. Dr. Kaufland said he would take care of it. I think there's some link to the mayor's office and he would hate to miss an opportunity to kiss his ass. Do you need anything, doctor?"

"No. I think I will give Jack a few more hours."

"Alright. Just holler if you need something."

Sara started walking away but stopped, turned around, and leaned closer to Nancy.

"Now that you mention it, could you do some online searching for me?"

"Sure. On what?"

"Try to find anything you can on Jack Karness, or any other Jack that looks like our patient. He grew up in suburban Detroit and went to the University of Michigan."

"You don't give a girl much to work with, but I'll let you know if I find anything," Nancy said.

Sara spoke with Abby for fifteen minutes or so before going back to her office.

As soon as Sara got there, Nancy was motioning Sara to her desk with an excited look on her face.

"Take a look."

Nancy laid some papers on the desk in front of Sara as she walked in. Nancy loved to help in some investigative manner and always got excited when she found something. Even though she knew she would never get the juicy details, she loved to be a part of it.

"This is everything I could find, which isn't much. Nothing with the last name of Karness, but I did find a Jack Thorn," Nancy said, almost dropping some papers as she spread them on the desk.

Sara rearranged them to suit her and looked them over. There were a few articles about Jack Thorn, but only one picture. A grainy unfocused one at that.

She picked up the picture and gave it a thorough look over. "Hmm. Hard to say. I guess it could be him, but the picture quality is terrible," Sara said.

"He wasn't in any of the yearbook photos either, but if that's him, he's one smart cookie. Finished top in his class. Though his degree was in art, he took his share of science and math classes and has a minor in both. Notice anything weird?" Nancy said.

"This article was printed almost twenty-two years ago. That would make Jack over forty. Does he look that old to you?" Sara said.

"You kidding? He looks like one of my grandchildren, but waaay better looking. Seriously, my grandkids are ugly. Maybe a relative or something?" Nancy said.

"Or he found someone with similar features to himself and is now trying to pass himself off as this Jack. Like I said, not dull."

"Anything else you want me to do, doctor?"

"No. Not right now. Thanks for the help."

Sara placed the new paperwork in Jack's file and sat at her desk for a few minutes, thinking.

Why the fiction? What does he hope to gain from it? He's obviously intelligent. Did he want me to find out, then call him on it?

When she made her way back to Jack's room, he was still in the conversation chair. She sat down across from him, trying to gauge him.

"Would you like to continue?" the doctor asked.

10

The streets of Ann Arbor were not so busy at night for a long time after that, but as time went on, everything went back to normal, as it always does.

The police never caught the murderer. It's not like in the movies where every bad guy gets arrested, and the survivors get closure. I was angry, depressed, and living in a fog for several months after that. I had never felt so empty. My mom was my rock, and someone had ripped her from my life. It was a dark time.

I went on to graduate, and it was one of the most bittersweet moments of my life. It's an odd feeling not having that home base you can always count on. It's like you're on a high wire without a net below. I think we all take our parents for granted, especially when we're young, believing they will always be with us. I guess that's like most things in life.

I was thankful I still had my room at Ted's house as he continued with his education. I knew I had at least another two years before being forced out into the real world. With very little money and a part-time job, I was in no position to make any life-changing moves. David apparently had so much debt, there was nothing left after everything was settled. If you have ever been that close to the bone, you know what a terrible feeling it is. When you have nobody but yourself to rely on, it puts things in a very different perspective.

After the craziness had settled down, I eventually adjusted to what had become my new normal. It was about this time that one short, strange encounter would mark the beginning of a series of events that would take me down the figurative rabbit hole.

11

One rainy afternoon, I went to a coffee shop downtown called The Art of Coffee. It had excellent coffee, great cappuccinos, and phenomenal art. It was my favorite of the dozens of coffee shops in the city.

When I walked in, I was glad to see it wasn't very busy. During the height of finals, there would be standing room only and getting a seat was like finding money.

"Hey, Jack, haven't seen you in a while," the girl behind the counter said.

Her name was Julie. She was cute, and I would usually try to make a little small talk, but I wasn't in the mood. I just wanted my coffee and a comfortable chair.

"Just been working a lot, you know how it is. Can I get a large dark roast please?" I said, trying my best to be polite.

"Sure," she said as she turned and got my order.

I grabbed my coffee from the counter and found one of the precious few comfortable chairs they had in the corner. There wasn't much I loved more on a rainy day than a super strong coffee and a good book, but I just couldn't get into it. I read a few pages before I set my book down on my lap and stared out the window at nothing. A weird feeling came over me and I looked over my shoulder. There was someone standing there, only a few feet from me.

She had light red hair pulled up in a ponytail, tight athletic clothing, and appeared to be in her late twenties. The look on her face matched that of her body language; unfriendly, bordering on hostile.

Her unspoken stare made me so uncomfortable that I had to say something.

"Can I help you with something?" I asked.

"No," she said curtly.

Her gaze turned into a more inquisitive look in a matter of seconds.

"Who are you?" she asked, as if I had just walked inside her house without permission.

"I'm Jack. Who are you?" I said, crossing my arms and leaning back in my chair.

I had a much shorter fuse post-murder, and I never cared for rudeness either.

She broke her gaze, turned on her heels, picked up her coffee, and walked out.

"What the hell was that?" I said out loud to no one in particular.

Julie gave me a terrible look. She must have assumed I insulted the redhead by the manner of our quick exchange and the way she walked out.

I turned to look back out the window, trying to make sense of this strange interaction. It was bizarre. I stewed over the whole situation for a few minutes before I decided to just go home.

When I stepped outside, I noticed the redhead on the other side of the street, about half a block up, standing under a canopy. She was facing the opposite direction talking on her cell phone. Before I took two steps, she turned to look in my direction. Though impossible, it almost appeared as if she heard me. I suddenly became aware of myself and tripped over my own feet. I caught myself just in time to prevent a headfirst nosedive, but the humiliation of it caused me to flush. I pulled my hood over my head in embarrassment, the rain being a convenient excuse, and turned down the nearest side street.

It was bad enough she was rude and unfriendly, but it made me angrier that I looked like an idiot in front of her. I know it doesn't make much sense, but that's how I felt.

Once out of sight, I felt the mild stress and anger dissipate. Was I blowing this whole thing out of proportion, or was it as weird as I thought? I shook it off and went home, thinking I would surely never see her again.

I walked into the house and saw Ted sitting at his desk doing some advanced mathematics. I'm smart, but Ted made me look like a child in comparison with anything math related.

"Thanks for the coffee. Set it on the table, I'll get it in a minute," Ted said with no trace of joviality in his delivery.

"You're welcome. It's urine flavor, your favorite," I countered. "Hey, what do you make of this? At the coffee shop, a gorgeous redhead approaches me, is rude as hell for no reason, and then leaves with no explanation. Thoughts?"

"What?" Ted said as he dropped his pencil and gave me his full attention. "Details, sir."

"She had to be a nut. It was the craziest couple of minutes."

As I explained the story, I started thinking about her eyes. I had never seen such a beautiful color before.

"Unfortunately, that's how God made the hot ones my friend. Just another way of letting all of us know we can't have everything. You want sane and well-adjusted, the library is your place."

"I do require mostly sane, but a normal librarian would be cool too."

"No argument here. I would be happy with a girl if she had all her own teeth," Ted said.

"Speaking of which, you want to head up to the Shillelagh tomorrow? I think some of the gang will be there."

The Broken Shillelagh was a favorite campus hangout. I hadn't been there in a long time, and having a few drinks with friends sounded like the perfect remedy for the blues.

"I don't know. Maybe," Ted said.

"Cyndi is going, and I am fairly certain she's single again."

It was no secret he had a crush on my friend Cyndi. She was the quirky, cool chic that everyone loved, especially Ted.

"Okay," he relented. "One beer."

Ted didn't get out much, and I believe I had only pried him out of the house, in a social context, a few times. Since the death of my mom, though, I think he attempted to become more adventurous.

"Great. It'll be fun, you'll see," I said.

I went into my bedroom to relax and get some rest. As I laid there, I couldn't stop thinking about the redhead. I don't know what bothered me more, being strangely and powerfully attracted to her, or that our brief interaction consumed my thoughts.

No doubt a girl that attractive is going to have an older, prominent boyfriend, who is probably super rich. Why did I even care if she was in a relationship? What the hell was all that staring about? I was minding my own business, wasn't I? I don't think I was rude, though she had no problem with rudeness. Forget about it, Jack. Just go to the library.

12

worked at the bookstore practically since I arrived at college. It was a good job with horrible pay, but I loved being around books and talking to people who also love books.

One afternoon, I was working the early shift, stocking the new arrivals, when my boss, Gus, asked if I would give the cashier a hand at the registers. The check-out lines could go from 0 to 100 in no time.

I walked behind the counter and gave the usual cattle call.

"I can help the next customer in line."

I was helping a nice elderly lady when I noticed a girl in line. She was about three or four customers back, and I couldn't be sure because of the distance, but she seemed to be staring at me. It wasn't the usual *please hurry up with your customer and get to me* kind of stare either. It was more like the crazy redhead but with less anger.

Her unique light brown eyes and high cheekbones made her pleasant to look at, but apparently her parents didn't tell her it was rude to stare.

When she made her way through the line, I got nervous that I might be the one to help her. It would have been awkward, but luckily, she ended up in Denise's line. She paid for her books, grabbed her bag, and walked right past me without a single glance in my direction.

My life has officially become weird.

"You know that girl, Jack?" Denise asked.

"No. Is it just me, or was she acting... strange?"

"That's putting it mildly. I thought there might be a few holes in ya after she left. Must be your cologne," Denise said with a wink.

Denise had no problem being inappropriate from time to time.

"We both know it's because of my nerdy good looks. Not to mention my apron goes perfect with my eyes."

Denise laughed, and we went back to the herd of customers. I rang up a few more people before getting back to my mindless book stocking.

My shift ended uneventfully, and I headed straight to the Shillelagh. I found my friends in one of the large circular booths. It was obvious they had a head start on the drinks, except for Ted, who still had on his jacket. The look he gave me when I got there was pure relief. I was his buffer, and he wasn't very comfortable with my other friends without me around. I couldn't blame him really; they could be a handful for the quiet and sober.

"Hey, everyone," I said as I jumped into the open seat next to Ted, pushing him closer to Cyndi.

"Glad you made it pal. Cyndi was just complaining that she was the only girl at the table," Ben said.

"What was that? It sounded like the chirp of a Benious Jackassious," I quipped.

My friend Ben was a character. If there was another person on this earth more assured of oneself, I've yet to meet that person. The unbelievable part was that he pulled it off without seeming like a total prick. Most times. He's genuinely a good guy, but you had to get past the somewhat rough exterior that rubbed some people the wrong way. I always thought he was funny as hell.

"Ben, you still planning to move to the Keys and live like Hemingway?" I teased.

"Right after I make my first million up here first. I can't move to paradise and live like you bums. Staying drunk twenty-four-seven takes cash. Dialysis isn't cheap."

Ben paused for a second and then changed the subject.

"Hey, is it true?"

"What's that?" I asked.

"Ted said some fiery redhead kicked your ass in a Starbucks the other day?"

Everyone at the table laughed.

Ted gave me a shrug as if to say, *sorry*.

"Wrong as usual. It was at The Art of Coffee," I said as I took a sip of the beer the server had just placed in front of me. I offered no further details, leaving everyone eager for more.

Cyndi was still laughing. "Stay away from redheads. They're all crazy, trust me."

"Spoken like a freshly dyed blond," Ben said.

"Easy hair club. I'm just enhancing the natural color of my hair which is still attached to my head."

We all cracked up. Ben couldn't deny quick humor, even at his own expense. He laughed harder than any of us.

"So, what happened? I gotta hear this," Ben pressed.

"I don't know. Just some wacko off her meds, I assume. There's no other explanation."

"She was hot though, eh?" he said with a sly grin.

"Gorgeous, I think he said," Ted added, happy to be part of the conversation.

"Hmm. Talk about a dilemma," Ben said.

"Could you be more shallow and stereotypical?" Cyndi said with a roll of the eyes. "Jack, you seeing anyone right now?"

"No. I'm having too much fun watching movies six days a week. I might be able to make a hole in my schedule. You know someone?" I said, trying not to sound too eager.

Cyndi had lots of friends, as she was by far the most outgoing and friendly. After my parents were killed, she tried setting me up a few times, but they were all disasters. My head wasn't in it, which made for lousy conversation and crappy dates. It surprised me she was willing to give me another shot.

"I might. I met a new girl in one of my classes. Attractive, smart, and seems nice enough. I'll call ya if we are all hanging out so you can *show up accidentally*," Cyndi said as she threw up the finger air quotes just in case I missed the obvious meaning.

"Please do. It wouldn't hurt to meet some new people, I guess. What's the worst that could happen?"

"She could knock your teeth out," Ben said, getting the reaction he wanted from the group.

Ted appeared to be enjoying the company and conversation, which furthered his confidence. He felt like a part of the group and not the focus of it. When you've been bullied, it's the little things that have the biggest impact. Cyndi even gave him a flirtatious smile here and there.

Ted got up to use the restroom that was behind our booth and down the hall. He was in his own little world, probably thinking about Cyndi, when he bumped into another patron. The guy was on the younger side but tall and muscular. The crew cut and tight college tank top screamed athlete.

"Dude!"

"Oh, I'm sorry, I didn't mean-" Ted said.

"Shut up, you fat bastard. They don't teach you assholes how to walk and look at the same time in your geek classes?"

Ted was about to apologize again, but the guy didn't allow him to say another word. He grabbed a beer from a nearby table, threw it in Ted's face, and then punched him in the head. Ted went down in a semi-conscious tumble, hitting his head on a high-top table as he fell. The guy must have thought he killed him because he ran out of the bar in a hurry.

I heard some commotion, and when I turned to see what was going on, I saw Ted on the floor in a terrible state. He stood up on unsteady feet and stumbled toward the front door.

"What the..." I said, as I ran to catch him before he left.

The rest of the group looked over the bench seat and saw me running toward the door.

"What the hell, buddy, are you okay?" I asked when I caught up to him outside.

"No. I just want to go home, is that okay, can I go home?" he pleaded.

"Of course. I'm coming with you. Hold on."

I ran back inside, left some money for the drinks, and told everyone that Ted wasn't feeling well. I thought it was better than telling everyone that my friend was a bloody mess, and I didn't know why.

Soon as we got home, I grabbed some paper towels and followed him to the bathroom to assess the damage.

"What happened?"

"I bumped into some goon, and apparently he didn't like my face. Or he was so jealous of my good looks that he felt the need to ugly me up."

"Next time, yell. Not that my skinny-ass would have been much help, but-"

"Ouch!" Ted said as he started wiping the blood from his head.

"You might need a few stitches, buddy. Your eye isn't too bad, but your head has a good size gash. You want me to call the police?"

"No. I feel like a big baby as it is. Sorry if I ruined your night out. I know it's been a while since you had some fun."

"You're not a baby and I had enough fun for one night. Another hour, and Ben would have been drunk and obnoxious. I think it was fortuitous you got your ass kicked when you did."

"Glad I could help," Ted said, wincing as I put pressure on the cut.

"Come on, quick trip to the emergency room. We'll be home before you know it," I said.

I took Ted to the E.R., where they patched him up in less than an hour. We took our time on the way back home, as he was in no condition to run or jog.

We were walking down Main when I noticed the antique store I went into last year to get my mother's gift. The window had a sign that read HELP WANTED. It was on the standard black and red sign, and someone had written in marker *experience a must*. If my childhood and college degree didn't make me qualified for such a job, I don't know what would. It was closed, but I made a mental note to come back.

I didn't know what a job at an art and antique store paid, but it couldn't be any less than my current salary. I remembered all the amazing pieces on display, and the owner seemed friendly, so I thought it was worth a try.

It was that one decision that may have altered the course of my entire life.

13

A few days had gone by before I went back to the art store. I was glad to see the sign still in the window. As soon as I cleared the door and my eyes adjusted to the lighting, I saw an employee standing behind the counter. It wasn't the man I had met before. It was a young woman, and she looked awfully familiar.

"Can I help you?" she asked as she was cleaning something from her hands with a rag.

"I saw your sign in the window the other day. Has the job been filled?"

"Is the sign still in the window?" she said.

"Um, yeah."

"Then no, it hasn't."

Great. Another smart-ass.

She threw the rag under the counter, grabbed a small bottle of hand lotion from behind her, and rubbed some on her hands as she spoke to me.

"Do you have any experience?"

"Well, not in the conventional sense. I've never worked in the business, but I think I'm more than competent in all things art-related. I even have a firm grasp of antiques as well. My-"

"The painting behind me," she said, cutting me off. "What can you tell me about it?"

It was a smaller painting, but the style was unmistakable.

"It's a Jackson Pollock," I said with a bit of a smug tone, knowing I was right.

She put her hand on her hip in such a disappointing way, I could feel her disdain.

"A first grader with a closed head injury could have told me that. What can *you* tell me about it?" she said as if I was wasting her precious time.

Feeling deflated, I thought for a second.

"Well, it's one of his earlier works. It has obvious Picasso influences, so it was before he went totally abstract. That would put it in the early 1940s, not long after studying under New York artist Thomas Benton. It's called *The Mask* if I am not mistaken."

She appeared to be thinking about what I said but seemed less agitated than before.

"Wait here."

She disappeared into the backroom, leaving me alone in front of the counter.

I had seen her at the bookstore just a few days ago. Why didn't she mention it? She had to have recognized me. She almost stared me to death.

She came back out and handed me a single sheet application and a pen.

"Have a seat and fill this out," she said in a business-like tone. She wasn't rude but she wasn't dripping with warmth and personality either.

I sat down and started filling out the paper. The girl took out her cell phone and walked into the back room with purpose. It only took me a few minutes to complete the simple one-page form, so after I finished, I got up and looked around. I waited a good five minutes before she came back and took the paper from me. She looked at the paper and then back to me.

"I'll give this to the owner," she said, making it clear the conversation was over.

"Okay. Thanks, Miss..."

"Bili."

"Thanks, Bili," I said.

I was about to leave, but the curiosity was more than I could stand.

"Didn't I see you the other day at the bookstore?"

"I don't recall. Thanks for applying. Someone will be in touch."

She turned her back on me and walked toward the back room again. I took the hint and left the store. A cold shoulder from a cute girl. What else was new?

It was nice out, so I sauntered over to the coffee shop to grab a cappuccino for the walk home.

I was lost in thought, wondering if I made a mistake applying for that job, when I grabbed the handle on the big wooden front door and pulled. The heavy door seemed extra light for some reason, and then I saw why.

As I pulled on the door, someone pushed on it at the same time.

"Oh shit," I said, as soon as I saw who it was.

The redhead.

A slight tremor of panic hit me. She stopped and so did I. The fraction of a second that neither of us moved and stared at one another seemed like an eternity. It was her that spoke first this time.

"It's you," she said.

Her smile caused me to pause, then stumble over my words.

"Uh, yeah, it's me."

I was unsure what direction this conversation was going to go. I wouldn't have been surprised if she punched me in the face.

"I owe you an apology. Jack, is it?"

"Yeah, but you don't really—"

"Please, of course I do. The last time I saw you, I was very rude. My morning started off horribly, I was in a terrible mood, and to make matters worse, I thought you were someone else. All of which is no excuse for my atrocious behavior. I was hoping I would run into you eventually, so I could say I was sorry. Now here you are."

She brought up her hand for me to shake, which I did instinctively. Seeing her smile changed everything. I looked at her in a completely different light.

"If it makes you feel better, apology accepted."

"It will. I'll sleep much better tonight now that I have this off my conscience," she said as she smiled and ever so gently brushed the hair out of her eyes.

She spoke in such a sophisticated and pleasant way I couldn't believe this was the same person. I couldn't find any words in that moment, and I just stared.

"Well, take care, Jack."

With that, the redhead gave me a quick apologetic smile and started walking.

"Whoa, wait. I didn't get your name." I said, not wanting her to leave.

She stopped and turned back to face me.

"How rude of me. You must see a pattern here. Don't worry, I'm probably only half as bad as I seem. My name is Viktoria, but everyone calls me Viki, or just Vik."

"I knew a Vic when I was a kid," I said.

"Girlfriend?" she asked.

"No. Neighborhood bully. *He* used to beat the hell out of me."

I got her to smile, which I took as a good sign. I was feeling bolder than usual, so I went for it.

"Are you in a hurry? I was just going to sit down and have a coffee. Care to join?" A slight fib, but it was all I could think of in that split second.

Viktoria was dressed in all black business attire, and I assumed she was on her way to work or something. I figured she would politely decline, which would have taken the pressure off.

"I have a few extra minutes. After you."

She opened the door for me, and we walked inside.

I couldn't believe she agreed, but I didn't let myself dwell on it too much, or I might have become overly nervous.

I grabbed a coffee, as she already had one, and we made our way to a table by the window. She sat first and I followed suit.

"You sure I'm not keeping you from anything important?" I asked.

"Nah, I have a flexible schedule."

"I'm guessing you're not a student. Did you go to U of M?"

"No. I went to the University of Pennsylvania. I graduated a few years back. Now I work for a financial company a few blocks from here."

"Impressive. The University of Pennsylvania is a great school. Did you know that it's one of the oldest colleges in the United States?"

"I think I may have heard that once or twice," she said, smiling.

"Of course, you did. You went there. Duh," I said, making fun of my own stupid question.

"What about you, Jack. You a Wolverine?" she said as she took a sip of coffee and sat back comfortably in her chair.

"Yeah. Graduated last year."

"Congrats. What field?"

"The most coveted of majors among the hip and homeless."

"Art History?" she said without missing a beat.

"Yep. Look out Wall Street. I gave myself a safety net, though. I dabbled a little in journalism just in case I want to write about life on the street."

"Smart," she said in a silent giggle. "I bet your parents are proud. U of M is tough to get into."

I never know what to say when the topic comes up. Do I go over the entire story? Do I lie and pretend they're alive so I don't make anyone uncomfortable? I just met this girl, and I didn't want to start off with a lie just in case I saw her again.

"They would have been. Well, my mom anyway, but they were killed last year. Please, please, don't feel bad. You didn't know," I said, trying to stop the guilt trip I most certainly just sent her on.

"I'm sorry."

"Thank you."

"Last year? It wasn't here in Ann Arbor, was it?"

I could tell she knew about it.

"Yeah."

"Parking structure?" she said with an oddly pleading look. It was as if *yes* was the last thing in the world she wanted to hear.

I just nodded. Being from the area there was no way she wouldn't have been aware of it, but her reaction was peculiar. She looked as though she was personally responsible.

"I'm so sorry, Jack. I feel like an idiot," she said as she looked toward her lap and then back to me.

"It's okay. Please, don't worry about it. There's no way you could have known. New topic. How about those Wolverines?" I said, giving her a reassuring smile.

"Football doesn't start for a few months," she said.

"I meant the women's field hockey team. They have an impressive starting line this year."

I made her laugh again, releasing some tension. I couldn't believe this was the same person I encountered the first time. She was utterly delightful.

"I'm almost afraid to ask but are your parents still around?"

"No, they both died a long time ago. I was very young, and frankly, I don't remember them very well. I don't even have a picture of them," she said.

"I'm sorry as well. Boy, what a depressing pair we make. We'd be a tremendous hit at dinner parties," I said.

Viki rolled her eyes playfully.

"Everyone would be in therapy within the first hour," she said.

Viktoria and I had a great talk for about thirty minutes, and I was surprised how smooth the conversation went. Her sense of humor was close to my own, and we picked up each other's sarcasm with ease. To me, there's no better sign you are compatible with someone.

Though everything was going great, I didn't want to be the guy who overstayed his welcome. If there are too many awkward silences or forced conversations, it would be a mood killer. I wanted to make sure this conversation, which was going far better than expected, ended before I ruined it.

"Thanks for the great talk, Viki, but I have to report to my meager underpaid job soon. Maybe I will run directly into you again sometime?"

"I could think of worse things," she said under her breath as she gathered up her things. I couldn't see her face when she said that, but it still shocked my system.

When a gorgeous woman drops a blatant innuendo like that, an outsider might see it right away. However, after the initial excitement, I decided it must have been an innocent remark with no sexual reference whatsoever.

I said goodbye and made sure I walked in the opposite direction from hers. Nothing worse than saying goodbye, only to step onto the street and walk awkwardly next to that person for three blocks.

Maybe she wasn't crazy after all.

I was feeling good about myself after I left, analyzing the hell out of the *I could think of worse things* comment, until I realized what an idiot I was. I never got her phone number. I was so worried about not looking stupid that I completely dropped the ball. What good was a great first meeting if there was no chance of a follow-up? Then doubt set in.

Maybe she wanted it that way. She never asked for mine.

Things happen for a reason, I told myself. It's always easier to blame fate when life doesn't go your way.

14

Later that week, when I was at work, I was restocking the cart of abandoned books, which was a tedious task but lately my favorite. It gave my mind all kinds of free time to daydream. Most of it revolved around a certain redhead.

I felt my phone vibrate in my front pocket, which snapped me out of my self-doubt and loathing exercise. It was a text with a return number I didn't recognize. It was local though, and my brain started its usual speculations. I called the number with hope.

The phone rang twice before a male answered the phone.

Damn.

"Piece of History, can I help you?"

"Hi, I just received a text from this number. My name is Jack."

"Yes. I'm looking at your application. Are you still interested in employment here?"

"Of course, yes, I am," I said.

"I was hoping you could come in for an interview," the man said in a pleasant voice.

"Absolutely I can. When is good for you, sir?"

"I'm here for the rest of the evening. Can you make it here before eight tonight?"

"Sure. I'm at work right now, but I won't have a problem getting off early. I could be there by 7:00 if that's okay?" I said, trying not to sound too excited.

"Very good. See you then."

I wasn't sure what a clerk in an art gallery made, but it had to be more than the 95 cents above minimum wage I was making at the bookstore. I finally felt like I was in a good place mentally, and now I wanted to be in a better place financially. Or at least a different place, as you never know where a new road may lead you. I needed to make some changes for the positive.

I walked over to Gus, who was doing some computer work at one of the terminals.

"Hey Gus. Do you mind if I skate out early tonight?" I asked.

"No problem, Jack. Hot date?" Gus said without looking up from his computer screen.

"You don't know how bad I wish that was true, but sadly it's just some personal matters."

I turned to leave when Gus stopped me.

"Oh, I forgot to tell you. Some girl was in here looking for you the other day," he said.

This grabbed my attention, and quickly.

"You get her name?" I asked. I think Gus could tell I was more than interested in this information.

"No. Denise is the one who talked to her, so I couldn't even tell you what she looked like. She'll have to fill you in."

I decided not to get my hopes up and be pleasantly surprised if it turned out to be *her*. The safer and more realistic assumption was that Cyndi came in looking to get a discount on some books.

The Piece of History was only about four or five blocks from the bookstore. Since Gus let me go early, I had enough time to run home and put on something more *interview* appropriate.

When I arrived at the store, I saw the same man who sold me the necklace for my mom. He was assisting a customer, a very wealthy-looking one at that, who appeared to be buying the Pollock Bili had quizzed me on.

He saw me standing off to the side and gestured to the back room with a quick tilt of his head. I picked up his meaning and made my way to the rear of the store.

I went through the ornate swinging wooden doors just to the side of the front counter. I was surprised at the size of the storage area and the amount of inventory he had. Among the beautiful pieces and stacked boxes, there was an office setting with no walls.

It was complete with a desk, an expensive-looking leather chair, and a bookshelf that was stocked with a very nice collection. I couldn't tell if they were for his personal reading or inventory. Regardless, they were impressive. I sat down in one of the smaller chairs that was in front of the desk.

"Sorry to keep you waiting," the man said as he walked in.

"No problem, sir," I said as I attempted to stand.

"Please, stay seated," he said, patting my shoulder as he walked by, reaffirming I shouldn't get up. He sat down and gave me a serious look.

"Jack, I will cut to the chase. I'm not looking for some mindless clerk to punch keys on the cash register for eight hours. I want a motivated employee with the knowledge and skills to run this business with little or no supervision."

He impressed me with the way he carried himself and his directness. There was an aura of confidence that permeated from this man. I liked him right away.

"We do much more here than just sell from the storefront. We have online sales, overseas contacts, and suppliers, and we have sold pieces to almost every country in the modern world. If you have half the knowledge I believe you have regarding art and antiques, I think you may be the person I've been looking for. Do you think I've overestimated my opinion of you?"

"No, sir. If there is one thing I'm confident in, it would be art. But as you can see from my application, I don't have any actual business experience. I just graduated college and have only worked part-time jobs."

"Yes, and you haven't picked up any bad habits, or think your way is better than ours. I believe you would be a perfect fit here. If you are interested in the job, I can start you out with a salary of $50,000 a year. That's until you complete your training, of course, and then we'll move you up to an appropriate salary. What do you say?"

50K a year?!

That was far more than I would have ever expected, let alone the possibility of raises. I tried to act cool, but I'm sure he could see through the facade.

"Yes. I would love the opportunity. Thank you..." I started to say, realizing that I didn't even know his name.

"Call me Theo. Welcome to our little family, Jack."

He stuck out his hand, and I gave him a firm handshake.

"Thank you, Theo."

"I know you would like to give your current job some notice, but I would like you to start as soon as possible."

"Yes, of course. That won't be a problem. I'll put my notice in right away."

"We open at ten in the morning. If I'm not here, Bili will help you get your feet wet," Theo said. "You will work with her most days, and she will handle the bulk of your training."

Miss personality. Great.

"Thanks again," I said as I left his office and made my way back to the front of the store.

I did a double fist pump and yelled a silent *Yes* as I walked toward the front door. That's when I noticed Bili polishing one of the tables just off to the side. She looked up for a second and then went right back to what she was doing. I tried to act as though she didn't see me acting like a fool, which I know she did.

I'm an idiot.

I left the store feeling like a million bucks. I couldn't believe my good fortune. I was hoping for a few dollars more an hour from my current job, but I would start out at more than double my current pay.

I couldn't help but feel proud of myself. David told me regularly that I wasn't worth a shit and wouldn't amount to anything. I didn't want to speak, or think, ill of the dead, but I could make an exception for David.

It had been a long time, but I was optimistically looking forward to the future and what it held. What the future actually held was so far beyond my wildest dreams, I hesitate to talk about it, even with you.

15

"What do you mean, *even with me*?" Sara said.

"I mean with a psychiatrist."

Sara stared at him, her eyes squinting as she cocked her head a little.

"Really?"

She knew a lie when she heard one, and this one involved her. She needed to see his response to her question, so she pressed him a little harder. This one detail could be important as it related to his treatment.

"Impressive doctor," Jack said. "Very intuitive. Have you always been like that?"

"What, able to read people? It's a necessary component of my job."

"I can see where that would be very advantageous. I'm sure you get lied too regularly. Some intentionally, some unintentionally, am I right?"

"That's true. Would you say that you fit into one of those categories?" Sara asked.

"No, I wouldn't. That being said, there may be one small exception."

"Which?"

"Patience, Doc. We're getting there."

16

Bili walked into the back room and sat in front of Theo. He was still sitting at his desk, deep in thought.

"Do you think this is a good idea? I know you are always twelve steps ahead but this..." she said.

"I believe him coming in here was serendipitous for several reasons. I know you may be questioning my motives, but things have changed, and this may be to our benefit," he said as he clasped his hands together and put his elbows on the desk.

The look on Theo's face concerned her.

"What's happened?"

"His existence has been made known."

"What?" Bili said, sitting up rigidly. "How?"

"I don't know, but it's just a matter of time now. Things are already happening," Theo said as he gave Bili a look that spoke a thousand words and she read every one.

"What are we going to do? Leave?"

"No. That would only delay the inevitable, and we wouldn't have the advantage of home ground. Besides, we would have to take him with us, or he would be in even more danger. We're left with few choices."

"You think he'll cause a shit storm?"

"If word gets out, which I'm sure it will, there are several individuals that might be an issue. So, yeah. A storm is coming."

"What can I do?"

"I know we can't watch him twenty-four-seven, but we have to do what we can. I don't believe any specifics about him are out, but those holes may not take long to fill in."

Bili just nodded. It had been a long time since she had seen Theo look this worried, and the last thing she wanted was to let him down. She owed him more than she could ever repay, but she would never stop trying.

"The problem is that he's different and conspicuous," Theo said.

"That's an understatement," Bili said. "I noticed him from over thirty feet at the bookstore."

"You be careful, Bilinda. You see or feel anything out of the ordinary, note it and let me know. Don't do anything rash," Theo said as he held her gaze to emphasize his point.

"Understood."

She never ran from a fight. Her only concern was failing Theo or letting him down. She would do whatever it took to protect Theo and anyone he held dear. Bili knew Theo better than anyone, but there was one small secret even she didn't know.

17

The next morning, while I got ready for work, there was a knock at the front door. I opened it, found a small package on the doormat, and saw a delivery truck pulling away.

I looked at the label on the package and noticed it had no *return* address, which I found odd.

I took the box to my room and opened it. I removed the packing paper and found only one thing inside. It was the necklace I bought for my mom that terrible night. I couldn't explain why, but the small piece of jewelry comforted me, especially when I held it in my hand, but it did. It made me feel as if part of my mom was still with me. Even though she never wore it, her reaction to it made it clear that it had some meaning to her. I hoped one day I would learn why.

"Hey, Jack," I heard Ted say from outside my bedroom door, which snapped me out of the dreamlike state.

"Come on in, buddy," I said, putting the pendant on my dresser.

Ted came in sheepishly, and I could tell right off he wanted to talk about something.

"New job today, eh?"

"Yeah, I'm kinda nervous. Does it show?"

"Yes, totally," he said with his usual dry sense of humor. "Should be right in your wheelhouse, though."

He paused briefly, then continued.

"Are you moving out?"

He asked this with a subtle sadness that moved me. I had told him I would be making a good wage, and I guess he thought I would want my own place. Though he was coming out of his shell a little more each year, he was still an introvert. I'm sure he felt if I left, it would be the end of our friendship. He was wrong.

"No plans to go anywhere, buddy. I love this place. I may never leave. Don't be afraid to raise my rent, though. You've carried me long enough," I said sincerely.

"Nah, I don't like change, you know that."

I finished buttoning my shirt and turned to face him.

"Think I'm overdressed for my first day?" I asked.

He looked me over for a second and then gave a light shrug.

"Do you sell gravestones there?" he asked, making fun of my all-black attire.

"Funny, but point taken," I said.

I changed my shirt, grabbed my keys, and then hurried out the door.

I showed up to work thirty minutes early, hoping to make a good impression on my first day. I found the doors locked and all the lights out. Since I walked to work, I just stood outside the front doors like a vagrant and waited. At 9:57, I heard the heavy lock opening behind me. Bili pushed the door open and held it without as much as a *good morning*.

The store was still dark, other than a few emergency lights. As we made our way to the rear of the store, Bili turned on several antique lamps in different areas, giving it a nice ambient light. When she hit the switches to the overhead lights, the room came to life.

I still couldn't believe the art Theo had in his store. He had at least one piece from most of the top masters, and a few worth millions. It didn't make sense for such a small art dealer. Or so I thought.

"I assume you know how to use a computer," Bili said.

It didn't come out as a question, but I answered anyway, not wanting to be rude.

She walked to the back, and I followed. Behind Theo's desk area was another small workstation among the inventory and storage. Two desks faced each other like something you would see in an old detective show. I imagined it was to take advantage of limited space, most of which we used for storage.

The desks were very nice. One of them had an enormous amount of paperwork, files, and office supplies, while the other was a clean slate.

"I guess this is my desk?"

"Theo was right. You are smart," Bili said as she stared at me for a second. I couldn't tell if she was serious or being a smart ass.

"Thanks, I like to think so."

"So do sloths."

That answers that.

"On your computer, you'll see several programs have already been installed. You will also see a contact list in there as well. Each person on that list has a personal bio attached to it. Study them and know them. Do you have a phone?"

"I do."

I proudly pulled out the phone from my pocket that I had bought recently.

"Ah, that's a nice one. Now, throw it in the trash or save it for a paper weight. Open the top drawer of your desk. In there, you'll find a proper phone. It also has the contact list already installed which will make your life much easier. We will pay the bill, so take your other phone back and cancel whatever plan you have. If there's a cancelation fee, we'll pay it."

"Thanks Bili," I said with sincerity.

The simple gesture made Bili pause. Later, I would understand why some small acts of kindness made her uncomfortable.

"It will be me and you working out of this store most of the time. Theo will drop by here and there, but he mostly works from home dealing with the overseas clients and the larger auction houses. We have pieces being sold at Sotheby's and Christie's regularly, and that keeps him busy."

I couldn't help but be impressed. The two biggest auction houses in New York only dealt with the best of the best.

My lack of experience made me feel self-conscious and out of my depth. As if on cue and reading my mind, Bili responded.

"Feel like going back to the bookstore and helping grandma find a cookbook?"

"I'm good. I can handle this."

I wasn't sure if I was lying or not. Time would tell.

"Alright, let's get to it," she said.

We went over every facet of the store's operations, while simultaneously assisting the walk-in customers. I couldn't believe what the business turned over in merchandise and profit. Just from what I learned my first day, the store alone had to be bringing in a small fortune. No wonder Theo could offer me such a great salary.

I learned a good deal about the art of selling from Bili as well. Watching her assist the walk-in customers showed a side of her I had never seen. She was a completely different person. The wise-ass I had come to appreciate vanished, and all that remained was a consummate professional. She worked with each customer differently and customized her sales techniques to that person. She could read them like a book, and they responded. Customers, who only came in to browse, would buy pieces they didn't even know they wanted. I knew I would learn a lot from this girl.

A FEW WEEKS had gone by, and one night, when we closed the store, I thought I would do something nice.

"Do you live around here, Bili? I could walk you home if you wanted?"

I felt like we were getting along well enough and thought it might be a nice gesture. I wasn't looking to pursue anything romantic, I just figured some after-work conversation would go a long way in getting to know each other better.

"I live in a condo three blocks from here. I'm sure I'll make it home without getting raped, but thanks," she said with the customary stone face.

So much for chipping away at ice.

"Okay then. Good night," I said.

I figured she had to soften up, eventually. I hoped for sooner but later seemed the better bet.

I walked over to the Art of Coffee for a late cappuccino. I was more than wishing to run into a certain redhead as well. No such luck. I decided to get a coffee and sit down inside anyway. While I sat there, something came to mind I was curious about. I googled *dumbest animal in the world*, and I wasn't surprised at the answer. *Sloth.*

Figures.

18

Another few weeks of work training had gone by, and I was getting in the swing of things. I enjoyed myself at the store, as well as watching my bank account grow at a steady rate. I know money isn't everything, but it sure can take away a few stressors here and there. Bili even showed signs of kindness as well. In small doses, of course, but I was happy for any improvement.

It was a quiet day in the store, and I was doing some research on the Asian art market while Bili worked the front. She was on the phone when I heard her say she was on her way.

"I need to run an errand. Think you can handle the floor while I'm gone?" she said.

"No problem. I will have it mopped and cleaned before you get back," I said as if I was completely serious.

She stared at me with a tilted head and her usual scowl. I knew this look perfectly.

"Relax. Joking. Yes, I can handle the customers and the phone at the same time. I'm even chewing gum."

I think she smiled but really it could've been a twitch.

"If someone comes in and wants to buy something you're not familiar with, call me. If you have any other questions, immediately lock the doors, go back to the bookstore, and beg for your old job back."

"Thanks. I can handle it. Get outta here."

"We'll see. And you better not be chewing gum, or you're fired," she said before leaving out the back door.

It stayed slow for the next couple hours. I was in the back room getting some cleaning supplies when I heard the front door chime. I made my way out to the front with haste. If it was Bili or Theo, I didn't want them to think I was screwing around in the back. Leaving the front area unattended for more than a few minutes was a no-no. Though most of the high-dollar items were closer to the back, there were still a few pieces near the door worth quite a bit.

I rushed through the swinging doors and stopped in my tracks. It wasn't Bili or Theo.

"Hey. Hi. What are you doing here?" I said, stunned. I was using every ounce of inner strength to remain calm.

"I came to see you," Viki said.

"How did you know I worked here?"

"The short answer is your roommate told me. I hope that's okay."

I couldn't wait to get home and kiss Ted on the forehead. The next question that popped into my mind was how she found out where I lived. I thought I would sit on that one.

"Of course. Now that you have successfully stalked your prey, what can I do for you? You need an end table or a Picasso?" I said, trying to act as casual as I could.

Viki laughed. Her smile was a joy to see.

"I was hoping I could take my homeless friend out for dinner tonight. Or does he have a reservation at the local soup kitchen?"

"He does not, and he would like that very much, as long as he doesn't have to refer to himself in the third person all night? Unless of course we are going to Cafe Tre' on Third Street."

Another smile and a laugh. Pure sunshine.

"Tell me there's no such place." she said with a straight face.

"No, but I think I've just found a way to make a fortune."

"No, you didn't. As your business adviser, I recommend you erase the idea from your mind immediately."

The ease of our conversations and the way she made me feel comfortable in my own skin was nothing short of miraculous. She was so far out of my league that it made no sense.

"What time do you get off work?" she asked.

"I'm stuck here till eight. What time did you have in mind?"

"How about I meet you at the coffee shop at nine? We can walk to one of my favorite places from there."

"That'll work," I said.

"This is a nice place, Jack," she said, looking around at the various works.

I walked her around the store showing her the nicer pieces, attempting to impress her with my art knowledge. She seemed to be interested and knew a fair amount about art herself. It only made her more impressive, as if she needed help.

"How long have you worked here?" she asked.

"I started shortly after our last coffee together. Maybe you brought me some luck."

"Maybe," she said playfully. "I'm going to leave you to your work and head home. See you at-"

The front door chime rang, stopping her thought mid-sentence.

It was Bili.

The two locked eyes on each other, and I could have sworn the temperature in the room dropped ten degrees. I could almost feel it in my bones. It didn't make any sense either because neither of them said or did anything that unusual.

"Viktoria, this is my boss, Bili," I said, hoping to get past the unknown weirdness.

"Viktoria," Bili said, but she never stopped to shake hands or offer anything further. She just kept walking.

"Nice to meet you, Bili," Viki said.

Bili walked straight into the back room and out of sight. I would have thought Bili was being very rude but that was her way. She obviously figured that Viktoria was not an actual customer, and therefore, she didn't feel the need to be at all pleasant.

"Please don't take offense. That's just how Bili is. Actually, she was more polite to you just now than she has been to me since I met her," I said, trying to lighten the mild tension.

Viki just shook it off.

"I understand. I work with many different personalities too."

"So, I will meet you at nine and then off to the unknown restaurant. Sounds very surreptitious," I said.

"Excellent word."

"Wait till you hear my synonyms for synonym."

What the hell am I talking about? I'm about to ruin the best thing ever with stupid chatter. Just say bye.

"Can't wait. See you in a couple hours," she said as she walked herself out.

I watched her as she left, unable to control my stare. I couldn't believe it. Not only did this beautiful woman attempt to find me; when she did, she asked me out on a date. There had to be an explanation. I just didn't care what it was.

The second she was out the front door, Bili reemerged from the back with some paperwork.

"Who was that?" she asked.

"Viktoria. Remember when I introduced her fifteen seconds ago?"

Then, just to satisfy my curiosity, I asked, "Have you met her before? I could have sworn..."

"No, never seen her before. Where did you guys meet?" Bili asked quickly.

"I ran into her at the coffee shop awhile back. Should've been there, it was a real treat. Then I saw her again, and she was a different person. I thought I would never see her again until she showed up here. Do you think it's weird she came here and asked me out on a date?"

"You never told her where you worked, and she just showed up?" Bili said as if it was the rudest thing she had ever heard.

"Uh, yeah. Well, actually, she showed up at my house, and my room-mate sent her here. So, I guess he's the rude one," I said, trying to make light of it. If I started dating this girl, I didn't want my boss to hate her. I could already see the drama on the wall.

"How did she know where you lived?"

"I wondered that myself, but I figured the internet. You can find anything there these days," I said, defending her.

I wasn't sure if I really believed it, but nothing was that difficult in the information age.

"Keep an eye on the sales floor. I have some computer work to finish up before we close," Bili said as she went back to her office area.

"Okay," I said to no one, as she was already out of the room.

The more I thought about it, the more I figured it was about Bili and her issues. How could it be about Viki? They just met.

Why did Bili care about this girl? It's not like she was jealous of her, was she? Why the third degree? She never asked me that many questions about anything. Why did Viktoria ask me out to dinner? That was a better question.

Bili and I closed the store as we did every night. She was more silent than usual, and it didn't go unnoticed. I finished the cleaning and locked up the more valuable items. I did one more check and then started walking to the front exit.

"See ya, Bili," I said as I headed for the door, not expecting her to answer.

"Good night, Jack. Be careful," she said.

It came out nonchalantly, but I couldn't help but think she meant it a little more literal. I guess she assumed Viki was going to break my heart and leave me more pathetic than she found me. I was way ahead of her as I already ran that scenario through my head numerous times.

I walked out the front door calmly and in no hurry until I knew I was out of Bili's sight. When I was, I bolted into a run. I didn't have much time.

19

got home and cleaned up as fast as I could. I was just out of the shower and getting my clothes together when Ted got home.

I heard his footsteps coming straight toward my room. My door was open, and I saw him look in cautiously.

"She came to your work, didn't she?" he said with an unsure tone. Obviously wondering what happened, and if I was upset about it.

"Maybe," I said, unable to hide my grin.

He relaxed when he saw my expression.

"Dude. You said she was pretty, but holy hot damn," he said.

"Makes no sense, right?"

"I guess there's hope for me yet. So, what did she want?" he asked excitedly.

"She asked me out to dinner."

As I said this, I looked at the clock on the wall and saw the time.

"Shit. I don't have much time," I said.

Ted followed as I hurried back to the bathroom to brush my teeth. After seeing her, I knew it piqued his interest. He needed details.

"She asked *you* out? I mean, she just went to your work and asked you out on a date? I never heard of such a thing. A woman like that should be dating pro athletes, not asking out regular guys. No offense Jack, you're a good-looking guy, but come on, she is rock star gorgeous."

Ted looked confused for a second. "I'm not sure if that's a thing but you get my point."

I spit out a mouthful of toothpaste and rinsed.

"She's just a normal girl, I guess," I said, wiping my mouth, "who happens to be genetically gifted. I would love to stay and ponder the query, but if I keep talking, I'm going to be late. I got news for you: I'm not going to be late."

I put my shoes on, grabbed my keys, and headed for the door.

"Make sure to wait up," I said, enjoying the moment more than I should.

The thought of someone else knowing that I had a date with a girl like Viki was icing on the cake. I know it's childish, but it felt good. It had been ages since I let myself get this excited about anything, and if nothing else, I felt happy. I needed happy.

I got to the coffee shop a few minutes after nine and I was glad to see she wasn't there yet. I grabbed an empty seat out of the way and sat down. I didn't have to wait long before I felt the draft from the door opening. Viki came into view a few seconds later, but she didn't notice me right away. In that fraction of a second, I was left bewildered.

Ted was right. What is she doing with me?

"There you are," she said as she turned in my direction.

As I stood up to greet her, she moved in and gave me a gentle but firm hug. She even smelled beautiful.

"You look amazing," I said, feeling proud that I got that out without stumbling.

"Thank you. You look handsome as well."

There was no way this was going to end well for me.

"You sure you're okay with me making all the dinner arrangements?" she said.

"Absolutely. You just saved us the twenty-minute, *where do you want to eat* volley."

"Good. I'm glad you're not one of those machismo idiots who think it's a blow to your manhood anytime a woman makes a decision or even a suggestion."

"Slow down. I never said I wasn't an idiot."

She gave me a playful push on the arm.

"You're funny. Now follow me, idiot," she said with a wink.

I followed.

We walked about two blocks before I could think of anything to say. I had always heard that the only thing worse than an uncomfortable silence is the idiotic attempt to break it with something moronic.

"You're not a vegetarian, are you?" she asked.

"God, no. If they stopped selling cheeseburgers, I don't think I could go on in this world."

"Good. This place is said to have excellent food. Not sure about cheeseburgers, but good nonetheless."

"No restaurant is perfect."

As we rounded a corner, two young men were walking in the opposite direction, and one of them ran into Viki. He held a plastic cup and whatever was inside spilled when they collided.

"Watch where you're going, you stupid bitch!"

It was clearly unintentional, and his blatant overreaction surprised me. And the insult pissed me off.

"Take it easy. It was an accident," I said to the guy.

"Jack, it's no big deal. Let's go," Viktoria said.

She grabbed my arm and pulled me along gently.

"Besides, it's probably the only female contact he'll get all year," Viki said as we were a few steps away.

We both snickered which only infuriated the guy further. They looked like two frat boys on the way to a party. Not uncommon on the streets of Ann Arbor.

"What did you say, filthy skank? You and your homo girlfriend think you're hilarious, don't you?" the guy said.

Viki stopped dead in her tracks. The look on her face changed, and it was obvious this guy had crossed a line with her. She turned around, slowly and deliberately.

"What?" she asked.

It was apparent that the guy was drunk. He was unsteady on his feet but clearly approaching us in an aggressive and hostile fashion.

The other guy, who was far more sober, tried to grab his loudmouth friend and prevent him from walking toward us. The bully yanked his arm away and kept walking closer until he was upon us.

"You heard me, bitch."

This was one of those scary moments when you know a confrontation is inevitable, and you hope it ends well. I had never been the guy who got into many fights, but this guy was way over the line. I resigned myself to the fact he was not getting away with this behavior. Though I was incredibly nervous, I was ready to do what it took to keep him away from Viki. I just hoped to high heaven I didn't get my ass kicked on our first date.

I tried to step in front of Viki to intercept the jerk from getting too close, but she moved too quick and got in front of me. Just as the guy came within arms-length of Viktoria, he dropped to his knees and started wheezing, desperately trying to get air.

"Are you okay, young man?" she said in the most insincere voice I ever heard. It was like she was talking to a small child.

I couldn't see what happened because of the lighting and the fact that Viki was directly in front of me.

The guy continued to gasp for a full breath and stared at the ground. When his buddy approached to help him, he pulled up short and stared at Viktoria with a weird look on his face. It looked like fear, but like I said, the streetlights were not bright in that spot, and this all happened in a matter of seconds.

"Let me help you," Viki said as she grabbed the guy by the wrist to help him up. The guy screamed in agony as soon as she touched him, so Viki just let him drop.

"Let's go, Jack. This guy seems to be lost for words now."

We walked away, and Viki couldn't have been calmer, considering the situation.

"That was crazy. What just happened?"

"I'm not sure. I was about to slap him when he fell to the ground. He must have asthma. Hope I didn't offend you. I know you were going to defend me, and I appreciate it. I just don't have any tolerance for that kind of bully behavior."

"I can see that. Remind me never to piss you off."

"I'm sure you'll never need reminding," she said as she playfully bumped into me.

Viktoria would not be boring. I could see that right off. As we walked away, I looked back at the guy, and he was still desperately trying to catch his breath. His friend was simultaneously pulling him up and yanking him in the opposite direction, presumably to get medical attention. He really did look like he was having a problem. I almost felt sorry for him.

We walked one more block when we came to a door between two storefronts. It was just a simple plain blue door.

"This is it. I hope you like it."

From the outside, it didn't look like any restaurant I had ever seen, but this was Ann Arbor, and anything was possible.

"Is this one of those restaurants you need a password to get in?"

I was only half kidding. There was nothing on or around the door but the address.

"You're not too far off the mark. It's an exclusive place. They don't let just anyone in."

Viktoria opened the door with a key, and we immediately came to a stairway going up. I could hear faint music in the background as I followed her up the steps. When we arrived at the top of the stairs, the loft came in view. Though it had a slight female flair to it, I would have had no problem moving right in and calling it home. It was very nice.

"Exclusive, indeed. I'm so gullible."

She smiled at me, taking pride in her little ruse.

The furthest corner from the stairs had a gas fireplace and large floor-to-ceiling bookshelves on either side. There was even one of those rolling ladders to reach the top shelves. The only enclosed areas were the master bedroom and the bathroom. The open kitchen, dining area, and living space all looked professionally done. It wasn't much in square footage, but it was enough.

"Interesting place," I said, walking around, taking in the space.

"Do you like it?"

"It's not bad if you're into everything that's cool."

There was a balance between modern and classic styles, with the furniture and the art alike. In the kitchen, she even had a small classic print of *Dogs Playing Poker*, but all the dogs looked like Alaskan Huskies.

I instinctively made my way to her bookshelves. Her collection was amazing. All the classics, of course, some obscure books that looked almost new, and some incredible first and second editions.

"You have to be kidding me," I said as I placed my hand on a book and looked at Viki. "May I?"

"Of course, this isn't a museum. You can touch anything you want."

Again, the half-smile just screamed flirtation, and it flew right over my head. Seems ridiculous, I know, but you really had to appreciate and understand the dynamics.

"Can I get you a drink?" she asked as she walked over to the large double door stainless fridge.

"Sure. If you have a light beer, I'll be your best friend."

I pulled the book off the shelf and saw that it was a first edition *Lord of the Rings*. She had all three volumes as well as *The Hobbit* and *The Silmarillion*.

"Do you have any idea what this one book is worth?"

She glanced over at the book I was holding, giving the slightest of shrugs.

"Not really. I've had most of these books for a long time. A couple grand, maybe? And yes, I've read them all. Twice. I have my nerd card."

I had to laugh at that. Where was she when I was in high school?

"A first edition set like this sold at auction recently for $70,000, and I'm sure they weren't in the same shape as yours. These look like they were just printed," I said, trying to not sound too excited.

"Hmm. That's nice," she said as if it was of no concern and then went back to getting our drinks.

The more I looked at her books, the more I was astonished. Not only the mint condition of the classics but the different genres of books. She had everything from the *Tibetan Book of the Dead* to newer fantasy novels I never figured someone like her to be into. It was as if someone designed the perfect woman based solely on everything I liked. I was starting to feel like the butt of a practical joke.

"Here you go," she said as she handed me a bottle of beer.

"Thanks. You are full of surprises, aren't you?"

"Maybe," she said sheepishly. "How do you mean?"

"I don't know. Just when I think I'm getting a handle on you, I see a completely different side."

"Keeps things from getting boring, don't you think? Besides, you haven't even scratched the surface," she said.

That smile again, I liked it a lot.

"I'm sure you have your fair share of surprises," she said.

"Pfft. I'm as normal and boring as they come. I'm sure I should keep such well-kept secrets to myself, but better you know up front."

I was trying to sound witty, but truer words were never spoken.

Viki walked closer to me, very close in fact, and looked me in the eye.

"You are far from normal and boring. One day you will see that."

Her stare was hypnotizing, and I could only stare back in silence. She broke her gaze and walked toward the window that overlooked the street below. I felt myself relax, not realizing I was holding my breath.

"How do you like working at the art store?" she asked over her shoulder as she stopped in front of the large plate-glass window that overlooked the street.

"It's great. I know it seems like a little store but it's a much bigger operation than it appears. I'm learning a lot about the art world I never knew existed. It really is a global market which makes it very interesting. I-" I stopped myself before I rambled any further. "In short, it's great."

I walked over and stood next to her, trying to see what she was looking at.

"Do you like your boss?" she asked innocently.

"Yeah. I know Bili seems like a hard ass, but she has a good heart when you get to know her. I'm assuming anyway, as I don't really know her that well. Still the new guy," I said, trying to make excuses for Bili's behavior earlier.

"She owns the store then?"

"Oh no. Theo is the owner. He's a great guy, but I don't see him that often. Mostly it's just Bili and me at the store. If you ever wanted to sell any of your pieces, let me know. I know we would get you top dollar for sure."

"I'll keep that in mind. Can I ask you something else?"

"Sure, anything."

She started to say something when her cell phone rang. She had one of those old school telephone rings from the seventies. Back when phones hung up and had cords.

Her phone was on the counter in the dining room, and she took her time getting to it. She stared at the screen for a long second before reluctantly answering.

"Hello," she said, then she mouthed the word *sorry* to me as she walked toward the other side of the loft, just far enough where I could barely hear her.

It seemed the other person was doing most of the talking because she hardly said a word. I didn't like the look on her face as she listened either.

I heard her say *I understand* several times in a rather aggravated manner before she pushed the disconnect button. She set the phone down and didn't move for a minute, as if she was collecting her thoughts.

"Everything okay?"

"No. That was my boss. I have to go into work. Some type of business emergency that apparently cannot wait until tomorrow. I'm very sorry, Jack."

I'm sure the disappointment was all over my face.

Viki walked closer to me and grabbed my hand.

"I had a nice time, please don't be upset with me," she said.

"I did as well. And work's work, I get it. Thanks for having me over. Maybe we can do it again sometime?"

"I really hope so," she said with genuine sympathy in her voice. "I feel terrible."

"Don't. Thanks for the beer and putting a hex on that guy earlier. Good times."

She gave me another warm, apologetic smile and squeezed my hand gently before dropping it, which I took as my cue to make a dignified exit.

I set my beer down on the counter and walked over to the stairs to let myself out, assuming she would be rushed. I turned around to say goodnight one last time, and when I did, I found her right behind me. Before I could say anything, she pushed my back up against the wall, ever so gently, and kissed me.

I have kissed a few girls in my day, but this was another level. Maybe it was the situation, the newness of the relationship, the fact that she was gorgeous, or all the above, but whatever it was, it was the greatest kiss of my life. Just long enough to let me know it wasn't generic, but it was short enough to make me mentally beg for more.

"So, I guess I will talk to you soon," I said.

"You will," she replied as she stared into my eyes.

I think it was the first time I really looked back into hers. They could tell a story themselves. It was like looking at the ocean surface at night. You know damn well there is plenty going on underneath and some of it dangerous.

I forced myself not to say another word, in fear I might ruin a glorious moment. Nothing else needed to be said. Maybe that was her plan from the beginning. Start the greatest date ever and then cut it short. If it was, it was genius. I ached inside as I walked out into the night.

20

was halfway home from Viki's when I got the feeling that I was being followed. It was odd because it was still early evening and there were several people walking about. I picked up my pace and looked around as I walked. I saw nothing.

I'm losing my mind. What's wrong with me? I need to see a shrink. Or a bartender.

When I reached the house, it surprised me to find several cars parked in front and the sound of a party. This was not Ted's usual evening at all, and my curiosity swelled. When I went in, I found Ted, Ben, Cyndi, and another girl I had never seen before, all playing cards.

"Hey, buddy," Ted said, grinning ear to ear.

The excitement on his face was obvious, as was the fact that he had had a few drinks.

Ted never had company over without me here. I didn't remember setting up any card games either. The situation was unusual at best.

"Hey, everyone," I said.

I immediately forgot about my paranoia, wondering more about how this impromptu party had come together.

"Hey, Jack. Glad you could make it. Sorry to ambush you like this, but we stopped by to see if you were home, and Ted was nice enough to invite us in," Cyndi said.

Ben, who is never one to pull any punches, made it instantly uncomfortable.

"Cyndi forced her way in with no regard to Ted's comfort level." Then Ben looked at Ted. "Nice house by the way. You never told us you were a frickin' millionaire."

Ted's ears became red with embarrassment.

"It's fine, really. I don't mind," Ted said shyly, glancing in Cyndi's direction every few seconds.

"He's a sweetheart," Cyndi said, patting Ted's arm.

Ted's entire face went red.

"Jack, this is my friend Ceana," Cyndi said, as she raised her eyebrows slightly, just in case I missed the fact that this was the girl she wanted me to meet.

"Nice to meet you," I said.

I walked over to the table and sat down next to Ted. I knew my presence would help him relax, though he seemed to be doing alright for himself tonight.

"Nice to meet you too, Jack," she said.

As Ceana smiled at me, I got another one of my Deja Vu feelings. There was something familiar about this girl, but I was certain I had never met her before. She had straight raven black hair past her shoulders, not much make-up, if any, glasses, and a slender build. The best way to describe her would have been librarian-goth.

"Have we met before?" I asked cautiously.

"Nice, Jack. You just get back from a date and you immediately start dropping cheesy pickup lines on Cyndi's new friend," Ben said.

The look Cyndi gave me was more surprise than disappointment. She prided herself as being my personal matchmaker.

"Damn, Ben. Just once when your head tells you to speak, ignore it," I said as I shook my head.

He just giggled to himself. Getting under people's skin was his favorite pastime.

"You do look familiar. Maybe we have met," Ceana said. "Do you work around campus?"

"I used to work at the bookstore on Liberty," I said, trying to think if that's where I may have seen her.

"Jack here actually landed a proper job that pays actual money. The amazing part is that his degree was of some actual use. Miracles can happen," Cyndi said, trying to make up for Ben's rude comment and build me up at the same time.

"Let me guess," Ceana said.

"Yes," I said, cutting her off, knowing she knew the answer.

She smiled flirtatiously, enough so that even I could pick it up.

"That's good to hear. It gives me hope. Philosophy major," Ceana said as she waved her hand as if outing herself.

Ben rolled his eyes.

"Great. Another one. Looks like Ted and I are the only ones who will pay any taxes so this country can function properly. Now, are we playing cards or what?"

We ended up having a great time that night. We played cards for hours, had some laughs, and Ted seemed to have the time of his life. I was happy for him.

I was cleaning up as the night was ending and Ceana helped me with the dishes. I saw Cyndi smile out of the corner of my eye, obviously pleased with herself, thinking she may have made a match. Though Ben told her I was on a date, she had no idea it was the best, albeit the shortest, date of my life. The last thing on my mind was trying to set up a date with Ceana.

"Where do the glasses go, Jack?" Ceana said.

"The cupboard above the sink, left side," I said as I pointed. "Thanks for helping but you really don't have to."

"I don't mind," she said. "You know, I think I have seen you at the bookstore. I'm in there all the time."

"Yeah, most students are."

I was talking to her in the bright lights of the kitchen, and I saw something that struck me as very coincidental. Her eyes had a thick black border around the iris. It was not the first time I saw this.

That's unusual.

I forgot about it quickly, and we finished the clean up together while the others played a three-hand rummy game. I knew Cyndi went through the trouble of setting me up on this quasi-blind date ambush, and I felt bad because I wasn't into it. I was polite though, thanked Ceana for the help, and then excused myself to my room. I could hear the party wind down soon after.

I laid down on my bed, not really trying to fall asleep, but was out within minutes. The dream that followed was so fantastic and disturbing, I will never forget it.

21

"What did you dream about, Jack?" Sara asked.

The question came out a little too hurriedly and with more than a fair bit of curiosity. It was a professional mistake and her patient picked up on it.

Jack crossed his arms as if thinking carefully about what he was going to say.

"Do you want to talk about it?" she prompted in a purposely stereotypical therapist fashion, trying to lighten the mild tension.

"No, I don't think we are far enough into the story where it would be appropriate or make sense. I think it would be a distraction. I'm sure you would like to explore the dream further and now is not the time."

"Okay. Just let me know whenever you feel comfortable, and we can revisit it."

"I will. Do you want me to continue, or do you need to do any of your doctor duties?"

The doctor felt as though she was getting close to some important information and didn't want to stop Jack's momentum. She also couldn't deny that he was an intense personality who was good with words.

"Not just yet. Please continue."

Jack took a sip of water.

"Good, because this is where our story takes some sharp turns, so hold on."

22

A light fog was settling over the city. It was that time of night when the very late and very early overlap, and there is just a silent existence.

The streets were vacant of any activity, and the only sound was that of hard-soled shoes hitting the sidewalk. The sound grew louder as it echoed off the surrounding buildings. She was close enough to smell now, and there was no doubt she was the one she was waiting for.

As the footsteps approached, she heard the subtle change in her gait and the speed of her walk. She knew she was there but continued.

She was waiting in front of a restaurant which had a doorway that was set back just enough to hide her physical presence until she was right in front of her. When she reached the opening, she stopped, turned, and faced her would-be assailant.

"I wondered if you were going to pay me a visit. Bilinda, is it?" Viktoria said.

Not a hint of nervousness in her voice or fear in her body language. Using Bili's real name was telling and no accident.

"I'm curious. You are one of a rare few I have ever come across in this area, and now you're dating Jack. Quite a coincidence, don't you think?" Bili said.

"I confess, I rarely go for his type, but then again, there is something different and familiar about him. Why do you think that is?" Viktoria said with raised eyebrows.

Bili could tell she knew something, but how much was the question. The last thing she wanted to do was give her information inadvertently she didn't previously have.

"Who are you working for?" Bili asked.

"I work for a financial company three blocks from here."

"You know what-"

"Yes, I do," Viki said, cutting Bili off. "I know lots of things. Do I know who he is? Of course, I do. That doesn't mean I'm the enemy."

She was telling the truth.

"Who's your maker?" Bili asked, changing the subject.

Viktoria's demeanor changed in a heartbeat.

"Nice talking to you, Bili. When you see Jack, feel free to tell him about this conversation," Viktoria said dismissively as she turned away from Bili and started walking.

Bili grabbed Viki's arm and pulled, causing Viki to whip back around, putting the two face-to-face. Their eyes locked unflinchingly. Bili knew she was playing a dangerous game with Viktoria.

"If anything happens to him, there will be no place on this earth you could run."

Bili's eyes were cold steel and deadly serious.

Viki peeled Bili's iron grip from her arm, slowly and deliberately, while staring right back at her. She was letting Bili know, in a not-so-subtle way, that when it came to the physical, Bili could not match her. Bili knew this as well, but with people she cared about, self-preservation was the last thing on her mind.

"Is it a sense of duty to Theodorus, or something else?" Viktoria said, tilting her head ever so slightly.

Viki took a few steps away from Bili and then stopped and looked back.

"Trouble is coming, but not from where you think. Keep sharp."

The situation was heating up. The dull and mundane life Bili had become accustomed to was over. She couldn't, in all honesty, say she was disappointed.

23

"Wait a minute, Jack. I have so many questions my questions have questions," Sara said, interrupting the story again. "Maker? What does that mean?"

Though Jack was not saying it outright, he was implying some incredible things. Usually in cases like this when the patient is beyond delusional, there are many natural breaks due to major inconsistencies and nonsensical ramblings. Jack's story was very different in that she had not yet found any. Though some of his implications seemed implausible, they were well thought out. That's why Sara found herself giving Jack a little more leeway than most.

Jack looked at Sara disapprovingly.

"I know what I said, but-"

"Doc, please," Jack said dropping his stare as to say *may I please go on?*

"Sorry, but-"

"Remember what I said. Though it may seem I'm not making sense, it will come together. Plus, after the next part of my story, you will have far more questions, as I'm sure you'll find it hard to believe. It will then force me to answer some of your doctor questions, so you won't think I'm utterly insane. It may take some doing, I'm afraid, unless I miss my guess."

"Okay," Sara said. "But I'm holding you to it."

24

t was a *dive bar*, in the purest sense. The kind you could find in any city on the verge of financial ruin. They haphazardly painted the name of the bar on the side of the building, along with some random graffiti.

Friendly's Bar.

The irony. It was not the place one would stop for drinks unless you were from the neighborhood, as *friendly* would not be what one would find. The exception being if you looked like Claude.

Even though he looked like he belonged in such a place, he hated being around such clientele. He found bars like this a breeding ground for the lost and forever hopeless.

If they only knew their potential, he thought as he looked at the customers and employees alike.

He had been drinking for hours waiting for the right time. People were coming and going, as with all bars, but he knew the difference between an individual being sent in, as opposed to wandering in. After seeing what he had been waiting for, he finished his beer, walked outside, and took a deep breath of cool air. He looked around momentarily and then started walking.

It was late, and he acted as if he was oblivious to his surroundings. Claude was never unaware of his surroundings.

He made his way to the motel across the street where he had rented a room. The Tiki Hut Inn was far from a tropical getaway, but it would serve his purpose. He checked in a few days ago after he discovered he was being followed. There were very few who could get the drop on Claude, as he was the best at what he did.

He did not relish this night or what it would surely bring, but lines were being crossed. If you crossed one with Claude, you had better be prepared for the consequences. Most weren't.

Once he was sure they were close enough, he made his way up the stairs to the second floor. All the rooms had outside entrances, like most low-rate motels. He also made sure his room faced the opposite side of the main road, which was a secluded alley that sat atop a freeway embankment. Not a popular area of the motel.

He unlocked the door with an actual key and went inside. He locked the door to keep up appearances and then sat in the lone ragged red chair in the corner. Claude wasn't reading, taking a nap, or watching TV. He was just sitting. He had done everything but lay a trail of breadcrumbs for these unfortunate souls. There was an element of risk, but one worth taking.

He could hear their footsteps slapping off the cement flooring of the second level.

Hard sole shoes and only two of them. Amateurs.

They were outside his door discussing the plan. Further evidence they were untrained and new to the life.

CRACK!

The door flew off the hinges and landed inside the room at Claude's feet. He didn't move a muscle as the two large figures walked into the room, full of confidence and swagger. They were acting strong and sure, and in most cases, rightfully so. It was obvious they didn't know who Claude was.

They were dressed almost the same, wearing three-quarter-length leather jackets and dark pants. The one on the left had a short buzz-cut, almost military style, while the other had longer hair that was pulled into a tight ponytail.

"Sorry about your door," Ponytail said insincerely.

Both intruders were very young, by Claude standards anyway, which can be a dangerous time. You feel invincible, and in most respects, you are.

"Get up!" Ponytail yelled. "Now!"

Claude remained seated and looked at them with mild interest. He could see this unnerved them. They looked at each other, wondering how to play this. Then Claude spoke.

"The problem with being a young pup is, not only are your tracking skills shamefully limited, you also do not understand your new world. Nor were you smart enough to notice your mark was tracking you."

Claude never lost eye contact with Ponytail, who was no longer filled with the same confidence he came in with. Claude had dealt with these types before, and the more he thought about the whole situation, the angrier he became.

Buzz-cut looked over at his partner, and his eyes said it all. He immediately felt over his head. Claude was sure that when they were recruited, they didn't know what they were getting themselves into. That didn't excuse their behavior, though.

"Who are you?" Buzz-cut asked, sensing something was off.

Ponytail wasn't having it. He tried to regain his authority, knowing it was still two against one.

"I said stand up."

Claude stood as the intruders watched in silent consternation. From the looks on their faces, they hadn't grasped the size of Claude from a distance. The dynamics of the room changed. Ponytail tried to appear fearless.

"They fed you lies, and you might even think what you're doing is right. Everything is not as it seems. I will make you an offer but only once. You will tell me who sent you here, and everything you know about them, and I will allow you to leave."

Claude said this in a calm and gravelly voice as he directed his stare to Buzz-cut, who appeared a little more open to reason.

"What if he's right, Alonzo? We never met this guy before. We don't even know if what they told us *is* true," Buzz-cut said, obviously hoping his partner would rethink their actions.

Alonzo ignored him.

"I know you're a traitor. The one who kills his own kind. That's all I need to know about you. Your only option here is to give us what *we* want, then maybe *you'll* live."

"No," Claude said pointedly.

Alonzo shifted his body weight by the slightest of margins, and Claude saw him grind his jaw. He was not taking his warning seriously. Worse, he was telegraphing his intentions and throwing away the only sliver of a chance he had.

Before another word, Claude sprang forward, caught Alonzo by the neck, and slammed his large body into the motel wall. The collision sounded like a wrecking ball hitting the side of a house.

Claude pulled him from the drywall and got behind him before his partner knew what happened. As Claude brought his boot down at just the right angle, the snap of Alonzo's knee echoed in the small room. All the aggression in Alonzo had vanished in a blink. Buzz-cut made no attempt to enter the fight.

"I suggest you reevaluate your future," Claude said as he snapped Alonzo's right arm, leaving it in an unnatural position.

The demoralized attacker did everything he could to stifle his yell with little success. Claude dropped him to the floor and stared into the eyes of Buzz-cut, who appeared stunned by the explosion of Claude's assault.

"My name is Claude. What's your name, young one?"

"Uh, Willis. I've heard of you. You're one of the Elders. They never told us."

"It's time you started making your own decisions in life. This is not your fight. You've been given the rarest of gifts. Do not piss it away."

Claude stepped over Alonzo and stood in front of Willis.

"Do you understand?"

He could only nod.

"I will allow you two to leave this room tonight, but you will need to tell me everything you know."

Willis couldn't talk fast enough, telling Claude everything he knew. Alonzo tried to quiet him, but Claude kicked him in the head so hard he went unconscious.

"If I find out that any part of this information is false or even stretched, I will find you," Claude said.

"That's all I know," he blurted.

Claude was confident that he was telling the truth. He wasn't as good as others when it came to reading people, but he was better than most like him.

"You can use this room to set your friend's limbs before they heal irregularly."

Claude stepped out of the room and back into the night. He had nothing of his in the room, as it was just a means to an end. He didn't get as much information as he had hoped, but it was not a total bust. One piece of information could prove very useful.

25

"Okay, Jack, I need answers. Claude is what then?" the doctor asked with more interest than condescending disbelief.

Jack contemplated his next words carefully.

"One of the oldest of his kind."

"Oldest what?"

"Some would call him one of the Vilkacis."

Jack waited to see if the term meant anything to the doctor.

"A wolf?" Sara asked with a squint in her eyes and a tilt of the head. "No. Werewolf, right?"

"Not one of your more commonly used words. May I ask how you know it?"

"I'm not sure, really. Maybe from a European Folklore class in college."

"Do you believe what I've just told you?" Jack asked. When he did, it was as if he was gauging, maybe even studying, her reaction and answer.

"I believe you believe it," she said, using a textbook doctor answer.

"Fair enough. Do you feel less comfortable around me now?" Jack asked seriously.

"I'm fine. Why do you ask? Are you a werewolf?"

"No, of course not," Jack said, dismissing the question as silly.

"Whew," Sara said, putting her hand to her chest in mock relief. "Do these wolves turn into anything? You know, like actual wolves, or hairy two-legged creatures you see in the movies."

"I'm afraid not. Nancy could be a wolf and you wouldn't know it."

"Sometimes I think she could be. You should work with her when she's in a mood."

Jack smiled.

"She is not, in case you were genuinely wondering."

"Good to know," Sara said, and then something occurred to her. "How do you know Nancy?

Without missing a beat, Jack responded.

"The other doctor, who *we* dislike, mentioned her when he came in earlier."

Though Sara was skeptical of several things, she did not write him off as psychotic or delusional. Maybe she was being swayed by his confidence and intelligence, or maybe a small part of her wanted to believe him. Who wouldn't want to live in a fantasy world where things like werewolves were possible?

Maybe Jack is telling this fictional tale to see what sort of response he would get. But why? Could he be some sort of plant to test me?

Sara wouldn't put it past Kaufland to set her up and try to sabotage her before she left. It was the perfect trap in her eyes. Have a patient, such as Jack, come in and bond with her over a common enemy. This could result in her dropping her guard just enough to make a mistake Kaufland could take advantage of.

The best course of action was to keep going, treat him like any other patient, and see where it took her. She would work it out eventually, as she always did. There was a reason she had a reputation. She was good.

"What about Viktoria and Bili? Are they like Claude? Because-" she started to say.

"I'm getting to that Doc," Jack said, cutting her off. "You wouldn't buy a book and start reading in the middle, would you?"

"No, of course not, but you said you would start answering some questions. I think it would be an important step to go over a few things before we went further."

Jack was about to respond but fell silent and sat back in his chair.

"What is it?" she asked.

A few seconds later the door opened, and a man walked in.

"Dr. Richards, can I see you for a minute?"

The man didn't wait for an answer before walking back out into the hallway, letting the door shut behind him.

Aggravation and disdain permeated Sara's face.

"Sure Dr. Kaufland, be right there," Sara said sarcastically, knowing he couldn't hear her.

"Everything alright?" Jack asked.

"Fine. Sorry for the interruption, Jack. I'll be right back."

Sara walked out into the hall where Dr. Kaufland was waiting. This seemed like a very convenient interruption in her mind.

"You mind telling me why you felt the need to disrupt my session?" Sara said.

"I'm still your superior, so watch the tone. You want to tell me what the hell you were doing in medical? I received a complaint that you were over there earlier questioning the medical staff like some sort of half-ass detective. Not to mention what you said to the social worker."

Sara knew damn well no one made a complaint. This was some sort of power play, and Kaufland was using it as an excuse to berate and question her.

"I was trying to get answers to accurately treat my patient. The same one you couldn't get a word out of, and as you can see, I'm making excellent progress."

She was past the point of caring what this man thought.

Spencer was fuming with anger but didn't let his temper get away from him. He was walking a fine line and he had to be careful.

"If you have questions, you bring them to me, and I will get them answered if it's important. Understand?"

"Yes, sir," she said mockingly like a new army recruit. The only thing missing was a salute and clicking of her heels.

"Aren't you leaving soon, anyway? Why are you bothering with this patient? You're more than welcome to use the remaining vacation time you have left. Maybe work on your defense for the lawsuit as well."

"How did you-? Tony. I should have known. Yes, I just turned in my notice to Mr. O'Rourke. And as far as the frivolous lawsuit, I have it well in hand."

"I bet you do," he said with an infuriating smirk.

"I still have two weeks and I will finish with *my* patients. Anything else?"

"Not at the moment."

Dr. Kaufland was about to say something but thought better of it. He held his tongue and walked off with purpose. Sara knew she hadn't heard the last of this. She went back to Jack's room, trying to shake off her aggravation.

"What an asshole," Sara muttered under her breath just as she opened the door.

Sara walked back to her chair and sat back down. Jack hadn't moved.

"Sorry about that," she said.

"Why? He is an asshole."

"I meant about the interruption," she said, looking back at the door. "I'm sorry you heard that. I shouldn't be talking like that about another doctor. It's not very professional."

"I promise not to tell," Jack said, making an x over his heart.

They shared a smile, helping Sara snap out of her mood somewhat. She also felt silly about her distrust of Jack. The theory that he was a plant to entrap her now seemed far-fetched.

Jack sat up straighter in his chair, as if about to emphasize a point.

"Listen. I know you have lots of questions regarding everything I've just told you, but if you let me continue, I think I might answer several as we get deeper into my story. And I will say this before I go on," Jack said, choosing his next words carefully. He had a way of creating suspense and curiosity like no other patient Sara had ever treated.

"What?" she pressed.

"I'm well aware my story seems unbelievable, and you are humoring me by not calling me out on some of these outlandish claims."

This was a tricky position. He was forcing Sara to either agree with him that she thinks he's lying or tell him she believes everything he is saying, which he would see as condescending.

"If you know this, then tell me how you think I should proceed as the listener to your story."

Jack gave Sara a look of appreciation.

"Well done. That was an excellent non-committal response."

Sara wasn't sure if Jack was being sarcastic or not.

"Well?" she said.

"I will say this. My story may in fact get even more fantastic. Rather than stopping me, as most psychiatrists might when hearing such ridiculousness, you listen as if it were all true. That doesn't mean you shouldn't ask questions, but if it's explaining why I think this or that is possible, it will ruin the flow."

Again, Sara was struggling with Jack setting rules, but her instincts told her to roll with it. She would figure him out eventually.

"Okay, Jack. Let's continue."

26

One Friday afternoon, Theo sent Bili and me on a delivery, as he did from time to time for our better clients. Bili was driving, and after thirty minutes of the silent treatment, which was a long time, even for her, I spoke up.

"What's with you?"

"What?"

"The attitude. Did I piss you off more than normal, or is it something else? It's hard to tell with you most of the time, but I know you've treated me differently since you met Viktoria. Does it have something to do with her?"

Bili looked at me and held her gaze. It was long enough that running off the road became a concern.

She opened her mouth as if she was going to say something but turned back toward the road in silence.

"What!?"

She refused to answer me, which fueled my aggravation.

We arrived at our destination and dropped off the piece to one of our regulars. The customer was nice, and Bili was even nicer, which irritated me that much more. I couldn't get the weather out of her, but Mrs. Turner and Bili talked about floor tiles for twenty minutes.

She invited us in for lunch, but we politely declined saying we had other stops to make. When we headed back to the truck, I got in the driver's seat without asking. I thought Bili was going to protest but she didn't. She just walked to the passenger side and got in without a word. I think I would rather she complained or physically punched me.

We drove for another ten minutes without speaking before she finally broke the silence.

"I'm not mad at you," she said in a manner that was bordering on apologetic.

"Does this have something to do with Viki or not?" I asked.

"If you want to date a woman who spends her days talking about cupcakes and unicorns that's your business. I just think there are a few things you ought to know."

"Like?"

"Everything, you idiot! You're..." she started to say.

Her raised voice tapered and cut off. Her anger didn't appear to be directed at me, even the *idiot* part.

"I'm talking about the things in this life you are oblivious to, and I think you should be brought up to speed, considering..."

"Considering what?"

"Nothing. You're right. I don't like the bitch. She looks like a high maintenance cheerleader that would spend hours contemplating toenail polish. I just got a bad vibe from her, that's all. Sorry."

Bili using the word *sorry* struck me as the most astonishing part of that sentence. I had never heard her apologize to anyone, let alone me, for anything, ever. After I got past that, I felt I needed to defend Viki.

"Well, I assure you she's not. You might actually like her if you got to know her," I said. "But it may be a moot point. I haven't heard from her since our last date. The same day you met her."

"Have you tried calling her?" Bili asked.

"Yeah, a few times, but her phone went right to voice mail. I left a message, but I hadn't heard back. It's weird because I thought our date went really well. Then she got called into work, I left, and that was the last time I spoke to her."

"Called into work?" she said as if I had fallen for the oldest trick in the book. "I thought you said she worked in business or something?"

"Her boss called when I was over her house. She said it was some kind of business emergency, but she didn't look happy about it. That gave me hope that it wasn't just a blow off move. What do you think?"

Bili just shrugged casually.

"Yep. Definitely a blow off," she said without batting an eye.

I stared at her until I saw that long-lost smidgen of a smile. She even let out a small laugh. Nothing seemed to make her happy like the misery of others.

"Don't worry about it. I'm sure it's for the best. Now speed up. If you go any slower, we'll go back in time."

"You would make an excellent social worker, you know that?" I said as sarcastically as I could.

That made her grin even more.

For the rest of the trip, Bili seemed in a much better mood. I guess sometimes you just need to talk things through.

When we got back to the store, Theo was there. He went over some online sales and research with me, teaching and testing at the same time. I was a quick learner, and I was seeing the trends he had been talking about. It was amazing stuff.

Though he wasn't at the store that often, when he was, he took the time to show me parts of the business few get to see. The amount of art that was bought and sold from country to country and dealer to dealer was amazing. There was almost nothing Theo couldn't get his hands on if he put his mind to it.

"Let's go," Theo said, throwing my jacket at me.

I saved what I was doing on the computer and followed him out the back door.

We drove to a rural town just outside Ann Arbor. After a few dirt roads we came to a long serpentine drive that led to a warehouse in the middle of nowhere. Theo hit a button on his visor and a large overhead door began rolling up on the side.

If the outside of the building was unremarkable, the inside was the polar opposite. It was breathtaking. Not only was it so clean you could eat off the floor, but it had an incredible amount of art and artifacts neatly stacked and stored. Theo shut the door behind us as the inside was temperature controlled.

"This is our main storage facility in Michigan. I figured it was time for you to see it," Theo said as he looked at me waiting for questions.

"I didn't know you possessed this amount of inventory in Michigan. Where does most of this come from?"

"A large portion comes from my supplier in France. but the rest I've had for many years waiting for the right time to sell. You must be mindful of the art market, as you are now appreciating. The prices rise and fall just like any other stock. Right now, sales on all things Picasso are soft, with a few exceptions of course. On the other hand, Salvador Dali pieces are ripe for selling. My associate at Christie's is waiting for us to ship most of our collection. I have them in the back, packed and ready to go. Though this place is secure, I have a little extra security for the most expensive items."

He walked me over to the large walk-in safe, which was conveniently out of sight from the main floor. There was a well-manufactured facade that looked like empty shelves. Once opened, the vault appeared, which had a hi-tech digital lock. Theo punched the access code right in front of me.

Theo must have seen the look of familiarity on my face.

"It's the address of the store, keyed in twice. Once normal, then reversed, got it?"

"Yes, sir."

"There will be times in the future when I'll send you here to pick up various pieces. Are you comfortable with that?" Theo asked, waiting to see if my face matched my answer.

"I think I can handle it. Thank you for the trust. I won't let you down," I said.

"I know you won't."

The way he said that made me feel good. Theo was the very antithesis of David.

We loaded up the paintings we came for and headed back. During the ride, I was staring out the side window, thinking about how fortunate I was. Something I never thought I would think about myself ever again.

"You are doing an outstanding job, Jack. Bili has had nothing but great things to say about your progress and work ethic."

Really?

"Thanks. I love the work. I never imagined I would be part of the art world in this capacity," I said sincerely.

"I told you when I hired you that once you were properly trained, I would move you to an appropriate salary," Theo said as he looked straight ahead, not taking his eyes off the road.

This day was getting better by the minute. I figured if he added a few dollars more an hour I would get close to $60K a year. The thought of it made me giddy.

"I figure a proper salary for your current skill level is a hundred and twenty thousand a year. Do you feel that is a fair wage?"

I was dumb struck. I couldn't even get an answer out right away.

"It's more than fair. Actually, I would say you would be overpaying me."

"You've seen the sales we do at the store. That's only a portion of what we do globally. It's a fair wage, and your direct deposit will start reflecting it as of your next paycheck."

Theo was not the sort of man you argued with, and though I was sure he was wasting his money, who was I to complain? Life had dealt me some terrible cards and maybe this was some sort of karma payback.

"I can't thank you enough, Theo," I said, still not believing what had just happened.

"You're a good kid, young man rather. You deserve it," he said as we pulled into the alley of the POH and parked.

"Now go in and help Bili close-up. I need to take care of some other business."

I shook Theo's hand, thanked him again, and went inside. I couldn't put my finger on it, but there was something different about Theo's demeanor. Nothing explainable, more of a feeling, but it was noticeable.

When I walked out into the showroom, I noticed the store had several customers inside. I stepped right into work mode, answering questions, and even selling a few nice pieces that turned a tidy profit.

We closed the store, and I said goodnight to Bili. Surprisingly, I got a response of *goodnight* in return. I locked the door behind me, as Bili stayed behind to finish some work. I only took a few steps when I heard a familiar voice.

"Thought you were never gonna leave."

I turned and saw Viki leaning up against the building just ahead of me.

"You don't like using phones very much, do you?" I said, trying to act unaffected by her disappearance.

"No. I feel some things are better said in person, especially when it's an apology. I know what you must think of me for not returning your calls, or worse, think I didn't want to see you again. I had some personal issues I needed to take care of, and it took longer than expected."

She seemed sincere, but the last thing I wanted to be was the sappy idiot who let a beautiful girl treat him like dirt. Everyone has their limits.

"There's nothing to apologize for. We went on one date. Half a date if you want to be technical. No big deal," I said as nonchalantly as I could.

"Well, I wanted to say I'm sorry. Can you forgive me?" she said as she walked up next to me and bumped her shoulder into mine.

When she approached me, she stepped into the light of the streetlamp. Her hair was hanging straight, and she was wearing glasses. I don't know how, but she looked even more appealing.

My attempt at ambivalence was crumbling by the second. I tried to stay stone-faced, though I knew it to be a lost cause. Maybe I was an idiot.

"Okay, I forgive you. What now?"

"I believe I still owe you dinner. If my place isn't on fire, it should be ready soon. Please let me make it up to you."

"Okay, but I just got off work and probably smell like old wood and furniture polish."

"You smell fine, but if you are feeling self-conscious, you can take a shower at my place. You wouldn't want my dinner to burn, would you?"

"No. Unless you're making hot dogs. I love those things burnt black," I said trying to be funny, but it was true. Burnt dogs are the best.

"Sorry, no hot dogs tonight. That will be date three and a half," she said with a wink.

I had a million questions running through my mind, and it took all my strength not to blurt them all out at once.

What kind of personal issues? Are you married? In the middle of a messy divorce? Do you have a dying relative you're taking care of?

As bad as it sounds, I was secretly hoping it was the sick relative. That would explain a lot, and I wouldn't have to deal with the anguish of her being with, or still in love with, someone else.

We came to her door and marched upstairs without the dramatics of my first visit. I don't know how to explain it, but when you are smitten with someone, the littlest things, or gestures, can make you feel like a kid on Christmas morning. A playful touch, a gentle brushing of the hand, or a simple hug was intoxicating. If you have never felt it, it would be hard to explain.

"Whatever is in that oven is going to be better than hot dogs, I'm certain."

"If it isn't, I'm going to have a word with the butcher at the market. Grab a beer from the fridge; I'm gonna change," she said as she walked into her bedroom.

"Can I get you something to drink?" I asked in a louder than normal voice as I opened the fridge.

"Beer is good. Be right out," she said, her voice echoing from her room.

I got two beers from the fridge and set hers on the granite countertop in the kitchen. I stayed put in the kitchen because she didn't close her bedroom door when she went in, and I didn't want to be *that guy*. The kitchen had no view into her bedroom, unlike the rest of her flat, and no chance of me looking like a perv.

She changed quickly and came out wearing a tight University of Pennsylvania T-shirt and a pair of black shorts. Even casual, she looked every bit a movie star. She walked over to the kitchen, grabbed her beer, took a sip, and then gave me a quick kiss on the cheek.

"Thanks."

She pulled the oven door open, took the glass cooking dish out, and set it on the counter.

The food smelled great, but it paled compared to the perfume Viki was wearing. Just the right amount so you could smell it when you were near her, but nonexistent from a distance.

"I like the T-shirt. It looks like one of those classic tees from the fifties or sixties," I said.

"That's the style. Everything old is now cool. It's amazing what you can get online these days," she said as she grabbed some plates from the cupboard. "You ready to eat?"

"Absolutely."

We had a great dinner and conversation. She was easy to talk to, just as before, and it was like we never had an issue.

She threw the dishes in the dishwasher and then sat on her sofa near the fireplace. She patted the seat next to her and looked at me. The universal sign of *come sit* was more than enough to get me to sit.

"I hope that was good enough to make up for the last dinnerless date?"

"It was great, really. I don't know who cooked that for you but tell them I said thanks. You owe them one."

She stared at me for a second, pretending to be mad before grabbing my little finger. She playfully twisted it, punishing me for my insolence.

We both smiled as our hands dropped, but she didn't let go of my finger. She got a better grip on it and pulled me closer. I didn't resist, and as soon as I was in striking distance, she kissed me.

I don't think the English language possesses the adjectives to describe that kiss. As ridiculous as it sounds, and I hate using it, *magical* is the only word that comes close. I didn't think the human body was capable of such emotion and feeling.

"Did you feel that or am I imagining things?" she said the second our lips separated.

She looked at me with those piercing gray eyes and I melted inside. Then I said the first dumb thing that popped in my head.

"Is this real?"

The question didn't really make sense and just came out. It didn't seem real. It was too perfect in too many ways.

In case it wasn't, I leaned in for another kiss. This one was longer and more passionate. She grabbed the back of my head and a handful of hair in the sexiest way imaginable. She pulled back, with eyes still closed, and then gradually opened them. She stared at me for a few seconds, and I could tell she was about to say something.

"What is it?" I asked, still trying to catch my breath and get my heart rate to a safe level.

"It's been a long time since I've dated anyone. Even longer since I went out with someone I cared about. Dating is... complicated for me."

"How do you mean? Because of work, or the personal issues you were talking about?"

I probably shouldn't have asked such a personal question, but I was hoping she would volunteer some information on her disappearance.

"Partly," she said, not specifying which.

She left the couch and walked over to the window, staring out into the darkness, apparently stalling for time.

"There is a lot about me you don't know. I mean more than the obvious things. Normally I wouldn't even mention it but... you're different," she said, looking over her shoulder at me.

I was a fair distance from her, but I could see the sadness in her eyes.

Coupled with all my recent bouts of phantom paranoia, which I was now questioning, I felt like I was in a fairy tale. This couldn't all be a coincidence. I walked over to where she was and stood next to her.

"Please tell me what you mean. Either I'm going crazy, or something weird is going on. I've been feeling like a fish out of water for some time now. I've heard and seen so many bizarre things lately, and it would be refreshing to hear the plain truth. I'm sure that whatever you're concerned about is probably not that big of a deal."

She turned to face me and grabbed my hand again.

"You have been through a lot, haven't you? But trust me, what I want to share with you is indeed *a big deal*. I've never been so torn in my life. There are things you may need..."

She stopped, rethinking her words.

"Wait. Wait a minute," I said. "What are we talking about here? I swear, I don't know who's more vague and cryptic, you or Bili."

I could see the change in Viki's eyes the second I mentioned Bili's name.

"What makes you say that?" she asked.

"Over the past few days, Bili has been talking in riddles and making odd comments, not unlike this conversation right now. Either you are both in on the same secret, or you are twins separated at birth."

Viki gave a quiet snort of a laugh.

"We couldn't be more different, trust me."

"See? Right there. You act like you know her, but you only saw her for a second or two. What aren't you telling me?"

When she didn't answer, I felt like I was being played for a fool. Like I said, I had my limits. Something was going on, and I was in the dark.

"Let me know when you want to have an honest conversation. Thanks for dinner," I said and then started for the door.

"Jack, wait," she said as she grabbed my arm and pulled me to her.

"I will have that honest talk with you, I promise. There's one thing I need to do first, and I can't do it tonight. Give me a few days. Please?"

I'm not exactly sure what I was going to say, but Viki didn't give me a chance. She kissed me again, pulled me to the couch, and pushed me on my back. She put her finger up against my lips as she straddled me.

I instantly lost my aggravation and curiosity. After another long kiss, she slid her head down to my chest and rested it there as I held her. My head, which had been a swirl of mixed emotions, now felt calm. I put all my questions aside, for now, hoping she would be true to her word and tell me what she was talking about soon.

The last thing I wanted to do was ruin the night by having her think I expected more. I decided I should leave.

"Thanks for a great night, Viki, but I'm sure you have to work tomorrow and it's probably better if I get going. Maybe next time we can finish our almost-talk?"

We got up in tandem and she was still holding my hand.

"We will, I promise," she said.

"Whatever it is, I hope you'll feel comfortable enough with me to talk about it," I said.

"Thanks for understanding."

I kissed her one more time, and she walked me to the front door. Once I got to the bottom of the steps, I opened the door to leave, but before I took another step, her hand came under my arm and pushed it shut. I froze in place before she spun me around for another kiss. This one was different, very different.

She grabbed my hand and walked me back up the stairs and right into her bedroom. It was dark, and the only light was from the moon shining through a sliver of window not blocked by her curtains. To say I was nervous didn't cover it by half, but her calming presence made me feel like I belonged with her.

She took full control, and I went without resistance. I'm not one to kiss and tell but I will say this, as cliché as it sounds, it was a night I'll never forget.

The next morning, I woke in the middle of an empty bed, and it took me a few minutes to realize where I was. I rolled over to the side and found a note on the pillow next to me.

Jack,
Stay as long as you like. Waffles in the freezer. xoxo
V

I stayed and ate some waffles. They were so-so.

27

The next day when I was walking to work, I was thinking about everything Viki had said the night before. I was analyzing every word and gesture and couldn't get over the similarities to what Bili had said. It couldn't have been a coincidence. I was going to hound Bili until the cows and any other livestock came home to get answers.

I arrived early so I could do all the prep before Bili got in. I didn't want her to have any excuses to make me wait. It was past ten, and Bili was still not in. I was getting aggravated to no end. The one time I wanted to sit down with her and have a conversation, she was late. She hadn't been late once since I've known her.

I was at the store by myself until Bili finally showed up around noon. I was waiting on two customers at once when she came in. She threw her things under the counter and took over one of the customers.

As the day went on, it remained busy, and I could never corner Bili for information. Day turned into evening, and I resigned myself to wait until we closed before I started my inquiries. That way there would be no chance of interruptions. I don't know why, but I felt certain I would get Bili to talk. I had a new confidence after coming off one of the greatest nights of my life.

"Did you get a hold of Leslie from Classic Interior Designs? She was due to pick up a few pieces for a client but they're still sitting in the back," Bili said.

"I left her at least four messages in the last two days," I said. "She may be a talented designer but she's a complete flake. Last week, she called me three times and asked the exact same question. I gave her the same answer every time, and each time it was as if she heard it for the first time."

Bili actually laughed.

"Before you started working here, she used to come into the shop more often. She was in lust with Theo, and of course he was never here, so I would have to listen to her endless natterings about cats. Did you know there are over one hundred different breeds of domestic cats?"

"I did not."

"I almost blew my brains out when she got into the fifties."

I let out a belly laugh. Bili was hilarious at times. Her cynical humor was like that of a New York City cop. She hated most people to begin with, but give her some ammunition, and she could be ruthless.

It was almost closing time, and we started placing the most valuable pieces away in the safe. The store was empty, and I couldn't wait any longer.

"Can I ask you something?"

"Sure, as long as it's not dumb. Contrary to what your Lit professor told you, there *are* dumb questions."

"The other day when we were in the truck, you were about to tell me something. What was it? And please don't give me some lame *I don't know what you're talking about* answer. You know what I'm talking about."

"Why do you ask?" she said seriously. I took this as a good sign.

"I was with Viki last night, and we had a conversation that was identical. And like you, she refused to finish her thought or tell me the whole story. I know something is up. I think I deserve to know, don't you?"

As I spoke, I raised my voice just a little. I wanted answers, but more than that, I needed them.

"I do. It's just that-"

She was about to talk when the front door chime rang, and two customers walked in.

Great.

They weren't in the store for more than a second when Bili grabbed my arm as I was about to walk out and assist them.

"Why don't you go home for the night. I'll take care of these two and close up."

"Go home? What about our conversation?"

"Tomorrow, I promise. I'll tell you everything."

Bili was talking to me, but she never took her eyes off the two guys that had just come in. They were making their way to the front counter, one slow step after another.

"Are you sure? Is everything alright? You look weird."

Bili turned and gave me a reassuring smile.

"I'm sure. Have a good night. Now get the hell out of here. Go out the back, too."

"Okay. Long talk tomorrow. I'm holding you to it," I said as I turned to walk toward the back.

"No need to rush off, Jack," one of them said as he approached.

I stopped walking and turned to look back at the approaching customers.

"Sorry, do I know you?" I said as I turned to face them.

The man that spoke was wearing a custom fitted button up black shirt and a look on his face that screamed *arrogance*. The other one was dressed more casually. He looked like he could be a student, an older football-playing student, but not totally out of place. They were both big but Black Shirt was far more menacing.

"I said I'll handle these two; now leave," Bili said, her voice raising and her look deadpan.

"I'm afraid you're not going anywhere. Neither are you whore," Black Shirt said.

What?

As the two got closer, I could see they both had the same color eyes. A very familiar color gray which made them even more glaring.

"I better call the police," I said as I took out my phone.

They were almost at the counter when Bili turned toward me, and in a split second, her face transformed into a combination of fear and anger as she stared directly into my eyes. She spoke the next sentence in a stern and deliberate voice.

"Jack, use the back door and run like hell."

Before I had time to protest, Bili shoved me with both of her hands to my chest area. The force of it felt like a car hit me. I went airborne, flying backward through the swinging doors, and into the back room. The phone in my hand flew from my grasp, and I assumed it landed where I had previously stood. I, however, landed a mere five feet from the rear exit. I must have traveled at least thirty or forty feet before I came to a stop.

I was on my back desperately trying to catch my breath as I had every bit of air knocked out of me, not to mention it felt like both of my lungs collapsed.

My mind raced as I tried to make sense of something that was beyond unbelievable.

How the hell did she do that?

I struggled to pick myself up off the floor, still gasping for air, and trying to regain my wits.

I could hear a commotion from the front area that sounded like multiple bulls in multiple china shops. It was not conceivable that people were making these noises, even in the worst of fights, let alone two guys against one small girl.

I was scared, almost to the point of being unable to move, like a nightmare you can't wake up from. I couldn't get over what was happening. When I did get up, I ran to the door, grabbed the handle, but froze before I pushed it open. I was scared to death and desperately wanted to run just as Bili instructed me to. So many things ran through my mind simultaneously in those few seconds. What if someone could have helped my mom but left because they were afraid? I had to go back. I couldn't leave Bili to die alone at the hands of those two maniacs.

I ran back and searched for anything I could use as a weapon. An art store is not rife with weaponry as you could imagine, but I saw an old golf club Theo had on his bookshelf. The plaque below it said: *Ben Hogan 1951*

Masters Champion, but I didn't give a shit. It was the only weapon I could find, and I grabbed it.

I gathered myself, took a deep breath, and walked back into the front portion of the store. What I saw defied all logic.

Black Shirt was bleeding from his nose and the other guy had a piece of a glass vase stuck in his head that he was pulling out as I entered. It appeared they had just gotten Bili under control. She had blood running down her face from several areas, but I didn't see any cuts. I had no idea what I was going to do but I tried to look as fierce as I could.

"I don't know what you guys want but take it and get the hell out of here!" I said as I held the club in a baseball stance.

The look on Bili's face wasn't fear as I might have expected. It was more of a look of disappointment and failure. The looks on the intruder's faces were just the opposite. Pure delight.

"Jack. Why didn't you leave? That was your chance," Bili said in a low somber voice as she hung her head in defeat.

The hulking man in the shorts dropped the shard of glass, and before it hit the floor, he was holding me by the neck. I barely saw him move it was so fast. The club hit the ground before I could even attempt a swing.

It was as if a steel vice was being clamped on each side of my neck as he squeezed. I could feel myself getting lightheaded from the slowing flow of blood in my carotid arteries. There was no fighting this monster. His strength was astounding. I felt like a child being led around by a steroid infused parent.

"There *is* something you can do for us, Jack," Black Shirt said.

"He doesn't know anything meat head. He's human, if you hadn't noticed," Bili said, knowing the road he was going down.

"Doesn't smell human but let's see. Franklin?"

The monster holding me punched me in the face, shattering my nose — then he squeezed my right forearm just below the elbow, snapping it like a pencil. It was such a surprise I didn't even feel the pain immediately. It didn't take long though.

"She's right, Kris. He's human, I guess," Franklin said sarcastically as he smiled a wide toothy grin.

Blood poured from my nose like a faucet for a few seconds before it slowed to a drip.

"This pathetic human, or whatever he is, is now in your hands, bitch. Tell me what I want to know, and you may live through this."

What does that mean? What does any of this mean?

"It's okay, Jack. It's gonna be alright," Bili said, trying to be reassuring. I'm sure fear was written all over my face as I hung from Franklin's hand.

"I hate to be the downer here, Jack," Kris said with a mocking frown face. "But I assure you, it's not okay, and it sure as hell is *not* going to be alright."

28

was still dangling from Franklin's grasp, while Bili was being held prisoner by Kris, though it appeared he wasn't hurting her at the moment. I figured they could kill us at any time, especially me, because apparently, I was the only human in the room. I was trying to deal with the pain and mentally process the bizarre situation I was in. I was not having much luck on either front.

"You idiots better think about what you're doing. If you think you can do something like this and just waltz outta here, you're dumber than you look, and trust me, you look du-"

Bili couldn't finish before Kris punched her square in the mouth.

"Sorry sweetheart, you were saying?" he said as Bili dropped to the ground.

He helped her up by grabbing a handful of hair as Bili wiped the blood away from a cut on her cheek that healed within seconds.

What the hell.

I didn't know what was more amazing. Bili taking punches from a guy this huge or the fact I had just saw a large cut on her face heal in seconds. If I wasn't in so much pain, I would assume this was all a dream.

As soon as Bili was upright, her defiance continued.

"I was saying, you two rockheads are—"

Smack!

Another boxer-style punch to Bili's face and then another to her stomach. She fell to her knees, coughing and spitting blood onto the floor. He wasn't taking into account she was female or half his size at all. The punches landed with a sickening thud that made me wince with sympathy pain. Though she was showing a tough exterior, he had to be hurting her.

"I was told you might be a handful," Kris said.

"Leave her alone! I'll tell you anything you want, please stop hurting her," I pleaded.

Franklin shut me up, and quick. A backhand to my face caused my head to whip back. I felt the orbital bone around my left eye shatter. Another cut opened and blood trailed into my eye and down my cheek.

Other than the beating, they acted as though I wasn't even there. All conversation was directed to Bili. Franklin held me as casually as a normal person would hold a broom stick. It was obvious I wasn't worth acknowledging. I had never felt as worthless as I did in that moment.

Seeing Bili taking abuse from this predator was making me mad. Though I was scared out of my wits, there was an anger building inside me. I felt a slight fever take over my entire body. It was the strangest sensation and I'd never felt it before.

"They're looking for someone," Bili said, glancing at me, and then she turned to Kris. "Isn't that right, genius?"

Bili regained her footing again and stared right into the eyes of this Kris character, showing no signs of fear. It was something to see.

"See Franklin? Not all leeches are complete idiots. Tell us where she is, and we'll be on our way."

She?

"So, after I tell you what you want to know, you leave us alone? Just like that?"

Bili couldn't have sounded more sarcastic or condescending if she tried. That's saying a lot.

"Yes. Well, one-arm here is coming with us, but you can go back to your normal pathetic life and go on doing whatever it is your kind do."

What did these guys want with me? I'm nobody.

Then something struck me. I don't know why but something Viki had said to me on our first date popped in my head.

You are far from normal, Jack.

"And I suppose you have her best interest in mind?"

The question came out completely rhetorical and with an added look Bili had perfected.

"Our business is none of your concern. Consider yourself lucky you are not part of our business."

"I feel pretty lucky, but nonetheless, I'm going to have to call bullshit on everything you just said. I have a built-in lie detector, or didn't your trainer teach you that? And you're not taking Jack anywhere, dipshit."

The way Bili said that almost made me believe her.

"We're done with this conversation," he said as he looked over at his friend.

"Franklin?"

Within a fraction of a second, Franklin grabbed me by the shoulders and squeezed. Both of my collar bones collapsed under his grasp. There was no delayed reaction to the pain this time. It was powerful and severe. I was shaking from the pain and agony. Saliva and blood were dripping from my mouth as I tried to stifle my scream.

"Stop this! I know someone else sent you assholes here and you obviously don't know who he is. You're making a grave mistake. Let him go and I'll talk," Bili said.

She had lost all her sarcasm as she pleaded with them to stop torturing me. Her eyes were still furious, but she attempted to regain herself for my sake.

"Where?"

Bili remained silent as she looked at me with worry. She knew what was coming.

Franklin moved me so I was facing him, and then he punched me in the face again before breaking my other arm. Every bone in my face felt shattered like glass. Blood was pouring down from several fresh cuts, leaving droplets all over the tile floor.

I was now as helpless as a newborn baby. It was as if I had been in a head-on collision going a hundred miles per hour with no seat belt. It was at this point I knew I was going to die. I could no longer even cry out. Franklin was the only thing keeping me from crumbling to the ground in a pile of immobile flesh and crushed bones. Tears and blood streamed down my face as I looked up at Bili. I just wanted to see a friendly face before I died. I had reached my limit and wished for the end. There was nothing left in me. I was emotionally, and physically, crushed.

That's when I heard it.

A sound came out of Bili that I had never heard before, anywhere, by anything. It shocked me enough to regain a brief burst of clarity.

Bili went for the throat of Kris quick as lightning and caught him by surprise. She took a bite out of his neck and drew blood, but the powerful creature pulled her off before she caused any real damage. The wound didn't heal as fast as Bili's, but it wasn't far behind.

He grabbed her by the neck and hit her in the face with a punch that appeared to be with all his power. I knew Bili couldn't handle much more of this. We were both going to die, and there was nothing either of us could do about it.

The last punch sent Bili to the ground at my feet with a thud. Kris grabbed her by the throat and picked her off the ground with one hand. Bili's feet were a good thirty inches from the floor as Kris looked into her eyes with unbridled anger.

"Last chance, whore. That's right, I know all about you. Where is she?" he growled.

Bili moved her head ever so slightly in the tight grasp of Kris's hand, trying desperately to look at me. The defeated look in her eyes said it all. I could see tears in her eyes as she could only silently mouth the words, *I'm sorry,* while in the grip of this madman. She had done everything she could to save my life but ultimately to no avail.

I stared at Bili a few seconds longer before finally hanging my head in defeat. Death was coming and I welcomed it with open arms.

But it didn't come. Not only that, something was happening. The burning sensation that started inside my gut earlier was back and spreading fast. It was intensifying at a steady rate. It doubled — then it doubled again. It became so acute that the pain in my arms, shoulders, and face disappeared in an instant. I had, for some unknown reason, regained a clear mind. The burning was now racing through my veins and into my extremities. No pain, no fear, just a silent, controlled fury throughout my entire body. I was seconds from death, I knew I was, but now I felt... different. Very different.

My eyes snapped open, darting from the ground to our attackers, and then back to Bili.

As Bili looked at me, I saw her somber face change into a devilish knowing grin. She averted her gaze from me, back to Kris. I couldn't believe it. Bili was now smiling at him, and just like that, the Bili I knew was back and defiant as ever.

Though my entire body was surging with this unknown rejuvenation, I felt a specific and strange sensation on my left foot. It was as if warm water had leaked into my sock and shoe. I looked down the best I could while still being held by Franklin's iron arms, and a realization washed over me like a tsunami wave.

The sadness in Bili's eyes wasn't because she was hurt and possibly facing death, though we both very much were. It was something else entirely. Something I just started to believe and understand. Though impossible, there was no other explanation.

Bili had bitten me on the ankle just above my shoe. The dark color of my sock had disguised the wound just enough that our attackers did not appear to notice. Not to mention she accomplished this with lightning speed when knocked to the ground at my feet. I never saw or felt a thing.

A change was underway and a rapid one.

Within seconds I could feel the bones in my arms set and heal. The collar bones popped back into place with perfect precision. I could feel my teeth harden and maybe even grow a fraction. I had that feeling in my jaw like I had just blown up a thousand tiny balloons. Every muscle fiber in my once-skinny frame swelled and tightened like stretched piano strings. The simultaneous feeling of euphoria and rage flushed over me as Franklin held me. The once immovable force of his hand now felt like a playful grabbing of a high school friend.

The smile on Bili's face enraged Kris and he was about to unload on her when she spoke.

"Okay. You guys win," Bili said, trying to sound thoroughly repentant. "I'll tell you where she is. It's not far from here."

"Where?" Kris said. He was obviously at the end of his patience.

"It's a high-rise apartment in Detroit near the train station, but getting there is complicated. That being said, I need to ask you a question."

"What?" Kris growled.

"If you were to get on a train in Ann Arbor and it's traveling at sixty miles per hour." Then Bili looked at Franklin, continuing in a tone of a first grade teacher. "And you were to get on another train in Grosse Pointe, traveling at eighty miles per hour, and the distance between the two is seventy-one miles, tell me this? Which one of you two fucking morons is dumbest?"

Bili looked Kris straight in the eyes with all the hatred and contempt she could muster and spit in his face.

Kris was so enraged his face went almost purple.

He slammed Bili's body against the hard floor with all his might, causing Bili to lose consciousness for a few seconds.

I knew exactly what Bili was doing.

Stalling.

Bili, whom I thought was the coldest, most uncaring individual in the world, was now risking her life to save mine. I had no time to ponder the question of why, as every thought and sense focused on this ongoing change.

I don't know how I knew this, but I did. I was seconds away from becoming just like Bili. This was not a dream. I was now something else. It was the only logical explanation. What I knew as impossible moments ago was now an absolute certainty.

After Bili hit the floor, Kris kicked her over and over. She was trying to protect herself as best she could, but the blows were connecting with horrific regularity. Then I saw the look in Kris's eyes.

"I've had it with you, bitch! Say goodnight!" Kris said as he raised his large black boot into the air, about to stomp on Bili's head as she lay helplessly on the ground.

Seeing the grin on Franklin's face, along with the beating Bili was taking, ignited my already burning fury like a powder keg.

The change was complete.

Franklin sniffed, as if he just realized a change in my scent. He looked into my eyes and saw something he didn't like. His smile vanished, and fast.

"What the-" Franklin started to say.

Before Franklin could finish or make a move, I broke his grip and charged Kris before he could kill Bili. I had no plan other than to hit that son-of-a-bitch as hard and fast as I could. I lowered my shoulder and with a speed I didn't have time to appreciate or comprehend, I hit him square in the chest. I sent him flying into the air, and his body crashed into a cast iron coat rack before hitting the wall. One hook pierced the back of his shoulder and came out the front part of his upper chest.

Bili stood up, shook off her beating, and didn't hesitate a second before attacking Franklin. Franklin appeared stunned by what happened because he failed to react until it was too late. Bili kicked Franklin between the legs so hard he came off his feet. No matter what powers he possessed, it was not enough to keep him from doubling over in agony. Bili followed up with a knee to the face that knocked him on his back.

Kris was struggling with his position as he tried to pull the curved steel rack from his body, while Franklin was trying to put his nose back in the correct position.

Even with Franklin and Kris stalled temporarily, a fight with them was too risky.

"Let's go!" she yelled.

I followed Bili to the backroom, and we headed for the rear door that I didn't use earlier. As Bili got closer to the door, she didn't slow to open it. She did the exact opposite. She sped up, lowered her shoulder, and hit the door with force. The doors flew open, leaving small pieces of metal everywhere.

Holy shit!

Seeing what Bili was capable of was hard to process but I didn't have time to think about. We were literally running for our lives. We entered the alley at a full sprint, but Franklin and Kris were now giving chase. The speed we were traveling was incredible, and I marveled at my own abilities.

We rounded the first corner, temporarily out of sight from our friends, when I heard Bili say, "Keep going; I'll catch up."

Bili slowed to a stop, grabbed a barrel of something that was behind a restaurant, and threw it in the path of our pursuers. When it hit the pavement, a dark black liquid burst from the barrel and covered the alley from end to end. They made the turn and didn't see the greasy substance until it was too late. Kris hit the cement, back first, and slid into a series of large garbage containers. Franklin kept upright only moments longer before falling face first and sliding into the same stockpile.

Bili caught up, just as she said she would.

"If we can get some distance on them after the turn, we can lose them in a vacant building two blocks up," Bili said.

"Right behind you," I said, surprised I could talk while running so fast.

Bili was in front of me, and as soon as we came to the last turn, I looked ahead and saw something terrible. Just when I felt we might get away, I saw a lone figure standing directly in front of us. A colossal lone figure.

My new sense of smell and instincts told me instantly that he was the same as Franklin and Kris, whatever that may be. This was bad.

We were lucky to get away the first time, but three of them would put a quick end to this fight, especially from the looks of this one. We were at a tremendous disadvantage now.

Both Franklin and Kris gained more ground as Bili and I pulled up abruptly before this ominous figure.

Bili slowed down to a walk but approached the roadblock of a man with no hesitation. I was a few steps back and if this was it, I guess we would go down fighting. Escape was not an option any longer. It was a small alley, and we would never get around this mountain before the other two were upon us.

We came to a stop in front of him, and my mind raced to come up with a plan to either fight or escape. That was until he spoke.

"Bili," the man said politely with a simple nod.

"Hey, Claude. You don't know how glad I am to see you," Bili said.

What?

Our attackers were now only about twenty yards from us and my apparent new best friend. Bili and I took a spot on each side of Claude and turned to face Franklin and Kris. They slowed to a crawl before stopping a good ten yards away.

"Kristov, I see you've met Bili and Jack," Claude said. His speech was deliberate and menacing.

How the hell does everyone know my name?

"Kristov?" I heard Bili say under her breath as she looked at Claude and then to Kris.

The name obviously meant something to her. If this person is famous enough to be known by name, rather than sight, it was not good.

"I see you've chosen the other side *again*," Kristov said, emphasizing the last word. "The lack of loyalty to your own kind has no limits."

If he was afraid of Claude, you would never have known it. He exhibited the same mixture of calmness and anger as he did at the store.

"What the hell happened to you?" Claude said. He looked as if he was disappointed in one of his kids.

"You *know* what happened. You abandoned me when I needed you most. Theodorus too, for that matter. But, whatever the fuck. I'm not here to reminisce. Give me the kid and we'll be on our way."

"No."

With my new senses, I could hear a low-grade growl from the gut of this Kristov. He seemed to be struggling with a decision he didn't want to make.

"You're not invincible, Claude. I need the kid. Give him to me and we'll leave," Kristov said.

The look Franklin gave Kristov was that of utter disbelief. It was obvious he didn't want any part of a fight with Claude, and Kristov seemed to challenge him.

Claude turned to look at me, stared for a few seconds, and then looked at Bili.

"Franklin was killing him. I had no choice," Bili said, as if reading his mind.

Claude turned his attention directly to Franklin. He became instantly pissed about something, and at the time I didn't have a clue as to why. I even thought I heard his teeth grind.

"Give him to me!" Kristov spat.

Claude, who appeared to calm himself, at least a little, continued, nice and slow.

"It's choice time. You are going to turn and walk, or we are going to see if you are as powerful as you seem to think you are."

Claude moved up one step, lowered his chin, raised his eyes, and produced a snarl that would have given my human self a heart attack.

"Choose," Claude growled.

Kristov tensed and moved forward. Franklin was preparing himself as well. Though attacking Claude didn't appear to be Franklin's first choice, he wasn't a coward. I had lost all my fear back in the store and I was ready for battle. I knew nothing of this Claude, but it was plain he was someone I wanted on my side.

I could see the slightest change in Kristov's eyes, his posture, and a few other subtle differences that I would never have noticed before. I was gathering information from the slightest moves and gestures as if someone was talking to me. Everything about him screamed a fight was imminent, and it was.

Just like that, Kristov and Franklin exploded into motion, heading right for us.

There wasn't time for any kind of plan, so I bent my knees and waited for impact. I hoped to use this newfound speed to my advantage and make them miss the first charge and then counter attack.

I was about to make my move when I caught a blur in my peripheral vision. I thought we were being attacked from behind until I heard and saw the collision of bodies in front of me.

Theo!

Even with the new abilities I now possessed, I knew the speed I had just witnessed had to be without equal. Theo colliding with both Kristov and Franklin created a unique and unusual sound. He caught them at just the right angle as to have them collide with each other, sending them both into another large steel garbage dumpster.

Theo regained his footing and made his way next to the three of us. Kristov and Franklin stumbled as they untangled themselves from each other.

"Sorry about that, Kris, but I've done you a favor. You too, Franklin, but don't worry, you can owe me," Theo said in his usual pleasant tone as if he was talking to an old friend.

Kristov was furious. When he stood up, he kicked the garbage dumpster he crashed into and sent it skidding across the pavement and into a brick wall. Shards of brick and sparks went flying in all directions. It was an impressive feat of strength.

"You think I'm scared of you, Theodorus?! You have no idea what I'm capable of!" Kris shouted with saliva spewing from his mouth as he spoke.

Kristov's teeth appeared to be more prominent and ominous as he yelled at Theo. I had never seen anyone or anything so irate in my life.

This time, Franklin grabbed Kristov and stopped any more forward movement. Less emotionally involved in the situation, Franklin was making better decisions.

"Kris! It's not the time," Franklin said.

Kristov stopped, regained his rational self, and stared at all four of us.

"Next time," he said, pointing his finger.

They backed away one step at a time before they turned and disappeared. They were out of sight in seconds.

Theo took a second to check his surroundings and then focused his attention on me. I was in a terrible state. Though I felt great, being covered in blood from my beating made quite the sight.

Déjà Vu.

"From the looks of things, I missed some excitement," Theo said, breaking the tension.

There was no one in the world at that moment I was happier to see than Theo. It wasn't just because he tipped the scales in our favor, which thankfully he did, but something less tangible.

"Bili, you and Jack go back to the store. I'll be there shortly," Theo said.

Bili and I did as we were told without question. Even though my mind was full of infinite questions, I felt a renewed sense of patience. I figured after the day's events, I would get answers sooner rather than later, for a change. At least one cat was out of the proverbial bag.

Bili and I made our way back to the POH in a silent march. After the excitement of potential death waned, I felt the physical changes that occurred over the last half hour. Most of them felt rather subtle, like the way I walked, and the thickness and texture of my skin. I also felt some internal differences as well, which would be very hard to explain, but they were there. Some changes I wouldn't notice until later.

When we got there, I did the best I could to clean the blood off my face with a wet rag, and then I boarded up the rear door as best I could with what we had in the storage area. Bili began clean-up on the broken everything in the front, and we both tended to our menial tasks in quiet reflection.

29

"Thanks, old friend," Theo said. "You saved their lives tonight. I owe more than I can say."

"Luck. I was coming to see you about another matter," Claude said.

Theo knew his friend would never take such credit. He never did. He looked around as if taking in the whole of the situation they now found themselves.

"They may have the advantage now," Theo said.

"Maybe," Claude said as he looked at Theo to make his next point clear. "Word will spread."

"Like wildfire," Theo said.

Claude nodded.

"You think the General is behind any of this?" Theo asked.

"He's in the States," Claude said. "Confirmed it yesterday. That's what brought me to your place."

"We need a meeting. Think you can find him?"

"Yes," Claude said. Then after a momentary pause, he spoke again. "Did you notice?"

"I did. Ever see anything like it?" Theo asked.

"Never."

30

The doctor was staring at Jack as he took a pause in his story. She was gauging everything about him, and he appeared to be doing the same.

Does he really believe this, or is it something else?

He wouldn't have been the first intelligent person, who appeared to have his full wits, to fall prey to mental disease. No one was completely immune. There was another part of her that was still suspicious of Jack.

"Ask," Jack said, breaking the silent stalemate.

"What are you then?" the doctor asked.

She asked this in a manner that revealed curiosity rather blatant disbelief.

"The name is so old it doesn't even exist anymore, but the closest modern term would be, vampire. Well, mostly."

"Vampire?"

Sara tried to keep the doubt out of her tone, but it came out that way regardless.

"I know how it sounds, trust me. The word itself conjures up so many fantastic images and stories, most of which is complete nonsense. But in fairness, several millennia of stories and folklore will do that to anything, as you can imagine."

"What do mean, mostly?"

"I'm getting to that. Do you believe me?"

This was another one of *those* questions. Any answer given would have its own consequences. Sara was still trying to get a read on her patient, who was still a mystery. This was the second time he put her on the spot with a direct question like this, and she could tell he knew what he was doing by asking it.

"If I said yes, would you believe I was telling the truth?"

"I would have to hear it."

"No. I do not believe you," she said bluntly and honestly.

Instead of being upset, Jack gave a look that said he expected this and understood.

"And for good reason. If you took a poll and asked a thousand people if they believed in ghosts, how many do you think would say they did?" Jack asked.

"Couple hundred."

"Agreed."

"If you said aliens, the Loch Ness Monster, or even Bigfoot, you may still get a fair amount. How many of those do you think believe in vampires? Real vampires, not the wannabees on Halloween."

"One, maybe."

"At best," Jack said. "My point is this. Without serious proof, no one would ever believe we exist. Our kind has evolved to where we are virtually indistinguishable from humans."

"The same goes for the wolves?" she asked.

"Yes. It's easy for humans to disregard anything that doesn't fit into a preconceived mold. It's just how your minds work," Jack said as he stared into the disbelieving eyes of his physician.

Jack looked away from the doctor, got up, walked behind his chair, and paced back and forth, gathering his next thoughts.

"So, why am I telling you this? Why would I try to convince you of something that I just told you we keep very secret?"

"My next question," she said.

Jack stopped, put his hand on the back of the chair, and gave Sara his full attention.

"There's a reason."

"Which is?"

Jack sat back down, eyeing Sara speculatively.

"Please forgive me, but I don't want to get into that yet," Jack said. "I know I seem unnecessarily evasive, especially after my big speech, but this is a point I must insist on. You will understand when the time comes, I assure you."

"Okay. Who was this *she* Kristov was looking for?"

Jack let out the slightest harumph. It was as if he was surprised Sara asked about this. His lack of a quick response didn't go unnoticed.

"Well?"

"I must say, you are a good listener. I will also say this, the answer to that question will change things."

"What things?"

Before Jack could answer, there was a timid knock. Both Sara and Jack directed their attention to the door as it opened.

"I am so sorry to bother you, doctor, but you are being summoned to the King's office," Nancy said, just above a whisper, trying not to intrude more than she already had.

Sara knew without even asking that she was directed to interrupt her session by him.

"Who did I kill in my former life to deserve this?" Sara said under her breath.

She had half a mind not to respond at all and ignore him altogether, consequences be damned. She reconsidered thinking of her patient. That would only result in further delays. She decided not to prolong the agony.

"I am so sorry, Jack. I'll be back shortly."

"Everything alright?"

"It would be if..." Sara stopped herself before saying something inappropriate.

"Yeah, it's fine. I'll be right back."

Sara made her way to his office, which was bigger and nicer than Mr. O'Rourke's. She always wondered how he managed that.

When she got to his door, she found it closed. Just another way of making her feel inferior to him.

She knocked.

Nothing.

She knocked again.

"Come," Spencer said, leaving off the *in* purposely to make it more of a command than a suggestion.

Bastard.

"You wanted to see me?"

Spencer pointed to the seat in front of him without speaking. He was still looking at some paperwork on his desk and didn't feel the need to acknowledge her.

Sara rolled her eyes and then sat down.

"I'm very busy, doctor. What do you want?" Sara said, trying to get this over with as soon as possible.

Dr. Kaufland continued writing in silence, ignoring her question. He finally closed the file and looked at Sara.

"I'm taking you off the John Doe. I'm taking over his treatment from here on out," he said.

"You mean Jack? And why would you do that exactly? He's my patient," Sara said, holding her anger as best she could.

"No, he's the hospital's patient and I decide who treats who. Though you think so, you are not in a private practice yet, doctor. There are rules to be followed."

"But-" She tried to say before Dr. Kaufland cut her off.

"Quiet! I'm not done. You've been attempting to undermine me since you got here, and I've had it. I'm still in charge and while I am, you will do as you're told."

"Wait just a minute."

"You're leaving, are you not? Why do you care about this patient so much? Is it professional, or is there something else I wonder?"

The suggestion was far from cloaked and insulting.

Sara could feel the tears of anger welling up in her eyes. The last thing she wanted was to give Spencer the satisfaction of seeing her cry.

"If that's your decision, I'll have the file brought to your office."

"No need. I've already sent someone for it. Now you can spend the rest of your time cleaning out your office," he said dismissively.

Sara got up and walked to the door. Before she left, she turned back to Spencer.

"I'll be making a formal complaint with the board. Now go back to pretending to work on that paperwork," she said, and then slammed his door.

When she got back to her office Nancy could tell something was wrong.

"That little weasel Tony just went into your office and took something. Is everything alright?" Nancy asked.

"No," Sara said.

She sat in Nancy's guest chair again. Thinking.

"Is he checking your work? You barely got started on treatment."

"He's not reviewing it. He's taking over my patient," Sara said, chewing on her pen.

"What?"

"I know," Sara said, staring off to the side, thinking. "If you find yourself in possession of that file again, could you make me a copy?"

Nancy smiled and gave a conspiratorial nod.

"I'll be right back," Sara said.

Sara grabbed her purse and left the hospital. She returned with a large bag and went straight to Jack's room. She bought Jack an early dinner from the restaurant across the street, partly as an excuse to see him one last time and explain why she wouldn't be continuing his treatment.

When she opened the door, Jack was lying on the bed. He got up when Sara came into the room and made his way to the chair.

"I hope you're hungry. I ordered way too much, as usual," she said.

"To what do I owe this unexpected pleasure?"

Sara couldn't hide the look of disappointment from her face.

"Since I will no longer be your doctor, I was hoping we could have a decent meal together and just talk as friends."

"Why is that?" Jack asked, wrinkling his brow with mild exacerbation.

This was unexpected, as Sara thought he may be indifferent about the change.

"The doctor in charge seems to think he's a better fit for your treatment and is taking over. I'm probably not even supposed to be here right now, but I didn't want you to think I abandoned you or didn't care enough to at least say goodbye. I'm really sorry, Jack," Sara said as she set her uneaten food down and ran her hands through her hair in aggravation.

"Is this a normal procedure?"

"Absolutely not..." Sara stopped herself again. She knew if she made this about her, it wouldn't help Jack. This was about him and his treatment, not about her personal problems at work.

"It will be fine, Jack. Dr. Kaufland is an experienced doctor and I'm sure he can help you. He has a different philosophy than me, that's all. C'mon, let's eat before it gets cold."

They ate with each other, talking only of unimportant things and nothing to do with Jack's story. The doctor enjoyed the company of this young man and regretted being unable to hear the end of his incredible story. Even though she knew it to be fantastic, she was certain that there were several layers of truth in there. One of which could be the key to his recovery.

The doctor cleaned up the takeout boxes and then stood up to leave.

"I wish nothing but good things for you, Jack. Something about you tells me you'll be okay," she said.

"Thanks, Doc. Thanks for dinner as well. Good southern cooking is a rare treat for me."

"You're very welcome. Is there anything you need before I leave? I'm not sure we'll get another chance to talk or see each other before they discharge you."

"No, I don't think so. Thanks for listening."

"My pleasure. Good luck in the future. I mean that."

"Thank you. I'm sure things will work out."

With that, Sara got up, walked to the door, stopped, shuffled her feet clumsily, and left the room. It felt so unnatural for Sara to leave a patient without the proper closure. She didn't like it at all.

She shut the door behind her and had a heavy feeling of sadness that she couldn't quite explain. She had never had an emotional connection with a patient in such a short time, and it bothered her she didn't understand why.

31

D r. Kaufland entered Jack's room with confidence and swagger. The first attempt to speak to Jack left a sour taste in his mouth, and he was looking forward to this next conversation.

Spencer would never allow a patient to make *him* look bad. He would finish Jack's treatment, even if he had to take some liberties, and then send him on his way. Either to another facility or back out on the street — it didn't matter to him one way or another.

Though Dr. Kaufland considered himself a professional, he was first and foremost a narcissist. Dr. Richards would not show him up by completing what he could not.

Jack was already sitting in one of the conversation chairs, staring at

Spencer when he entered the room. It was as if he was waiting for the doctor.

"I'm glad to see you are feeling better... Jack?" Dr. Kaufland said.

"Yes, I am feeling better. Dr. Richards is an excellent doctor."

"Ah, you talk. I had a suspicion you might. That's great. It will make things much easier for both of us."

Spencer sat in the chair opposite of Jack and got comfortable. He organized his file, put his glasses on, and prepared for the session.

"Well, maybe not for both of us, Spencer," Jack said, using the doctor's first name as if he was a subordinate.

The look on Dr. Kaufland's face changed, along with his body language. He looked Jack in the eye and saw a sinister look that made him uneasy. It even gave him a slight chill, but he knew better than to show any signs of weakness.

"What do you mean? I hope that's not some thinly veiled threat. Your stay here could be substantial with that attitude."

"I doubt that," Jack said, sitting up in his chair and leaning toward Spencer.

Spencer frowned but Jack continued before he could speak.

"I know your kind all too well and I know you," Jack said as he raised a single finger and pointed at Dr. Kaufland. "This may not be the usual doctor-patient conversation you are used to, but I suggest you listen and listen carefully."

"No, you listen-"

"Shut up!" Jack snapped. It was just under a yell but with a sternness that couldn't be denied.

He shut up.

Jack regained a softer demeanor about himself. He laced his fingers together in front of him, taking on the mannerisms of a stereotypical psychiatrist about to start a session.

"You've been a doctor at this hospital for seven years," Jack began. "And in that time, you've made some excellent strides, considering your meager abilities and pedigree. The online University of Wright & Anderson doesn't open as many doors as one would think, does it? Yet you still did okay for yourself, didn't you? It wasn't without its roadblocks, though."

Dr. Kaufland squirmed in his chair. He didn't like what he was hearing at all.

Jack continued.

"The sexual harassment complaint from your former secretary, Ann Pearless. That was a close one, but she withdrew her complaint after she received a visit from a stranger in the night. How about that suspicious fire at your failed practice? Remember your partner, Martin Scofield? Apparently, he fell asleep on one of the sofas that night and never made it out, making you the sole beneficiary of the insurance. Then you thought it would be a nice resume builder if you were the head of a large psychiatric facility. The first two didn't work out, but you figured out an easier way to get what you wanted. How many private investigators did you have to hire before you finally got something on Mr. O'Rourke? He's a good man, but you got something on him just embarrassing enough to get the job you wanted.

"Then there are the underage girls, drugs, and the contents of your home computer. Not the desk-top mind you but the laptop hidden in the closet. Naughty boy Spence, very naughty indeed," Jack said, shaking his head with disappointment.

Dr. Kaufland was speechless, but inside he was angry. He wasn't the guy who was the victim. He made others the victim. The weak, the lambs, the ones who didn't matter. He was tired of listening to this. He was in charge.

"Who the hell are you?" Dr. Kaufland asked, attempting to regain his control.

"No one of consequence," Jack said casually.

"I don't care what you think you know. I could have you locked away for the rest of your life with a snap of my fingers. Look around you. This is a secure facility, and I hold all the keys!"

Jack appeared to be waiting for this. The attempt to regain his position of power.

"You're right. I'm here. However," Jack said, "my associates are not. You may have dabbled in the realm of intimidation and coercion, but trust me Spencer, if we need to pay a visit to 534 Townsend Lane, it will not end well."

The look Jack gave Spencer unnerved him but not as much as Jack knowing his home address.

"What do you want?" Spencer asked.

"Always the pragmatic. Good boy. First, you will draft your letter of resignation and give it to Mr. O'Rourke before the end of business today. You will tell him you're sorry for your immediate departure, but you will have to resign right away. Something tells me he'll be okay with it. Then you will make the lawsuit against Sara go away. Yes, I know it was you that fabricated the anonymous information to the press and Michael's parents. Failure to do any of these will forfeit the deal."

"Deal?"

"Yes. The one where you do as you're told, and I let you go about your miserable existence relatively unscathed. Now move your ass, Doctor."

With fury in his eyes, Spencer grabbed his file, got up, and walked to the door. He opened the door and looked back at Jack with defiance in his eyes.

"Don't do anything unwise, Spence," Jack warned. "I'll know."

Spencer was ready to do what he was told, but the more he thought about everything, the more he figured it was a ruse. He was the doctor, and he would not be told what to do by a psychiatric patient. He didn't give a shit how much he knew about him. There were several plausible explanations for how he could obtain the information he had. Jack was in lockdown, and if Spencer gave the word, they would send him to a maximum-security facility. The inmates do not run this asylum.

32

Sara was eight hours into a twelve-hour shift when she received a call from Nancy. She looked out the door and saw she wasn't calling from her desk.

"Is something wrong? You sound... weird."

"You could say that. You need to go to Dr. Kaufland's office right away," Nancy said, and then she hung up.

What's this about? He already took my patient.

Sara planned to give Spencer a piece of her mind, and if he said one cross word, she was quitting on the spot. She marched down the hall with vigor and purpose.

She got to his door and didn't bother knocking. She wasn't about to allow him to humiliate her again by making her wait outside. She stormed inside and found Mr. O'Rourke and Nancy waiting for her. They both had odd looks on their faces.

"Well... what do you think?" Mr. O'Rourke asked.

"What?" Sara said.

Mr. O'Rourke looked to the front of the desk, gesturing to the plaque centered in the middle. The plaque had a long piece of computer paper taped to it.

Director of Psychiatry – Dr. Sara Richards

Sara stiffened as she read it twice.

"Has a nice ring to it for sure, but-"

"No buts, just say yes. I know you planned to leave, but I'm hoping this new position, and a nice raise, will keep you here. Sorry about the crude paper title, but I didn't have time to have the plate engraved properly. What do you say?" he asked, almost pleading.

Sara was in minor shock. She had been all set to leave and now this.

"What happened to Spencer?" Sara asked.

"That's a mystery," Mr. O'Rourke said. "I received his letter of resignation less than an hour ago. Effective immediately. I'm not one to look a present horse in the face, or whatever that dumb saying is, I'm just happy he moved on. I have to think you are too."

"Mouth," Sara prompted.

"What?"

"Gift horse in the mouth," Sara said.

"Face, mouth, nose, whatever. Do you accept?"

"I accept, I accept. Thank you," Sara said with a wide grin.

"You're welcome. I'm afraid we are going to be short a doctor for a while until you can hire someone, so you will have to take over any patients Spencer may have been treating. Is that okay?"

"That won't be a problem," Sara said. "We only have a few patients right now."

"Oh yes. I heard there was a new mysterious young man who came in yesterday. I've heard more than a few people make mention of him. Anything to it?"

Nancy looked at Sara and smirked.

"We'll see. It's early," Sara said, hoping Mr. O'Rourke didn't press for further details. He didn't.

"Good luck, Dr. Richards. I mean, Director."

33

Sara was in her old office boxing up her personal items to move into her new digs. She couldn't believe how much crap she had in her cramped space.

Nancy walked in to help with the packing.

"Nancy," Sara said, almost as a whisper. "Any idea what really happened to Spencer? It doesn't make sense."

Nancy became serious and lowered her voice.

"I have contacts everywhere at this hospital and no one, and I mean no one, knows anything."

"I can't believe he would just quit," Sara said.

"I agree. If I hear anything, I'll let you know."

"Other business," Sara said, changing the subject. "You're getting a raise. Move your things to our new office as soon as you can. Oh, and tell Tony he is now your personal assistant."

"In that case, you deal with your patient, and I'll finish up here."

"Thanks, Nancy."

Sara wanted to get back to *her* patient, knowing that she had lost some valuable time. Jack's story was taking some surprising turns and she felt she was getting somewhere. She also knew that too much delay could impede progress. Sara grabbed her essentials and made her way to Jack's room.

She gave a quick obligatory knock and then went in. Jack was standing at the window, looking out.

"Good afternoon, Jack. Any blue jays?"

Jack turned to look at Sara.

"There was one earlier, but he just disappeared."

Jack sat down in the conversation chair without being asked.

"Are you just visiting, or is it something else?" Jack asked.

"Apparently things *worked out* after all. I will resume as your doctor for the rest of your stay."

"Hmm, what changed?"

Sara looked at Jack suspiciously. She wasn't sure if it was the way he spoke, the comment about the bird, or the fact that he wasn't surprised to see her, but something was off.

"Do you know anything about Dr. Kaufland?"

"What do you mean?"

"Did he talk to you earlier?" Sara asked.

"He did. He came in here, made some threats about keeping me locked up indefinitely, and then left. He couldn't have been in here five minutes."

"He threatened you?" Sara said. "I'm sorry about his behavior, Jack. Rest assured you will no longer be dealing with him. He quit today."

"Can't say I'm sorry to hear that. How do you feel about it?"

Sara smiled a half grin.

"It may not be very professional to say so, but I'm not sorry either."

"Do you have somewhere to be, or would you like to get back to our story?" Jack said.

Our?

"I do not. Do you remember where we left off?"

34

Theo walked in the shop while Bili and I were still cleaning up the shattered glass and debris scattered everywhere. It was no surprise as to the amount of devastation done to the store.

"Jack," Theo said softly as he headed toward the back room. I followed behind him to his desk.

He motioned to the seat with his hand, and I sat. He sat as well, giving me a knowing and apologetic look.

I was in the same chair I had my interview. This conversation was going to be very different.

"It seems you had quite a night," Theo said with a gentle smile. "How are you... adjusting?"

There was no confusion as to what he was talking about, and I grew excited about the conversation we were about to have.

"Okay, I think," I said, unsure how I was supposed to be feeling.

"It will take some time for you to get a grasp of the magnitude of tonight's events. I'm sure your imagination is working overtime, am I right?"

"Yes, sir. It is."

"You've only glimpsed the new world you have been... born into, for lack of a better word. I will do everything I can to help with this transition."

I nodded in thankful agreement but kept quiet as I wanted him to continue.

"I want you to know something, Jack. This was not part of any grand scheme, but if there is one thing I'm certain of, it's that nothing in life is certain, or in anyone's complete control."

"So, you knew who I was before I started working for you?" I asked.

"Yes."

"How? Why? I'm nothing special."

"Nothing could be further from the truth."

"Really?"

"How do I explain this? I learned that your existence had leaked, and it was likely certain individuals may come looking for you. When this happened, I started keeping closer tabs on you as a precaution. Like an invisible security detail. I didn't know if they would ever find you, so I kept my distance, watched, and waited. I wanted to be close enough to help if the need presented itself."

My new cognitive skills were very efficient, and I was thinking crystal clear, which made several things come to light. I wasn't paranoid after all. I was being followed from time to time. There was one word that stuck out, and I had to ask.

"My *existence*?" I said, not hiding my ignorance.

"Yes. Though not directly, you are part of a larger story that goes back many years. We don't have the time to go into it all right now, but I will do my best to answer the immediate questions bubbling to the surface."

Theo leaned back in his chair and collected his thoughts for a second. It was obvious he was going to be careful how he approached the enormity of it all.

"The most immediate problem is that, because you are special, you have caught the attention of others and not all of them are friends."

"Kristov and Franklin definitely hammered home the *not all friends* part," I said.

"I'm sure they did." Theo said with a smile. "You will have to tell me all about it sometime, but there are more important things to discuss at the moment. So, let's get the obvious questions out of the way,"

"You and Bili are vampires or something, and unless I am dreaming and about to wake up, I am as well."

It came out almost as a question.

"That would be the modern generic term for us, and for your understanding and current knowledge base, I would say that would be close enough."

"I assume that Kristov and Franklin are some type of wolf derivative and so is your friend. I don't know why I assume that, but..."

"Also correct, but again with the same disclaimer. The younger ones of both clans identify as you do because of the era they were born, but some elders would take offense to such names," Theo said.

I looked at Theo with my new eyes, and it was as if I was seeing him for the first time. I was looking at someone with a world knowledge few would believe.

"Are you immortal?" I asked, still not really associating myself as being the thing same as Theo.

"No. Well, not in the absolute literal sense. It's possible for us to die, but we are much less fragile than our human counterparts. We are comprised of the same genetic material as anyone else, for the most part. We are just blessed, or cursed, depending on who you ask, with a certain gene or genes that affect many attributes of our being. Our overall anatomy is much stronger, and we can recover from most injuries quite fast. The same unique gene also stops the aging process. That being said, if we sustain massive trauma to the heart or brain, it's good night."

"I feel silly for asking but do we drink blood? Cause the thought of it still doesn't sound appealing. At all."

Theo grinned. I think he was waiting for this question.

"No. Many of the legends and historical inaccuracies of our kind have stemmed from centuries of storytelling and the mentally unbalanced. The most famous being Vlad, who was human by the way. He wanted to be a vampire in the worst way when he learned of our existence, but he was so far gone mentally that no one wanted anything to do with him. Ask Claude about him one day.

"Some legends may have had some historical basis at one time, but like all living creatures, we have evolved to blend better with our surroundings."

"What about the wolves?" I asked.

I wasn't sure what I was asking about in particular, but Theo took my meaning.

"Same rules apply, but again, with a few variants."

"They don't change...?"

"No. However, as you could see when Kristov became furious with me, there were some minor changes in his physical makeup. Most of it very subtle, but a few things were more than obvious to your new eyes. Am I right?"

"His eyes seemed to change color slightly, and his teeth looked fuller, sharper," I said.

"Yes. When this happens, the wolves can be a handful. There are exceptions to every rule, but here are a few basics. The wolves are slightly stronger than most of us, but on the contrary, we are faster, have more acute cognitive function, and have a few other skills you'll soon discover. They do have one very distinct advantage, though. When the moon is full, their strength and speed increase. Mind this if you find yourself in a troubling situation. There is a time to fight, and there is a time to run," Theo said with a very stern look.

"Understood," I said.

"Good. Listen, Jack, I don't want to scare you, but these are troubling times. Things may escalate before they get better. I don't know how this will all play out, but I'm fairly certain we haven't seen the last of Kristov, and some others, I fear."

"Aside from Claude, do all werewolves hate us?" I asked.

"No. There was a time long ago when war was common between our clans, but over the last millennia, we had moved past that and even worked together quite well. War between us does not benefit anyone. In this current climate, though, things could change."

"Who am I?"

"Ahh. That's the one I've been waiting for."

Theo put his hands together on the desk in front of him and took a deep breath.

"If only the question was as easy to answer as it was to ask. It's... complicated."

"In what way?" I asked.

"In every way."

My entire life, I had thought I was just a normal kid, and now I felt like I had just stumbled down a supernatural rabbit hole. It's an odd feeling, to put it mildly, seeing the curtain pulled back, exposing a world you thought only existed in books or movies.

"Perhaps if I explain some things about us as a species, it will shed some light. Relationships between humans and our kind are extremely rare and almost nonexistent. There are all the obvious reasons but also a few not so obvious. When the transformation takes place, for us and wolves alike, we become sterile. On top of that, we develop a strong aversion to the human odor. But like I told you before, there are exceptions. There have only been a few cases that I'm aware of where individuals remained fertile. There may be others, but like I said, most of those very few wouldn't know it because of what I just explained. It's chemistry, you could say. The possibility of a relationship existing and producing a child is nearly unfathomable."

"I'm a product of one of those rare relationships?"

"Yes."

My mind was racing from this and hanging on every word Theo said.

"How... who...?"

"I'm afraid that information will have to wait. I'm sorry, Jack. I don't enjoy holding back secrets any more than you like waiting, but there are reasons for this. Patience."

Though disappointed, I trusted Theo had my best interest in mind, so I relented and changed the topic.

"I know I am new to this life, but I hope you will allow me to help in any way I can."

I didn't know what kind of reaction I would get from him. He may very well have told me to go home and not worry about it.

"You will be an integral part of the events to come, that I can assure you. First thing you need is rest. You need to complete your transformation and the only way to do that is with sleep. I have an apartment upstairs

I want you to use. It's the one with the green door that looks like a storage closet. It's not."

Theo threw me a set of keys he had on his desk.

"Go rest and unwind. Sleep will take you before you know it. I suggest you get your things from your house soon as well, preferably when your friends are not around. In all the excitement, I'm sure you haven't noticed the changes in your physical appearance. It will be easy to explain these things to your friends, but only after a lengthy absence. The changes are not something that could occur overnight," Theo said.

He held his gaze, making sure I took his last point seriously.

"Understood."

"We'll talk more later, I promise," Theo said as he motioned for me to head upstairs.

I took the keys and started to walk away. I stopped and turned back toward Theo.

"I hope I haven't become a burden."

Theo's look spoke a thousand words, and I felt better instantly.

"Get some rest."

I did as I was told and went to the upstairs flat. I had seen the green door on my first day of work, and he was right, I thought it was just a storage closet we never used.

Though the flat was small, it seemed to fit me like a glove. I took it in for a minute, looking around at everything, and then dropped in the most comfortable leather chair I ever felt. I sat in quiet contemplation about everything that had happened in the last few hours. What I saw tonight couldn't exist. I couldn't exist.

35

Bili was out on the showroom floor, pulling pieces of glass and ceramic from the drywall and throwing them into a garbage can in robotic fashion. The worry on Bili's face was palpable. She knew what she had done, and though she would do it again under the same circumstances, she couldn't help but feel responsible for what was sure to come. The worst of it, though, was what she had done to Theo.

Theo approached her, knowing what she was thinking. He got within arm's length before Bili stopped what she was doing and turned to face him. She started to say something but swallowed the words. She didn't cry, but her eyes were red with a thin glaze.

"I'm so sorry, I .." she tried to say, but Theo cut her off.

"Shh," Theo said as he grabbed her in a tight hug. Nothing needed to be said. He knew the situation had to be dire with Kristov involved.

"Don't worry about this mess. I'll take care of it," Theo said.

Bili didn't argue and walked to the back to get her things.

Theo sat down in one of his expensive antique chairs like it was a piece of lawn furniture and stewed over the night's events. Though he was not showing it on the outside, he was livid. Bili was like his daughter. And then there was me.

Theo was not just going to look the other way and wait for another attack. It was time to go on the offensive. He needed some help to get answers and he was going to call in a few favors.

36

heard the footsteps long before the door handle moved. As soon as the door cracked open, the smell of her reached me before she came into sight. I couldn't help being impressed with it all.

"Do you mind if I come in?" she asked.

I could see the redness in her eyes. It was unusual to see Bili in this vulnerable state.

"Please do, seeing that it's not my place."

She walked over to the footstool that was on the other side of a small coffee table and sat.

"I hope you can forgive me," she said.

"For what? Saving my life?" I said in earnest. "I was at death's door."

"There may come a day in a few hundred years when you look back on this day and wish it had ended differently. This life doesn't suit everyone the same."

As she was sitting across from me, something occurred to me.

"My girlfriend is one of *them,* isn't she?"

"Yes. I wanted to warn you about her several times, but there was no way without raising suspicion or telling you the truth. Now you know why."

"You think they sent her to kill me?"

"No. Neither does Theo. If that was the case, we would have taken measures. That being said, I'm sure meeting you was no coincidence."

"You think everything about her is bullshit?"

"Not sure, but it may surprise you to know how rare a relationship between humans and-"

"Yeah, Theo mentioned it. And yes, in hindsight, I'm sure none of it was an accident. But if she really wanted to do me harm, she could have done it easily on numerous occasions. That's the part that makes no sense."

"Maybe she was just the watch dog who relayed your every move back to whomever is holding her leash," Bili said.

I wasn't sure if her disgust was with the wolves in general, or Viki in particular. She seemed to like Theo's friend well enough. I can't imagine the life she has led to this point. She could be centuries old and have seen things I have only read about.

"That would make the most sense, I guess."

It hurt to think about it. *Was I being set up? Did she really not care? Was I just a mark to be played?*

Bili was looking at me, wanting to say something, but held her tongue. I was deciphering the smallest movements in her face that seemed to give away one secret after another. It was amazing what I was picking up from non-verbal cues.

"Is there something else on your mind?"

"I'm sure Theo will fill you in on the rest when he thinks you're ready, but our little adventure tonight is just the beginning."

"Yeah, he mentioned that as well. You sure that's it?"

"Enjoying your new gifts, are you?"

"Yes. Especially when talking to you."

I couldn't help but be a little smug. Bili had the best poker face I had ever seen, but now there were cracks, and I could read them.

"Look, I'm far from the sentimental type, but I want to apologize for how I treated you since you've been here. I have reasons, none of them good, but they're reasons."

Bili stood up hesitantly and walked to the door. She reached for the handle, then turned back to look at me.

"You have no idea how your life has changed tonight. You may think you do, but you don't."

I nodded, not sure what to say.

She opened the door, about to leave.

"Bili?" I said, stopping her.

"Yeah?"

"Do you ever regret this life?"

She gave me a sly smile.

"Never."

She closed the door, and I fell asleep within seconds.

37

When I awoke in the chair, my heart was pounding, and I was covered in sweat. I was so disoriented that it took a full minute to realize where I was. It's always a strange feeling waking up in an unfamiliar place, especially so while in the seated position.

Was everything a dream?

I was thinking I was in some sort of accident or something. Maybe Bili and Theo are just regular people and I dreamt everything else. Kristov, Franklin, and Claude could have been imaginary. The feeling that I may have lost my grasp on reality was bizarre, but it did not seem far-fetched.

I reached for my phone that was sitting on the table to see what time it was. I had to look twice, not because of the time, but the date. Unless I was still in this dream world, I had slept for almost two full days.

I stood up and instinctively headed for the bathroom to wash my face and clear my head. Maybe the date on my phone was wrong, or I just forgot what day it was. I was coming up with several possible solutions to what I thought I had experienced, the last of which was that any of it was real.

I entered the bathroom, and when I shut the door, I saw myself in the full-length mirror on the back of the door. I knew in an instant I was wrong. It *was* real. All of it.

I stared in complete disbelief. It was as if the person in the mirror wasn't me but a stranger mocking my movements. I wasn't completely different, but to me the changes were glaring.

The first thing I noticed was that my once hazel-brown eyes were now a silverish blue with a distinct thick black border. The same as with Bili and Theo's eyes. After I got past that, I couldn't help but notice that I gained a few pounds of body weight and all in the right places. I felt as fit as an Olympic athlete.

I could see why Theo wanted me to wait awhile before seeing any of my friends. There was no way something like this could happen overnight.

I took a quick shower and got dressed. I worried that something may have happened while I was asleep. After getting my things together, I walked out of the flat. Before I took two steps, Bili was grabbing my arm.

"About damn time. I've been waiting for twenty hours. Let's go," she said.

We got into Theo's Cadillac and took off like a bat out of hell. Something was happening, and I knew it was significant. We were on a familiar road, and I knew right where we were going. When we pulled into the parking area of the warehouse, I saw several cars I didn't recognize.

"While you were napping, a few things have happened," Bili said as we stepped out of the car. "The meeting is wrapping up, but Theo wanted to make sure you met everyone."

I couldn't help but notice that Bili, although still herself, didn't treat me like she used to. I almost felt as though she was treating me as an equal. It was as if I had passed the last initiation of a secret club. In some respects, I guess I did.

When we walked in, I immediately felt the heavy weight of numerous stares upon me. As I scanned the crowd of onlookers, the whispers began, and I heard them all. *It's him, it's true,* and *look at them* were repeated most.

Them?

Theo broke the ice to get past any further awkwardness.

"Everyone, this is Jack," Theo said in a minor grandiose way, as if he was introducing me to a panel of judges. He met me near the door, then made a point to introduce me to each of them.

I could see Claude standing behind everyone, or more accurately, towering over everyone. He was working on a laptop, not paying attention to the group.

There were five unfamiliar faces and all of them vampires. Three were females and two were males.

"Jack, this is Lucinda and Miah," Theo said.

I shook Lucinda's hand and felt a hint of apprehension in her grasp. It was an odd sensation. She was taller than me, had jet black hair down past her shoulders, and dark brown skin.

Miah was shorter and had short brown hair, straight edged bangs, and dark green eyes. The thick black border around the iris of their eyes was obvious, as it is with all of them.

"Nice to meet you, Jack," Lucinda said.

She held her stare longer than normal, but it wasn't unfriendly, just longer.

"Nice to meet you as well," I said.

Miah shook my hand next.

"How was your transformation? Everyone adjusts at different speeds."

"Good, I think. Haven't had time to think about it, really," I said, not sure how she meant the question.

"Of course. Considering how you were turned," Miah said as she shot a backward glance toward Bili.

I couldn't tell what it was specifically, but the look she gave Bili was not a warm one. Bili's subsequent look was just as telling. They were not friends.

Theo moved me along.

"And this is Harold, but everyone calls him Steve."

"Hi Steve," I said, shaking his hand.

He was the youngest looking of the bunch by far. He looked about my age, or even a year or two younger. He had short blonde hair that was strategically mussed, not very tall, and just a ball of pure energy. He looked like a California beach bum with a better tailor. I liked him right away.

"Hey. Never met a... I mean, I've heard, but... wow. Nice to meet you."

"Likewise."

Steve was about to say something else, but then he became distracted, and it was as if I had disappeared from the world.

Bili had walked up next to me to the obvious delight of Steve.

"Hey, Bili. How've you been?" Steve said with a huge grin. He didn't shade his feelings. You didn't need special abilities to see he had a thing for her.

I looked at Bili and saw the look of mild embarrassment and aggravation on her face. I relished it.

"Steve," Bili said curtly.

"Harry, get over here," Claude said from the back of the room.

He never looked up from the computer and didn't raise his voice, but it was clear he wanted Steve to assist in something.

Being called Harry caused Steve to stop smiling.

"Stop calling me that, ya giant gorilla. I'll be right there," Steve said.

The quick exchange told me that those two had a history and comfortableness with each other I'm sure few have with Claude. Either that or Steve had a death wish.

"Nice to meet you, Jack. We'll talk more later. You too," Steve said as he shifted his look to Bili. Then he winked.

I think I heard Bili's eyes roll.

Steve made his way over to Claude's location, bumped Claude out of the way, and jumped on the laptop he was working on. Claude smiled at him and messed up his hair, causing Steve to swat at his hand.

I was staring at Bili with a wide smile which resulted in me being punched in the chest. This made me laugh, and Bili walked away shaking her head. It was totally worth the hit.

Theo came back from talking to Miah and walked me over to the last two he wanted me to meet.

"And here we have Andrew and Allison," Theo said.

I could tell right away that they were together. The only way to describe them would be *Hollywood Perfect*. Both were attractive and well-to-do looking, even though they were dressed casually. I could tell from the subtle gestures and the way Theo spoke to them they must be longtime friends. They also exuded the same familiar serenity and good nature as Theo.

"It's a pleasure to meet you. We've heard a lot about you," Allison said as she shook my hand.

Andrew stepped closer and shook my hand next.

"We heard you had an exciting first day as it were. I'm glad you are still with us," he said.

They both had the same English accent that gave them a royal flair for lack of a better description.

"Thank you, I am as well. Thanks to Bili, Theo, and Claude," I said.

"Yes, of course. That incident has caused many of us much concern. It's our hope we can get this matter handled before it gets worse."

Allison put her hand on Andrew's arm, and he got the meaning right away.

"Yes, dear," Andrew said looking at Allison. "Sorry Jack, but I'm afraid we must take our leave."

"It was nice to meet you both," I said.

They smiled in tandem and then looked to Theo.

"I will let you know if we find anything," Andrew said.

"Be careful," Theo said.

Andrew and Allison excused themselves and left the warehouse shortly after we met. They had obviously discussed some plans prior to my arrival and were on a mission.

Theo walked to the back where Claude and Steve were working, and I followed.

I saw Lucinda and Miah make their exit too. Before she walked out the door, Miah gave me one last look. I picked up several mixed signals in that quick moment and planned to ask Bili about it later. I would forget to do that, and it would be costly.

38

Steve was working fast, and the look on his face said he was close to something interesting. The slight creases in his brow, the narrowing of his eyes, and the tightness of his mouth were as telling as if he were talking in a loud voice. This ability was something else, and it made me wonder what else I was capable of.

"Sometimes our subculture is more prone to rumor mongering than a group of teenage humans. It's embarrassing," Steve said. "In fairness, it's been a millennium since... well... since a situation like this has presented itself. Let's just say you have caused a ripple effect unseen for some time."

Steve shot me a quick glance, but it was as if he was verifying something rather than the usual generic look.

Theo interjected.

"We believe someone is trying to exploit this situation. When the rumors about you had originally leaked, they were mere whispers. Now that you've been turned, those whispers have exploded into screams. Someone is trying to make you famous."

"I think that ship has sailed, Theo. Just look at him," Steve said.

"Why would anyone want that?" I asked.

"With this kind of fame, you get two things: fear and jealousy. Both can be used in a sinister manner if stoked properly, and it seems someone is doing just that," Theo said.

"We are tracking all new arrivals in the city using the Dark Web our kind are prone to use. I don't expect to find a direct connection, but I can sort through the peripheral pretty well and link information together. Though most of us are smart enough to avoid detection, there are always *those* few," Steve said with a slight shake of his head.

I watched as Steve typed on the computer keys like he was playing a video game. The speed was amazing, but not nearly as remarkable as the way he navigated the different websites and forums, barely slowing to read. My mind was working efficiently, but Steve's was on another level.

Steve stopped typing and smiled.

"And Bingo was his name-o. You are a piece of work, aren't you, *TruVamp69*? Kids these days," Steve said as he rolled his eyes.

Steve highlighted the post for all of us to read.

"Like I said. Always a few."

The post read:

Heading to Ann Arbor. Let you know if this is for real. Staying near the Stadium. Be in touch after I get in contact with her and get paid.

"This was posted this morning," Steve said.

"There can't be too many hotels near the Stadium. Most of them are closer to the freeway."

Claude collected his things and headed for the door. He wasn't wasting a second.

"Steve, when Claude finds Mr. TruVamp, and he will, be prepared to do the forensics on his phone and computer. Feel free to finish your work here or go back to my place. Anything new develops, let me or Bili know," Theo said.

"Will do," Steve said, throwing up one of his hands in a quasi-salute, without looking away from the computer. He was in a heavy work state and focused.

"Her?" I said, referring to the post.

"Interesting. This may be the break we needed," Theo said without elaborating.

Theo told Bili and me to go back to the Piece of History. He had a few inquiries to look into.

After our meeting and listening to all the mutterings under everyone's breath, I was bursting with curiosity. As if I didn't have a million other questions about my new life, the vagueness of my so-called special heritage had me dumbfounded. Bili drove us home, and the second the doors were shut, I began.

"Okay, what's the deal?"

Bili didn't answer right away, and I could see that she was contemplating what, or how much, to tell me.

"You're a little different," she said.

"No kidding. What does that mean? The other night, Theo explained that I have some immortal ancestry in my family tree, but how does that make any difference. I was still human in every way just a few days ago."

"No. I just meant you're a little odd. You know, like a weirdo."

She could only keep a straight face for a fraction of a second before she burst out laughing. I had never seen Bili let out a full laugh before, and even though it was at my expense, I was glad to see it. I tried not to follow suit, but her laugh was infectious, I started chuckling to myself, and then before I knew it, I was laughing as hard as her. It was just the pressure release I think we both needed.

"Theo will tell you when you're ready. Be patient. The answers are coming, trust me," Bili said.

"I get it, it's just..." I trailed off, letting the matter go.

I sat quietly for the rest of the ride, thinking about what may lie ahead. It was the first moment I had to myself, mentally, since all of this happened. I was a part of what had to be the biggest and best kept secret of all time. Or was it? Could there possibly be more? Hell, anything was possible. I was a goddamned vampire, and don't think that thought hadn't crossed my mind.

We arrived at the POH, and before I got out of the car, Bili grabbed my arm.

"One more thing," Bili said. "As soon as you can do it discreetly, Theo wants you to move into the store loft. Sooner rather than later. I'll be moving in there as well. He wants us close until this all blows over."

"I'll go when I know my roommate will be out," I said.

She nodded once, removed her hand, and stepped out of the car.

The simple gesture could have been as meaningless as a kiss from a great aunt, but other than when she bit and punched me, I think it was the first time Bili ever touched me. It wasn't a romantic touch by any means, but it made me feel like we had grown closer. It must be like the camaraderie of soldiers in battle. We shared an experience that could have easily been the death of us. There's no question such things bring about a significant bond.

39

T he next day, I called Ted and told him I was moving out and I
would be by in the afternoon to get my things. He worried he had
offended me because I was offering nothing in the way of an
explanation. He also assumed it may have something to do with Viki.

She had been on my mind, and I knew I would have to talk to her
soon. I guess I didn't want to know the truth. It only seemed logical that I
was a job and nothing more. It was painful to think about, so I made a
choice not to speculate until I knew for sure. She tried calling me several
times since my encounter with Kristov, leaving me several touching voice-
mails. It filled me with mixed emotions when I heard them. Since I
couldn't see her face, I couldn't detect deception, but knowing what I did, I
felt it was just part of the act.

The next morning, I took the work van to the house when I knew Ted had class. I didn't have much, just a few small pieces of furniture, clothes, and some personal items. It didn't take long to gather my things, and I had everything packed in the van in less than fifteen minutes. I went back inside to do one last walk through when I heard the front door.

Damn.

I knew it was Ted before the door handle turned. His smell was as distinct as burgers on a grill. This must be what the senses of bloodhounds are like. Almost everything was unique, unmistakable, and overly pungent.

I could have easily fled without being seen but didn't. I felt I owed him. He was a great friend, and I couldn't bring myself to flee like a burglar in the night. I was still me, wasn't I?

I stepped out into the hallway and saw him peering into my room.

"Hey," I said.

"Shit!" Ted said as he turned to face me. "Sorry, you scared the hell out of me."

"Sorry, Pal. How are you?" I said, remaining a good distance from him.

"Good."

He started walking toward me and then stopped. The changes in my appearance became clear and unsettled him.

The look, or rather looks, on his face were screaming many things at once.

Confusion.

Apprehension.

Nervousness.

Scared.

Surprise.

"How are *you,* is the question?" he asked.

"I'm good. Just grabbing my things. Sorry, but I thought it might be better this way."

"I thought you might do something like this, so I cut
my first class."

He was still trying to work out in his head everything that was wrong with the situation as a whole.

"You always were the smart one."

Ted inched forward, unable to look away. The most obvious alteration was literally staring him in the eye.

"Everyone has been asking about you. I've never had so many people come to my house before. Is everything alright? You had us worried."

"Tell everyone I appreciate their concern, but I'm fine."

"I can see. You look... good. Real good," Ted said with a confused stare.

He didn't know what to make of me. The change in eye color, physique, and demeanor was more than obvious to someone I had spent an enormous amount of time with.

"Where have you been?"

"That's a long story and a good one, and one day I promise to tell you all about it, but now is not the time."

I could sense him bursting with curiosity and questions, but to his credit, he held on to them.

"You're a good friend," I said as I walked up to him. He fell silent as I patted him on the shoulder, gave him a reassuring smile, and then walked past him toward the door.

I don't know why but it hurt me to leave him like that. He was one of those rare friends who truly cared and never had an agenda. He deserved better.

Maybe one day I could tell him something remotely close to the truth, but at that moment it was best to let him come up with whatever explanation his mind thought feasible. Steroids, surgery, or even heavy make-up would all be more probable than the truth.

I was about to walk out when I stopped and looked back at Ted.

"Can I ask a favor?" I asked.

"Anything."

"If anyone asks you about me, and I mean anyone, just tell them you haven't seen me, and you don't know where I am. This is very important. Can you do that for me?"

"Yeah, I can do that. In fact, that's exactly what I told that girl we met awhile back. What was her name? Cierra?"

Ceana.

The image of her became crystal clear in my mind. I can't believe I didn't think about this before, but in fairness, I'd been a little distracted with new events.

"When was she here?" I asked.

"The second night you left. I thought it was strange, but you've been doing well with the ladies and-"

"What did she want?" I said, cutting him off.

"She asked if you were home, and when I said you weren't, she wanted to know where she could find you. Of course, I had no idea where you were and told her as much."

"Keep it that way. If she comes back, do not answer the door under any circumstances and call me right away. Understand?"

"Sure. Did I do something wrong?" he asked.

My tone and stern look must have scared him, but I needed to drive this point hard. If he spoke to her and lied, he could find himself in severe trouble. This was important information that the group would want as soon as possible. This was not another odd coincidence.

"No. Just remember what I told you".

I hurried to the van and made my way back to the POH as quickly as I could.

40

J ack stopped talking for a moment, prompting the doctor to speak, "Is something wrong?"

"No. It's just that the next part of my story is a little more personal. I haven't spoken about it in a long time," Jack said.

"You know you can tell me anything, but only if you feel comfortable doing so."

Jack nodded and thought for a moment.

She was giving him an out but hoping that he didn't take it. Most times, pressing for details could cause some to shut down.

"Do you want to take a break?" she said.

"No. It's better if I get through it now. In some respects, this was a turning point for me in several ways."

Jack took a deep breath, and his face became solemn. The doctor could tell that he was about to enter a painful area, and she couldn't help but feel a little excited. These were often the times when real progress happened. Sara swelled with anticipation.

41

T hough I had been very busy with everything at hand and adjusting to my new self, there was one thing I had to deal with. I hadn't seen or spoken to *her* since it happened, and I was at a point where I wanted to know. No, that's not a strong enough word. I *needed* to know what her involvement was. Though Bili and Theo didn't think Viki was an immediate danger, that didn't mean she was completely innocent either.

One evening, I told Bili I had an errand to run. She wanted to come with me, but I assured her it wouldn't take long. Bili could tell I wasn't being entirely forthcoming, and I think she knew what I had to do.

When I got to Viki's apartment, I could see she left one of her windows open. This made it very easy to get in undetected. No one was home, so I walked around the place looking for any clue that might give some insight as to her involvement.

Her computer had every security measure, and I had no chance of searching it. At the time, I secretly hoped she kept a diary like a thirteen-year-old girl from the fifties. No such luck.

What I found was one memory after another. The book we talked about, the kitchen where we ate together, the couch... the bedroom. Mixed emotions were fighting for space in my head, making clear thought difficult.

I decided not to dwell too much on the *what ifs* and took a seat in one of her chairs near the corner where it was darkest. The only light on in the whole place was the small kitchen sink light that barely lit the counter.

I heard the metal sound of the key hitting the door lock, and my senses grew sharp. Once she was in her loft, she threw her keys on the kitchen counter and then hung her purse over the chair. She knew someone was inside but didn't tip her hand until she felt ready to defend herself.

"Show yourself or I promise you it will not be pleasant when I find you," she said in a calm voice.

As I stood from the chair, the sound of leather brought her attention on me. I walked toward her, and I could see she was ready for an attack, or to be the attacker. I got to a point where the light was just bright enough that she could make out her would-be attacker. Her posture and expression changed in a blink.

"Jack?" she whispered.

"Surprised?"

"What happened? I tried to..." she trailed off as she looked at me closer, obviously seeing the changes. Though the room was dark, she could tell.

"What happened? That's a good question," I said as I walked past her without stopping until I was a suitable distance away. I wanted some space between us as we spoke.

When I passed her, I took her scent in as I never had before. Memories flooded my mind, but I pushed them away. I didn't want to think of those things now.

"Here's another," I said as I turned to face her again. "Was the plan for Kristov to kill me, or did you have something else in mind?"

Even though I didn't think she was working with Kristov, I felt that her motives regarding me were less than truthful. She was hiding plenty, and I doubt they sent her to be my bodyguard, so the alternative seemed bleak. That's why I accused her of more hoping to see a reaction.

"Did he..." she started to say. "No, he couldn't have."

She wore a confused look, trying to make sense of something.

I ignored her question and asked one of my own.

"Was everything a goddamn farce?" I asked with more vigor than I intended. I felt my canines sharpen as I said this. My face flushed with anger, but I controlled it. I was furious thinking she could be in league with who was behind all of this, no matter how trivial her involvement.

"No," she whispered.

She said this without a hint of hesitation or dishonesty that I could detect.

"Are you willing to hear my side, or did you come here for some other reason?"

I knew what she meant. Even now, the thought of hurting Viki was unthinkable. Being here again in her presence was harder than I thought it would be. My feelings were swirling like the wind, but I held them tight to my chest.

"By all means," I said.

She took a step closer, and I took a step back. She stopped, respecting my need for distance.

"A friend of mine contacted me and said he was looking for someone. A human someone. He didn't say who, or why, just that I would know if I got close enough. He assured me it was for informational purposes, and he meant that person no harm. He knew I wouldn't help him if it meant hurting the innocent."

"Who's this *friend* of yours?"

"I guess he would be the same as the person who is responsible for your new look." Then her demeanor changed. "It was Bili, wasn't it?"

Jealous.

"Go on," I said, ignoring the question.

"I asked how I would know, and he explained that the person he was looking for was an *anomaly*, and it would be obvious. I had heard of such a person but never thought I would meet one in a million years. There are only stories and legends of such individuals. He had information that such a person may live in the area. That's why he contacted me."

"Anomaly?"

"You still don't know, do you?"

"I was told I'm different. Something about my family tree, but I don't know why it's such a big deal."

"That's true, you are different, but that's hardly the extent of it," she said.

I thought she was going to elaborate on what she meant but she didn't. I was going to come back to that later.

"Anyway, after I relayed the message that I found *something,* gave him what little information I had, I was told to stay away from you. I did just that, but it never sat right with me. Then I saw you again at the coffee shop. I was looking for you, like I said, but for other reasons."

"What reasons?"

She shifted her stance, and again, her demeanor changed. It was subtle, but I could read it.

"I had to understand," she said.

"Understand what?"

"Why I was attracted to you when I shouldn't have been. I should have been repulsed, but I was drawn to you like no other before. It wasn't normal. I don't know if you know this-"

"I got the Cliff Notes, but yes, I know such a thing is rare."

"Yes, you could say that. After our talk at the coffee shop, the pleasant one, I knew something was there. This also confused me. I thought I might be making a mistake, so I kept my distance again."

"Then you came to the store."

"I did. I couldn't stop thinking about you."

She looked down, blinked a few times, and then looked me in the eye when she spoke again.

"Did Kristov hurt you? I know his reputation," she asked as she took a step forward.

I didn't move.

"It was his friend Franklin who took that pleasure. At Kristov's orders, of course."

"What happened?"

I told her the short version of the story, and as I did, I could see the emotion in her eyes.

"I'm so sorry, Jack," she said.

Her sincerity appeared to be authentic. I was new to this life and trusted my new abilities, but I didn't know if others like us could successfully lie to our kind. I hadn't been around long enough to know anything for sure.

"That pain was nothing compared to the thought you might be involved, but as you can see, I'm much better now."

I was trying to change the subject and appear unaffected. That I detected no signs of deception when she said she was attracted to me only made this more difficult. I don't know what I thought was going to happen when I came here, but this wasn't it.

"You have to believe I had nothing to do with the attack on you and Bili," she said. Then she spoke a little softer. "I'm glad she was there to save you. She'll never know how grateful I am."

"What we had, was any of it real, or was I just a task to be completed?" I finally asked.

She moved closer again and I let her get within arms-reach this time.

"Very real. I know I didn't tell you the whole truth, but now you understand why. The more I got to know you, the more I wanted to tell you everything. I came close once, if you remember, but I knew you wouldn't believe any of it."

Her eyes were pleading for forgiveness. I could feel it to my core. It was the first time I had heard raw emotion in her voice. Every new sense I had said she was being truthful.

Her eyes were now tear-filled to the point of spilling over. I came here intent on hearing the worst, for whatever reason, and I was mentally prepared for that. This made the situation far more complicated. Either she was the best liar in the world, or it was something else. I was not ready for the something else.

Viktoria's tears were at a constant drip now. I had never seen her so vulnerable. I didn't know how to deal with this.

"I want to believe you," I said.

My walls were being torn down, and it was obvious to anyone with eyes. She didn't hesitate.

"I know you know I'm telling the truth," she said with certainty, aware of my new abilities.

She took a deep breath and wiped the tears from her cheeks before she spoke again.

"I've been by myself a long time before I met you. I didn't think my match was out there. Then a silly human came along."

When I said nothing, she took one more step and looked me in the eye.

"Even if you can never forgive me, leave here knowing that my feelings for you were... are..." she said lightly, shaking her head, unable to finish her sentence.

She partially covered her face with one hand as she silently sobbed.

I couldn't let this go on. I had never known love, but it had to be something like this. Seeing her cry was too much for me.

I moved forward, took her in my arms, and held her tight. She returned my embrace, and we held each other motionless. I didn't know if this was going to work, but I felt she was worth the try. My feelings for her had not diminished one bit after my transformation. If anything, they intensified.

Was this normal?

"Please forgive me, Jack, please," she said with her head on my shoulder. I could feel her warm tears soak through my shirt.

I lifted her chin up with a light finger and kissed her. It was a kiss of forgiveness, and I think she knew it. I did believe her. I had to. I never felt this way about another person in my life.

She relaxed, wiped her eyes on her shirt sleeve, and pulled back just far enough to look into my eyes. It was still very dark, but I could see her forcing a thin smile.

When she moved her head slightly, a partial ray of light from the kitchen illuminated my face. She looked at me, and I saw her smile turn to a look of concern. She noticed something peculiar.

"What is it?" I asked.

"Your eyes. I thought it was unusual that you put on some weight, but now I see your eyes," she said looking confused.

"I assumed it had something to do with my transformation," I said, not sure what she was getting at.

"It does, but—" she started to say, but stopped mid-sentence.

Just as she stopped talking, I heard a faint sound of glass breaking.

I looked up just as a small piece of glass fell from her front room window and hit the floor with a soft crackle.

"What the hell was that?" I said, momentarily distracted.

Viktoria didn't answer. When I returned to look at her face, it faded from a bleak smile to a blank, unfocused stare. She dropped, and I raised my arms just in time to catch her before she fell to the floor. When I grabbed her, I could feel the warm drops of liquid hitting the backs of my hands.

The blood was spilling faster by the second.

"Viki!"

I didn't hesitate as I picked Viktoria up in my arms and carried her out of sight to the bedroom. I laid her on the bed as the blood continued to pour from her head. I tore a large piece of cloth from the quilt, rolled it up, and used it to put pressure on the wound. The void in the back of her head was alarming. From what little I knew about us as a group, the weapon used had to be a powerful one.

"Viktoria!" I said again as I shook her.

I still did not know the full extent of the healing powers of the wolves and clung to an irrational hope that she would heal and wake up. The burning rage within me was starting as it did before when I became angry.

I wrapped Viktoria's head as tightly as I could with the sheet from her bed and gently laid her down.

I was tired of losing people I loved, and I would be damned if this son of a bitch was going to get away with it. Knowing that there was nothing I could do to help Viktoria other than wait, I bolted out the door faster than I had ever moved before.

I ran as fast as I could down the steps, outside and across the street to where the bullet may have come from. There was a fire escape that led to the roof of the four-story building directly across from Viki's apartment. I was up the ladder in a blink, and when I reached the top, I knew I was in the right area. I could still smell the gun powder residue from a spent shell casing in the air, but there was also another unmistakable scent. I followed the scent trail across the rooftops and down the backside of a three-story building which led to a parking lot. The scent stopped there.

I was irate that the killer had gotten away, but I couldn't waste any more time looking. I wanted to get back to Viki and do what I could to help her. As I ran back, I envisioned her sitting on the couch complaining of a mild headache.

When I got there, I couldn't believe what I found.

Nothing. She was gone.

What the hell?

I took out my phone and made a call. It rang once before it connected.

"It's me. I need your help."

42

t had been months since Viktoria's murder, and her body still hadn't been found. It was hard to mourn her when I didn't know what really happened. Could she still be alive? Even though all my senses and instincts said she was dead, I wanted to believe she wasn't.

Right after she was shot, I called Bili, and she was at Viki's within minutes. She brought supplies and we went to work. I got the feeling this wasn't her first *cleaning*, as it were. She wanted to make sure if the police looked around, they wouldn't find any signs of a murder, which could lead them to me.

A week after it happened, one of her co-workers notified the police after she failed to show up to work several days in a row. I heard they classified her as a voluntary-missing person, as there was no evidence of a crime. The fact that her apartment was a rental, no signs of foul play, and she held a foreign passport, which we found and took, only added to the speculation she left willingly.

Viktoria didn't tell anyone at her work about me, which was fortuitous, so the police never contacted me.

Even though I knew exactly who shot Viki, as his scent was unmistakable, word had spread throughout the wolf community that I killed her. Theo said the propaganda was the whole point of the murder which made it even tougher to take. I felt wholly responsible. Everyone kept telling me that none of these events were my fault, but it sure felt like it.

Claude was successful in finding this General I had been hearing a lot about, and Theo decided to move forward with a meeting. Theo wanted answers, and the past needed to be settled to get them. I was still in the dark on much of this at the time.

I was riding with Theo on the way to the summit of sorts. Arranging the meeting was just the first hurdle. The second was surviving it. Theo had mentioned that there was an unpleasant history with the General, and that was putting it in the mildest of terms.

If this meeting turned ugly, which was a real possibility, Theo gave us a fifty-fifty chance. Not a comforting statistic when you're talking about your life.

We were about ten minutes into a thirty-minute ride, and neither of us had said a word. I knew we had some time, and there were just too many things I wanted to know to let it get wasted. I rarely had Theo to myself where I could talk to him freely.

"Can I ask you something?"

"Always."

"Why is Bili the way she is? There has to be a reason."

"There is," he said without hesitation.

When he didn't expound right away, I felt I may have overstepped myself. These two have probably been together for centuries, and here I come asking all kinds of personal questions.

"Sorry. I shouldn't have presumed-"

"No. You should know. You are family, Jack, and you spend the most time with her. A little background may give you some perspective."

Just hearing him say I was part of his family gave me a feeling I had missed for a long time. It's one of those things you just don't understand unless you've experienced incredible loss.

I felt honored that Theo trusted me with what was sure to be a personal story.

"It was in the mid-seventeenth century, and Bilinda, as she went by in those days, was married to a minor English Lord named Landell Ainsworth. He was the bastard of all bastards. He treated her as though she was put upon this earth to be the object of his physical and mental torturous whims.

"I had come across them by pure happenstance. I was on an errand for General Treville, protecting a small consort of dignitaries through some hostile territories. After completing my mission, I checked into the local inn for the night. I was about to leave when Ainsworth arrived, literally dragging Bili behind him. After I witnessed just a few of the abuses Ainsworth conducted in public, I decided to stay a little longer than planned. I dislike the mistreatment of women.

"One afternoon, I saw Ainsworth leave without Bili, giving me the opportunity to check on her. When I got to her door, I heard muffled sounds, so I forced the door open and went in. What I saw infuriated me. He tied her to the bed with her hands and feet pulled tight to each bedpost. The room didn't have a fire going, and the air was frigid. Bili was gagged, bleeding from her mouth and nose, and both eyes were swollen shut. She shivered uncontrollably, as she didn't have on a stitch of clothing. I wanted to track down Ainsworth and kill him where he stood, but the priority was that poor girl."

Listening to Theo talk about Bili that way was hard to believe. To me she was almost indestructible, both physically and mentally. Right now, though, I just felt like giving her a hug.

"What did you do?" I asked.

"I untied and clothed Bili as quick as I could and took her back to my room to warm her up and treat her wounds. She had several fresh injuries and numerous other partially healed wounds, including a few broken ribs. Once I tended to her immediate needs, I headed for the door to take care of Lord Landell. I do not take pleasure in hurting others, but that would have been an exception. Before I reached the door, Bili stopped me. She didn't want to be alone. I guess she wanted to feel warm and safe for as long as she could, fearing it wouldn't last and she would return to Ainsworth before long.

"I did as she asked and kept her company, telling her very little about myself. I got her to talk about how she ended up with Ainsworth and the grim reality of her life.

"She had been born into a noble family, but her father was a first-rate bastard as well, who squandered what little money the family had. He didn't give it a second thought when Ainsworth offered to pay him for his daughter. He traded her for a few gold pieces like she was livestock. Bili was just nineteen, and the years of hell she endured since that day would have killed a lesser person."

"I hope there is a special place in hell for people like Ainsworth," I said, shaking my head.

Theo continued.

"I stayed with Bili all day and night, mending her as best I could. I told her I would take her to another village, give her some money, and help her start a new life without Ainsworth. She thanked me earnestly, but sadness covered her face. This poor girl had nothing, nowhere to go, and no family to turn to. Back then, a woman with no support or family would eventually be forced to turn to her last alternative when she ran out of money."

My heart broke for Bili. I couldn't imagine the hardships she must have endured in those days. As bad as I thought my life had been, I still had fond memories of those I loved. Her life was far and away more tragic.

"When I saw the distant sorrow in her eyes, I knew right then what she needed. Something she had never known and something she may have thought didn't exist for someone like her. She needed freedom. Not the kind a prisoner gets when they are released from jail, but true freedom. The kind that allows you to distance yourself from the past and take control of your future.

"I sat on the bed next to Bili and told her the truth about what I was. I told her I could give her a life she never thought possible and all it would take is one bite. I explained what life would be like afterwards, both good and bad, then asked her one simple question. *Do you accept?*"

I hung on Theo's every word as he went on.

"Not once did she question my sanity, ask if I was serious, or doubt what I said. Without hesitation, Bili rolled up the sleeve of the over-sized shirt I had given her, stuck her arm out, wrist up, and stared me straight in the eye and said, '*what are you waiting for?*'

"Now that sounds like the Bili I know," I said, smiling.

"Some people just need a sliver of hope and opportunity, and when they get it, they never look back."

"Please tell me Bili dealt with Ainsworth." I pressed.

Theo gave a sly smile and shrugged.

"That's a story for her to tell."

43

We arrived at the meeting location, and though I was nervous, it excited me at the same time. We were meeting an individual of some significance which could result in a positive resolution or the death of us. It surprised me that I was even a part of it to be honest. Theo told me that if not for me, he wouldn't have even tried to talk to him. He didn't explain what he meant, and it was clear he wasn't going to until the time was right.

Theo dropped me off at the meeting location, which was an abandoned park in the city.

"If everything goes as planned, I should be back in less than twenty minutes and well before their arrival. I have a few arrangements to make beforehand. Questions?" Theo said.

"I have a hundred," I said.

"Claude should be here soon, ask him. He loves questions," Theo said with a crooked smile.

"Funny."

"Sit tight," Theo said, and then he sped off on a mission.

I sat on a splintered picnic table in the middle of the inner-city park. The grass almost swallowed the few remaining swing sets and slides scattered about. The basketball court was hardly noticeable amid the shrubs and weeds. The hoop-less backboards stood tall out of the grass as a reminder of how things once were.

I was sitting quietly, alone with my thoughts, trying to remain positive. It was seconds later when I smelled him. We picked this park for several reasons. One being the seclusion, and second, if anyone saw anything, they would likely keep it to themselves. When you live in a place like this, you get very good at minding your own business. If things turned deadly, it would appear to be common inner-city violence and not a raging war of immortals.

I was hardly surprised when I saw him making his way towards me. I looked like I just stepped out of a GAP store, and I couldn't have been more conspicuous. I was hoping to avoid this.

City youth are good at sizing up their targets with little more than a glance. Living in neighborhoods like this one was Darwinism to its core. The strong and ruthless preyed upon the weak, and that's just the way it is. A mistake in evaluating your victim could be costly.

I knew I had to deal with this quickly and quietly. We did not want an audience, or a commotion, that would disrupt this meeting.

"Wussup," the approaching thug said. "You have the time?"

So unoriginal.

It's either the *time* or *do you have change*? One to get your wallet out, the other your watch or phone, but both to distract you from what was about to happen.

He was a young-looking kid, about eighteen, but tall and muscular. He was wearing a tight white tank-top with a Tiger's cap.

"No time, sorry," I said, not looking at him or acknowledging his presence further. I also did not appear to be worried, and I could tell this confused him.

"Everyone has the time. Check your phone," he said, now trying to sound a little tougher.

"No phone, either," I said, again with no emotion or eye contact.

I knew at this point there was nothing I could say to scare this kid or change his mind. Not with words, anyway. He was committed. There was only one solution to this equation.

I waited until he pulled a weapon, which happened to be a knife. The second the knife caught daylight, I grabbed the hand that held it. I squeezed as I stood up and faced my new acquaintance. I looked into his eyes, and I could see the fear take over as he tried to move his hand. He couldn't. Though I wasn't trying to break bones, I made sure he knew who was in control.

"It's never too late to change your life, young man. This world goes well beyond the neighborhood you know. There are mysteries and wonders all around you. Do you hear me?"

He stared back, giving me a slight nod of understanding.

I released my grip, and when I did, the knife dropped. He did not pick it up. He turned around, almost afraid to run, and walked away. It was a quick walk, and I saw him look back numerous times. I never stopped staring at him until he was gone.

I may have overdone the dramatics of it, but I couldn't help myself. And who knows, maybe this bizarre and unreal experience would change his life in a positive way.

I waited another fifteen minutes before Theo came back. He was now driving a Bentley. I heard he had one but had never seen it until now. It was something to see. Not the most inconspicuous set of wheels, but knowing Theo, there was a reason he brought it.

He pulled up next to me, and I got in.

"Any problems?" he asked.

"Nope. All quiet."

44

As I said, this meeting was a complete unknown. Theo had no way of knowing how it would turn out, but it had to happen. We needed information and to find out the full extent of this individual's involvement.

We drove to the other side of the park where I imagine Theo thought would be more advantageous and waited.

"I like your car."

"I don't take it out much, but I figured it was right for the occasion. Better to have the locals get the wrong impression of us. Plus, it has a few other special qualities I hope we will not need."

"You think he'll listen?"

"That's the question, alright. When emotions get involved, anything can happen. With our history, well…"

"Emotions?"

"We don't have much time, but I will try to give you a brief history lesson that may shed some light."

I had only heard bits and pieces about this person we were meeting. He was quite the legend from what I was hearing.

"Claude and I go way back, as you probably guessed, but there was another close to us. His full name is Murdoc Rieger, and in 731 AD, he was a General in the army Claude and I fought for. War was common back then and it had spread throughout our homeland. We received word that the enemy had made their way into our village where Rieger's wife resided. Because I was the fastest, Rieger sent me to get her to safety, but when I got there, I was too late. I won't go into the details, but the enemy did not show anyone in the village mercy, including Ayla. To make things worse, she was nine months pregnant with Rieger's child. To this day, he blames me for not saving her. No more than I blame myself."

"Is he like us?" I asked.

"No, he's a wolf."

"His wife?"

"Human."

"So, *he's* one of the exceptions," I said.

"Yes. One of only a few I have ever encountered in all of my days."

"How old are you?" I asked.

"2,496 years old," he said without a moment's hesitation.

I stared at Theo in complete disbelief, though I knew it was the truth. The things this man must have seen throughout history. I couldn't even imagine the stories he could tell. I fought the urge to ask about every historical incident that I had ever read about in college and focused on the present. We had enough on our plate.

"Do you think Rieger is the one behind the attack on Bili and me?" I asked.

"He certainly has motive, but I presume nothing. We've been looking into this situation for some time and only getting fragments of information. I was hoping to avoid this conversation, but we have come to an impasse. This may be our only way through."

"Any chance he won't show?"

"Doubtful. Claude went to a lot of trouble setting this up. He rarely fails to deliver."

As if right on queue, I saw a black SUV approaching from a distance. Claude, who was on a motorcycle, followed. He was unmistakable, as he never wore a helmet.

As the car approached, I could see four large bodies inside. The vehicle pulled up in front of us, nose to nose, about twenty feet apart. Claude rode up a little more, almost between us, threw the kickstand down, and got up from the bike.

The wolves in the SUV exited. All four were impressive, but one of them stood out. It was obvious he was the leader and not someone to be taken lightly. He was one of the most intimidating figures I had ever seen. I would say even more imposing than Claude, and that was saying something.

"Are you ready for this, Jack?" Theo asked.

"No."

"It's just a walk in the park," he said, grinning at his obvious pun.

Rieger approached us, and his companions fell into place at his side with military precision. It surprised me not to see Kristov and Franklin as there were rumors they may be working for the General.

We walked toward them, and they walked straight for us. We stopped about ten feet from each other.

Claude walked over to the side. He appeared to be acting as an unofficial referee. The one I assumed was Rieger stared holes into Theo before turning his attention to me.

"So, this is the heir?" Rieger asked with an accent I was very familiar with.

Heir?

Even though I was incredibly nervous, I got that burning inside as I thought about my mother, Viktoria, and the beating Bili took. The burning calmed the nerves and filled me with more confidence.

"My name is Jack," I said, staring back into his icy gray eyes.

"The only reason that you both are not dead right now is that Claude insisted I hear what you have to say. What is it you could possibly tell me, Theodorus, that could make me forgive you? Not to mention what this *thing* has done," Rieger said, gesturing toward me again with a tilt of his head.

Rieger took a couple slow steps toward us, muttering something low under his breath. I heard it clear as day.

"Je n'ai pas peur de mourir," I said in response. *I'm not afraid to die.*

He stopped and looked at me again. This time, the look was different. He was still angry, but there was something else.

"Just say the word, sir, and I'll finish him," said one of Rieger's lieutenants.

Rieger just held up the back of his hand, which was more than enough to keep him quiet.

"I think we both have been getting fed malicious lies, and to this point, the *why* escapes me," Theo said calmly.

"Did you have Viktoria killed?" I asked, unable to hold my tongue.

"Jack!" Theo snapped.

I knew I shouldn't have spoken without Theo's leave, but I couldn't help myself. I knew we were playing with fire, but I was at my breaking point. I knew it was Franklin who killed her, and there was a possibility that *he* was working for this Rieger. The burning was spreading again.

"You're the one who killed her, you little piss ant! Either by your own hand, as I was told, or by your filthy existence. I'm her maker, boy, so don't test my fucking patience!" he spit out.

Not only did he think he was telling the truth, but he was also on the verge of attacking. His teeth were full and looked as sharp as broken glass. They grew even more than Kristov's and looked far more intimidating. My new senses were on fire and everything about this situation screamed *danger.* I was no longer scared and more than ready to fight if it came to that.

Out of the corner of my eye, I saw Claude set his feet, ready to move. Rieger noticed this as well. I was less than sure of Claude's allegiance at the time.

"General! Don't make the biggest mistake of your life," Theo yelled.

"The biggest mistake of my life was trusting you to protect my Ayla!"

"You're right, I couldn't save her. I tried, but I couldn't. But I did save Aleana," Theo said.

Rieger stopped in his tracks and stared at Theo. His expression changed in a heartbeat. That name meant something to him.

"You better explain yourself, Theodorus," Rieger growled.

"When I got to our village that night, I found Ayla, as I told you then.

What I didn't tell you was that she was on the verge of death, but still alive and conscious. By some miracle, the baby had not been injured in the attack. Ayla was strong and gave everything she had to deliver your child, and she succeeded. She was a beautiful little girl and a living miracle at that," Theo said.

I was completely in the dark now. I knew these two had a past, but the depths were far beyond what I imagined. Rieger's lieutenants seemed more interested in Rieger's reaction than the possibility of a fight. This information was something I gathered no one was expecting.

Theo continued.

"Ayla's dying wish was that I take your baby somewhere safe, far away from the fighting. Though she loved you, she knew you wouldn't quit the war to do what was necessary to raise a child without her. She made me promise to take Aleana to a church to be raised away from the horrors of the time. She made me swear on your daughter's life right before her last breath. Right or wrong, I gave her my word. Ayla swore in time you would understand and forgive her."

The look on Rieger's face was a mix of sadness, guilt, and fury. You could have heard a whisper from a hundred yards. The world seemed to have stopped as Theo went on.

"She put me in an impossible moral dilemma, but in the end, I did as she asked and honored my word," Theo said as he hung his head.

Pain and regret permeated Theo's face.

"I knew that one day we would be here, now, just as we are. I know you can never forget; I do hope you can forgive."

If the wolves had half the clarity we had, I'm sure Rieger was remembering this event as if it happened yesterday and not centuries ago. Though Rieger was still bordering on furious, I sensed something else in his demeanor. Centuries of believing something only to find out it was not the truth can make anyone question their beliefs.

"There's more."

This simple statement grabbed everyone's attention as if he yelled *fire* in a theater.

"Go on," Rieger said.

"Look at him," Theo said.

Look at who? What was Theo talking about?

Rieger was not in the mood for more secrets and losing his patience.

"And what am I looking for?" Rieger said sharply.

"Please, just look."

Rieger looked back at me and stared. His face went from hatred to something else in a fraction.

"He can't be," Rieger said, almost to himself.

"He is."

"No," Rieger said, but with less conviction this time.

I was looking to Theo this time. What was he talking about?

It's complicated, alright.

"The second he was changed, his eyes went from brown to that. It was never my intention for him to be turned. If Kristov and Franklin hadn't been sent to kill Bili and kidnap Jack, this would never have happened."

"Kristov?" Rieger said. It came out like a question.

"They're not working for you?" Theo asked.

"He hasn't worked for me in over two centuries. Is this some sort of ruse, Theodorus?"

He was telling the truth again.

"It's true," Claude said.

Theo and I looked at each other, thinking the same thing. If Rieger wasn't behind this, then who?

"What brought you to the States, General?" Theo said.

Theo obviously had a lot of respect for this wolf, and now I understood why.

"I received some anonymous information that you had an heir in Michigan. That's when I contacted Viktoria to keep an eye out. Viktoria told me she found something and would contact me when she was sure. The last time I spoke to her, she told me I should come to the states because there was something she wanted to discuss with me. Something important. It was a short time later that I received news that Jack killed her."

Just hearing him mention her that way caused my heart to break all over again. I knew rumors were spreading that I killed Viki, but I couldn't believe it had reached Rieger overseas.

Rieger continued to stare at me as he walked closer. He looked into my eyes, unblinking.

"You have her look, young one," he said. His tone was much calmer now.

I just stared at him, not knowing what to say.

Who's look?

I was completely in the dark.

"What happened to Viktoria?" Rieger asked.

I told the story, trying not to leave out any details as I thought he may be able to provide help if he had all the information. My eyes teared up as I recounted the moment of her death. I was reliving it all over again and it was just as painful. When I told him it was Franklin who killed her, because his scent was unmistakable, his eyes held murderous intentions.

"Are you sure it was him?" he asked.

I could see he was getting angrier, and the fact that it was another wolf who was responsible only added to his anger.

"I am. The son of a bitch fled like a coward, but that was apparently part of the plan," I said.

He had a confused look. Then I told him about when I got back, she was missing without a trace. When I told him this, he got a look about him even I couldn't decipher.

"I will find him, as well as any others who may have played a part."

"Sounds to me as if someone is attempting to start a war and about to pull it off," Rieger said as he looked back at Theo. "I have received reports of conflicts in Europe, as well as Asia."

"I have as well. May I ask how you received your information about Jack?" Theo said.

"It was a letter, typed, of course. All it said was *Theo has an heir in the states: Ann Arbor, Michigan.* That was over two years ago. No return address but mailed out of New York."

"If this doesn't get dealt with soon, there will be a conflict of which we haven't seen in over a millennium," Theo said.

"I think it's time we had a meeting with everyone we can trust. We need to spread the word about what's happening," Rieger said.

"Agreed. Claude and I will arrange it. We also have a few leads that may provide some information. If we get anything useful, I'll keep you apprised," Theo said.

Rieger nodded, looked at me one last time, and then got back in his vehicle with the others and left. Once the vehicle was out of sight, Theo, Claude, and I took a second to digest what had just happened.

"I guess that could have been worse." I said, looking at Theo.

"Indeed. We're still alive," Theo said.

Claude was contemplating something, and Theo saw it right away.

"What do you think?" Theo asked.

"I have more questions than answers, and I don't like it," Claude said as his phone chimed.

Claude looked at the text and then put the phone back in his pocket.

"That's some intel I had been waiting for. This may be something we can use. I'll call you soon."

He got on his bike and sped off with purpose.

"Let's get back. We have work to do," Theo said.

45

We got into the Bentley and started driving. I was bursting with curiosity and questions after our little meeting, but before I could even ask, Theo beat me to the punch.

"He's your grandfather. There are too many *greats* in front of the title to mention but you share the same blood," he said.

I was a distant relative to Rieger? What did this mean, was I half wolf?

"The story I told Rieger was the truth. What I didn't elaborate on was the fact that I have been keeping tabs on every descendant of Aleana's since. Trying to keep them safe and helping when I could," Theo said.

"So, my real father was the descendant?"

"No. Your mother."

This was incredible information. The thought that my mother had the blood of an immortal made me wonder about a variety of *what ifs*.

"Did you know my mom?"

"Yes."

There was something in his look when he said that. I could tell that he knew I sensed it. Things started to piece together in my mind. All these seemingly random events I thought were coincidence were finally connected.

"How?"

"Like you, she worked for me at one time. She was a fantastic woman. I'm sure I don't have to tell you."

Hearing him say nice things about my mother brought back a flood of memories, and I had to fight back the tears.

"They killed her because of her bloodline, didn't they?"

"I believe so, but until we discover who is behind these other events, we won't know for sure."

After he said this, I could see his demeanor change.

"I'm sorry, Jack. If I had known her identity was compromised, I would have taken more precautions. I failed your mother, and there is no apology that could make up for it. I hope you can forgive me."

"It's not your fault, Theo. There is evil in this world, plain and simple, and there always will be."

Knowing Theo, I realized his guilt must have been eating at him something terrible. There was no way he could be everywhere at once, but I could see that he felt directly responsible for her death.

This also made me think about the look Viki gave me when I told her about my mother. She must have known it was an immortal and probably suspected it was a wolf, or wolves, involved.

"What am I, Theo, some freak of nature?"

"No, you are a gem of nature. A very rare one at that. There are legends of individuals like yourself, which is why you are causing such a stir throughout the community. If you haven't guessed, the fact that you have taken on some wolf traits after your transformation has many worried and others curious. Both can be troublesome. Everyone fears what they don't understand. We all know what happens when people fear things."

He didn't have to elaborate on that last point. The message was loud and clear.

"What happened to the others like me? Any still alive?"

"No one really knows," Theo said.

The attention I was getting overwhelmed me, and I had only been dealing with it a short time. I wouldn't have doubted the others went into permanent hiding. The thought crossed my mind a few times.

There was one question I needed to know, but I wasn't exactly sure how to approach it. I tossed it around in my head for a second or two before just spitting it out.

"When Rieger spoke about the letter he received, he indicated I was *your* heir," I said.

"Yes. That someone knows our history enough to fabricate an appropriate lie is wearisome."

"Then I'm not...?"

"No."

Though I observed no trace of deception in what Theo had just said, I felt like there may have been more to the story. I didn't press the issue.

"I'm going to drop you off at the warehouse where Steve is currently working. Give him a hand for a while if you don't mind, and if you find anything, let me know."

"I will."

"You did well today, Jack. I'm proud of you," Theo said, and when he did, he gave me a reassuring smile.

To the average person, those words may seem mundane or cliché. To me, they couldn't have been more special. I had never had a father figure in my life, a good one anyway, and those simple words went straight to the heart and choked me up. I kept quiet and nodded.

46

Theo dropped me off, and I found Steve working on the computer again. He was on the floor with his laptop sitting on his legs.

"Hey, Jack!" Steve yelled as soon as he saw me walk in.

Steve always seemed to be in a good mood, and it was hard not to follow suit when in his presence.

"Any luck?" I asked as I walked over to where he was working.

"Not yet, but the day is young, my friend."

Steve and I chatted while he worked, mostly about Bili and how I was dealing with being famous. Those were his words, of course, and the thought that I'm something other than the norm in anything made the entire situation even more unbelievable.

It had been hours now, and I was walking around the warehouse checking to see if anything new arrived. I heard Steve chuckle to himself, and I walked back over to him. He stood up and turned his computer screen toward me so I could see what he was looking at.

"TruVamp was a decent lead, but take a look at this Jacky boy. I think we may have something we can work with. It posted an hour ago," he said.

I looked at the screen and then back at him.

"I think you're right. We better call Theo right away," I said, reaching for my phone.

Steve grabbed my arm before I could make the call.

"I may be overly cautious, but this group seems to have quite a knack for obtaining information, which leads me to believe they are tech savvy. Cell calls are not that hard to intercept with the right scanner equipment. Just text him the gist for now."

I texted Theo, and a few minutes later, I got a return text that just said:

Bili's apartment ASAP!

"Okay, let's get going," I said.

He threw his computer in a backpack, and we went out the back door. His car was in back, and it didn't surprise me that he drove a Beetle. It fit him like a glove.

"Where are we going?" Steve asked.

"Bili's."

His eyes lit up.

I had to wonder how long he had been pursuing her. Was it months, years, centuries? It was obvious from the first meeting at the warehouse that it wasn't the first time Steve had fawned over her.

When we arrived at Bili's apartment, I saw Theo's Caddy parked out front. I had never been inside Bili's place before, and I was curious to see it, as was Steve. It was a third-floor unit of a luxury condominium complex only a few blocks from the Piece of History.

Bili had been staying in the POH flat with me, so I was assuming there were things we needed for this mission at her place. Bili opened the door before we even knocked and then continued gathering what she needed.

"Where's Theo?" I asked, thinking he might be here.

"With Claude. We're gonna meet up with them."

I took a quick glance around the place, noticing something odd. To put it politely, she lived simply. The walls were bare, no TV, and no proper furniture to speak of other than a small couch and a reading chair. She had a few unpacked boxes on the floor next to the balcony door wall and not much else. It looked like she had moved in this morning. The only odd thing that stood out was a large vase with fresh flowers.

"Were you robbed?" I asked.

"Shut up," Bili said without looking at me.

"Love your apartment, Bili. I don't like clutter either," Steve said, grinning.

"Thanks," she said, distractedly.

Bili grabbed the last of the items we needed and headed for the door.

"Let's go," she said.

Steve and I followed Bili down the stairs to the ground floor. The elevator would have taken too long.

I looked at Bili in a whole new light as I thought about what Theo had told me. I wanted to tell her how sorry I was for everything that happened to her. I know it was centuries ago, but the thought of anyone hurting her that way was hard to think about. This girl saved my life, giving no thought to her own survival. I was in her debt, and I hoped one day I could repay her.

"What's the plan?" I asked.

"The information you got produced results. I'll fill you in as we drive," she said.

Bili tossed me the keys to Theo's Caddy.

"You're driving. Steve, you're in the back."

I felt for Steve. I'm sure he didn't know her past. The walls he would have to hurdle to get remotely close to her would be herculean.

We got in the car and headed out with purpose.

"Where are we going?" I asked.

Bili gave me a general location and said that we would get more specific instructions from Theo shortly.

Steve was sitting in the back but leaning forward between the seats like a teenager trying to be part of the front seat adult conversation. I could see in the rearview mirror that he was staring at Bili.

"Heard you had an interesting visit with Rieger," Bili said.

"Holy shit! Murdoc Rieger? Really?" Steve said excitedly. "What was he like? I've heard stories. Did he kill anyone?"

Apparently this Rieger was a big deal. After meeting him, I can see why. He did little to give the impression that he was someone to trifle with. I wanted to say that the only person he almost killed was me.

"He wasn't a ball of laughs, that's for sure," I said.

"I can believe it. He's the most notorious wolf that ever lived. His reputation is worldwide," Steve said as he shook his head, still not believing what he'd heard.

"Did you know about the other thing?" I said as I looked at Bili.

"Which?"

"That he's my grandfather," I said.

"What?" Steve said, again in disbelief. The look on his face was pure shock.

"Yes. I told you a long time ago..." Bili started to say.

"Commpliiicaaated," I said in a drawn-out mocking tone.

"See. Now you're getting it."

"Is there something else? As shocking as it was to find out I have wolf blood, I sensed there was more to it."

"Hmm," Bili said.

"Hmm? What do you mean, hmm?"

I noticed a slight hand twitch as Bili grabbed a piece of her hair and twirled it. Both small signs I have picked up from Bili when she is hiding something.

Poor Steve was in the back dying to ask a million questions. I'd never seen someone fidget so much in my life. He was on the verge of exploding.

"I don't know everything, Jack," Bili said.

"You know a lot."

"Most of which you ended up learning the hard way. Remember?"

"Hey. It's Steve, from the back seat. I still can't believe what I just heard. That explains the eyes, I guess. And why you're still alive. So, he isn't the one trying to kill everybody and start a war?"

"Doesn't look that way," I said.

"Slow down; we're almost there," Bili said. "I need to contact Theo for his exact location. They were on the move in this area."

We pulled into a vacant lot and parked as Bili sent Theo a text. He responded with his location.

"You know where the *Downs* are?"

"Yeah. Less than five minutes from here."

"Approach from the north. There's a hill that overlooks the parking area," Bili said.

"Got it. I know right where they are."

47

The City of Northville is very nice and upscale. It's known for nice restaurants, coffee shops, clothing stores, and a few pubs. The city had one large attraction that was a boast for some and the bane of others. A horse racing track.

When I circled the far perimeter of the northern lot, I could see Theo's work van parked amid a few other vehicles. It didn't have any markings, and from the outside, it looked like any other plain van. It was white and blended in nicely with the surroundings. The sun was facing the front windshield, and I figured this was no accident. Anyone looking in this direction would get a bright mirrorlike reflection of the sun for the next hour or so.

I pulled behind the van, attempting to conceal the Cadillac as best I could. I figured whatever he was looking for was near the main building or stables. Claude opened the rear door and waved us inside.

The three of us made our way into the van via the rear door, and Steve closed it behind us.

"Hey, Theo," Steve said. Then he looked at Claude. "Sasquatch."

Claude didn't move or respond. He didn't take his eyes off whatever he was watching.

"Excellent work, Steve. You never cease to amaze." Theo said. "After we received your text, we broke off the surveillance we were doing and came here to wait for the new mark. A short time later, that truck showed up."

"Who's driving it?" I asked.

With my new eyes, I could see the occupied truck, but not much else. It was a good distance away and parked at an awkward angle.

"TruVamp," Theo said. "Even better, it was the vehicle we were following originally. Imagine our delight when it pulled in and parked."

"So, you found him? Thought you were losing your touch," Steve said, looking at Claude.

Claude gave a grunt that could have been interpreted in several ways.

"The real prize in all of this may be the one who is coming to meet him," Theo said. "The fact that we had time to set up and do surveillance will help us get a better look."

I felt like we were about to get somewhere. Whomever was behind this had made it very personal when they killed my mother and Viki. I wanted to know why. Then I wanted something else.

Claude looked over at me.

"Have you adjusted, young man?"

"Yes, sir. I believe so," I said.

I didn't know if the change was complete, or if I had some growing pains yet to endure. Theo said it was a little different for everyone, but my unique bloodline made it even more unpredictable.

We weren't waiting for more than another ten minutes before Theo saw something of interest.

"White Jaguar pulling in from the west entrance," Theo said as he sat up.

The Jag pulled into the parking lot and headed straight for the brown truck. Even with our vision, we were too far to get a clear look at faces, but it was obvious the driver of the Jag was female. She pulled next to the truck and spoke with the driver without ever getting out. She was cautious. She also had on sunglasses, which made it harder to recognize her.

"You recognize the car?"

"No, but the driver has a familiar look about her. We need to get closer," Theo said.

As I focused on the Jaguar, Bili noticed something else.

"What the hell is this?"

Another white vehicle pulled in from the opposite side of the lot, not driving slow or cautious. Even from a distance, you could see the two individuals in the car looked larger than average.

Wolves.

They were in a mid-size four-door vehicle, not designed for the girth of the passengers.

I looked over at Steve, and he just shrugged. This was news to him as well.

"This is going to complicate things," Theo said.

The wolves pulled alongside the truck, opposite the Jag, and parked. It looked as though they exchanged something, and within moments, all three vehicles took off in different directions.

"Shit!" Bili said.

"Bili and Steve, come with me. We'll take the wolves," Claude said, taking logistical lead of the situation.

Without a moment's hesitation, Theo and I jumped out the back door and into the caddy.

We were playing the odds that the Jag and the wolves would produce better results. The woman in the Jag was a complete mystery and appeared to be of some importance.

The engine roared as Theo floored it, launching us like a bullet. We headed west, hoping to pick up the Jag as it came onto the main road. We passed a row of tall office buildings, and when we came back out, the Jag was nowhere in sight.

"Theo, turn right. There's a back road that may cut off her route," I said.

I knew the area well, and unless this person was heading toward the countryside, they had to be going back east to pick up the freeway.

Theo turned on a dime and cut through the historical neighborhood. We were about to reach the highway when the Jag burst right in front of us. This time the driver was close enough to get a good look. Her hair was now blonde, but there was no mistaking who she was.

"What the hell?" Theo and I said simultaneously.

We looked at each other, wondering how the other knew this person.

"You know her?" Theo asked, turning his attention back to the road, still driving like a professional. The Jag was pulling away from us which said a lot about the car and driver.

"That's Ceana," I said. "The girl I told you about that came to my house."

We went around a tight corner, and the Caddy held without sliding out of control. The speed we traveled concerned me, but not as much as the fact we weren't gaining on the Jag.

"Damn, she's fast. Her name is Parrus, and I thought she was dead. Trust me when I tell you, I was much happier when I believed that to be true," Theo said.

We could see the Jag in the distance, but we weren't gaining ground. There were some train tracks approaching, along with a slight increase in grade. Theo didn't slow down, and when we hit the tracks, I believe all four tires left the earth for a moment. When this happens in real life, it's far more concerning than it appears in the movies.

The road we were on was one hill after another. We would see the Jag, and then it would disappear the next second. After we crested the last hill and the road became flat, the Jag was no longer in sight. There was a freeway ahead and several directions it could have gone.

The look on Theo's face said it all. He wanted to catch her in the worst way. I could tell he knew this woman well. I figured her to be a major player in this conflict.

"Who the hell would she be working for," Theo said, thinking out loud.

Theo's frustration was obvious as he pulled over and put the car in park.

"Who is she?"

The question seemed to bring him out of a deep thought.

"She's one of our kind, as you may have guessed. She's not as old as I am, but not too far behind. Her entire family has been a plague on this earth. I had some dealings with her for a short time. Once I discovered she was psychotic, and evil to her core, I cut all ties. I hadn't seen her in centuries, and then I heard some wolves killed her in France. Though she's insane, she's very intelligent. Can you think of a more disturbing combination?"

"What do you think she wants?" I asked.

"That's the question alright. Her motivations have always been an enigma. You could never tell what she was after or why. I know one thing for certain, she's not working alone. She always finds someone of extraordinary means and does their dirty work."

Theo looked at his phone.

"They have one of the wolves and they're not too far."

48

Theo turned off the highway and into a small out-of-the-way neighborhood. There was an old elementary school that appeared to have been closed for some time. Weeds overgrew the parking lot and there wasn't another car in the area other than the white van.

Theo and I parked the car next to the van at the rear of the school and made our way to the blue door that Bili was holding open. We walked down the hall and into a small gymnasium. Claude and Steve were standing in front of their prisoner, who was in a solo chair.

"One got away after the crash," Claude said. "But as you can see, one did not."

"What's this one's name?" Theo asked.

They bound the wolf to the chair with rope and extra tough tape to add a little more security. Not that we were in danger from him, but rather to keep his attention where it should be.

"This is Alonzo, my friend from the motel," Claude said as he walked past his prisoner. If intimidation was Claude's objective, I was sure he accomplished it. Alonzo watched his every move, knowing he was in a bad way.

"He is also not as fast as he thought he was," Steve said with a grin. "A girl caught him."

Alonzo was the more aggressive of the two wolves that attempted to ambush Claude. This resulted in a few broken bones, but apparently it did nothing to change his mind about what he was doing.

"Alonzo, I am Theodorus. I understand you are on the young side and may have never heard of me, like you had never heard of Claude before your last meeting. He gave you some sage advice that you chose to ignore."

Theo walked around the back of Alonzo, grabbed a chair that was against the wall, and then moved to the front of him and sat. Theo stared at Alonzo, unflinchingly, for what seemed like forever. This was a side of Theo I had never seen before, as he had a threatening look about him that was frightening.

Alonzo's face was a mix of emotions. He didn't want to appear scared, but I could sense it.

"Who are you working with?" Theo asked.

Alonzo sat in silent defiance. His facial expression was almost a smug smile.

Mistake.

Theo grabbed him by the ear and yanked it clean off in a split second. I don't think that Alonzo knew what had happened until Theo held it up for him to look at. Alonzo let out a growling, agonizing yell.

I think I was as shocked as Alonzo. No warning, no threats, no nothing. Theo dangled the ear in front of the wolf before tossing it on the hard tile floor as simply as tossing an apple core in the woods.

"We can heal from most anything, as you're probably aware. What you may not know is that when a piece is removed from the body for an extended period, the cells deteriorate and die, making regeneration impossible."

Theo kept his icy stare directed at Alonzo, letting him know who was in charge and that this was not a two-way conversation.

"You may consider yourself tougher than most, but I assure you, if we start down the path of body part removal, you will get tired of losing parts well before I get tired of removing them. You have fifteen seconds to think it over before I start this process. Just so you know, your right hand is next. Sorry, but fingers just take too long."

Theo pulled out a large knife that could have been from his antique collection. It may have been old, but it looked heavy and sharp as a razor.

"Oh, so we are clear. A lie will earn you the same result," Theo added.

Alonzo's mind must have been spinning, but he knew that this was not a bluff.

"Who are you working with?"

"My maker," Alonzo said. Sweat was now dripping from his forehead.

"Which is?" Claude said.

"His name is Kristov. I don't even know if that's his first or last name," Alonzo said as he kept looking at the floor. "I'll talk. Can I have my ear back?"

Theo ignored the request.

"Continue," Theo said.

"After he turned me, and a few others, he took us to meet a woman."

"What woman?" Claude asked.

"I never got a full name, but Kristov called her Paris, like the city. The bitch at the track."

"Parrus Truzic?" Claude said, looking at Theo.

"The Jaguar," Theo said, looking at his friend.

"Shit."

"Indeed." Theo turned back to Alonzo. "Go on."

"They gave us limited information about what we were doing, but it was clear that she wanted information on you," he said, looking at Theo. "She also wanted you dead as soon as possible," Alonzo added, looking at Claude.

"And you just did as you were told, like a mindless idiot?" Bili interjected.

"We were told this was the price for our new immortality. She said you were all evil to the core, and we were doing society a favor. It was also heavily implied that if we didn't do as asked, it would be a death sentence. So..." Alonzo said, raising his eyebrows.

He was telling the truth.

"Why were you meeting Parrus at the track?"

"I don't know," Alonzo said hesitantly.

Before Alonzo finished his lying sentence, Theo brought down his knife on Alonzo's wrist and separated his hand cleanly from the rest of his arm. The hand still gripped the arm of the chair, but now there was a minor gap from hand to wrist. Blood dripped from the hand portion but spurted from the arm.

"Ahhhh, grrrr!"

Alonzo screamed and growled in equal measure.

"Someone has a short memory," Bili said calmly.

"Okay! After we failed to take care of him," Alonzo said, nodding toward Claude, "she killed my partner and gave me another chance to redeem myself."

"By doing what?" Theo pressed.

Sweat covered Alonzo's forehead, as he looked from Bili, to Theo, and then to the knife.

Theo raised the knife, slow and deliberate.

"I had to kill her," Alonzo said, looking at Bili and then back at Theo, "and I had to make it look like you did it. She said she had the perfect plan to execute this, which is what I was picking up. Then-"

"That girl kicked your ass?" Steve said, enjoying the chance to talk about Bili again.

Claude opened the small envelope he found in Alonzo's pocket and showed Theo the contents.

I didn't like the look on Theo's face.

"Did she say why?" Theo said.

"No, she never told us shit!" Alonzo yelled angrily. "I heard her say she was after someone named Jack, but after Kristov fucked up the original plan, things changed. That's all I know!"

Claude looked at Theo, who gave a nod, letting him know that everything he had just heard was the truth.

"Where's Kristov staying? And how do you contact him?" Claude asked.

"I don't know exactly, but it's somewhere downtown, near some baseball field. Cork something."

"Corktown?" Theo prompted.

"Probably. Listen, his number is in my phone, take it. That's all I know. Really!"

Theo backed up, and Claude stepped in front of Alonzo. The nervous look on Alonzo's face said he should have taken Claude's advice the first time.

Claude punched Alonzo in the face so hard that I thought his head may come off. It took a few seconds before his face was the proper shape again. It was the oddest thing I had ever seen at that point.

"Listen carefully," Claude said.

I guess that was Claude's way of getting his attention. He got it.

"The first time we met, you thought you knew better. You don't. We better not meet again," Claude said as succinctly as ever.

Claude looked over at Steve.

"Cut him loose."

In an excited hurry, Steve tripped and fell into Alonzo, knocking him and the chair over. Alonzo's hand went flying onto the dirty floor not too far from his ear.

"Shit, sorry," Steve said as he awkwardly pulled Alonzo back up.

Bili cringed.

Steve brushed off the dirt from his pants absentmindedly, seeming to forget what he was doing.

Claude made a throat clearing sound.

"Oh. Yeah."

Steve pulled out a small Swiss Army knife and cut away the ropes and tape which took a full minute. When Steve got through the last of it, he backed up and stood next to Claude.

"There you are, sir," Steve said as if he had just brought up Alonzo's car from the valet.

Alonzo stood up, looked around at each of us suspiciously, but didn't move.

Bili opened the door and motioned with her head and eyes, as only Bili can do, and said, "Beat it, dipshit."

Alonzo bent down, picked up his ear, and put it in his pocket. He grabbed his right hand with his left, which was a surreal sight, and then he edged toward the door. I think he felt we would attack at any second. We just stood, watching him.

He pressed his hand against the bloody stump, and it fused right away.

He took two more steps before he burst into a sprint. He was out of sight in no time.

"You think he will go back to them?" I asked to no one in particular.

"Only if he is the dumbest wolf alive," Bili said.

"We're counting on it," Steve said, grinning. "I put a tracker on him. C'mon, you think I'm that clumsy? I'm not a wolf."

Steve punched Claude in the arm, with no power at all, mocking the punch Claude gave Alonzo.

"Excellent work, Harold," Claude said.

Steve's grin softened. I think that name was the only thing that upset that guy.

"Even if he finds it, it may give us a direction," Steve added.

"I wondered why you were so nice to him," Bili said, directing her attention to Claude.

Nice? He about decapitated him.

Claude walked to the window and opened it to let in some fresh air. We gathered in a circle to discuss our options.

"Parrus? I thought that crazy bitch was dead." Claude said, looking at Theo.

"Me too. You think you can find Kristov's place in Detroit?" Theo said.

"Read my mind. You guys take the vehicles. I'll get my own ride," Claude said, before rushing out.

"See ya later, Claude; be careful. You too, Steve. You're the greatest by the way. Oh, stop," Steve said in mock conversation, playing both his and Claude's part.

That even got a smile out of Bili.

"Bili, can you and Jack take Steve back and then head to the POH? I'll take the van and meet you two there later. Keep your eyes peeled. This situation might have accelerated."

"Mind if I stay at the warehouse?" Steve asked.

"Anywhere you like. Anything catch your eye?" Theo asked.

I wasn't sure what he was referring to until Steve answered.

"I like the Lichtenstein you had hanging in the back, but not picky," Steve said.

I couldn't tell if he was serious or not.

"Bili, give Steve the *Drowning Girl* when you get back," Theo said.

That answers that.

"Thanks, Theo," Steve said nonchalantly as if he had just given him a cup of coffee. That painting was worth a fair amount. Theo took care of those close to him.

It was hard not to like Steve, as I said. He was the epitome of good nature and positivity that most people like to be around. Unless you're Bili, of course, who I think despises both qualities.

We got in the Caddy and made our way back to Bili's, where Steve had his car. On the way, Steve made one last effort to get Bili to have dinner with him, but in standard Bili form, she impolitely declined.

Bili was starving, so when we got to the POH, we called in some takeout from her favorite Chinese restaurant. While we ate, I prompted Bili again, hoping to get her to talk to me about my new world, and she did. This world we live in is truly a remarkable place. It's a shame so few ever get to see or experience the whole of it.

49

J ack took a deep breath and then sat back in a more relaxing posture. Sara followed suit and sat back in her chair as well. True or not, she found herself engrossed in Jack's tale.

"What did Bili tell you?" Sara said.

"Another time. How about a coffee, Doc? I'd buy, but you guys confiscated everything," Jack said.

Sara grinned at him.

"Good idea. I think I can spring for it."

"Any chance you have access to anything other than vending machine coffee?" Jack asked.

"Don't care for an eight-ounce cup of stagnant brown water?"

"Not a fan."

"Ah, a fellow coffee snob. There's a good coffee shop across the street from the hospital. What would you like?" she asked.

"Dark coffee. Large and strong please. One raw sugar if they have it. If not, black is fine," Jack said.

"Okay. I'll be back in a little while. Get some rest," Sara said as she gathered up her paperwork and went back to her office.

She sat at her desk, still amazed at her new digs. She logged in the progress she had made and typed her notes. Even though she recorded her sessions, she wanted the highlights at her fingertips.

Nancy poked her head into the office.

"Is your patient glad to have you back?" Nancy asked, hoping for any details about Jack. The buzz around the hospital was still picking up.

"I hope so," the doctor said, not elaborating.

"I also wanted to tell you I have a contact at the police department who said she can get you that letter of his. I'll let you know when I have it. Should only be a few hours."

"That's great. Thanks, Nancy. I'm going to grab some coffees, want anything?"

"Sure. I'll take one of those fancy cold coffees with whip cream if you don't mind."

"You got it."

Sara finished up some typing and then made the coffee run. She returned in short order and went right to Jack's room.

"The coffee they had brewed was a medium roast, so I had them throw in a shot of espresso. I hope that's okay," Sara said.

"Perfect, thank you," Jack said as Sara handed him the coffee. "This should get the blood moving."

"I think we have time for one more session before we call it a day. Are you okay to continue?" Sara said.

"I am."

Jack took a long sip of his coffee and then began.

50

Theo organized the meeting just as Rieger suggested. He contacted everyone I had met at the warehouse and a few others he could trust. He also rented a log cabin, through a third party, that could accommodate the group comfortably. It was in a country setting but very close to the city, making it convenient for everyone.

If the meeting went as planned, and everyone could get along and work together, there was a good chance the combined efforts of the group could turn the propaganda tide. And find out who was behind all of this.

Theo, Bili, and I drove to the warehouse to pick up Steve and Claude, who had been working throughout the night. While we were on the way there, Theo told us Steve had made several valuable discoveries.

We walked in to find Claude gathering up a few things and putting on his jacket.

"Well?" Theo asked.

"Found the bitch," Claude said. "And several possible associates."

"You're kidding." I said instinctively.

Claude, Bili, and Theo all looked at me at the same time with the same blank stare. Apparently, *kidding,* was not something Claude did. Thankfully Theo spoke, mercifully diverting the attention from me.

"If we can get everyone on board, do you think we will have enough bodies to conduct a proper offensive?" Theo asked Claude.

"If the General and his men commit, we will have more than enough."

This was a huge break, and the excitement showed on Theo's face. The possibility of ending the feud, as well as catching those responsible for the senseless violence and killings, was indeed a positive. This meeting was going to be bigger than originally expected.

"Where's Steve?" Bili asked.

"He left just before you got here. He needed to talk to Miah, but she wasn't answering her phone. He was gonna try and catch her at her house before the meeting," Claude said.

"We have to get going. We're running late as it is, and Rieger is not overloaded with patience," Theo said.

Claude followed the three of us on his motorcycle as he did most trips. I got the feeling he liked his solitude. Not to mention, they did not design vehicles for his frame.

The mood among the three of us in the car was upbeat for a change, and we talked about work and maybe even taking a vacation when this was all over. My lack of travel experience excited Theo and Bili, as they both had several *must visit* destinations they were adamant I see as soon as possible.

We were almost at the cabin when I caught a dreadful scent in the air. When I looked at Theo and Bili, I knew I wasn't the only one. No one said anything, hoping there was a good explanation.

After breaching the thick forest, we came to the clearing where the cabin was located. My heart sank.

"No, no, no, no!" Theo said as we approached, each *no* getting louder and louder.

Flames engulfed the entire cabin, as well as several vehicles parked in the driveway. The fact that we didn't see anyone standing outside was alarming but not near as disturbing as the smell.

Flesh.

That and the fact that two large box-vans were parked in the front and rear of the cabin. They were big enough to block the two doors as well as the two windows big enough to escape through.

Theo was the first to spring into action, and we followed his lead. He ran around the cabin looking for a way inside. They must have used an accelerant, as the flames felt unnaturally intense.

The cabin was built like a tiny fortress; good for keeping people out, but unfortunately, excellent at keeping them in as well. I noticed a few small gaps in the side that looked as though someone started a hole but was unable to finish. The fire must have been quick and ferocious to keep them from getting out.

Claude ran to the truck blocking the front door and began pulling from the rear bumper. The tires on both trucks were all flat and looked to have been done so purposely to make them harder to move.

Claude's skin sizzled and blistered as he tried to pull the truck away from the door. We ran over to help him, and just as the truck started to move, it exploded into a ball of flame. We were all blown clear of the blaze.

We circled the cabin several times looking for a solution that just wasn't there. The fire was so intense and hot that just being within ten feet made your skin burn and peel. Though it would heal when we backed off, I instinctively knew that if burned too badly, there would be no recovery.

The lack of noise other than the crackling sound of wood and embers made it obvious no one was alive.

The four of us stood there, mesmerized by the dancing fire, looking like we had just crawled out of a dirty chimney. The faint sounds of sirens echoed in the distance.

Theo had streaks of ash and tears down his cheeks as he stared into the fire with a fury equal to those of the flames. He was squinting and grinding his teeth, using every ounce of strength not to scream in rage. It was clear he was at his breaking point.

Bili and I shared a concerned glance toward each other as we were on either side of Theo. He had set the place and time, and somehow the enemy got the information and used it against us. I know he would forever feel responsible.

"We need to get out of here," Claude said as the sirens were getting closer by the minute.

Not knowing for sure who was inside was unsettling, but time was up. We had to go.

It was a somber trip back, and we rode in silence as the fire trucks passed us, adding to the eerie helpless feeling. They would put out the fire and find the remains of our friends, all of whom had died in what had to be a most horrible death.

Theo got a call from Claude, who went to Miah's to look for Steve. He found him and told us to get there right away.

Miah and Lucinda lived in the city of Wixom, which is only thirty minutes from Ann Arbor. They had a large plot of land for the area, and their driveway was almost a quarter mile itself, making the house well out of sight from the neighbors.

When we arrived, we pulled up, parked behind Steve's car, and got out. When we did, we saw Claude standing further up the drive, motionless.

Steve's disheveled and lifeless body lay on the gravel, just in front of the house. The rocks that surrounded Steve's head were such a dark red they almost appeared black.

I watched Claude as he stood over Steve's body in silence. Though he wasn't saying anything, his body language and face were screaming. Even at the fire, he seemed somewhat emotionally unaffected. Not now. There was anger in his eyes that chilled me to the bone, and a subtle sadness that was heartbreaking. I had a feeling from the way they talked to each other that they may have been close, but it wasn't until that very moment I understood.

Bili brushed past Claude and knelt down beside Steve's body. They had shot him in both eyes, but his face was otherwise the same. The damage to the rear of his head was another story and obviously why he couldn't recover. Like Theo had told me before. Massive trauma to the head or heart, and it's all over.

Bili reached down and grabbed Steve's hand. I thought she was going to move him, but she just held it as gently as she could.

"You idiot," Bili said, almost with contempt. "Why didn't you just come with us? You never did anything right, did you?"

I saw her eyes mist up as she continued.

"Your stupid flowers, your moronic text messages with hearts in them. Why did you waste your time on me? I treated you horribly."

My heart wept as I saw Bili do something I never thought I would see her do. She bared a piece of soul, which is tough for anyone, especially her. She went on.

"I never told you, but I loved the flowers," she said in a softer voice now. "You never gave up on me when you should have. I wanted to tell you... I just..."

I wasn't sure what Bili was referring to, but I felt for her just the same. Viki's death was still fresh in my memory, which added to the sadness of the situation.

My sadness was now turning to anger. If my mom, Viki, and the cabin weren't enough, this seemed to be the proverbial last straw. I know I wasn't the only one thinking this either. This nice and considerate person did not deserve this, nor did any of the others. So much loss, and for what?

Bili set Steve's hand down on his chest with a soft pat and stood up. Still looking at Steve, she took a deep breath and spoke with a vengeful tone.

"How do we get these sons of bitches?" she said.

It was only a few seconds later when it came to me.

"I know how."

51

J ack stopped talking, stood up, stretched his legs for a moment, and then sat back down.

"Are you okay? Do you want to take a break?" Sara asked.

"No. I'm good. I was wondering, though, can I ask you a personal question?" Jack said.

He was so casual with his request that Sara wondered what harm it would cause. Sara certainly wouldn't get too personal, but a little background might be okay. Even though she didn't like to do it as a rule, she hadn't broken new ground in her field by not taking chances.

"What would you like to know?"

"Where did you grow up? Were you always a country girl?"

Sara chuckled as she covered her mouth with her hand. This struck her as very funny.

"Goodness no. I don't think I saw real grass until my teens."

Jack smiled along with her and asked another seemingly simple question.

"What do you remember about your father?"

This caught Sara off guard and stunned her to silence. Her smile faded, and she glared at Jack. Her look was a serious one, bordering on angry. It wasn't just the question itself but how he phrased it. It was a knowing and presumptuous question.

"Why would you ask me that?"

"You really don't know, do you?"

"I don't. Tell me."

She had lost a little of her doctor professionalism at the mention of her dad.

"Tell me what you remember, and I'll explain," Jack said.

"I remember he left his family like a thief in the night."

Sara regretted going down this path, but Pandora's Box was open. She crossed her arms and raised her eyebrows, waiting for Jack to speak.

"You were very young and never truly knew him, which is an absolute shame. But if you think he left his little girl because he wanted to, then you don't know anything. He was an extraordinary man."

Tears welled up when Jack said those kind words. The anger was still there, but she wasn't as sure about herself as she was just moments earlier.

"Did you know him?" she asked.

Sara knew it was a ridiculous thing to ask but her need for information was greater than logic.

"No, but I know of him. His heroism and bravery are legendary and the reason you are here now."

Sara shook her head, ever so slightly, with her eyes closed as if trying to clear it or remove a bad memory.

"Stop! Stop this! There is no way you could know anything about my father. I have been listening patiently, and even enjoying your story, but this is..."

"Impossible?" Jack finished for her.

He looked at her with sorrow and understanding that only made her angrier.

Sara stood up and walked around her chair in aggravation, pacing back and forth. Her mind was a storm of confusion and questions.

What's happening here? Who is this person?

Sara questioned everything at that moment in time. This had put her in a quandary, and for the first time, the treatment of Jack took a second chair.

"Yes. It is impossible. Almost everything you are telling me is impossible. I want to help you, Jack, but I have... I mean... I'm not sure if this is a good idea. We are treading dangerous ground here."

"Sit down, please," Jack said.

The look he gave Sara was pleading and thoughtful.

Sara stopped pacing but she didn't sit.

"I know what it's like hearing things you don't want to hear, or things you can't understand, but you have to let your prejudices go," Jack said. "And, so you are aware, I'm not telling you this to upset you or for some unnecessary drama."

Sara sat back down when he said this and looked straight at Jack with tear-laced eyes and spoke with a tremor in her next words.

"Why, then?"

"That right there is the question," Jack said, holding up a single finger. "When you understand that, everything will become clear."

"You can't just tell me? You sound like a shrink."

Sara said this without a hint of humor in her voice.

"I can tell you this. If you can get past what I have just told you, and let me finish my story, there will be more answers than questions by the end. That, I promise."

"What do you mean?" she asked, sitting back a little with a squint in her eyes.

"I don't just know things about your *father*, Sara."

The simple implication was loud and clear. He knew things about her mother. The mention of her father was a sore topic, but her mother was something else entirely. There was no fighting back the tears now. The mere thought of *her* was an avalanche of emotions that couldn't be stifled. The deep seeded memory of her mother's disappearance had been a source of great anguish over the years.

"You were raised by Emily after she went missing, who was a

wonderful woman, but she was not your mother. I'm sorry for your loss by the way."

Sara knew better than anyone how easy it can be to manipulate someone with the right information, and she was well aware Jack could be doing that to her right now. The rules of psychiatry be damned. If he had information about her parents and the mysteries surrounding them, she would hear him out.

"Did you know *her*?" she asked again, not sure if she wanted to know the answer.

"Yes. Very well, in fact."

Sara was about to launch into a thousand questions but stopped cold. She would have to take this slow, and she knew it. As soon as she found a hole in his story, she would call him out. There was no way Jack could have known her mother. He was younger than she was. She had to keep her emotions in check.

"Okay," she said.

"Okay?" Jack repeated.

"Yes, okay. You have my attention. I will hold my questions until the end of your story, but when we get through it, you will tell me everything you know," Sara said, almost as a threat.

Jack didn't flinch at the comment.

"Agreed. Back to the story then."

52

Claude, Bili, and Theo listened to what I had proposed and thought on it for a few minutes.

"I don't like it," Theo said.

I could tell by the way he spoke it wasn't the plan he didn't like, but the risk involved. My plan wasn't too complicated, and the gist of it was putting myself in a position to be taken by the enemy.

"What choice do we have?" I began. "It's just us now and we don't even know who is pulling the strings. This will be the quickest way to get from point A to point B. Steve believed that the enemy was very tech savvy and has probably been monitoring us this whole time. This would explain why they have been one step ahead of us. We can use this to our advantage."

The truth in what I said struck a chord. The enemy had the drop on us at every turn, and we were chasing our tails.

"What you are proposing would require a large group in order to do it properly. Even then..." Theo said, shaking his head as he looked off to the side.

"What if you're wrong, and they no longer want you alive, then what?" Bili added.

"Then I'm screwed, I guess. Anyone else have a better idea?"

The silence said it all. Though it had a risk factor no one was comfortable with, it had merit.

"There's one problem with your idea," Bili said.

Bili made a significant point, but it was my plan, and I didn't want anyone else in harm's way.

Since I started talking, Claude remained quiet.

"I think this may work, and I have some ideas to reduce the risks as well," he said.

Theo shook his head but less convincing than before. He knew it might be the only way to get the information we needed.

When we partially agreed that this was our best last option, Claude went on to explain a plausible, albeit theoretical, plan of execution.

53

We went about our lives as best we could. Theo added some security precautions to the store, and we opened back up for business. It didn't take long before we were moving art just as we had before, and the market was the best it had been in years. Theo worked with us at the Piece of History almost every day, forgoing other aspects of his business for the time being.

Bili and I were still sharing the flat in the storage room, which wasn't too bad as we made every attempt to give each other some space and privacy. That being said, there were a few awkward moments when Bili was changing clothes or coming from the shower. She didn't walk around naked, but she didn't exactly have self-image problems either, as I noticed she seemed perfectly comfortable in her underwear with me in the room. I tried not to stare, but I couldn't help but notice her... physique, let's say.

After more time had passed, things were almost as they were before I was turned. Theo was leaving the office more, and Bili moved back to her apartment. Theo made certain it had the best security measures possible, including a panic room. Bili hated the thought but didn't fight Theo on it. Theo told us that Claude had left Michigan but had planned to return before too long.

Bili and I were doing computer work in the back when Theo approached us.

"I just got off the phone with Mr. Hendricks, and he wants the Whistler. Do you two want to take a ride and deliver it to him?" Theo said.

"To the crazy Highland house?" she asked.

"Yes."

"Is that the older guy that gets your name wrong every time he comes in?" I asked, looking at Bili.

"Yeah. He's... on the eccentric side. That reminds me," Bili said, turning her attention to Theo. "Your favorite designer called. She may stop in later to see you."

"She's nice. Just a little lonely," Theo said.

"I'm sure she is," I added with raised eyebrows.

I looked at Bili and we both snickered like little kids.

"Go deliver you two," Theo said in mock anger.

I think it was the only time I saw Theo close to being embarrassed. I don't know why, but it made the whole situation funnier, and no one laughed harder than Bili.

We packed up the painting, got in the van, and headed out.

"Wait till you see this place. It looks like Graceland dipped in puke-green paint," Bili said.

It was only about a thirty-minute drive, and when we got there, I pulled into the long horseshoe driveway. Though it was ugly, it was obviously expensive.

We cautiously checked our surroundings before exiting the van and making our way to the front door. Even though things had relaxed, Theo always reminded us not to let our guard down.

I carried the large piece of art, which was still crated for protection, up to the front door. It was an original James Whistler, and it was rather expensive.

I got a funny tingling feeling in my hands as we made our way to the door. I think Bili noticed me stretching and wiggling my fingers.

"You alright?" she asked.

"Yeah, fine. I feel a little different, not bad, it's... I don't know what it is."

"Puberty is a natural part of life, Jack. Later on, we'll have *the talk*," Bili said in her most teacher-like expression and tone.

"You really should do stand-up."

"Who says I haven't?"

Bili stared at me with a sly grin as she pushed the doorbell with an exaggerated point and push of her index finger.

The doorbell rang, but instead of a standard ring sound, it was a brief excerpt of "Hound Dog". That caused me to burst into laughter. All professionalism straight out the window. I was thankful that Mr. Hendricks didn't answer the door right away, giving me time to compose.

After the second encore of Elvis, Mr. Hendricks answered. He was about sixty-five or seventy with solid white hair and a slender build. He looked like a retired CEO of something.

"Hello Mr. Hendricks?" Bili said. "We have something for you."

"Hello Betty. Please come in. Who's your friend?"

"This is Jack," Bili said. "He works at the store as well."

"Oh, yes, of course."

The micro wince on Bili's face at the error in her name didn't go unnoticed. She hated the name Betty, which only made it more humorous. I also noticed something else unusual about Mr. Hendricks but didn't give it too much thought. He was elderly.

"Bring it to my study. It's in the back."

There it was again. He looked as though he was ill and trying to hide it. To the average person, he had the perfect stone face. Not to us.

Bili and I looked at each other, thinking the same thing.

"Are you okay, Mr. Hendricks?" Bili asked.

"Fine, fine. This way please."

We followed Mr. Hendricks down the hallway, which led into an open living area.

"You have a very nice home, sir," I said, doing my best not to sound sarcastic. Mr. Hendricks didn't respond and kept walking.

I could see the study off to the right, but Mr. Hendricks didn't walk that way. He walked straight toward the large door-wall that led out to a huge backyard.

"It's very warm. I'm just going to let some air in," he said as he opened the sliding door.

"I see the study, Mr. Hendricks. Do you need help hanging this piece? Bili and I aren't very good at it, but we wouldn't mind practicing with your Whistler." I said, attempting to make a joke.

Mr. Hendricks walked back toward us without saying a word. I thought that was one of my better jokes too.

Bili looked at me again and then back to Mr. Hendricks.

"Are you sure you're all right, sir?" Bili said in an above normal voice, trying to get his attention.

His face was white as a ghost, and I thought he might be having a stroke or heart attack right in front of us.

"I'm-"

Before he could utter another word, an arrow flew into the house and struck Mr. Hendricks in the back of the head. He dropped to the ground with a thud as blood spread across the floor.

"Run!" Bili said.

I dropped the million-dollar painting as if it was a worthless paper print and bolted to the front door with Bili close behind. I pulled it open and stopped where I stood.

Kristov!

He was standing in front of us with another wolf even bigger than him. We backed up and turned to assess our options. Just then, two more wolves appeared from behind, coming in through the sliding door Mr. Hendricks had just opened. I didn't recognize the first one. He'd apparently killed Mr. Hendricks, as he had a modern version of a crossbow slung over his shoulder. As he walked, I could barely see the other wolf behind him because of his size. I say barely because I only needed a glimpse to recognize that son-of-bitch.

Franklin.

The sight of him made my blood run hot. I don't mean metaphorically either. I felt my core temperature rise several degrees.

Franklin was carrying an odd-looking, but very large, short-barrel rifle. I wanted nothing more than to charge and kill him with my bare hands.

"Hey, Jack. Did you miss me?" Franklin said with his usual sarcastic smile. The obvious double meaning only added to my burning fury.

"I did. Never figured you for a coward," I said, shrugging my shoulders as nonchalantly as I could. "Guess you're just a sack of yellow piss when Kristov isn't around to protect you."

Kristov chuckled at this as he made a show of his entrance into the house, his back-up close behind. Franklin's smile faded as fast as it came, and though he kept quiet, I could tell I angered him. I was baiting him, hoping to get him to make a mistake we could capitalize on, but he didn't fall for it.

"Thanks for coming all this way to meet us. Saved us another trip to that stupid city," Kristov said.

"Not to mention you got your ass kicked the last time you came to Ann Arbor," Bili said, looking at Kristov.

We were in a terrible situation, but Bili wouldn't give him any satisfaction. I was so far beyond angry that I could hardly think straight.

"What do you want this time, Kristov? The usual?" I asked.

"I'm afraid things have changed since our last meeting. My employer has had a change of heart and a much more pragmatic solution to this problem," Kristov said.

I saw a look on Franklin's face that was troublesome.

"Which is?"

I knew damn well where this was going, but every second I could stall him the better. I knew from our first meeting that Kristov loved the sound of his own voice, and I was going to exploit it as much as I could.

"Apparently you have become more trouble than you're worth, so, we're taking the long road."

"That doesn't even make sense, you witless frickin idiot," Bili said, squinting her eyes and shaking her head. "You really are one big dumb sack of shit, aren't you?"

Kristov shook off the insult with nothing but a mild grunt of a laugh. This concerned me the most.

"I would tell you to give Theodorus a message for me, but since I'm going to kill you, don't bother," Kristov said.

"Franklin."

Kristov gave him the look I was all too familiar with.

As soon as he said this, I knew what was coming, and it wasn't broken bones or punches.

This was not how this was supposed to play out. My mind was racing, trying to figure out what to do next. Bili gave me a quick glance and I could tell she was doing the same. We were no match for the four of them and we had no escape route. Time was up.

Franklin raised his gun and leveled it at Bili's head with that shit-eating grin on his face. That was more than I could take, and my body flushed with heat. I no longer cared about myself and if I was going to die, I was going to do everything I could to give Bili a chance. I owed her that much.

I set my stance firmly, about to sprint forward, when I felt a gust of wind, followed by a blur of motion.

Just as Franklin was about to pull the trigger, he disappeared. Not in the magic trick sort of way but by sheer speed and force.

The open rear door-wall and long hallway provided the perfect runway for gathering speed, and Theo used it to perfection. Franklin was standing in just the right spot for Theo to hit him from behind at a dead sprint. It was nothing short of incredible. When he hit Franklin, the two of them shot forward and through the small front plate-glass window like a bullet, taking a large portion of drywall and brick with them.

Kristov and the other two wolves stood stunned for a second, trying to comprehend what had just happened. On the contrary, Bili and I were far from surprised by this, other than we were expecting him a little sooner.

Bili and I were already moving. We tackled Franklin's partner and pushed him out the rear door-wall where Theo had just come from. This left Kristov and his partner alone inside the house. Well, not exactly alone.

Kristov was about to help Franklin when he heard the heavy footsteps coming down the stairs which stopped him in his tracks. He motioned for his back-up to stand next to him.

The other wolf had short red hair and an even darker red beard. He appeared confused when he saw Claude walking down the steps. This wolf knew who Claude was.

"This is between me and him," Claude said, pointing to Kristov, but looking at Redbeard.

After assessing the entirety of the situation, I'm guessing Redbeard figured he wasn't being paid enough for this kind of fight. He took off through the hole created by Theo and Franklin and probably didn't stop until he hit one of the Great Lakes.

Kristov just stood and watched his former companion run with a look of disgust. He turned back and faced Claude with utter defiance.

"Go to hell," Kristov said.

54

If you didn't know whether 50,000 volts of electricity would be enough to stun an extra-large muscle-bound wolf, let me tell you, it is. Prior to our trip to Mr. Hendricks' home, we scouted the land and placed several helpful items around the grounds *just in case*.

Stun guns, rope, double heavy tape, and 1000 CC's of Propofol were the items of choice. The plan came together, but it was far from perfect. Mr. Hendricks getting killed was not part of the plan and was a heavy loss we all would have to live with. I still carry that guilt with me today.

It was not luck that we were ready for such an attack but rather the culmination of endless preparations. We had prepared for this type of event on several occasions, knowing it was only a matter of time before they struck again. It was also the first trip Bili was with me on the delivery.

Franklin and his partner, Will, were still unconscious when we tied them up and sat them on Mr. Hendricks' couch.

Claude was just finishing the final restraints on Kristov, who started to wake as well. Claude didn't use any of the items I mentioned as he insisted on the old-school method of beating him unconscious. Kristov was secured to a separate chair made of heavy steel, a few feet from the other two.

"I thought you were in Europe." Kristov said, as he regained consciousness.

"I know," Claude said tersely.

Bili walked slowly toward Kristov, who eyed her every move. She stopped right in front of him and hit him in the face as hard as she could.

His head whipped back as if a large man hit him. Her hands were tiny, but they were strong. It was because of her tiny hands that I think she lacerated his face from ear to nose. Bili did not forget or forgive.

Kristov smiled as the cut healed quicker than what I thought was normal for the wolves. It was then that something occurred to me.

It was a full moon.

"That all you got?" Kristov said.

"No," Bili said.

She left it there, allowing Kristov's mind to wonder what she's capable of. Her eyes said *plenty*.

Franklin had a different look on his face when he woke up. He was scared, and he was right to feel that way.

"Hi, Franklin," I said.

The look I had on my face must have stirred something in him, as all pretense of playing it tough vanished.

"It wasn't my idea. I never wanted to hurt her."

"Shut up, you coward!" Kristov spouted.

I turned to face Kristov, and without a hint of anger, or raised voice, I spoke.

"One more word and I will tape your head so that the only airway you have left will be your left nostril."

He must have believed me because he shut up.

Our plan was to take Kristov to one location and the other two to another. Theo figured it may take some time to get answers, so we needed a place more suited to our needs. Claude had a plan in place for just such a scenario. It was just a matter of getting them secured for the trip, and then we would be off.

Bili and I were watching them while Claude pulled the van to the front door and Theo packed up the rest of our gear. Like I said, we had items in several places, and we weren't leaving any trace we were there.

Franklin squirmed where he sat, testing the strength of the rope and tape. It was Kevlar rope, and the tough tape we used was almost as strong. Claude figured the combination of both should be adequate to hold them for the trip.

"You were saying?" I said, looking at Franklin. I wanted to know why he killed Viki, and Franklin was in a talking mood. If he didn't tell me now, he damn sure was going to tell me later.

Franklin looked over at Kristov, who glared back at him.

"He's not the one you should be worried about," I said.

"Sorry, I don't mean to interrupt again, but there is something I need to say," Kristov said.

"Me too. What color tape do you want?" I said, not looking at him. I was still waiting for Franklin to answer me.

Kristov cracked a hint of a smile that I caught out of my peripheral vision, and then he said something that I will never forget.

"Do you think your mother misses her little goofball, or do you think — who gives a shit? She's dead." Kristov said.

Time stopped. I turned and gave him my full attention.

"What the hell did you just say?"

I couldn't believe what I had just heard. The magnitude of it caused every rational fiber of my being to be suspended.

"Ahh, so it's true. I wondered. The bitch kept babbling something about her *little goofball* right after I ripped her fucking throat out. It was more of a gurgle really, as you can imagine. Oh, that's right, you don't have to imagine. You saw," Kristov said, grinning.

"Jack, no!" Bili said, knowing what I was thinking before I did. She jumped in front of me, trying to stop whatever it was I was going to do. Just then, Kristov burst free from his bindings with a roar. He knocked Bili out of the way, sending her to the ground.

A fire exploded inside me like never before. So much so, I didn't feel like the same person. I got tunnel vision, and I shut the world off. There was just Kristov. He didn't have time to utter another word before I grabbed him by the neck and picked him off the ground. I held him in the air with one hand while he gasped for breath, clawing at my hand to break free. I felt like I had the power of a hundred men.

Claude and Theo had just walked in to see Kristov wiggling wildly in my grasp.

"Jack! Don't kill him!" Theo yelled.

I couldn't hear him as my thoughts were of those I lost. I became blind with rage.

"Why did you kill my mother?" I growled.

My teeth and jaw ached something terrible, and I wanted nothing more than to rip Kristov's throat out.

Kristov was still trying to breathe and in no position to answer. I didn't want an answer, I just wanted him dead. I wanted him dead more than I wanted anything in the world at that moment. I could see the look in Kristov's eyes as I held him as easily as a newborn. Vampires should not be this strong, and it confused him as much as scared him.

Exceptions to every rule.

I was about to snap his neck, which I knew I could do at any second, when it happened.

I felt the spray of blood hit me before I heard the distant popping sound of the gun. Franklin's head all but exploded and he slumped over where he sat. The other wolf tried to stand while still tied and took four or five shots almost at the same time. A few through the chest and the rest through the head, causing him to crumble to the ground.

This happened so fast I barely felt the bullet hit my arm that held Kristov in the air. It tore through the skin and bone of my forearm, causing me to drop Kristov.

My arm was dangling awkwardly as I hit the floor. It amazed me how fast it healed. It was good as new within seconds. I knew this was not the norm, but I had no time to ponder it.

More shots sprayed overhead, shattering everything in their path. Kristov wasted no time and sprinted to the rear of the house in a crouched fashion. He took several bullets to the back but apparently not hitting anything vital because he never broke stride. He escaped out the back door, and there was nothing we could do.

The bullets filled the air, keeping us pinned down for another minute or two. Long enough to give Kristov enough of a head start that chasing him would have been pointless.

Just as quickly as the shots started, they stopped. We gave it another few seconds before we got to our feet. The damage the bullets caused, not only to Franklin's head, but the house itself made it obvious that the weapon was tremendously powerful. Claude guessed it was military grade.

"That was fun," Bili said sarcastically as she stood up, brushing glass and drywall from her hair and clothes.

Theo came over to me, gave a quick glance to my arm, and then put his hand on my shoulder.

"You okay?"

I know my arm wasn't what he was referring to. I nodded once.

"I'm sorry. I lost control," I said.

Guilt was already upon me as I couldn't help but feel I screwed things up by losing my temper.

"You have nothing to be sorry about," he said with a pat on my back.

Our plan had worked, and we were close to getting some answers. Even when we got the upper hand, we found ourselves one step behind.

"What just happened?" I said, mostly to myself, as I looked around at the carnage.

"I'm guessing someone else wants us dead," Bili said.

"Or it was the same group assuring we didn't get answers from Kristov," Theo added.

I saw Claude take a deep breath and blow it out his nose. It made me take notice and I don't think I was the only one either.

"What do you think old friend?" Theo asked.

"It may be time to see the Witch," Claude said.

Theo gave Claude a serious look accompanied with a small shake of the head, in what I could only surmise as apprehension of the highest order.

"Too risky," he said.

"What options do we have?" Claude said.

"The cost?"

Bili looked at me with confusion which made me glad. Finally, I wasn't the only one in the dark for a change. The fact that this person gave Claude and Theo pause said a lot. I was also curious if that was a nickname, or if she was an actual witch.

"What if I took Bili with me?" Claude said.

Theo thought about this for a moment, and though his look said the idea was a good one, he was not okay with it.

"I see the wisdom in the idea, but I still don't like it," Theo said.

Bili looked back and forth from Theo to Claude, reading the unspoken words.

"If this woman can help us, I want to go," she said as if it was a done deal.

"That's because you know nothing about her," Theo snapped.

This was the first time I heard Theo talk to Bili with a sharp tone that was parent-like. Bili didn't like it one bit.

"I appreciate your concern, but look at us. We are falling apart and holding the shit end of the stick once again. Can this woman help us or not?" she asked plainly.

"Maybe," Theo said.

"Then it's settled. When do we go?"

Theo wasn't happy, but considering our position, it was hard for him to argue the point. We were indeed at the end of our rope, and someone had just greased it.

"Okay," Theo said, relenting. Then he stood directly in front of Bili to get her full and undivided attention.

"Listen to me carefully. Do not underestimate this woman. She will talk in riddles, and you will get the impression she's your friend. She is not. She will be drawn to you for several reasons which may help in retrieving information, but let Claude do the talking."

"I got it. Don't worry. I'll be fine," Bili said.

"Do not get baited," Theo added. "She will tempt and taunt you at the same time."

"I got this. Relax."

Bili patted Theo on his shoulder. Though done somewhat mockingly, it made Theo concede. He gave her a thin, tight-lipped smile and squeezed her hand that was on his shoulder.

Theo looked at Claude.

"Jack and I will handle this mess. Good luck."

55

Claude and Bili hit the road right away and drove for ten straight hours before they arrived at their destination. It had been over a century since Claude had seen her, and now that he was on her doorstep, he realized that a hundred years wasn't long enough.

Amalasuintha was one of the few wolves who was far and away above the norm on the intellectual scale. She was old and powerful, which is why some feared her, but those who knew better feared her for her intelligence and irrational behavior. If she chose to help, you would get quality information. If.

Information was her business, and how she obtained it was a source of much speculation. She rarely left her little neck of the woods, but she was always on top of current events. Though unconfirmed, it had been long rumored that she was a billionaire which would explain her resources.

There are few of Claude's kind older than him, but she was one of them. She was one of the first to migrate to the United States as well and landed in Massachusetts. She fell in love with it and never left, even during the era of the Salem witch hunts and trials, which some speculate she played more than a small part in.

Her house was set back among a small orchard of willow trees that danced on the wind. The best way to describe her place would be to imagine a stereotypical haunted house in the middle of a three-acre grave-yard. Just update the home, remove the gravestones, and what remained would be her estate.

Claude and Bili walked up to the door, and within a few seconds, someone approached them from behind.

"Comment avez-vous ete Claude?" a female voice said in perfect French and then she spoke English. "Do my eyes deceive me?"

Though relatively young-looking, maybe early thirties, she had the demeanor and mannerisms of someone much older. She was wearing a black evening gown, and her dark hair looked professionally done.

"Pour mieux Amalasuintha. How are you?" Claude said.

"I'm fine, as no one is trying to kill me. Call me Cynthia, please. We are old friends, are we not?" she said casually. "You brought me a guest I see."

Her movements were graceful and almost ballet-like. The muscles in her shoulders and back were like those of a gymnast. She exuded power and confidence.

She opened the door to her home, walked in, and motioned for Claude and Bili to follow.

Bili shut the door behind her, and when she turned back around, Cynthia was standing directly in front of her. Cynthia stood a few inches taller but had a kind look.

"You and I are a lot alike, young one," she said, running the back of her hand along Bili's face, shoulder, arm, and then very close to Bili's breast. Bili held still and kept quiet.

"I know things that may interest you, Bilinda," Cynthia said, bringing her eyes back up to Bili's.

Bili was about to say something, but Claude didn't let her. The last thing he wanted was for Bili to get in over her head. Any lengthy conversation with Cynthia would almost certainly fit that category.

"Another time, Cynthia. We're here on other business."

Cynthia looked disappointed and made no bones about showing her disapproval. She moved over to the sofa in the living room and sat down, calmly and smoothly.

"Yes, I guess you are," she said.

"Who's bankrolling the initiative against us?" Claude said.

Claude didn't waste time explaining the details, as he was more than optimistic that she was aware of the issues at hand.

"That is one question but hardly the most important."

"Why are they?" Bili said.

Cynthia's eyes lit up with enthusiasm.

"Ahh, smart too. I knew I liked this one," Cynthia said with a grin. "Please, sit down, you two."

Claude walked around to the side of the fireplace and faced her. He remained standing. Bili plopped down in the loveseat next to the couch as if she was testing the durability of the cushion.

Cynthia put her hand to the side of her mouth and spoke to Bili in a mock attempt to keep Claude from hearing her.

"He never likes to sit. Been that way forever," she said, almost at a whisper.

This made Bili smile.

"Why, then?" Claude asked.

Claude was not much on patience, but even he knew better than to rush Cynthia. If they could get any information and leave without a future problem, it would be a victory.

"What does the big bad wolf have to offer?" she asked flippantly.

This is what he didn't want to hear.

"What would you like?"

"A pint of Jack's blood," Cynthia said without a hint of hesitation.

"Why?" Bili asked incredulously.

"Not the right question this time, sweetie," Cynthia said as if she was talking to a young child.

Bili scowled, but she remained quiet. She'd made a promise to Theo, and she would keep it.

"He's an anomaly, but not an unprecedented one," Claude said.

It was no accident that Claude worded his statement this way.

"No?"

Her answer was obvious.

"What makes him so special," Bili asked.

"Do you know who Ayla is?" Cynthia asked.

"Rieger's deceased wife," Claude said.

"Yes, but what do you know about her?"

Claude thought hard, trying to figure out where she was going with this. As far as he knew, she was a human of humble origins. He shrugged.

"Hers is the bloodline you might want to research. It was not a coincidence Rieger fell in love with a human. That is all I will say on that. Now, about the blood."

"No blood. What else?" Claude asked succinctly.

Cynthia's brows furled in disappointment. Then quick as a blink, she smiled and looked at Claude.

"A favor then," Cynthia said.

Claude had traded this item before, and it nearly cost him his life. Still, considering their circumstances, it was a simple decision.

"Done," he said.

"Not from you. Her," Cynthia said, turning to look at Bili.

Bili didn't see why it was such a big deal. It seemed like a break. Getting what they came for and the only thing she had to do was a favor to be named later.

"Sure," Bili said.

"No," Claude said abruptly, almost talking over her.

Bili looked at Claude with a confused look. She would do anything to help Theo, and this couldn't have been a better deal in her eyes. It was a no-brainer.

Bili got up and stood next to Claude.

"Claude, let me do this. We have lost too many friends already," she said, knowing she was right.

Claude thought hard. He knew Bili was right, of course, but would Theo understand? Theo only suggested Bili come along to help soften Cynthia and help Claude negotiate. She was not there to use as collateral. He felt the weight of the world on him at that moment.

"No. I will offer two favors," Claude said.

"Sorry, honey bunny, that's not an option. It's her or no deal. Take it or leave it," Cynthia said apologetically.

"I agree," Bili said, not giving Claude a chance to answer for her.

Cynthia smiled and gave a minor bow, letting them both know the deal was done.

Claude was about to object, but he knew it was too late.

"This is my choice. Theo will understand," Bili said unwaveringly.

Claude shook his head, knowing full well the consequences of what Bili had just done. If Bili knew then what those consequences were, she never would have agreed.

56

"This may be a good place to call it a night, I'm getting a little tired," Jack said.

Sara looked at her watch, surprised at the late hour.

Where had the time gone?

After the bombshell of Jack's knowledge of her parents and Emily, Sara was looking forward to getting home and doing some investigating of her own.

"Okay, Jack. Is there anything you need before I leave for the day?"

"Any luck getting the letter back?"

"Let me check. Nancy said someone from the police department should have dropped it off."

Sara went into her office and found a plain manila envelope on her desk. She opened it, saw it was the letter, then pushed it back inside. Sara stood there in her office contemplating the right thing to do.

Sara knocked on Jack's door and then went in carrying the letter at her side.

Jack was still sitting in the chair and didn't say a word as Sara sat down in front of him and handed him the letter.

"Here it is. Sorry for the delay in getting it."

Jack studied Sara's face, not looking at the letter at all.

"You didn't read it."

It wasn't a question.

"I was going to, but no, I didn't. If this is a very personal letter, and I believe it is, I don't think I should, doctor or not."

"It is very personal, just not to me," Jack said seriously.

Sara gave Jack a confused look.

Jack stood from his chair, touched Sara on her shoulder in consoling fashion, and then handed the letter back to her.

"This will be harder than you ever imagined. Goodnight Sara," Jack said, and then he walked over to the window and looked out into the emptiness of the night without explanation.

Sara was about to respond but stopped herself. She got up with the letter in hand and left without another word. She went to her office, thought about opening the letter but changed her mind. It was late and she wanted to get home. She put the letter in her purse, grabbed her jacket, and headed home for the night.

When Sara arrived home, she got into some comfortable clothes, poured herself a glass of wine, and sat on her couch with the envelope in hand. She pulled the heavy piece of paper from the thick envelope and unfolded it on her lap. It looked to be old and stained from time and lack of care. As soon as she read the first few words, tears filled her eyes.

My precious baby pumpkin,

I am so sorry I wasn't there for you when you needed me most. Leaving you the way I did was the hardest thing I ever had to do, but I was left with little choice. I did what I thought I had to do to keep you safe. I know you may never understand, and that will probably be for the best. For if you ever do, the cost could be greater than the price I had to pay for your survival. Sometimes our best intentions result in our greatest regrets, and I have too many to count, but keeping you safe will never be one of them. Only time will tell if what I've done was worth all the pain.

If you can understand, at least a little, that I did what I had to do, then maybe you can forgive me. You will always be my special little girl, and special you are. If only I could have seen what you have become. Love you forever.

Mom

The *mom* was somewhat smeared, probably from a tear as it was written. One of Sara's hit the same spot.

How?

Sara set the letter down and began to cry.

This can't be.

57

DAY TWO

Sara woke up feeling confused, and the wine she drank the night before was only partly to blame. She had been up most of the night thinking about the note from her mother. She came up with several outlandish theories of how Jack may have obtained the letter, but now that it was morning and she was sober, none of them seemed plausible. She found little joy in a problem with no rational solution.

Sara grabbed a couple aspirin for the headache and went straight to the shower to clear her mind. She let the streams of hot water pour over her as she thought about the prior day in detail. After her mother disappeared all those years ago, there wasn't a single piece of evidence that indicated she was still alive. Though not conclusive, the letter suggested she wrote it after she went missing. This could also mean, though unlikely, she was still alive today. Sara considered for the briefest of moments contacting the police but thought better of it.

Nothing in her training had prepared her for the likes of this new patient. It was far too coincidental to believe Jack ended up in her care by accident. The why would be the hardest part to uncover. She still hadn't completely dismissed the possibility Jack was a plant to test her, or worse, get her to commit an ethics violation and lose her license.

Jack could have just made an appointment to talk to me if that's all he wanted. Why the charade? Why make up this ridiculous story about a secret world filled with vampires and werewolves?

Sara got dressed, grabbed her keys, and walked outside. The second she closed the door behind her, she saw a black vehicle parked just down the street from her house. It took off before she made it two steps from the door, leaving an eerie feeling in the pit of her stomach.

The closer she got to the hospital, the less she thought about the car and focused on her approach to Jack. He had proven himself stubborn but open to reason, lending the situation to more than one possible option.

When she arrived, she didn't waste any time with emails or paperwork, as she normally would before seeing patients. She dropped her work bag on the floor of her office, grabbed her folder, and walked straight to Jack's room.

She decided that she would let Jack continue with his story, but she was going to press him harder for any information relating to her parents. She was going to find out where and how he got that letter.

58

Sara was almost to Jack's door when a loud scream sent chills throughout her body. There was only one room it could've come from. Abigail's.

Sara dropped what she had in her hands, burst into a run, and headed straight for Abby's room. She got to the door, swiped her access card, and rushed in. When she got inside, Abigail was sitting on the edge of her bed, rocking back and forth, crying. The tears streamed down her face, one after another, as she sat with her arms wrapped tightly around her legs which were pulled up against her chest.

"I'm here, Abby, I'm here," Sara said as she sat next to Abigail, rubbing her back to comfort her.

"They're never coming back, are they?" Abigail said, sobbing as her body shook.

"No, honey, they're not," the doctor said plainly. Though this was a very painful event for Abigail, this is exactly what Sara was hoping for. This was a breakthrough and a big one.

"Why... why would-"

Abigail tried to finish her thought but couldn't. She trembled harder as the emotions took over, causing her to cry in earnest. This was a release mechanism that would start the healing process for the better.

"Sometimes there are just no answers," Sara said, doing her best to reassure her patient, who had come into clarity and realization. Both of which can cause great pain to the human mind. If the mind can withstand that pain, healing is all but certain.

Sara stayed with Abigail for another thirty minutes. She was getting close now, and Sara was very optimistic about her recovery. She had bonded with Abigail and wanted nothing more than to help her mend. She was far too young not to have a chance at a full and normal life.

"Get some rest, Abby. We'll talk more later."

Abigail forced a smile and nodded as she wiped the tears from her red cheeks.

"I will. Thanks."

Sara backed out of the room and made her way down the hall. She picked up the folder she had dropped in her haste and approached Jack's door. Her heart picked up a beat with every step closer. She took a deep breath, grabbed the door handle, and went inside.

59

Jack looked as though he had been up for a while even though he was still in bed. He also looked like he didn't have a care in the world. This behavior was far from typical and another indication that she was correct in her assessment about him.

"Good morning, Jack."

"Good morning to you," he said, sitting up to greet the doctor. He had a mild look of concern when he saw the doctor. "You look tired, Doc. Did you get any sleep?"

"Enough, thank you," Sara said. "Appears you've been up a while. Did you eat?"

"I did. I also got a lovely escort to the showers by three large men," Jack said lightheartedly.

Sara gave a knowing smile and nodded her head.

Jack ran his hands through his partially wet hair as he got up and walked to the chair and sat down across from Sara. He leaned forward and his smile vanished. He put his hands together in front of him and gave Sara a sympathetic look.

"I want to apologize," Jack said.

"For what?"

"I dropped some heavy emotional bombs on you yesterday, and for that, I'm sorry. I want to make sure you understand I didn't do it with malice or without careful forethought," he said sincerely. "I take it you read the letter?"

"I did."

Just thinking about the letter took Sara back to her last memory of her mother which was referred to in the letter.

Sara's mom, Clara, had taken Sara to the zoo one afternoon when she was younger, and it was one of best days of her life. They walked around for hours looking at all the exotic animals, but what made the day special was that Clara spoke to Sara like an adult for the first time. She instilled a few life lessons she wanted Sara to remember, and she did.

They were about to leave when Sara begged her mother to let her go into the butterfly solarium. It was an enclosure that contained hundreds of beautiful butterflies. Clara was tired and ready to leave, but she relented as Sara pleaded for this one last stop.

The exhibit was packed with kids, so Clara told Sara to go inside without her, and she would meet her at the exit in ten minutes. Sara agreed and ran into the exhibit. The colorful winged creatures fascinated her as they flew around. There was this one beautiful yellow and purple butterfly that landed on her hand and refused to leave, making Sara feel like its caretaker. It enthralled and captivated her so much that before she knew it, a good thirty minutes had gone by. Sara reluctantly sent the colorful creature back into flight and made her way to the exit. When she came out, she was fearful her mother would be mad at her for staying too long. That fear quickly became irrelevant.

Sara walked around the outside of the exhibit, several times in fact, looking in vain for her mother. Panic set in as she walked down one paved path after another, frantically searching all areas of the zoo. Her mother was nowhere to be found. Sara found a zoo employee, asked for help, and they took her to the office. They paged her mother several times over the intercom system but to no avail. Clara was never seen or heard from again.

"Where did you get that letter?" Sara asked, fighting her emotions.

"From a mutual acquaintance," Jack said softly. His eyes looked as if he shared the pain Sara felt.

Sara blinked a little more, while using her palms to wipe the corners of her eyes. Sara was about to start some inquiries when Jack spoke again.

"Listen, Doc. You know more than anyone that some information needs to be taken in small doses. Too much too soon can be a hindrance because of the emotional pain."

"In some cases, yes, but I also know that information can manipulate as well," she said as she sat back, crossed her arms, and looked at Jack as if that's exactly what he was doing.

"True. This is what I propose. Let me continue, and though some of it may be hard to hear, I will give you the answers you have dreamt of for years. Some of which you had no idea you wanted or needed," Jack said.

"What does that mean?"

"Before this day is over, you'll have a far different perspective about life and what you consider most important."

"Could you be more vague?"

"In due time it may not seem so unclear," Jack said, not elaborating.

Sara stared at Jack, irritation clearly seeping into her demeanor.

"In due time? What are you, a hundred?" Sara said, shifting in her chair. Her frustration was plain.

"No."

That's all Jack said as his expressionless stare waited for a response from the doctor.

Sara thought about this carefully. She wanted to know what Jack knew in the worst way, but this was a delicate game of wills. Appearing more desperate than she already had would put her in a bad way, making Jack feel as though he had the control.

"Okay, let's get back to it then," Sara said.

"You're sure?"

"Yes, let's move on. Do you remember where you left off?"

"I believe I do."

60

Deaglan had only been to the United States on a few other occasions. He liked it well enough, but he preferred the rolling green hills and pubs of his homeland. Mostly the pubs.

He lived a modest lifestyle, roaming from one rural village to another, every decade or so. When he ran low on money, he would take a high risk, high reward job, and repeat as necessary.

This particular mission was a novel experience for him. He wasn't adept in new world technology, and getting documentation for ease of travel was foreign to him. He was skilled at traveling by boat or train without getting noticed, but walking into the first-class accommodations of an airline was a pleasant change. The fact he wasn't paying for any of it made the experience even better. He had a new passport and credit card in the name of Seamus O'Hara.

Could they have been more bleddin stereotypical?

He enjoyed himself immensely during the long plane ride. The free drinks fueled one hilarious story after another with those lucky enough to be seated around him. He made plenty of friends, both male and female. He even had a few phone numbers passed his way before they landed.

Once off the plane, it was a quick walk to short-term parking where the car of his choice awaited him. His eyes lit up when he saw the candy apple beauty glistening in the sun. He ran his hand along the side of the car, checking every detail of the classic Mustang before grabbing the handle. The car wasn't his to keep, but he had it for the duration of his assignment. The keys were in the center console, just where she said they would be, along with a thick envelope that contained instructions and American cash for incidentals.

He made his way to the hotel, which was much nicer than the *motels* he was used to. After he checked in and settled into his extravagant room, he went over the documents for the job. This was the most dangerous job he had taken in centuries.

I hope you know what you are bloody doin Deg.

To pull off a job like this would take intelligence, fortitude, and a fair bit of luck as well. His skill and Irish luck were legendary, and he would need both in excessive amounts just not to get killed.

The next day, he got to the meeting location earlier than suggested, far earlier as a matter of fact, but waiting in a pub during the morning hours wasn't foreign to him. In some regards it was preferable.

He saw her walk into the sparsely lit tavern and though he had never met her in person, he knew it was her. She was more infamous than him, and that was saying something.

She surveyed her surroundings, thoroughly checking every inch of the room, as well as the other two patrons sitting at the bar. She sat across from Deaglan and watched him closely as he took a long drink from the dark beer which was as unmistakable as his reputation for drinking it.

"Change of heart?" she said.

"The money was finally at a level worth risking my pale white Irish arse for. Going up against Theodorus and Claude is no small undertaking, not to mention, I'm hearing some interesting things about this bloody Jack fella."

She slid him a large manila envelope that was bursting at the edges.

"Assuming your drunken Irish arse is worth a shit, and your reputation isn't all fluff, this will be just a taste," she said looking at him expectantly.

He grabbed the envelope, moved it up and down as if weighing it, and then smiled. He finished the last of his Guinness in one big gulp and then winked at her as he wiped the frothy suds from his lips.

"I'll let you answer that question for yourself when you see what I have for you. Feel free to double my pay if you are so inclined," he said as he stood up and gestured for her to follow with the slightest tilt of the head.

She wore a confused and concerned look, as she was there to go over some details regarding his mission. But knowing she had checked the surroundings before going inside, she felt comfortable no other immortals were around.

He started walking toward the kitchen area, and she trailed behind him, double checking every area of the bar. She was suspicious of everything, but nothing appeared to be out of order.

"Another pint, mate. I'll be right back," the Irishman said with a friendly nod to the man behind the bar.

The bartender went to the tap and started building the Guinness as the two of them entered the employee area. Deaglan held the door for her as any polite gentleman would as she walked past him, entering the room first. She turned the corner and saw she wasn't alone. When she turned to leave, the sound of steel slapping together confirmed Deaglan's betrayal.

61

"Parrus."

"Hello Theodorus. Lovely seeing you here," she said as if she had just run into an old friend.

Parrus turned to face Deaglan with a look that would have killed a mortal man. He gave her a toothy grin, followed by a half-hearted bow. She turned her attention back to the four of us, knowing she had no recourse. Claude, Theo, Bili, and I were standing in front of her, blocking any possible exit.

"Hi Deaglan," Bili said politely as she leaned to the side looking around Parrus.

"My dear Bilinda, nice to see you, lass," he said, tipping an imaginary cap.

Parrus rolled her eyes at the exchange of pleasantries.

"So, what now?" Parrus said defiantly and nonchalantly in equal measures. "We going to start talking about the weather?"

As casually as reaching for her cell phone, Bili grabbed the gun from the counter behind her and shot Parrus in the chest with no further discussion. The large dart stuck, and within seconds the dark liquid emptied itself into its target.

"Sleep tight, bitch," Bili said.

Parrus' eyes fluttered for a second before falling shut. She fell to the floor, soft and gentle, as if she was performing a ballet move. The plan had come off without a hitch. It was time to get some answers.

62

When Parrus awoke, she found herself in strange surroundings. It was a house, but the interior of the large living room had been modified with a steel cage. She got up and walked around each section of her cell, looking for any weakness in the construction, including the ceiling portion.

"It's secure, I assure you," Theo said from a chair on the other side of the room.

"Just checking," she countered softly, still acting as if she was unconcerned with his presence. "I'm curious how you got the better of me. I should have smelled at least one of you before I even walked in that shithole. Care to share?"

"It's something my good friend Steve developed before you had him killed," Theo said, not masking his displeasure.

Parrus walked toward Theo. When she reached the bars, she leaned her head against the steel like a prisoner in an old western movie. She didn't deny Theo's claim.

"Come closer. I want to see your face."

Theo got up and walked within ten feet of Parrus, the overhead light now illuminating his face.

"Come now, after all we've been through together, you won't come just a little closer," she said with a sinister smile Theo had seen too many times.

"What's your game, Parrus?" Theo said curtly.

"Are you going to start chopping things off if I don't tell," she said with raised eyebrows.

She knew Theo all too well, both personally and professionally, and he knew her. The usual methods of interrogation would never work with Parrus. Things needed to be handled much differently and far more delicately. She would die before she gave in to the use of force or torture. Her will and resolve were unmatched. Everything was a battle of wits with her, and she was always willing to play that game.

"No, that won't be necessary. I think you want to tell me, so just tell me."

"Oh, you know why. You may not know *which* why, but you know," she said with suppressed grin. "Is Jack with you? I would like very much to talk to him again."

"Why is that?"

"Didn't really get to discuss everything I wanted the last time we were… together," Parrus said, trying to get under Theo's skin. "He really is a handsome one, don't you think?"

There were traces of hidden knowledge in almost everything Parrus said. Much of it sounded like nonsense, but only a fool would disregard even the smallest of details as unimportant. She relished the gamesmanship in everything. She would gladly risk everything for the chance to say I told you so later. Theo was all too familiar with every evil aspect about her.

"How did you find out about him?" Theo asked, not expecting her to give him an honest answer, but the more she talked the better.

"Let me go and I'll tell you."

"I'm afraid that will not happen. Help us stop this war that you have almost certainly helped to start, then give me the name of your employer and you'll be free in no time."

"What, and miss the best part?"

"What do you mean?" Theo asked.

Parrus walked backward and sat down on the floor with her back against the bars and stared at Theo. It was as though she had dropped her eccentric façade and became a real person.

"You hurt me you know."

She wasn't lying.

"You didn't leave me any choice, did you?"

"You know more than anyone, Theo my dear, there is always a choice," Parrus said, with a slight tilt of her head to emphasize her point. "You and Claude with your self-imposed moral code bullshit. You live just like them."

There were several double meanings behind that statement alone, but Theo didn't dwell on it. He needed information, and sooner the better.

"Who are you working for?!" he snapped.

"Someone who understands this world far better than you. This world is cruel, and it's time you figured that out."

This was more of a threat than a statement, and Theo knew it.

"One day you will come to realize that self-loathing and destruction are tiresome, costly, and no good for anyone."

"Let me guess. I'm only hurting myself?" she said sarcastically.

Theo shook his head and gave her a look of pity as he turned and walked away from her.

This infuriated Parrus.

"Don't you walk away from me, Theodorus!" she yelled as she stood and hurried toward the front of the cage. "You can't hold me! You're all dead!"

Theo walked out and shut the door behind him, hearing her threat through the door. He made his way down a long hall and into another large room where the rest of us were waiting for him. It was far enough that even Parrus couldn't hear us talk.

After Theo came back into the parlor area where the rest of us had gathered, he sat next to me on one of the larger couches. Everyone else gathered around, waiting for an update.

"Other than the threat to kill us all, did she say she was sorry, offer a detailed explanation of her actions, as well as everything she has planned for the future? Oh, and a list of all the players involved?" Deaglan asked before Theo spoke.

That made Theo smile.

"She talked in riddles as she always does."

"Anything we can use?" Claude said.

"Maybe," he said, giving his big friend a familiar look.

"How long do you plan to be in town, Deaglan?" Theo asked.

"Well, I just got a large bundle of cash from our friend in there, so I may fancy a holiday in the States. What do you need?"

Deaglan was talking to Theo, but he was staring in my direction an awful lot. This little ruse had come together rather fast, and I didn't get an opportunity to talk to him. I had heard some very interesting stories about him, and I was curious how many of them were true.

"Considering your abilities, if you come across any discernable information..." Theo said, knowing Deaglan could fill in the blanks.

"Of course."

Deaglan walked up to me curiously and stuck out his hand for me to shake.

"Don't hold back, young man," he said.

I gave a quick glance to Bili, trying to see if he was serious or not.

"Um, Deg," Bili said, trying to interject, but he disregarded the half-hearted warning. She smiled and watched.

I shook his hand firmly and held it. He stared me in the eyes intently for a good fifteen seconds before he relented.

"Bloody hell," he said with a grimace as he pulled his hand back and shook it gingerly.

He patted me on the shoulder in what I assumed was a confirmation of something he suspected. He then turned to Theo.

"I'll let you know if I hear anything, mate," he said. "I'm gonna bugger off and spend some of this hard, unearned cash of mine."

Deaglan nodded to the rest of us and then left.

"I see what you mean. Is it possible not to like that guy?" I asked.

"He has a gift," Theo said. "And more times than not, he'll produce some good intelligence."

"What's our next move," Bili said out loud, but to no one in particular.

Claude was the first to speak up.

"We get moving on the last piece of information we received from the Witch."

Bili nodded in agreement.

I was unaware at the time of what Bili promised the Witch, but I had overheard enough from Bili and Theo's conversation to make me believe Theo didn't think it was worth it. With the capture of a main player in this conflict, it said volumes about the reputation of the Witch, and Theo's concerns. His worry was not unwarranted, and unfortunately, a time would come when he was proven correct.

"Okay," Theo said. "This will take some prep. You two head back to work while Claude and I make the arrangements. I would also like it if you two didn't go anywhere alone for a while. This lull may be coming to an end."

Bili and I made the lengthy drive back to Ann Arbor with very little in the way of conversation. I did ask her what this Witch was like, and Bili said she was like any other wolf, just weirder. I got the impression she didn't want to go into it, and from what I was picking up from her haptics, I knew there was far more to the story.

We got back late, and Bili dropped me off in the alley next to the rear door of the Piece of History. I saw she was going to ask me a question, but she bit her tongue and settled on a simple goodnight.

Ever since I was turned, reading people's secrets became much easier. I could tell if someone was lying as easily as if I could read their mind. That being said, there was a hierarchy of such. Humans were the easiest, wolves second, younger vampires third, and Elders last. Any immortal over two thousand years old were considered Elders. There was some speculation on my part regarding Elders altogether in that sense, and I would learn later I was on the right track.

63

The doctor gave a slight wave of her hand, letting Jack know she had a few questions.

"Sorry Jack, but something's been bothering me since yesterday, and I'm having a hard time concentrating. I know you want to wait, for whatever reason, but..."

Sara dropped her head slightly, trying to get the words out properly. She was about to start again when Jack spoke.

"You want to know if your mother is still alive, or at the very least, what happened that day at the zoo, am I right?"

His delivery was very matter of fact, it took Sara a second to process the magnitude of what he said. Not only was the zoo a particularly sore topic; Sara never spoke of it with anyone but her late stepmom.

How could he know this?

Sara's desperate need for information about what Jack just asked her, overrode logic, which prompted her next question. Though simple, just by asking it would change their relationship permanently. She didn't care.

"Is she?"

Sara knew her anticipation of hearing the answer to this question would give away some portion of her power and authority. Again, she didn't care. She hung on Jack's next words as if they were life or death, and in some fashion, they were.

"Forgive me, but we're not ready to go into that right now."

Sara let out a breath of relief, though she was not relieved. It felt more like a short reprieve from the truth. It only took a second for disappointment to turn to anger.

"What do you mean, we?"

"*I* am not ready to talk about it, and *you* are not ready to hear about it. *We.*"

Jack's refusal to disclose information she was anxious for aggravated her, but not hearing the word *dead* eased the tension, if only a little.

"Can you tell me why you think that?"

She was attempting another classic diversionary tactic widely used in her profession.

"It would be counter-productive, it's that simple. However, I can tell your mind is somewhere else, so maybe a little information wouldn't hurt."

She hated that her patient had the ability to hold her mentally hostage. It was not a situation she had ever come across, and it was testing her professionalism to its core.

"Tell me what you can then," Sara said, fighting the urge to beg for more.

Jack nodded, appearing to be happy with the doctor's acceptance.

"Did you ever wonder why Emily moved you from one city to another after your mom went missing? How many times do you recall moving?"

"Four or five, maybe," she said, doing her best to recall where and when they moved. "Emily had to move us because of her job."

"That's not the reason."

"Why then?"

"To protect you," Jack said plainly.

"From what?"

"Those who would do you harm," he said, as if the answer was obvious.

"Why would anyone want to hurt me?"

"Because you are your mother's daughter."

"What the hell does that mean? You're just playing with words now. I know these tricks."

Sara's aggravation had reached a boiling point. She hated Jack's ability to manipulate her emotions so easily. If she wasn't so upset by this, she would be in awe of his skill. It was a genuine gift. She didn't wait for a response before she spoke again.

"Can you just drop all the nonsense and tell me what you know about my family?"

"No," Jack said succinctly.

"No?" Sara repeated bitterly, raising her eyebrows.

"Yes, no."

Sara shook her head in disgust as she stood up. His blatant refusal to tell her what she wanted to know set her off.

"Tell your story to someone else then," she said as she turned and headed for the door.

She looked back one more time before exiting, only to see Jack steadfast in his silence. Sara left, slamming the door behind her. She went back to her office and sat at her desk, rocking back and forth in her new, and very expensive, leather chair. Her mind scanned through her childhood, searching for anything that could shed some light on what Jack had just told her. She sat there for a good ten minutes before she heard a light rapping on her open door.

"Come in."

Nancy peeked her head inside with a worried look.

"Are you okay, dear?"

"No," Sara said, as she rested her forehead on the palms of her hands. "Come inside and shut the door."

Nancy walked in, gently closed the door behind her, and took a seat in front of Sara. Nancy watched with concern as the doctor leaned back and rubbed her eyes.

"What do you think really happened to Spencer?" Sara blurted out.

"I don't know, but I'm glad he's gone. Aren't you?"

"Of course, that's not the point. I can't stop thinking that there's more to the story. I can't tell you why, but I feel as though my patient may know something about it."

"How do you mean?"

Sara looked toward the door nervously and then back to Nancy.

"I shouldn't be discussing this with you, but certain events have me questioning everything."

"And you think the beautiful man has something to do with it?" Nancy asked in a low conspiratorial voice.

"Maybe. He's not a typical patient, and I'm definitely understating this fact. I do not believe his being here, at this hospital and in my care, is random. He planned it, and for the life of me, I can't figure out why."

"What makes you say that?"

Sara thought about what she had promised Jack that first day before he began his story. *Do not talk about this with anyone.* Then she thought of how Jack hasn't been upfront and honest since he got here. The fact he might not even be an actual patient in need was more probable than not. His being here could be a complete sham, or worse, a setup of some kind.

"Jack seems to know an awful lot about me and my past. I also get the impression he may know something about Spencer's odd departure as well. I know this sounds crazy, but the evidence suggests-"

Sara stopped herself before going too far.

"Do you think Spencer set this up himself?" Nancy said, eager to keep the conversation going. "That's exactly the kind of crap he is capable of, don't you think?"

"I thought that at first as well, but now I'm not so sure."

Nancy thought for a quick second.

"The fact he isn't from around this area, which I'm more than certain of, does seem suspicious."

"I agree."

"What does he know about you, if you don't mind my asking?" Nancy asked, not sure if she would get an answer.

Sara looked at Nancy with a serious expression.

"Things I've never told anyone. I can't explain how he could have obtained this information."

Sara sat back but kept a hand on her desk, fingers tapping the wood nervously.

"Has he said anything else out of the ordinary?"

"Pfft. You wouldn't believe me if I told you. I don't..." Sara stopped herself, again. She would not get into the details of her sessions. That was too much, as she already felt as though she had crossed a line.

"I could ask my friend on the police force to look into the Spencer thing if you want."

"Please. Anything that could shed some light on this situation will help, but please do not mention why you are asking or anything about what we've just discussed, okay?"

"Oh, of course not," Nancy said, miming the classic locked lips with her hand.

Nancy leaned over the desk, patted Sara on the hand, and gave her a sympathetic nod. "You are one smart cookie. I know you'll figure this young man out."

With that, Nancy left the office, shutting the door behind her.

Sara considered her next step carefully. Her next move was important. She was upset, but instead of letting her anger fester, she made herself settle down and take a different route. She would do whatever it took to get her answers, even if it meant breaking protocol.

After another twenty minutes, Sara went back to Jack's room, gave a quick knock, and walked in. She was carrying two large coffees from the gourmet coffee shop across the street. Jack was standing near the window but walked toward Sara as she held out the coffee for him.

"This is an unexpected surprise," Jack said as he took one of the coffees from the doctor. Jack looked at it suspiciously. "Should I be worried about drinking this?"

"I deserved that," Sara said. "I'm sorry for my outburst earlier."

Sara sat down in the chair, and Jack followed, sitting at the same time.

"Apology accepted, but unnecessary. I understand, and considering everything I've told you, I'm surprised how well you're taking it."

"Thank you. Now, let me make something perfectly clear. There are far too many coincidences for me to believe you are here by accident. In fact, I think it's fair to say that everything leading up to you getting admitted here has been a complete farce. This also leads me to believe you are not someone who genuinely needs psychological help. The ruse to get in my care is blatantly obvious at this point, but the why is the most troubling. This leaves us in a precarious situation," Sara said, almost as a question.

Jack was hiding a thin smile and nodding along as Sara spoke.

"You're right, on all fronts," Jack said. "The way I see it, we have two options. One, I do my remaining time here, answering only questions asked, if you would even have any at this juncture, and then leave, never to be seen again. Or two, you listen to the rest of my story as you have been. If you choose option two, you will receive almost every answer you ever wanted to know regarding your past."

"Almost? Why almost?"

"Because there are some questions you don't even know to ask, but like I mentioned before, those may be the most important."

"I want to know what happened to my parents," Sara demanded.

"We all want things, isn't that right? From a clinical perspective that is."

The sarcasm was veiled, but thin was an understatement.

"Goddamn you."

Jack simply shrugged at the comment.

Sara got up again, clearly frustrated. She grabbed her coffee and walked to the window, ignoring Jack for the moment. She was sipping her coffee when something caught her eye. A bird. It was on the bird bath, taking a sip of water, and then turned its tiny head toward the building. It was as if it was looking into the window, straight at Sara. For some odd reason, Sara was able to suppress her anger. She couldn't explain it, but this seemingly casual and inconsequential event had just calmed her to the core. She returned to her chair and sat.

"Let's get to it then," Sara said. "Finish the damn story."

Jack raised an eyebrow.

"And you are okay with the pace I choose to tell it?"

"Yes."

"Good, because things are about to get very interesting."

64

The next day, Bili and I were working together at the store.

"Are we still doing the detail later?" I asked.

"Yeah. Meet me at my apartment at 9. I'll drive."

"Groovy," I said, and then changed topics. "Hey, I have an errand to run. Can you close up without me?"

"Hmm, I'm not sure," Bili said, putting her index finger to the side of her chin. "I've only been doing this job for a hundred years."

"If you ever answer me with a normal, non-sarcastic response, I will know for sure you've been kidnapped and replaced with a shape-shifting alien."

"You can't have too many safety nets for such events," she said, heading to the back room to get a replacement piece for a painting she sold.

I went to the loft and changed my clothes before I left. I made one quick stop, and then it was a short drive to my destination. I parked and walked on the grassy hill until I found what I was looking for. Theo had replaced the tiny stone with what he called a more appropriate memorial to an exceptional woman. The marble structure was unbelievably ornate and beautiful. It had a carved picture of my mother on the front and above her picture was a moon and rose. It looked just like the pendant I'd bought for her the night she was murdered. I still didn't know the significance of it at the time, but I loved it on there just the same.

I talked to my mom as though she was there, speaking of the changes in my life, large and small. Before I left, I made a promise to her I would find that son-of-a-bitch, Kristov, and finish what I started. After he confessed to killing my mom, I was within seconds of killing him before he escaped in a hail of gunfire. I said goodbye to my mom and then went to Bili's.

Bili and I made our way to the jailhouse to feed the prisoner. Per Theo's instructions, I conducted the perimeter check and acted as lookout, while Bili went inside to take care of Parrus. Bili threw together a quick dinner and slid it under the small gap in the bars.

"Thank you, Buh-linda," Parrus said sardonically when Bili gave her the food.

"Enjoy. Tomorrow it might be dog food," Bili said as she started walking away.

"I see why Theo likes you. He was always one to pick up strays and keep them as pets."

Bili stopped, turned around, took a step toward Parrus, and gave her a mock confused look.

"Which one of us is in a cage?"

Parrus smiled and nodded her head, conceding her situation.

"Theo doesn't have what it takes to win this war. He's weak. That he makes you come here is proof of that. You on the other hand…"

"Kindness is a weakness? Only an evil psychopath, like yourself, would look at it that way. You're right about one thing though, I would gladly starve you, or just kill you for the fun of it," Bili said unwaveringly as she stood in front of Parrus' cage.

Parrus raised her head and nodded, as if she had just remembered something.

"Ah, yes. The computer nerd, I almost forgot. Harold, was it? Why did you care? Not your type from what I've been told," Parrus said with a wink.

"His name was Steve, and if you mention his name again, I will remove your ears."

"You have spent a lot of time with Theo."

"I have, which begs the question. Are you doing all of this because he dumped you? Wouldn't it have been a lot less hassle to just find someone else? Or get fifty cats, like all the other crazy bitches?"

Bili had enough of the conversation and turned to leave. Just before she got to the door, Parrus spoke.

"Did I smell Jack with you? What do you think of our handsome young man? I know he's not your type either, but he does have something, doesn't he?"

Bili would have left, but there was something in Parrus' tone that made her stop. Having Bili's attention, Parrus continued.

"What? Don't tell me you didn't know," Parrus said. "I thought you were Theo's nearest and dearest.

Bili crossed her arms and reluctantly responded.

"Know what?"

65

had just completed a large lap around the house, making sure it was clear, and waited another five minutes before Bili came out. She walked straight past me toward the car and got inside. There was no mistaking that her look and mood had changed from when she went in.

"What took so long?" I asked when I sat down in the car.

"Let's go."

Bili avoided looking at me, and her body language suggested many things as well, but one thing was clear, she wasn't happy. As I drove, there was a deafening sound of silence I couldn't ignore. The look on Bili's face became so distracting that I had to ask.

"What happened in there?"

"Yeah, fine," she said, looking out the passenger window. "Drive."

What?

I let it go, making no mention of her weird response. We can detect deception, but unfortunately we can't always fill in the blanks.

"I never told you how sorry I am," Bili said, breaking the long silence.

"About?"

"Viktoria. I know how you felt about her, and... well, I'm sorry," she said, brushing her hands on her jeans. Nothing was there, but I sensed it was a subconscious response to something she would never mention if she could help it. I thought she was going to say more, but she let the matter drop. Since she was talking, I prompted a new topic.

"How's the apartment since the remodel?" I asked, moving the conversation to safer waters.

"The same, except now it would take a pack of rabid wolves just to get past the screen door. I think Theo went a little overboard with the security."

"He cares about you. It's nice," I said, thinking about my mom. I think Bili sensed it as well, giving me a sympathetic nod in response.

"Do you want to grab some food and watch a movie at my place?" Bili said as if it were no big deal.

This simple gesture threw me for a loop. I never thought Bili was capable of anything so mundane and normal. It was ridiculous, but I just pictured her doing one of two things in her spare time; reading or training to hurt people.

"I didn't think you had a TV?" I said, remembering the last time Steve and I were in her apartment.

"Theo put one in when he updated the security. He even stocked the entertainment center with movies, apparently to keep up appearances. I'm sure there's something in there worth killing two hours while we eat."

"I'm in then."

We stopped for some pizza, took it to go, and then we actually watched a movie. One I suggested, of course, as she was completely out of touch with what was a viewable film. Most of the movies she knew were in black and white and not in her collection.

She was quiet during the entire movie, and I think she may have even enjoyed it. I also felt like I was picking up a few gestures that suggested something else was on her mind. I asked her about it, and she shushed me, raising her eyebrows and tilting her head toward the TV.

When the movie ended, I cleaned up the kitchen and grabbed my jacket to leave for the night. I enjoyed her company, and considering where we had started, it said something about how far we had come. I think you could say we were indeed friends now.

"I'll see you at work tomorrow," I said.

When she didn't answer, I turned to make sure she was still in the room. When I did, Bili was mere inches from me, staring me in the eye. This startled and confused me. Before I had time to blink, she kissed me. It wasn't a deep passionate kiss of lovers, but it wasn't a friendly peck on the lips either.

"Bili, I-"

Before I could finish my sentence, Bili opened the door and shoved me into the hall with such force that I damaged the drywall on the opposite side. The door shut just as quickly.

I stood there trying to understand where that came from and what it meant. Even with my abilities, I never saw that coming. I walked back to the store where I had taken up permanent residency in the loft and thought about the entire night. Something happened to Bili at that house.

I had never thought of Bili in that way before, and this had my head spinning right until I fell asleep. I had several bizarre dreams that night, the most vivid involved Bili and Viktoria violently fighting each other. It left disturbing images in my mind, and I did my best to forget about it.

When I woke up the next day and walked out of the loft, I saw Bili had already done the prep and opened the store an hour early. She said good morning and acted as if everything was normal. No hint at all that she was thinking about what happened.

"Hey, Theo called. He's going to pick you up in an hour or so," Bili said.

"Work, or other?"

"Other. I wanted to go, but apparently, it's too dangerous for a girl," she said.

"Really?"

"Of course not, don't be stupid," she said, only halfway paying attention to me while thumbing through some paperwork.

"Good one. Hey-"

Bili put her hand up.

"Stop, right there," she said. "I don't want to talk about it."

"But-"

"Jack, no," she said, now giving me her full attention and the most serious of looks.

We stared at each other for a second, and I could tell she was not budging on the topic. I shook my head in frustration, knowing it was a lost cause.

"Fine."

I walked away and jumped on the computer to get some work done. I could feel Bili looking at me as I did. I thought she was going to say something, but again, she didn't. She was as protective of her words as the Vatican is with their scrolls.

When Theo arrived at the store, he gave Bili a list of instructions, some work related, some not, and then we were off. He had the Bentley again, which made me wonder what he had in store. The last time he brought it out, we came close to dying. I hoped this trip was going to be different.

We weren't in the car for five minutes when we pulled into a bank parking lot. I looked over at him, waiting for some sort of explanation as to what we were doing here. He just smiled and tilted his head toward the front doors as a non-verbal command to follow him. I did, and when we entered the bank, we were met by one of its representatives right away, who took us into a private room.

The employee had two stacks of paperwork on the table, ready for dates and signatures. Every line that needed to be signed had a sticky yellow arrow in front of it. I signed them, one after another, not really taking the time to read most of it. I could tell what kind of transaction it was, and I trusted Theo had my best interest in mind.

"Okay, Jack. If you could just sign these last few forms, I think we'll be all set," the lady said as she placed the last of the pages in front of me.

"Congratulations, I hope you will be happy with your new home," she said, as she handed me a set of keys.

"Thank you, I'm sure I will."

I was bursting with curiosity but waited until Theo and I walked outside.

"I bought a house?"

"No, a condo. I figured you were tired of living at work, so, as a bonus for all your hard work, I bought you a new place in Bili's building. Don't worry, it's on another floor, so you will have some space from each other."

I wondered if he could tell what I was thinking. I suddenly got a slight guilty feeling in the pit of my stomach. Maybe because I knew Bili was like a daughter to him.

"I don't know what to say, Theo. It's too much."

"Hardly, and it's long overdue. I stocked it with a few essentials, like a bed, couch, and television, but you can fill it in as you see fit."

"Thank you so much," I said, looking at the keys in my hand. It was an unbelievable surprise.

I had been on a roller coaster of highs and lows in my crazy new world and the thought of a place of my own was just the thing I needed. I don't think I knew it until just that moment, either. Before I even said a word, Theo answered an unspoken question.

"Yes, I wanted you close to Bili for safety reasons, and that building is the most secure in the city. Don't hold it against an old man," Theo said as he put his arm over my shoulders as we walked to the car.

On the way to my new place, I wondered if Bili was aware of this development, and if not, how was she going to react. She might very well throw me off the roof, feeling that I was crowding her. I needed time to reflect on all the new developments, and little did I know I was about to get that time.

66

J ack stopped talking, and his attention veered toward the door. Sara turned to where Jack's attention went and then heard the muffled commotion outside in the hallway. Just then, she saw someone run past the small window in the door. The urgency in the run was noticeable in that quick second, and Sara knew something was wrong.

"Excuse me, Jack, I'll be right back," she said as she moved swiftly to the door and out into the hall.

Sara was almost knocked over by another orderly running past her in haste.

"What the hell is going on?"

"New arrival. He's big and violent," the orderly said, as he glanced back toward Sara as he ran.

Sara ran to her office, frantically searching her cabinet before finding the bottle and syringe she was looking for. She filled the syringe with the clear liquid as fast as she could, tossed the small glass container on the floor, and then sprinted toward intake. Once she cleared the double doors, she saw two police officers and three hospital employees struggling with the huge man.

The massive shirtless patient was tossing the cops and orderlies around as if they were small children. He was bald, sweaty, and absolutely furious about something. The man was yelling and throwing punches at anyone who got near him. He wasn't saying anything legible, just yelling in a disturbed manner. The staff were justifiably horrified and did everything they could to stay out of reach from this man.

With needle in hand, Sara ran toward the man just as the officer tried to get him to the ground by the legs. The officer failed to take him down just as Sara approached the crazed subject. The man towered over Sara, but without hesitation, she jabbed the needle toward the man's exposed skin. The maniac caught Sara by the wrist before the needle could find its mark and squeezed, forcing her to drop the syringe. The man picked Sara up over his head and threw her against the wall and into a glass framed picture. The glass shattered and covered her body as she fell to the ground. This dazed Sara for a moment, but she got to her feet as the man ran toward the interior of the hospital. Sara, the police officers, and the orderlies gave chase. They had just burst through the closed double doors when they found him.

The large man was lying on the floor, unconscious.

Sara's eyes drifted from the man to the door right next to him. Jack was inside his room, looking out the small window in the door.

The man began to move and groan, causing Sara to regain her wits. She ran back to intake, grabbed the syringe that was on the floor, and before the violent beast woke, she had the needle in his arm. He went limp in seconds. The relief of all involved was palpable.

"What the hell happened, Kraminski," one officer said to the other.

"Heck, if I know. He was calm as a lamb when we brought him in, so the nurse asked me to take the cuffs off. In less than a minute, the guy got a weird look on his face and all hell broke loose. He just went crazy," the officer said, and then he looked at Sara. "Sorry Doc, you know what I mean."

Sara had met this officer once before, as there weren't that many on the force in Franklin.

"It's okay. Did you see what he was looking at?"

"Nothing I could see. Other than us, the room was empty. Maybe it's a full moon. You know what they say," the officer said.

"Yeah, I do," Sara said, as she looked at Jack again. "Thanks for the help, officers."

Sara brushed off some loose glass from her jacket and then opened the door to Jack's room. Jack moved to the side and followed her to the chairs and sat.

"Want to tell me what just happened?" Sara asked, rubbing her wrist subconsciously.

"My guess is drugs, but I'm not a doctor."

"You had to see him. What happened?"

"He ran through the doors and then fell to the floor in a heap."

Sara looked for any signs of deception, trying to see if he was telling the truth, but saw none. Even still, the story didn't add up.

"Really?" she asked suspiciously. "The monster just passed out right in front of your door?"

Sara walked back to the door, which seemed to be in working order, and tested it several different ways. She didn't find any obvious damage.

"Yes."

Sara walked back to her chair and sat down gingerly, now feeling the bruises from being tossed like a stuffed animal.

Jack was about to say something but diverted his attention to Sara's forehead.

"You're bleeding."

Sara brought her hand to her head, and when she lowered it, she saw the bright red confirmation on her fingertips.

"Oh, it's nothing," she said dismissively. "I'll…"

That was the last thing she remembered before waking up on the bed in Jack's room. Sara felt her forehead again, but this time she found a clean dressing covering her cut.

"How long was I out?"

"Just a few minutes," Jack said. "Blood is not your thing, I see."

"Nope. Especially when it's mine."

"How is she?"

Sara heard a female voice coming from behind Jack.

"I think she'll live," Jack said, as Nancy walked around him and into Sara's view.

"Nancy was kind enough to bring you a few bandages after you decided to take a nap."

"Funny," Sara said as she sat up and put her feet on the floor. The dizziness was still there but faded with a few deep breaths.

Nancy walked to the sink in the bathroom and wrung out a towel, sending the light pink liquid into the drain. She threw the towel in the bin and sat on the bed next to Sara.

"How did you know what happened?" Sara said, glancing at her friend.

"I saw some blood on the floor under the picture that was shattered. When Tommy told me how you were thrown by the bald maniac, I thought I better check on you. As soon as I peaked in the window, you passed out. How's that for timing?"

"Impeccable."

Sara got up and walked back to her chair. Nancy followed, making sure she didn't faint again.

"Do you want me to get a doctor from medical to look at you?" Nancy asked.

"No, no. I'm fine. Wasn't the first and probably won't be the last."

"If you're all set, I'll get back to work." Nancy said, rubbing Sara's arm, while looking at Jack.

"Thank you. I owe you one," Sara said, breaking Nancy's minor trance-like state.

"Of course, uh, yeah, work," Nancy said as she left the room, leaving Sara back where she started.

Sara felt her head once more before she looked at Jack and spoke earnestly.

"Why are you here?"

It was the first thing that came into Sara's aching head.

"Because-"

"Stop. Why?" Sara said, knowing that Jack was about to give some fabricated answer.

Jack appeared to contemplate his answer carefully.

"Because, I have to be, and because you need me to be," Jack said, sincerely.

"You're not-?"

"No. Are we going to go through this again?"

Jack took a deep breath and shook his head with a tight-lipped grimace.

"Listen, I told you before the day is over, you'll have answers, and you will. If you can give me a little more latitude, you will understand why I'm being less than forthcoming."

Sara had never felt less in control than she did now. Even though she knew Jack wasn't a real patient, so to speak, she was still his doctor for the moment.

"Okay, okay."

"Are you sure you don't want to have those cuts looked at by a professional before we continue?"

"I may not be a wolf, but I'm not a dandelion either. Start talking."

Jack smiled.

"The dandelion is one of the most stubborn flowers in the world, did you know that?"

"Okay, maybe I am a dandelion. Now get to it."

Jack gave the doctor a sly smile, accompanied by a simple nod.

"Yes, ma'am."

67

Ted walked into the Broken Shillelagh and saw Ben sitting at his usual barstool, sipping on his usual drink, at an unusual time. Ted knew that if there was one person who may take him seriously it just might be Ben. Though he was not one to pull punches, and honest to a fault, he was loyal to his friends.

"You always drink at ten in the morning?" Ted said as he sat down on the barstool next to him.

"No, It's the earliest this bar opens," Ben said in a manner that Ted couldn't tell if he was serious or not.

"Another Manhattan, Mike, but no cherry this time. The last one tasted like it came out of a leprechaun's ass," Ben said, wiggling his empty glass to the bartender.

"Okay Ritchie Rich, what's so important I had to meet you right away? I was perfectly happy drinking breakfast with Mike."

Ted stalled, appearing to be thinking about what to say. His face remained stoic.

"Nothing? C'mon, that was funny."

Ted tried to force a smile, and Ben saw right through it.

"What?"

"It's Jack," Ted said, rapping his fingertips on the bar, and chewing on his bottom lip. "Can I get a beer? Arbor's Best, please."

The approaching bartender grabbed a mug and started pouring.

"Atta boy," Ben said with an appreciative smile. "What about him? I thought you said you talked to him, and everything was cool."

The bartender handed Ted his beer and he drank half in one go. Ted hesitated, but only briefly.

"I didn't tell you the entire story before because he told me not to, but now I... I think he might..."

Ben moved his hand and index finger in a circular motion. The universal sign of get to the point.

"I think he might be in some kind of trouble."

Ted told him about the meeting at the house, as well as my stern instructions regarding Ceana. Ben listened carefully and took him seriously, which was a pleasant surprise to Ted. He thought Ben might dismiss him and act as though he was being paranoid. He couldn't have been more wrong.

"Any idea where Jack is now?" Ben asked.

"No, and I haven't heard from him in ages. I was thinking of going to his work, but I wasn't sure if it was a good idea. Like I said, he told me-"

"Hell, let's go."

Ben was never one to worry about overstepping himself or hurting feelings. He was the person who got things done. Ben and Ted finished their drinks and then started the four-block walk to the Piece of History.

"Oh," Ted said, just before they reached the shop. "He told me before that his boss is a real hard ass."

"Don't worry about it. I've dealt with pricks like that all my life."

"It's a woman."

"Oh. Well, I've dealt with plenty of bitches too."

When they got there, Ben took the lead and Ted followed behind sheepishly, feeling as though he might have made a mistake telling Ben.

They walked in and saw an attractive woman standing behind the counter, who watched them as they approached. This made Ted even more nervous. Not Ben, though.

"Excuse me, young lady, is Jack working today?" Ben said.

"Who's asking?" the woman said.

"Two very good friends of his. May I ask, who's asking, who's asking?" Ben said, not to be outdone by anyone in the sarcasm department.

"No, and he's not," she said without elaborating.

"Can we speak to the woman in charge then?"

"That's me."

Ben turned to look at Ted, who nodded in affirmation.

"Interesting," Ben said with a smile forming.

Ted cleared his throat and spoke up before Ben went any further.

"You're Bili, right? Jack told me about you. I'm his roommate, or I used to be. Listen, I'm really worried about him. Could you please tell him we were here? If you see him, I mean."

Bili rolled her eyes, but something about the pitiful look on Ted's face made her pause. That and the fact that I told her to send them back. They never heard a thing.

"Wait here," she said as she walked into the back room, where we had a quick discussion.

Ben looked at Ted with a nod and a smile, accompanied by a pat on the back.

A minute later, Bili came back out.

"Go on," Bili said, motioning with her head.

Ben and Ted started walking.

"Hey, Mr. Rogers, don't touch anything," Bili said, looking at Ben, referring to his red sweater.

Ben grinned even wider at that. She instantly infatuated him with her tough, sarcastic demeanor. They walked through the swinging doors where I was waiting for them.

"Excuse me pal, we're looking for-" Ben began, but stopped when he realized it was me.

Ben shook his head as if he was seeing a mirage.

"Holy shit. Jack, is that you? You weren't kidding," Ben said, looking back at Ted.

"What are you guys doing here?" I snapped.

Ted's face flushed.

They had just inadvertently put themselves in peril by walking in the front doors.

"Sorry, but I was worried about you. I know what you said, but-"

"What I said was for your own safety." I stopped myself from getting angry, knowing it was no use yelling about it now. The damage was done. "I'm sorry, I appreciate the thought, but I'm fine, really."

"Whatever," Ben said. "Let's get back to the fact that you look like some freakishly good-looking male model. Where'd you have the work done? I'm making an appointment tomorrow. Good thing Cyndi isn't here, or she just might-"

"Got it," I said, cutting off whatever inappropriate comment he was going to make.

"Listen. I know you two have a million questions, trust me when I tell you, I know the feeling, but now is not the time. Set up a night out next week, and I'll meet with you and explain everything, okay?"

They both agreed without too much fuss. Then Ben asked a Ben question.

"What's with the warden up front?"

"She's the female version of you. You like her, don't you?" I said, knowing the answer.

"I'm so attracted to her, I would have her babies."

Ted and I let out a good laugh which eased the tension somewhat. I was grateful for my friends, but in this climate, such things were dangerous and potentially deadly.

"All I can say is, good luck."

I walked them back to the front, hoping I could get them out of the store as soon as possible. I thought about sending them out the back, but that would make it even more obvious they weren't just regular customers. Ben passed Bili, and in his usual subtle manner, he spoke.

"You, I like," he said with a point of his finger. Then he smoothed out his sweater with the palms of his hands as he winked at her.

"See you guys later," I said as they left the store.

Once they were out the door, Bili looked at me incredulously, as she sat on a small stool we kept behind the counter.

"You're really going to meet with them?"

"Maybe. I know it's not a good idea, but coming here again would surely make them targets, assuming that ship hasn't already sailed. We don't have the time or resources to watch them too. This puts me in a tough spot."

I could see Bili thinking.

"What?"

"I have an idea," Bili said. "You may not like it, but it just might help them and us."

She was right. I didn't like it, but all things considered, our choices were limited and out of our control to a certain degree. We knew, or assumed anyway, that the enemy was always watching and/or listening. If we could use that to our advantage, no matter how small it might be, it just may give us a leg up. Bili pushed the issue by going outside and waving to them as they walked down the street.

Though it didn't happen right away, it did give us something, but a leg up might not be the best way to describe what happened.

68

Kristov waited on the park bench tossing tiny pieces of bread at the ducks. His shaved head, accompanied by the long beard and mustache, drastically changed his look. With the baseball hat pulled low over his eyes, he was unrecognizable. If not for his bulky frame, he would have looked like a common truck driver.

The meeting was a risk, but the alternative was even worse. He couldn't have put himself in a worse situation if he had tried. Kristov detested this modern world, and his inability to adapt caused his continued failures.

"You shouldn't be doing that," an elderly woman said as she watched Kristov throw the bread. "The ducks will get used to the food, and it will change their eco system."

"Go buy some yarn and knit a muzzle, ya old bat," he said without looking away from his task.

The woman was aghast at the comment and walked away with a scowl.

A minute later, a wire-thin man in an oversized rain jacket shuffled over to the bench and sat next to Kristov. He was too close, which prompted a reaction.

"Jesus Christ, can't I get a break? Excuse me, but can you fuck off. I'm waiting for someone."

The man didn't move. He also kept his eyes straight forward.

"Indeed, you are," the man said, not elaborating.

"I'm not in the mood, so don't make me hurt you. It's bad enough I'm sitting next to a pile of garbage in this shit-hole city."

The man turned his head toward Kristov, revealing the right side of his face. It was a mass of scars that was highlighted with a solid white eye.

"Mr. Mouglish, sorry, I didn't know it was you," Kristov said, changing his attitude in a hurry.

"You have been granted one last chance," he said, ignoring the threats.

Kristov felt a wave of relief but did his best to conceal his emotions. His reputation for being fearless was all he had left in this world.

"So, now what?"

Kristov did not like the fact that he had to talk to this man in this fashion, but he was no ordinary human. The fact he was even being cordial to this person, in Kristov's mind, was the equivalent to begging for his life. He hated it, but this was one human you did not mess with. His reputation was worldwide, and more importantly, so was the person he worked for.

Mr. Mouglish pulled an envelope from the inside of his jacket and handed it to Kristov, who took it apprehensively.

"If you succeed, all is forgiven."

"If not?" Kristov asked.

Mr. Mouglish didn't answer. He gave Kristov a quick stare, stood up, and walked away from him toward the street. An approaching Cadillac SUV pulled up alongside him. Mr. Mouglish disappeared inside, and then it sped off. The answer was obvious.

Kristov opened the suspiciously thin and weightless envelope while still sitting on the bench. He unfolded the single piece of paper as the wind rattled it in his hand. There was a single sentence.

When he read it, he dropped the paper on the ground.

"Fuck."

69

had moved into my new place, and I couldn't have been happier. After I added a few things to make it more me, it was a home I could live in for years to come.

One afternoon, I came home to find a housewarming gift from Bili. It was one surprise after another with her and this one went beyond extravagant. She already had it hanging in the living room, perfectly centered, and spaced.

It was an original Picasso from the blue period, which is far and away my favorite era of his. It was a smaller painting that I had seen in a competitor's store awhile back and mentioned it in small talk. Bili had it framed, which she had an eye for, and it looked beautiful.

I wasn't sure how to interpret a gift like that, especially from her. She had a post-it on the frame that simply said, welcome home. Was it just a friendly gesture, or something else? Regardless, I prayed there was never a fire in this building.

As the days went on, Bili and I still acted as though the kiss never happened and continued to do the feeding detail at the jailhouse. Theo was nothing if not civilized. He would rarely treat the worst of his enemies, as they would undoubtedly treat him.

Bili and I had our routine down to a science. We parked near the road, and while I did a perimeter check, Bili went inside and fed Parrus. We were usually back on the road within minutes. We never did this at the same time and not every day.

When we got to the house, I started my check as Bili went inside. I made a wide circle around the house and the wooded area it sat on, checking for anything out of the ordinary. I found something I didn't like and hurried back to the house. Just as I approached the front door, Bili came out of the house. I could tell instantly something was wrong.

"What?"

"We have a problem," she said, motioning for me to follow her.

There was a large hole in the rear of the house with wood and brick scattered about the yard. There was also a long and very thick chain outside as well. It looked as though they broke out the window, attached the chain to a segment of the cage, and pulled it apart with a large vehicle. One with torque and horsepower enough to mangle the thick bars of steel for Parrus to fit through. The dust mites in the air said this little event must have happened recently.

We were hoping to break her down and get enough information to not only stop this war but find the person responsible. Someone was bankrolling an expensive operation and had no problem hurting people in the process.

"I thought I smelled something familiar near the far edge of the property," I said.

"How could they have found her? We took every precaution."

Bili started shaking her head, as if trying to remove a terrible thought.

"It has to be someone we know," she said. "There has to be a leak."

I couldn't think of anyone who could, or would, betray us. The thought was too disturbing to consider. Just then, I saw something on the floor that caught my attention. Just outside the cage area, there was a small circular piece of metal on the floor. I picked it up and almost dropped it because of some slippery substance that covered it. It was blood.

"This is how they found her."

Bili came closer, took it from me, and shined a light on it.

"A GPS tracker. That bitch must have had it implanted under her skin. They knew where she was this entire time."

Bili called Theo to let him know what happened. He told us to repair the house as much as possible as not to gain attention if anyone was to walk by and then get back to his house.

We did just that, which took two trips to the hardware store, and every bit of four hours. We did a quick clean-up and headed to Theo's.

Theo's place was beautiful, not to mention a virtual fortress. It was on a large pond, or rather a small lake, and no neighbors to speak of. There was an iron fence with a rolling gate blocking the driveway.

It was the five of us: Claude, Deaglan, Bili, Theo, and I. We were just standing around his kitchen counter in no discernable fashion. After the pleasantries and a few other odd pieces of business, Theo handed me two airline tickets.

"I thought about cancelling this trip in light of recent events, but I think it may be even more important now. I need to stay here and deal with this mess, and I want you to go in my stead. Deaglan has agreed to go with you."

I knew there was something planned overseas, I just didn't know any of the details. Deaglan would fill me in during the flight.

"Deaglan is completely up to speed and more than familiar with the area you'll be visiting. He also has more contacts in the area than anyone, including myself," Theo said. "You'll be in good hands."

I nodded, and then looked over at Deaglan, who gave me a quick nod of assurance as well. I know Theo must have full trust in Deaglan to give him this kind of responsibility. I didn't know the full extent of our mission, but I knew it could be vital.

This was my first journey abroad, and I was very excited about it. London was one place I had always wanted to visit, and even though we were on business, for lack of a better word, Deaglan was sure he could provide a suitable travel experience. I didn't know what that meant, but trust me when I tell you, traveling with Deaglan was an experience alright.

70

The plane ride was smooth and landed without crashing, which is really all I want out of any flight I take. We arrived at Heathrow around midnight, and the airport was relatively empty. I was a little nervous going through customs, when thirty seconds before, Deaglan told me his passport and ID were fakes. This declaration was proceeded by, *you may have to make a run for it*. Unsurprisingly, he charmed his way through without so much as a suspicious look.

Theo had booked us at a hotel in Chelsea, but we promptly disregarded those reservations and checked ourselves into a different one on the other side of London. We had learned too many times that the enemy was exceptionally adept at gathering information on an expert level. Theo went overboard on security and safety ever since the fire at the cabin. Claude and

Theo were no amateurs, but even they couldn't fathom how information was being obtained and used against us.

We had only been in our suite, which was more like a full-scale apartment, for thirty minutes when there was a knock on the door. Deaglan and I looked at each other thinking the same thing. We both shook our heads, letting the other know that we weren't expecting anyone.

Deaglan walked to the door cautiously, making sure to not stand directly in front of it. It was then I noticed the details in the simple things he did. Deaglan took nothing lightly during our trip, especially with tactics and safety. I wasn't aware of his past, or experience, but his tradecraft was vast and meticulous. I was learning a tremendous amount just being in his presence.

"Sorry, but neither of us are decent. Who is it?" Deaglan said.

"Now, I really want you to open the door," a female voice said.

I looked at Deaglan with a confused look, and he smiled at me as he unlocked and opened the door.

"I would know that voice anywhere, and if it wasn't for all this bloody potpourri in here, I would have smelled ya, love," he said as the door opened, revealing an attractive woman on the other side.

I was standing on the opposite side of the door from Deaglan, but several feet back. I walked closer, revealing myself to this person. As soon as she caught site, she locked eyes with me. Her piercing gray eyes stood out from her caramel skin and long black hair. The woman started walking in, but Deaglan put up his hand, blocking any further advancement.

"Not so fast, lassie. We weren't expecting any visitors, so to what do we owe the pleasure?" Deaglan asked.

His voice was pleasant, but I could tell his guard was far from dropped. He knew this woman, but if he wasn't expecting someone, you better believe he was going to find out why she was there.

"Claude thought I could be of use," she said, still focusing on me. "You're him, aren't you?"

"Claude said nothing to me, dear."

"Check your phone," she said, speaking to Deaglan, but still looking at me.

Deaglan pulled his phone from his pocket and looked at it. After approximately thirty more seconds it chimed with a text message from Claude. He just sent the letter T.

"Before you ask, he had to contact me through a third party, or maybe even a fourth, to make sure they didn't intercept the message," she said.

Deaglan thought it over for about three seconds, before deciding it made perfect sense.

"In that case, Jack, this is Tanzy. Tanzy, Jack."

Tanzy was already walking toward me as Deaglan was doing the introduction.

"I know who he is," she said.

She stuck her hand out to shake, which I did. She was not interested in testing my strength as Deaglan was when we first met. Her grip was altogether different but just as telling.

"Nice to meet you, Tanzy. Your name is very fitting."

"Smart, too. My, my," she said as she brushed her hair over to one side with her fingers. "Yes, if my parents only knew."

That one little gesture said many things simultaneously, and I don't think she cared I could read them. I put that out of my mind as we were here for a reason, and I had to stay focused.

"Okay, okay, try to keep your knickers on, eh. If you are here to help, fine, but we are on tight schedule," Deaglan said.

"Again, I know. Do you think I came here to do my nails?" she said, finally breaking her stare, directing her attention back to Deaglan. "I have your vehicle... ready and waiting."

She looked over her shoulder at me just as she said the last part. I fully believe that my former naïve, and all too human self, would have picked up that one.

"Great, why don't you wait downstairs, we need to bloody unpack. Thirty minutes or less, alright lass?"

She gave Deaglan a bit of a scowl but didn't argue.

"I'll be in the lobby then."

Tanzy walked out and shut the door behind her. Deaglan was looking at me, smiling from ear to ear.

"What?"

"What indeed. You're not used to that kind of attention, that tis plain as day. You may be before long, especially since you have both clans intrigued, in more ways than one."

We dressed in what Deaglan called "you never know" gear and headed to the elevator. Just as the door shut, I got some last-minute advice.

"Tonight will be the trickiest by far, lad. If everything goes well, it will set the tone for the rest of our stay, making things much smoother. Bodicea has this island in the palm of her bloody hand. If we get rejected by her, the others will most likely follow suit."

"Then what?"

He shrugged.

"Good chance we all die in the end."

This statement troubled me for one simple reason. I couldn't tell if he was joking or not.

He bumped my shoulder and gave me a wink. "It'll be fine."

I think everyone in the modern world knows when someone uses the word fine, they rarely mean it. I wasn't exactly sure what Deaglan meant by his *fine*, but our night was about to get very interesting.

71

Ted was in his usual Thursday class, packing up his notebook after a long lecture. He stood, about to leave, when Cyndi came up next to him and pulled him back down into his seat.

"Hey," Cyndi said. "Have you heard from Jack?"

He was unsure how much to tell Cyndi, but in his mind, a couple of facts influenced his decision. She was a close friend of mine, but the most dominating factor was that he had a terrible crush on her. So, he pretty much told her everything, including what happened at the store.

"Wow, are you serious? Have you heard from him since?" she asked curiously.

"Yeah, I just received a text from him yesterday. Ben and I are meeting him at the Pour House next week. I think he's out of town right now, but he should be home soon. You want to join us? I'm sure he wouldn't mind," Ted said.

Cyndi appeared pleasantly surprised by the offer, which in turn made Ted happy.

"I would. I also wanted to talk to you about something. Something important. Can I stop by your house in a little while? I'd rather not talk about it here."

"Yes, of course. Everything alright?"

Though Ted was over the moon that Cyndi wanted to come to his home, for any reason, he couldn't think of anything so important she couldn't just talk about it right there.

"Yeah, fine, it's just that I had the weirdest conversation with... Listen, I don't want to go into it right now. Is an hour enough time for you to get home and get situated?" Cyndi asked.

"Yeah, an hour should be enough time."

Cyndi leaned in, gave Ted a quick hug, and patted him on the shoulder. "Great, see ya in a few."

Cyndi left with purpose, looking over her shoulder at Ted a few times before she reached the lecture hall doors.

Ted left the hall right after, using the opposite doors, as his house was on the other side of campus. He was in his head the entire time about what Cyndi wanted to talk about. That she was coming to him for any kind of help or advice was a victory in his mind.

Ted took a quick shower when he got home and even changed his clothes. He wanted to look his best, just in case. The closer it came to the hour mark, the more nervous he became.

Any anxiety, however small, upset Ted's stomach. He went to the kitchen to get a soda and a few crackers, hoping to settle it before Cyndi got there. He opened the fridge, grabbed a ginger ale, and drank it down with the door open. It helped cool him off after a hot shower. The last thing he wanted was to have sweaty armpits when she arrived. After a few more seconds of extra cooling, Ted shut the door. When he did, he found he had a visitor, but unfortunately, not the one he was expecting.

"Hey there, Teddy Bear."

Parrus was sitting in one of the kitchen chairs as casually as could be. Although she looked very different, professionally made over and older looking, he knew who she was. Ted's mind raced, unsure how to respond to this woman. In the best of circumstances, this would have made him extremely nervous. This was not the best of anything.

"H-hey," was all Ted could get out. His eyes darted around the room. He searched in vain, hoping to see Cyndi, or anyone else that would explain why this woman was in his house.

"What's wrong sweetie, you seem... tense," she said as she arose from her chair and sauntered closer to Ted until she was within inches. "It's okay, really, I just have a few questions, that's all."

Parrus was so close, Ted could smell her spearmint-flavored breath as she ran her fingers through his hair. As she played with his hair, her other rested comfortably on his chest.

"Love, love, love the red hair. I would kill to have hair that color."

The way she spoke was most unsettling. Ted remembered what I had told him about Ceana which scared him even more.

Do Not let her in and call me immediately.

She put her hand on the side of Ted's flushed face as if appreciating the clean shave and then let it drop softly to his shoulder.

"Where is Jack?" she asked delicately and intimately.

"I don't know. I haven't seen or heard from him in a long time," he said as he backed up from Parrus, doing his absolute best to sound confident. He failed.

Parrus moved forward with him until he hit the counter, stopping his retreat.

"I thought you were Jack's best friend? You really don't know where I can find him?"

"No, no. He moved out, and I haven't seen him -- I have to ask you to leave. I'm sorry, but I have company coming over," Ted said, trying to regain some authority as the homeowner.

"Didn't Jack tell you that lying to me was a terrible idea?" she said calmly. "Oh, and our friend Cyndi isn't coming, sorry."

Ted was now beyond nervous and well into scared.

Parrus moved her hand around Ted's shoulder in a warm, caressing manner. Ted shook physically as she did this. Her hand rounded the top of Ted's upper chest and without a whisper or warning, she dug her thumb through Ted's shirt and deep into his flesh.

Ted yelled in agony, but Parrus slapped her other hand over his mouth, stifling his scream. Ted swung wildly with his fists in an instinctual, self-preservation fashion, but it did nothing but mess her hair up a little. That was enough for her to dig her thumb in deeper to stop the flailing. It stopped.

"Let's try this again," Parrus said as she blew the hair out of her eyes that Ted had mussed. "I know you went to see him at his work, and I'm thinking he agreed to meet you at some other time, yes?"

Ted nodded his head vigorously as tears streamed down his face.

"See? It's really just a question of motivation," Parrus said calmly. "Now, I have a few ideas on how we can use this information to our benefit. You don't mind me including you, do you?"

Ted couldn't think clearly as the intense pain spread throughout his upper body. Her thumb was grinding a nerve cluster that surely was causing the severe agony he was experiencing. Though Ted didn't answer, Parrus acted as though he did.

"Great. Now, I'm going to remove my hand. If you yell, I will pull your lung out through your rib cage. I do not mean that metaphorically. Are we crystal on this?" Parrus said, with a quick raise of her eyebrows.

Again, Ted nodded quickly, and Parrus slowly pulled her bloody thumb from Ted's shoulder and uncovered his mouth at the same time. Ted had a look of horror on his face, and Parrus seemed to revel in this. He reached up with his off-hand and tried to put pressure on the open wound.

Parrus leaned over Ted's shoulder, pressing her breasts against his chest to grab a dish towel that was on the kitchen countertop.

"Excuse my reach, honey," she said as she grabbed the towel.

She wiped the blood from her thumb with a mock scowl on her face.

"Kinda gross, isn't it?" she said as she tossed the towel into the sink. "Yes, I know, you can't believe this is happening, and no, you're not dreaming, blah, blah," Parrus added with a roll of her eyes.

"I thought you liked Jack. Why are you doing this?" Ted asked.

When confronted with the supernatural, so to speak, the rational mind does everything it can to make sense of it. Though Ted had a million different questions about what Parrus was, and how she was able to do these things, he could only ask simple, mundane questions.

"Your next question will be, why are you pulling my limbs off, if you waste my time with ridiculous drivel. Understand?"

Ted nodded. Then his attention drifted ever so slight. Parrus noticed this and saw something she didn't like. She turned just in time to see Claude walk into the house, moving directly toward her.

If Parrus was shocked by this, she hid it very well. She smiled, and quick as a whip, she grabbed Ted by the throat. She picked him off the ground by his neck as Ted grabbed at her hand with both of his, trying to release her grasp. He could barely make a wheezing sound, due to the tightness of her grip.

"One more step and I kill Red," Parrus said calmly.

"So," Claude said, casually.

Ted was sure the end was coming when the big man continued his approach toward Parrus. If she was good to her word, he was seconds from death.

Parrus stared directly at Claude, and just like that, her serious look left and a wide, toothy grin appeared.

"I was expecting someone else, but you'll do fine," Parrus said.

The back door opened, and two wolves and a vampire walked in together. Claude knew the vampire, but not the wolves. Parrus had learned her lesson about traveling alone.

The vampire, who walked in first, appeared to be in charge, as the wolves followed closely behind. Both wolves looked to be recent turns and perfect for manipulation.

"You're not the only one who can plan a counter strategy," Parrus added.

Claude had been in some dangerous situations before, but sometimes your luck runs out. He had limited options and very little time to think.

"The big bad wolf doesn't look so tough now," Parrus said with a snicker.

Claude didn't waste another second before he burst into action. He sprinted forward and grabbed Ted from Parrus' control just as he kicked her, sending her into the glass cabinets. Claude picked up Ted and threw him right through the nearest plate-glass window and into the backyard.

Ted's unconscious body hit the dirt in a bloody heap and rolled awkwardly to a stop. The double-plated glass window was more than enough to knock Ted out cold and cut him to shreds as he went through it. If the window cut a major artery, he would bleed out in seconds.

Claude turned to face his assailants. He should have made a run for it, but it just wasn't Claude's way.

"That was a mistake," Parrus said, regaining her footing.

Parrus watched as her three escorts rushed Claude all at once. Claude made a good showing of it and almost prevailed, but in the end, they were too much. The vampire was behind Claude, with a vice-like choke around his neck as the two hulking wolves held his arms in a spread-eagle fashion. Parrus stepped in front of Claude, relishing the moment.

"You don't know how long I dreamt of this moment," Parrus said, not hiding her contempt.

"Shut up and get on with it," Claude said, refusing to give Parrus any gratification.

Parrus smiled and nodded.

"I guess begging was too much to ask, but no biggie. killing you will be just as satisfying."

Parrus looked up at the vampire choking Claude.

"You heard him brother, let's *get on with it*," she said with a sinister smile.

With no further discussion, the vampire started squeezing and pulling on Claude's head with everything he had. Claude was fighting with all his might, but he was losing consciousness. When that happened, it would be all over. As soon as he was out, his muscles would relax and that would be it.

Just as Claude was about to black out, he was hit, and hit hard. Claude found himself on the floor, now freed from his captures. The wolf that had held his right arm was just getting to his feet. Claude grabbed him and broke both his legs and an arm in seconds, leaving him temporarily helpless.

A new wolf had just entered the house and now stood next to Claude. His clothes were in tatters, covered in blood, and far too small for his frame.

Ted was no longer a paunchy, out-of-shape book nerd, and that's putting it in the mildest of terms. Though he was completely in the dark, instincts took over after the change, compelling him to help Claude, who had bitten him before his trip through the window.

Claude knew this was the only way to save his life and maybe even his own. Claude would later tell me it was only the second time in his long life that he turned a human, and by far his best choice.

Claude looked at Ted and then at the other wolf on his right.

"You take care of him," Claude said. "And I'll handle these two."

Claude directed his attention to Parrus and her brother with a look of pure seething fury. He was ready to unleash every ounce of bottled-up hatred he had for the entire Truzic family, and there was plenty of it.

Parrus sized up the situation within a fraction of a second and gave the word to run. The three of them fled out of sight, leaving the fourth on the ground at Claude's feet. Ted was about to give chase when Claude grabbed him and shook his head.

Ted stopped, shut the door, and went back to Claude's side.

Claude directed his attention to the wolf on the ground that had just straightened his limbs. He tried to regain his footing and escape, but Claude grabbed him by the hair. This wolf was going nowhere. Well, nowhere good.

72

Bili and Theo were at the store before it opened doing some paperwork.

"Why didn't you tell me?" Bili asked out of the blue.

"About?"

"Jack," she said succinctly.

Theo took a deep breath and let it out slowly.

"So, Parrus did know. That's troubling," he said, knowing it had to be her that told Bili. "What else did she tell you?"

"Bitch called me your pet," Bili said, before shifting back to what was really bothering her. "Didn't you think you could trust me?"

The tone in her voice and look on her face saddened Theo to his core.

"There is no one in the world I trust more," Theo began. "I thought I was protecting both of you by keeping this information to myself. I'm starting to think I've made a mess of things."

"When are you going to tell him?"

"Soon. I was hoping to get through this conflict first. He has a big enough target on his back already. If this information gets out in mass, which I'm guessing is a real possibility, it will only make it worse."

"Maybe Parrus was hoping to leverage this information against you."

"Possible."

Bili could tell why Theo was apprehensive, and she could see what he was thinking.

"He'll understand you know."

"But will he forgive, is another question."

"It's Jack, you know he will."

Before Theo could respond, his phone rang.

He spoke to Claude for no more than sixty seconds, which was a long conversation for Claude.

Bili could obviously hear both ends of the conversation clearly.

"That psychopath has a twin brother?"

"Yes. His name is Quintas, and he is just as bad, if not worse. The day she was turned, she turned him. They are, and have always been, two twisted peas in the same deluded pod."

"Should we tell Jack about his friend?" Bili asked.

"Let's wait till he gets home. He has plenty to deal with right now in England."

"Didn't sound like Claude was able to get much information."

"I think the enemy has been recruiting from halfway houses," Theo said. "The arbitrary *turnings* are worrisome."

"Who's the woman Claude mentioned?" Bili asked."A friend of his that agreed to help Jack and Deaglan. She's adept in the art of procurements, plus, the extra body couldn't hurt if things get complicated."

"Ah."

"Is there something you want to tell me?"

"No. Well... I kissed Jack. I know I shouldn't have, but I was curious."

"Does he know?"

"No."

Theo let it go, knowing Bili was maxed out on the personal questions for one day. He had always worried that her lack of connection with others would be detrimental in the long run.

"Let's get going, we have a few things to do."

73

eaglan said the restaurant we had a reservation at was a common retreat for the wealthy and sophisticated of our kind. He knew Tanzy wouldn't be happy about it, as she was familiar with the place. Though not totally prejudiced against non-wolves, she preferred the company of her own. Deaglan had filled me in on some information as to Tanzy's past. She had a tough upbringing, and though it was nothing like Bili's, it had left some scars and trust issues. She also had a few negative experiences with some unsavory vampires, which contributed to her general apprehension. I got the impression there was much more to the story, but we didn't have the time to get into it.

We had arrived at our destination, the Harbor House Restaurant, somewhat later than we had planned. They aptly named the place, as it was on the water in one of the most picturesque areas in England: Weymouth Harbor.

We didn't take any weapons, but we had something almost as good. The odor evaporator, which was invented by our late friend, Steve. It went on like sunscreen and lasted almost as long. You would have to be right on top of us to tell us apart from humans. An observant immortal could most likely spot us by sight, but they would need a good long look to do it in a dark restaurant.

"I hate this place," Tanzy said, shaking her head as she looked around at the clientele.

Deaglan smiled at me, taking pleasure in his correct assumption about Tanzy's comfort level.

The crowded restaurant consisted mostly of humans, with the odd pair of vampires scattered about. They were eating, or otherwise engaged, and hardly gave us a backward glance. They appeared comfortable in their surroundings, further indication that we had gone unnoticed. The loud clatter of dishes and conversation was fortuitous, as it made it easier for us to talk without being heard by others with our unique hearing abilities.

Though Deaglan was always smiling and looking for a laugh, he took his business seriously. He watched everyone in the place like a hawk. He took into consideration the smallest of details, such as ordering a Pale Ale, as opposed to his preferred drink. He told me that when playing a game of life and death cat and mouse, he who makes the least mistakes, lives. Knowing how old he was, I believed him.

Tanzy was in the middle of telling us the best places to eat, when Deaglan rapped his fingernail on the table twice. We stopped talking, and when I looked in the direction he was in, I noticed a small group that had just walked into the restaurant. They had to be our mark.

There were four of them altogether, and it was obvious they were of some importance. The staff, and clientele alike, seemed to treat them as if they were the royal family themselves; especially one in particular. She had a smoothness about her that made her stand out.

Deaglan had given me a brief background on the key player. She was very wealthy, and by all accounts, the oldest and most powerful vampire in Europe. She went nowhere without a security detail, and just getting an audience with her would be a challenge. Deaglan wouldn't tell me the details, but he said he had a sure-fire plan that was certain to get us in front of this woman.

The four of them, three females and one male, went straight to the back of the restaurant which I suspected was a VIP room of some sort. People like that do not eat among the regular folks. The look of disdain from Tanzy said it all. She loathed every aspect of their fancy existence. Once they were out of sight, Tanzy and I looked to Deaglan for instructions.

"Okay, you two go out the front door and move around to the right side of the building. There's a side door that goes directly to the room they just went in. If everything goes as planned, I will open it in less than five minutes," he said confidently.

"And if you don't?" Tanzy asked.

"I suggest you go straight to Heathrow and get out of the bloody country."

"I'm not on holiday, Deaglan, I live here," she said, trying to keep her voice down.

"Oh, then you just go home, and you," Deaglan said, looking over at me, "go to the airport."

Tanzy looked over at me, shaking her head in disbelief.

"Is he serious?" she said.

I just shrugged. I didn't know if he was serious or not, and with my abilities, it spoke volumes about Deaglan. It also made me wonder about a few other things I had been curious about. I was starting to doubt my abilities to read people.

Tanzy could only roll her eyes as Deaglan stood up and motioned for us to head outside. She looked at me to make sure I was going through with this seemingly half-assed plan. I gave a quick nod, and we were off.

We were just out of our seats when we were stopped, mere feet from our table. What we thought to be just other patrons of the restaurant were nothing of the sort. I knew they were immortals, but they played the part so well, I was sure they were just out for a bite to eat. Only five of them were standing, but I was certain they had backup within the room. They did this so discreetly, none of the humans in the room seemed to notice a thing.

"Bodicea would like to speak to you," the man said, looking at Deaglan.

"Great, I would like to speak to her as well. Wait here you two, I'll be right back."

"All of you," he added, directing his attention to Tanzy and me.

"Even better, I'd hate to be the only one killed tonight," Deaglan said.

Again, couldn't tell if he was joking, but the fact he was smiling eased the concern, at least a little. I couldn't help thinking this was oddly similar as to how we captured Parrus. Not a pleasant thought.

"Brilliant plan, Deaglan. Who helped you with it?" Tanzy said as we marched toward the back room.

I saw a smirk from one of our escorts.

It was sarcasm to rival Bili's, but I didn't have time to appreciate it, as I was thinking about all possible means of escape. They had all avenues covered and covered well. The person in charge was no amateur. I just hoped they were reasonable.

We walked into the banquet size dining area and only saw one dining table. There were several people eating at it, but what was more telling was the amount of security standing around the interior of the room. There were no less than two guards per door, and a few in between, spaced accordingly. There was an excessive amount of open space between the door and dinner table, which made little sense, but it was about to.

The one I believed to be Bodicea sat on the opposite side of the table, so she was facing us as we marched in. She locked eyes on me when we entered the room, noticing my unique peculiarities. The humming of conversation stopped the second the door closed behind us.

"Everyone, we have guests," she said.

The sophistication and confidence displayed by this person reminded me of a female Theo. She demanded respect, and she got it in droves.

Deaglan appeared overly calm considering the dynamics of the room. This was not a pleasant situation, and for the first time, I doubted Deaglan's abilities.

"Before we speak, I'm curious about a few things," Bodicea said, placing her hand on her chin, nodding to one of her associates.

Without missing a beat, Deaglan dug our hole a little deeper.

"Most lasses are," he said, giving Bodicea a wink and a nod.

I had a feeling that might have been a mistake, which was confirmed when I saw the look on Bodicea's face.

"Could you two take a few steps back," Bodicea said politely, looking at me and Tanzy.

I looked at Deaglan, who nodded. We stepped back against the wall, leaving Deaglan alone in the center of the room, in front of the table.

Her associate, who was sitting across from her, motioned to the two guards near the rear door. They snapped into action and approached Deaglan in a quick and aggressive manner. He didn't let them get too close before he responded. And what a response it was.

The two vampires that attacked Deaglan were fast, but Deaglan was faster. I had observed a few fights among both wolves and vampires, but I never saw anyone move like Deaglan. His combative arts were something to behold. I can only liken it to that of a kung-fu master in a cheesy TV movie. I know it sounds corny, but you really had to see it to appreciate it. There were no wasted movements, and his defensive and countering abilities were amazing. Theo said he was a good fighter, and that was why the enemy tried to hire him, but *good* was a gross understatement.

"Enough."

As soon as Bodicea spoke, the two guards picked themselves up from the floor and stepped back to their post. I heard the guards fix more than one broken bone as they did so.

"Jack, is it?" she said, waving me forward. She shooed Deaglan backward with a couple flicks of her fingers.

"Yes," I said, moving to the same spot Deaglan had been.

She looked at me more inquisitively than with hostility. She said nothing, but again looked to her subordinate across from her. He stood up, slowly and methodically, before he approached me. Not out of fear, as I could tell that wasn't the case. He was trying to psychologically intimidate me. He was the biggest vampire I had ever laid eyes on. He was every inch as big as Claude, and maybe even a little heavier.

He stood in front of me, sizing me up with a less than impressed look about him. I got the feeling he had heard of me, but I don't think I met his expectations. The smirk on his face said it all. I was beneath him in every sense of the word. He was a full head and a half taller, and as he looked down at me, I became angry.

Without a word, he grabbed me by the neck, with both massive hands, and squeezed with all his might. He raised me up in the air, making a show of his strength and dominance. I was struggling to breathe as I dangled a foot from the floor.

I could see the look on the other patrons' faces, and their snickers echoed throughout the room. Worse than that were the ones shaking their heads, feeling sorry for me. My body flushed hot, and I felt a surge of power.

I grabbed the arms of my attacker with all I had. I squeezed the smallest portion of his wrists, and when I did, I could feel the bone and tendons collapse in my grip. His hands became free from my neck, and I slowly lowered myself back to the ground until my feet were safely on the floor. His facial expression changed, as did everyone else's in the room. He couldn't believe what was happening to him and neither could his associates. The snickering stopped cold, and several of the guests were looking to Bodicea to stop it. She just smiled.

I let go of his wrists and grabbed the large vampire by the hair with one hand and the belt with the other. I picked him up over my head and slammed him down on the tile floor, shattering several squares of what had to be expensive Italian marble. I reached down to grab him again when I saw several guards produce and level large weapons at me.

"I think you've made your point. Let him go," she said.

I did just that and stepped back from the large beast, who scooted away from me on his elbows. The look of the other dinner guests suggested they didn't know who we were, as there were several audible gasps and nervous chatter. Bodicea, on the other hand, did not appear surprised in the least.

"I see the stories about the both of you have not been exaggerated. This puts things in a proper perspective, I think," Bodicea said in her refined English accent.

Tanzy, who had stood by quietly the entire time, walked out onto the floor where I was standing and stood next to me. She was tired of being ignored.

"And what perspective is that darling?" Tanzy said, copying Bodicea's English accent perfectly.

Though Tanzy lived in London, she did not have an accent. If I had to guess, she was American, and probably lived on the east coast most of her life.

Bodicea stood from the table and walked toward us. She made a small motion with her hand, and they ushered Deaglan next to Tanzy and me. She studied all of us for a few seconds before speaking.

"I was told you two were coming, I think that's obvious," she said, and then she looked at Tanzy. "Not you though, which is vexing, but irrelevant."

The comment was dismissive and condescending. I could hear Tanzy's teeth grind.

She continued.

"I was advised that the best course of action was to kill you immediately. Not doing so would be at my peril."

Deaglan and I looked at each other, obviously wondering the same thing.

"Why are we still alive?" Deaglan asked.

"Theodorus and I have not always seen eye to eye, but he is the most honorable being on this earth. He would never sanction an unsolicited attack on me, or any of my associates, without just cause. I know there is no such cause, so this has me questioning this unsolicited information."

Bodicea walked closer and stood directly in front of me. "Why would someone want you dead? Deaglan, I can
easily understand, but you..."

Deaglan smiled and shrugged.

"You got one chance. Why are you here?" Bodicea asked me.

Deaglan started to say something, but she silenced him quickly. Talk about pressure.

"To save you," I said calmly.

The fact that she knew I wasn't lying intrigued her greatly.

"Explain."

"Why do you think you were advised to kill us on sight without talking to us? I can only guess how you received this information, but something tells me it wasn't a face-to-face delivery. Ridiculous propaganda has been spreading throughout the States in the same manner," I said.

I was looking at Bodicea, but I spoke to everyone in that room.

I went on.

"I'm sure you're aware of the conflicts occurring around the globe. How does this benefit us? And if it doesn't benefit us, then it must benefit an individual. Who? Why?"

I left that last question hanging in the air for everyone to consider for themselves. I could see nodding and other smaller gestures among those in the room.

"Why indeed," Bodicea said.

"If Theo and Claude can be targeted for assassination, what makes you think you're safe?" I added.

Bodicea's look was serious, and I think she understood how dangerous a rogue individual could be, especially if they had money and power.

"Sit down and have dinner with us, all of you, please," she said, giving Tanzy a look that could've been considered apologetic in nature.

The mood among everyone changed in that moment, and the three of us sat. After a long night of eating and drinking, we learned several things about Bodicea, or Dee, as she insisted we call her. First, she was brilliant. Second, she didn't like anyone manipulating her. Lastly, she liked to drink. I think Deaglan may have fallen in love by the end of the night. The funny thing was his charm had no influence on her. She was indeed powerful.

Dee agreed to pool resources and information with Theo and Claude. She planned to have a secure dialogue with Theo as soon as possible. She was a businesswoman and a successful one. She didn't have time for this sort of meaningless nonsense, as she referred to it.

We ended up staying in London a few extra days, making as many connections as we could, letting them know what was going on. The trip was an overall success, but in the grand scheme of things, we still had work to do. The false propaganda campaign was larger than we thought. Even with Bodicea's help, it would be an uphill battle to stop this madness from spreading.

I also made a good friend in Tanzy, who was not only an excellent ambassador to the werewolves throughout Great Britain, she was fun. I enjoyed her sense of humor and got the impression she was open to a more, let's say, personal relationship. Had we had more time, who knows what would have happened. I was worried about my friends and looking forward to getting home. I was excited to share what we had learned on our trip. Little did I know, I was about to receive some interesting news myself.

74

Once we arrived back in the states, Deaglan told me he was going to track down an old friend of his. From what he told me, he sounded exactly like the ally we needed. He said to tell Theo that he was going to see the *wolf*. I had no idea what that meant, and the word "wolf" seemed overly generic, considering, but I did as he asked.

Theo picked me up from the airport, and I relayed Deaglan's message. Theo seemed to know who he was talking about and agreed it was an excellent idea, in theory. I got the impression he felt Deaglan was over-reaching somewhat. Theo was pleased with our success and optimistic about collaborating with Bodicea.

It was late when I got home, and all I wanted to do was take a shower and get a good night's sleep. When I got to my door, the first thing I saw was a note taped to it.

I grabbed the single sheet of paper and opened it.

If you haven't eaten, feel free to order something and bring it with you, I haven't eaten either. Third floor in case you forgot.

While away, I had thought about Bili a fair amount. You could say I missed her quite a bit. I wasn't sure as to my feelings about her, but we were far closer now, and I liked being around her.

I went inside, took a quick shower, and ordered a pizza from her favorite place. The food arrived shortly after I got dressed, and I walked up the one flight of stairs to the third floor.

I knocked on her door which was actually closed. She always had the door open when she was expecting company. I couldn't wait to ridicule her for not knowing I was coming.

It took a full minute, but Bili answered, wearing an oversized flannel shirt that went almost to her knees.

"About time," she said. "And if there are mushrooms on that pizza, I'll kick your ass back to London."

"Nope, just the usual Hawaiian Style that you and three other people in the world, outside of Hawaii, like. You're welcome," I said as I walked past her to set the pizza on her kitchen counter.

When I didn't get a response to my Hawaiian joke, I turned around and saw she was sitting on the couch. I could tell from her facial expression and her body language something was weighing on her.

I walked over and sat next to her.

"Okay, what is it?"

She stalled for another few seconds and then let it out.

"You're probably wondering why I kissed you that night, and strangely enough, I've been wondering that too. This is what I've come up with."

"I-"

"Let me finish," she snapped.

Her eyes said that what she was about to say was important to her. I kept quiet.

"You probably noticed that I don't have many friends. If you don't count Theo and Claude, you could argue I have none. There are a few reasons for this, but the most prominent is, I just don't like most people. Or they don't like me; whatever, semantics. But I like you."

Bili stopped talking when she said the last part and looked down at her hands.

"I like you too, Bili."

"Jack, I'm gay," she said bluntly. "Or lesbian, as the kids say today."

"Oh. Okay."

The fact that she was gay was not a problem. I was just confused about the situation as whole. She sensed it and continued.

"I have feelings for you, just not *those* kind. You are the first person I ever connected with, and I like spending time with you."

I could see tears forming in the corners of her eyes, and it saddened me.

"From your perspective this may seem ridiculous, or not a not a big deal, but to me it couldn't be more important. Do you understand?"

After what Theo had told me about her life, and ex-husband, it wasn't hard to see how she got to this point. No matter how much time had passed.

"Yeah, I think I do."

"Good," she said as she stood up. "let's eat."

She wiped her cheeks with her palms, walked to the kitchen, and grabbed some plates from the cabinet.

I walked up behind her, grabbed the plates from her hand, and set them back on the counter. She didn't resist. I stepped in closer, and without hesitation, I grabbed her into a soft, but firm, hug. She didn't move, arms still dangling at her side, for what seemed like minutes. As soon as she sensed I was going to release her, she brought her arms up and latched on tight. Her body shook as I held her, and her silent sobs broke my heart.

She must have had this bottled up for years, if not centuries. I felt a mixture of gratitude and empathy, but the overwhelming feeling was that of love. The love of a friend who had saved my life with no regard of her own. Few can say that when push came to shove, they were there till the end. Bili was, and I will never forget it.

She let go and grabbed her plate.

"You tell anyone about this, I'll set your Picasso on fire."

"Don't worry. Vault," I said, pointing to myself. "Hey, does this mean we can watch football together?"

She punched me. "Yes."

75

A knock on the door caused Jack to stop his story.

Sara became instantly aggravated.

"What now," Sara said under her breath.

Sara got up and walked to the door. When she opened it, she saw it was the intake nurse, Cheryl. She looked anxious.

"Sorry to interrupt, but there's a problem with Abigail."

Sara looked back at Jack.

"I'll be right back."

Sara quick-stepped it behind the nurse, who was already heading toward Abby's room.

When Sara went in, Abigail was flipping her bed over, completing the destruction of her room. There wasn't a lot in there, but what there was, she broke. She wasn't yelling, screaming, or even crying. She was silently and methodically tearing her room apart.

"Abby, settle down, please. Talk to me," the doctor said.

Abigail looked at Sara, brushed the hair out of her eyes, and then sat down right in the middle of the floor. Sara waved to the nurse, letting her know everything was okay and she could go back to her duties.

Sara plopped down next to Abby, not asking anything, or saying anything.

"What's the difference," Abby said. "Break some shit, don't break it; it doesn't really matter either way, does it?"

Sara had seen this behavior before, and it was not uncommon with such a case as Abigail's.

"If this was yesterday, I would have given you a very good textbook answer why it does matter. But today, I'm wondering that myself."

Abigail glanced over at Sara, seeing the distant look in her eyes. She appeared to notice a change in her doctor.

"Keep that up and you'll be rooming with me."

Sara turned, and as soon as they caught each other's eye, they both burst into laughter.

"You don't know how true that statement is, you really don't," Sara said, still smiling. "You feel like talking about any of this?"

"Nah. It will give me something to do. I haven't cleaned anything myself in ages. I can handle it."

Sara patted Abigail on the knee and got up.

"Hey Doc," Abby said, before Sara got to the door. "Thanks for everything, really."

Sara knew right then Abigail was going to be okay. It made her happy to see the changes for the better.

"I will start the paperwork. I think we could have you out of here in a few days. How does that sound to you?"

"Sounds good. I think I'm ready."

Sara gave her another nod and left the room. Before she took two steps, she ran into a strange man standing in the hallway. He was in a suit and looked to be a business executive or something.

"Can I help you?" Sara said curtly.

The man produced a small wallet, opened it up, and showed the doctor a badge and an ID that said Detective.

"Are you Doctor Richards?"

"Yes," Sara said, now a little confused.

"I'm Detective Manillo, from the State Police," he said. "Is there somewhere we can talk? In private?"

"Of course, follow me."

The officer followed, keeping a steady eye on the doctor.

"Sorry if I'm interrupting, but it's rather important," he said.

Sara opened her office door and shut it after the officer walked in.

"Have a seat, please," Sara said, gesturing to the guest chair.

The detective sat down and opened the folder he had with him. He leafed through a few pages before he found what he was looking for and placed it on top.

"What can I do for you," Sara asked as she sat as well.

"When was the last time you saw Spencer Kaufland?"

Sara immediately became nervous. Just having suspicions that Jack knew something about Spencer made her feel like she was hiding something. She also had to think about every legal obligation she may have regarding such a situation.

"It was yesterday, around midday, I think."

"Do you know where he is now?"

Sara sat back in her chair and crossed her arms in front of her.

"No, I don't."

"What did the two of you argue about yesterday?"

Sara could see right away where this was going, and it wasn't good. The detective had obviously spoken to other employees and decided that Sara might know something.

"It wasn't an argument. It was a disagreement regarding the treatment of my patient."

"What kind of disagreement?"

"He wanted to take over after I had already started treatment; breaking every protocol we have."

"And this upset you?"

"Of course."

Now, there was no doubt about it. These questions were not mundane, and Sara felt like a suspect.

"You argue about anything else?" the detective asked innocently.

Sara was a skilled interviewer and well-aware of the tactics taught to the police regarding interview and interrogation. She knew when a fishing expedition was taking place.

"No."

"Did you find it suspicious that Dr. Kaufland quit with no notice to the hospital?"

"If you knew Dr. Kaufland, it wouldn't surprise you."

The detective stopped writing and gave Sara his full attention.

"How so?"

"He was selfish. If it benefited him, he would have no problem leaving the staff short-handed."

"So, you don't know where he is?"

"I already told you, I don't know."

Sara was becoming less nervous and more agitated.

"What are you really asking me, Detective?"

Sara was no amateur at mind games and more than prepared to go down that road if needed.

"Just questions, that's all."

"Sounds more like accusations from here. Did something happen?"

"You could say that," he said, not tipping his hand. "So, you have no knowledge of Dr. Kaufland's whereabouts?"

"For the third time, no. If you tell me what happened, maybe I can help you."

Sara said this with genuine interest, hoping to get some information. She had questions herself, and any clues were welcome.

"It's an active investigation, and I'm not at liberty to discuss much. If you hear anything, anything at all, would you let me know right away?"

The detective handed Sara a business card that had his name and phone number on it.

"I will. Sorry I couldn't be more helpful."

"Would it be okay if I contacted you again, if I have further questions, that is?" he said with a soft smile.

Sara nodded, "Yeah, that would be fine."

She stood up, and the detective followed suit. He gave Sara a quick handshake and let himself out. Sara sat back down in her chair to think.

Why am I feeling guilty? I had nothing to do with Spencer leaving. I damn sure have no idea what happened to him. Like Jack said, he was here the entire time.

Sara shook it off and went back to Jack's room. She sat down and shuffled her pen and papers distractedly. Jack seemed to take notice.

"Don't worry, doctor. The police are flying blind and don't have a clue what happened to our friend."

This statement was disturbing and gave Sara pause.

"How-"

"I saw you two walk by. That was a cop if I ever saw one."

"Jack, listen to me. If I believe a patient of mine has anything to do with a crime, especially a serious one," Sara said, leaning forward to press the point of the last part. "I am bound, by law, to report it to the police."

"I know. I told you I had nothing to do with it, and I didn't. That's all you need to know."

Sara thought for a moment and decided to let the matter drop. She was eager to get back to Jack's story. She would cross the Spencer bridge later if she had to.

76

So, the night at Bili's ended on a positive note, and I felt much better about our relationship. I was glad that she was comfortable enough with me to have an honest discussion about herself and her feelings.

The next day, we were back at the office preparing for a large shipment of Egyptian artifacts from Cairo. We had to clear a large portion of floor for its arrival, which isn't as simple as piling things on top of one another. When you're dealing with very expensive pieces of art, you must be meticulous and organized.

I knew the shipment was due to arrive soon, so I unlocked the rear door and started to open it. As soon as the door cracked, a strong and unmistakable smell sent me into immediate defense mode. I slammed the door shut and hit all the locks.

The sudden movement on my part caused Bili to react, move into a better position near the door, and prepare to fight. I moved to the other side, waiting for the enemy to make their move. With the newly constructed doors, it would be a difficult task to gain entry, even for several large wolves.

I was about to run to the front and bolt the door when we heard a casual knock. Something a wolf with ill intentions would probably never do. The hair on my neck settled as well, especially when I saw Bili's face, which showed signs of recognition.

Bili stood casually, and while looking at me sympathetically, she unbolted the door and swung it open. What I saw before me left me speechless. I barely recognized him.

"Can I come in?" he said.

Bili gave me a soft smile and tilted her head toward the loft.

"I'll take care of the order when it gets here," she said.

"Thanks."

I gave my friend a wave inside.

"Get in here," I said, opening the door further to accommodate his size. This was a story I was most eager to hear. I couldn't imagine the scenario that led to this, and how, or why, I hadn't heard about it.

As Ted entered, I picked up numerous clues from his face and body language. Now I knew how he must have felt the first time he saw me in my new state. It really is unusual to see someone you know very well instantly changed. Though I could tell this was my friend, the changes were far more drastic than mine. It was the first time I was witness to a change from human to wolf and didn't know if Ted's was the norm.

I took Ted into the loft apartment, so we could have some privacy. I motioned for him to have a seat in my favorite leather chair which I had already received permission from Theo to take back to my new place. As soon as he sat, I immediately regretted it, because the wood screamed for mercy as his weight rested on it.

"Sorry, pal. You gotta get up. If you break my favorite chair, I won't be able to go on in this world," I said as I gave him the universal sign of wiggling fingers upward in quick succession.

I said it jokingly, but I really loved that chair. He was gracious about it, got up, and switched to the ottoman on the other side. The ottoman wasn't fairing any better, but I didn't care if he shattered that or not. I sensed some pride in his smile that his muscular frame was an issue. Something I'm sure he'd never thought would be a problem. It was bizarre seeing my friend like this. His entire demeanor and the way he carried himself had changed drastically.

"Seeing your new look, and the fact you're not dead, I'm guessing you met my friend, Claude?"

Ted nodded casually.

"I did. Right after I met your friend Ceana, excuse me, I mean, Parrus," Ted said, holding up his index finger to make a point. "For the record, she let herself in, and I didn't have time to call."

That forced a smile and a stifled laugh as I thought about the instructions I gave him. I was glad to see his sense of humor was still intact because he was going to need it.

"Now do you see why I was trying to keep my distance?"

"Well, maybe if you would've mentioned that you were part of an ongoing war consisting of vampires and werewolves, I might not have talked Ben into coming here."

"Hindsight is a bitch, isn't it?"

"True, but I think Parrus has hindsight by a landslide."

I laughed and nodded. "I'm sure she does."

It felt good to banter back and forth with my friend. I had missed him terribly.

"Where is Claude now?" I asked.

"He's meeting Theodorus, which has to be the coolest name ever, by the way."

"Isn't it though?" Then I changed the subject as my curiosity was killing me. "Okay, let's hear it. Leave nothing out."

Ted went on to tell me everything that happened and how it felt when he awoke on the lawn after being bitten. I was curious to hear the details, comparing the similarities and differences to my own experience. I was surprised at the amount of differences, as I assumed most turns would be the same for wolves and vampires alike. I was wrong.

"I helped Claude with a few other odd jobs, if you know what I mean, and then he told me to see you when you got back. I guess he figured you would be the best person to help me get acclimated. I heard you had an interesting trip abroad as well."

"I did. You would have loved it. The history alone was amazing."

I filled him in on the highlights of the trip and then went on to give him as much information as I could regarding his new world. He listened intently for over two hours. We had a few laughs as well as a few somber moments when I told him about the tragedies we had endured as a group. I also gave him the same advice I received about seeing and/or talking to friends and family. I don't think I had to press the issue, considering how drastic his changes were.

I would find out later that not all changes were as significant as Ted's. Apparently, it makes a substantial difference if turned by an elder. That goes for both groups.

After our talk, I gave Ted the keys to my place and sent him there to hang out until I got off work. I also made him take my chair with strict orders to stay off it.

It was the next day that Theo gave Ted an accounting position with the company. There was space in the warehouse that became Ted's new office. He fit into our little group seamlessly, both professionally and personally. He had made some suggestions to Theo regarding overseas transactions that ended up saving the company a large sum of capital. Theo promptly rewarded Ted with a significant bonus. A new Mercedes SUV.

If not for this damn war, and the problems surrounding it, everything would have been perfect. Things were not perfect though, and about to get worse.

77

As soon as Deaglan turned onto Fulton Street, the enormous building came into view. The magnificent structure looked like it should be in Washington, D.C., not Atlanta. Deaglan had never been there before, but he was one of a very few that knew the location of this individual. It had been centuries since he had spoken to him directly, and he wasn't sure what kind of reception he was going to get. If he hadn't been a relative of this person, he wouldn't be privileged to his whereabouts.

Wolfgang Gregorn was not your typical librarian, and that was the understatement of all understatements. He kept a low profile, and few of either clan were familiar with him. That was not by accident, and Wolfgang took careful steps to keep it that way. He was not overly friendly, or good with others of any species, which is why he preferred the company of his books. Wolfgang had published several books himself, under different pseudonyms, and many of them had become best sellers. He lived off the royalties, which was more than enough for a lavish lifestyle if he chose it, but he preferred to live simply.

Deaglan had walked down several aisles before he saw, and smelled, who he was looking for.

"Oi! What would happen if I shook this?" Deaglan said as he grabbed the bottom of the ladder Wolfgang was standing on stocking books on the upper shelves.

"I imagine I would fall, you Irish dolt," Wolfgang said without even looking down. Apparently, Deaglan's voice and accent were a dead giveaway.

"Get your arse down here before I start randomly creasing the pages of your books."

Wolfgang shelved the last book diligently and then made his way down the ladder as if he was getting paid by the hour to do so.

"For heaven's sake. If your bloody name wasn't ironic enough, you move like an obese mongrel with two prosthetic legs."

Wolfgang continued his descent, making no attempt to hurry for Deaglan's sake.

"Everyone is always in such a damn hurry. Of all the beings on this planet, why do the bulk of us feel the need to rush all the damn time? How's that for irony?" he said when he reached the bottom.

"That is an excellent question, but not one of the more important ones at this time."

Deaglan purposely left the statement open, gauging Wolfgang.

"You referring to this business with the supposed anomaly?"

"Not supposed. I've met the lad," Deaglan said seriously.

"Have you now?" Wolfgang said, looking at Deaglan with a little more interest.

"He's as green as a Galway pasture, but he's a terrific young man with a kind heart. There is no telling what this lad will be capable of if he isn't killed first."

Wolfgang sauntered over to a nearby table and sat down gingerly. If you didn't know better, you would think he was suffering from some degenerative bone or muscle disorder. He brushed the hair from his eyes and adjusted the glasses he was wearing, presumably to look the part.

"Then the whispers of war are true as well?"

"Aye. There has been trouble on both sides of the pond, and South America is seeing its share of problems as well. The conflicts are gathering steam, and it won't be long until it's unstoppable."

"Is this kid really worth it? Sounds to me if he's sacrificed, this war ends. Wouldn't that be the expedient thing to do?"

"And if it were Jane, or Scotty?"

Wolfgang's eyes narrowed. He was stung by Deaglan's comment and made no attempt to hide his displeasure.

"Don't."

It hurt Deaglan to bring up the dead, especially since he knew what had happened to them, but he needed to make this personal for Wolfgang. His participation could be crucial.

"I miss my sister and nephew too, mate, but this is a good kid. If you met him, you would've never asked that question."

"Is it true Theodorus and Claude killed Rieger and his men?" Wolfgang asked, changing the topic.

"Come now. You know Theo better than that."

"Do I?"

"Yes. Everything being spread is propaganda, bullshit." Deaglan said. "You're the smartest of all of us. What do you think will happen if stories like that keep rearing their ugly bloody head?"

Wolfgang was thinking, not really paying attention to Deaglan anymore. It was as if he was working out multiple math problems in his head simultaneously.

"What do you want from me, Deaglan?" he finally said, cutting to the chase.

"I want you to figure this shit out. Who is doing this and why? You guessed it has something to do with the kid, and you're probably right, but my gut tells me there is more. I figure you've already worked out a few probabilities just since we started talking. I know you like it here in your safe little corner of the world where nothing bad happens," Deaglan said, raising his hands and looking around the beautiful library, "but how long do you think it will be before someone comes looking for you?"

Wolfgang shook his head in frustration. He wasn't happy, but his options were few. Wolfgang wrote something on a piece of paper and handed it to Deaglan.

"Have Theodorus send everything, and I mean everything, to this email. It's secure, so make sure he doesn't use his home computer, or one remotely connected to him."

"You got it. Anything else?"

"Yes. Please do not come back here again."

Deaglan tipped his newly purchased Atlanta FC cap in pure Deaglan fashion and left without further discussion. Once he convinced Wolfgang of the truth, which was easy, the rest would take care of itself.

If anyone could crack this mystery, it just might be the most introverted vampire that ever lived. Deaglan was sure Wolfgang would find something, and it wasn't long before he did just that. The first thing he uncovered was not only shocking, but equally disturbing.

78

got a text message from Theo that said Claude would be picking me up shortly and taking me to meet someone. Being with Claude was unpredictable, so I wanted to have something on that was a little more durable. I was both nervous, and intrigued, at what this was about.

I was glad to see Claude didn't have his motorcycle when he arrived. That would have been awkward and uncomfortable. He was driving an older pickup. The kind with no back seat, just one large bench made for two or three people. In Claude's case, the two of us were pushing the limits of said bench.

Claude drove in silence for most of the trip, which was the norm for him in any situation.

"I wanted to thank you for what you did for my friend," I said. "He's like a brother to me."

In typical Claude fashion, he nodded once in acknowledgment.

It really was fortuitous that Claude was even there. After Ted and Ben came to see me at the gallery, we figured there was a chance they could become targets. With our limited resources and time, we tried to keep an eye on them when we could, but it was sporadic at best. Claude, being the best at calculating odds and probabilities, picked the right place and time. However, his misjudgment in numbers nearly cost him his life.

Claude pulled into Theo's driveway and right into the garage.

"There are reasons for everything young man. Some reasons just take longer to understand. Someone is inside waiting for you," he said, pointing in the direction of the inside garage door with his head and eyes.

I just nodded in confirmation, got out, and proceeded inside. The scent trail led upstairs and that's where I went. As I reached the top step, I saw only one room with an open door. I instinctively walked directly to that room, even though part of me was hesitant to do so. I knew Claude would never send me into any sort of danger, but I approached the room like it was plagued. As I crested the opening, I saw a woman standing by the window. I couldn't believe my eyes, thinking I was surely looking at a ghost.

I lunged forward and grabbed her in a tight hug, hoping my arms didn't go through her like an apparition. When I felt she was indeed flesh and blood, my eyes filled with tears of joy. I pulled back, holding her at arms-length, so I could see her face.

"My, what a handsome young man you turned out to be. Your mother would be so proud of you," she said.

"How... why?"

I wasn't exactly sure what I meant by those two words, but Helen seemed to understand. She smiled kindly as she stared into my eyes. The thick border around her eyes caught my attention right away, as well as her overall being.

Vampire.

Other than the eyes, and a different hair style, she looked the same as I remembered her. She did not seem near as old, or old at all, now that I was older myself. When you are a preteen, anyone over twenty seems ancient.

"My, where to start," she said. "I guess I should start with the fact that I'm not your mother's friend."

When she saw the confused look on my face, she explained.

"I'm a proud aunt to an extraordinary young man," she said, placing her hand on the side of my face.

I didn't have to be a vampire to know she was telling me the truth. I felt it to my bones. I think I even sensed it when I was younger, as she had always felt like family.

"What happened?" I asked.

I knew I was being vague, but I wanted to know everything that had happened since she left.

"This will take some explaining, so bear with me," she said as she sat on the edge of the bed, patting the seat next to her. I sat. "Your mother was always the most adventurous person I ever knew. Even at a young age, she wasn't scared of new experiences. She also knew she wanted to move to the United States since she was very young. When our mother and father died, she applied for, and was granted, a Foreign Exchange Student visa. She fell in love with America and never left. She obtained her citizenship after completing college, and that's when two things happened simultaneously that changed the course of her life."

I was dying of curiosity as she continued.

"She met your father, and not long after that, she got hired at an art and antique shop in Detroit. You can guess who owned it."

"I can. What about my dad? Who was he? Mom never spoke about him, ever. Well, I take that back. We had dinner together the night she was killed, and one of the last things she said was a reference to my real father. We were supposed to talk about it the next day, but we never got to finish our conversation."

"So, you don't know anything?" she said, shifting her position on the bed.

The look on her face spoke a thousand words. I could tell this made her instantly uncomfortable.

"Nothing. Do you know what happened to him?"

"I do, but I don't think I should be the one to talk to you about it. Theo has the most information regarding him, and I'm sure he would be happy to fill you in if you asked. I'm sorry, Jack, but I hope you understand."

I knew she was telling the truth, so I didn't press the point. I was curious how Theo knew my father and why he never brought him up.

"It's okay. Please, go on."

"Your mom worked for Theo for several years, and during that time she became pregnant with you. Right before she gave birth, she quit working there, and never went back. Knowing Theo as you do now, you won't be surprised to know that he gave her a nice retirement package; what she would allow him anyway, and your mom moved on. The rest you know, it was just you and her until I could move to America."

"Why did you leave?" I asked, not able to conceive any possible answer to that question on my own.

"I had every intention of returning to Michigan after my visit, but something happened while I was gone. Patricia told me I absolutely could not come back. She apologized profusely but wouldn't tell me why. She just said it wasn't safe for me. The only other thing she said was if anything ever happened to her, I should contact a person named Theodorus. She provided his contact information and told me to write it down in a safe place and hold on to it for dear life. She also made it clear we shouldn't have any contact with each other for the foreseeable future."

This information was astounding, and even though I had a million questions, I kept quiet.

"I did make it back to America, although I never told Patricia, and ended up in New York. It was hard at first, but I started a life of my own. It was several years later when I heard about what happened to my baby sister. I was crushed and furious because I felt robbed of several good years with you and her. The absence of any closure as to why she was killed made it worse."

I nodded as she spoke, knowing exactly how she must have felt.

"It was a few months after her death that I remembered what she had told me. I had to dig up my old phone book to find Theo's number. Even when I did, there was a moment when I thought about not calling him. If I knew then what I know now, I don't know if I would have made that call. It was after that conversation that I was forced to make some of the hardest decisions of my life, causing me the greatest pain and regret."

Helen looked down as soon as she said that last sentence, and when she looked back up, tears were streaming at a steady rate.

"It was less than a year later when I experienced the worst day of my life."

"What happened?" I asked, hanging on every word.

"I had taken my daughter to the zoo, and it was one of the best days of my life, until it became the worst."

79

"What did you say?" Sara asked, sitting up in her chair.

Jack's last sentence caused Sara's back to stiffen as if touched by electricity. He not only had her attention, but he had tapped into an emotional powder keg.

"She had taken her daughter to the zoo," Jack said simply.

"Who took her daughter to the zoo?" Sara asked, raising her voice.

"I promised you answers," Jack said. "I also told you that some of it may be hard to hear."

Sara shook her head, not believing what she was sure to hear.

Jack leaned in toward the doctor ever so slightly.

"I told you that my story was true, and it is, except for one small lie. My aunt's name is not Helen, it's Clara."

Sara's eyes were fixated on the floor as she started shaking her head.

"I don't know how you know these things, but you cannot know my mother. You can't," she snapped, now looking at Jack.

Jack took a deep breath and gave Sara a consoling look.

"But I do."

"No," Sara said, as if it was a fact. She stared Jack in the eyes as anger built up inside her.

"If you are playing me for a fool or if this is some sick game..."

Sara stood quickly, sending the chair flying backwards.

"It's not," Jack said calmly, leaning back now that he had to look up at the doctor.

Sara pointed her finger straight at Jack's face.

"I'm not like you, I can't tell if you're being truthful just by looking at you. Are you fucking lying to me?!"

Jack sat still, saying nothing. He just shook his head gently.

"I don't believe you," Sara said, now pacing back and forth. "I can't."

"Why?"

"Because, if I say I believe this, I'm essentially saying that I believe everything else you've said. Since I don't believe you're a vampire, and I don't believe in werewolves, how the hell can I believe anything you might tell me about my mother?"

"That's your analytical mind trying to override the rational. Your heart tells you what I'm saying is true. Am I right?"

"Nothing about any of this is rational, Jack."

"I guess that's for you to decide. We all have to make choices, do we not?"

"Here's a choice. Go straight to hell," Sara said as she turned around, kicked the chair out of her way, and headed for the door.

Sara slammed the door so loud it shook the walls. The stunned employees in the area were silent as Sara passed by and went to her office.

She shut her office door, sat in her big leather chair, and cried. All the emotions, pent up for over a decade, came bursting out. After a good ten minutes, she calmed herself and thought carefully about everything. She used all her training to separate emotions from facts. It's easier said than done when you are personally involved.

The knock on the door jarred Sara out of her thoughts.

"Come in," Sara said, wiping her eyes.

Nancy peeked inside.

"I know this is a bad time, but I have some…" Nancy started to say as she opened the door. Once she saw Sara's face, she started to close it again. "I'm sorry, honey, I'll come back."

"No, please, come in," Sara said, waving Nancy into the room.

"It's about Spencer," Nancy said, hesitantly taking the seat in front of the doctor.

"What did you find out?"

After the visit from the detective, this information became much more valuable.

"His home was a disaster; broken furniture, bullet holes in the walls, it looked like something out of the movies, I guess."

Sara sat still and listened but said nothing.

Nancy went on.

"The officer I spoke to said they called in the State Police to help with the investigation. I figure it required a little more expertise in the forensics department. You don't think Jack really knows anything about it, do you?"

The doctor didn't respond right away, lost in thought.

"Doctor?"

"Sorry," Sara said, blinking away her thoughts. "No, no, I'm sure he had nothing to do with it. Please, don't say anything to the police about what I told you, okay?"

"Of course not. I told them Spencer left suspiciously and without much warning. Knowing him, I bet he was into something illegal."

"Good. And you're probably right."

"Is there anything else I can help with, Doctor?"

"No, you've been a great help. Thanks for everything, really."

"I know you have been through a lot, dear, but I think good things happen to good people. You are good people," Nancy said.

This made Sara force a smile.

"Thank you."

Nancy went back to work, while Sara sat and tried to come up with the best course of action. The line between personal and professional was now blurred. She wanted to know what this man knew, regardless of the consequences. Sara tried to understand why she got so upset before Jack even told her what he knew about her mother. The answers to every question she ever had might be at her fingertips. The truth, if that's what was waiting for her, had to be dealt with.

Sara went back to Jack's room and sat down. Jack was still in his chair, sitting quietly. He didn't appear to hold the torrent against her.

"So, we're what? Cousins?" Sara said. It was more of an icebreaker than an actual question.

"We are. I know how this sounds, but if you can get past your skepticism and prejudices, you just might come to see things a little clearer."

"Okay, clear it up. Tell me what happened to my mother."

"You sure you don't want to take a break?"

Sara peered at Jack, fervently.

"Alright. Let's keep going."

80

Clara was waiting for you outside the solarium when she decided to walk to a drinking fountain which was about a hundred feet away. It was that one decision that might have saved both of your lives that day.

She got her drink, and when she stood up, she saw two men approaching her, and they didn't appear to be there for the animals. They walked straight past the solarium you were in, making their way directly toward Clara. Even though they were a good distance away, Clara knew she was in trouble. Everything about them fit what Theo had warned her about when they spoke.

She knew she couldn't lead them to her daughter, so she walked in the opposite direction, trying to appear as normal as possible. That she didn't openly panic says a lot about her strength and courage. She walked straight to the parking lot and made it to her car as calmly as she could. She watched and made sure they were still following her and not heading back toward her daughter. She backed up out of her parking spot and then made her way to the exit. When she saw them get into a vehicle, she sped up and hit the gas.

She immediately called Theo, which was made easier, as he insisted she put his number in her phone.

"I'm being followed by two large men. What do I do?" Clara said urgently.

"Is Sara with you?" Theo asked calmly.

"No!" Clara said as the tears filled her eyes. "I left her in the zoo trying to lead them away from her, but I can't leave her there, Theo, help me, please!"

"I will. Stay calm, and I will get you out of this. First thing, you cannot go back, if you do, your daughter will be in grave danger. Do you understand?"

"Yes."

"Where are you now, exactly?"

"I'm about to pull onto the I-95 service drive, approaching Marmion."

"Okay, that's good. I know right where you are. Get onto the freeway proper after the next light. Run the light if you must and then go fast, and I mean fast."

This was exactly what Clara did not want to hear. Her heart was breaking as she got onto the freeway, getting farther from her daughter.

"Do you see any vehicles driving erratically behind you? Keep looking in your rearview mirrors," Theo directed.

"No, nothing," Clara said, looking at all three mirrors in quick succession. When she didn't see anything, she thought maybe she had overreacted, leaving her daughter alone for no reason.

"Keep looking."

"Still nothing," she said, searching for anything unusual. "What if I made a terrible mistake and -- wait. Shit! There they are. They're in a black car weaving through traffic. It's catching up."

"You put that gas pedal to the floor. Now!"

Clara did as she was told, and before she knew it, she was doing over a hundred miles per hour.

"The East 175th exit is within the next mile. Get off the freeway and turn right."

"They're getting closer, Theo. It's definitely the same men from the zoo."

Clara was staying extraordinarily calm considering the situation, but she was still human and prone to simple mistakes.

"I got off the freeway."

"Did you turn right?"

"Shit, shit, shit! I went straight. Should I turn around?"

"No. Tell me the next major street you come too?"

Clara was doing her best to drive and look at street signs at the same time. Not an easy feat while being chased.

"Carter Road," she blurted out when she saw the long green sign.

Clara was watching behind her when the car appeared again. It was passing cars on the shoulder and even running others off the road. Their intent was blatant.

"They're gaining quickly, Theo. I don't think I'm going to make it."

"Yes, you are. Turn right on Carter and you give it everything it has. What kind of car are you in?"

"Blue Ford sport utility. I'm sorry, Theo, I should have listened to you. Tell Sara that I love her and I'm sorry."

Clara had the accelerator to the floor, but they were almost on her bumper now. They were close enough for her to see the ill intentions in their eyes. She was as good as dead, and she knew it.

"Focus, Clara!" Theo yelled. "Are they directly behind you?"

"Yes."

"Hit your breaks, now!" Theo yelled through the phone.

Clara did just that, and the black vehicle smashed into the rear of her Ford. The force of it caused Clara's head to whiplash and the car to shoot forward, but she maintained control.

"Now punch it!" Theo yelled into the phone.

Clara hit the accelerator again, which created a gap between the two vehicles, but not as much as Clara had hoped for.

"It didn't work. They're still behind me, Theo."

"Not for long."

Just as Theo said those words, Clara looked in the rearview mirror and saw a large van smash into the side of the black vehicle. The van hit the driver's door and sent the car flying onto its roof, skidding along the pavement. The van, which was heavily damaged, came to a stop, and the driver got out and took off running.

"Alright," Theo said. "Come to me. We need to talk."

"What about Sara?"

"I'm already taking steps to ensure her safety. She will be fine, trust me."

81

J ack stopped talking for a second and took a drink of water. When he didn't continue with the story, Sara became frustrated.

"That's it?" Sara asked.

"No, of course not."

"Are you going to tell me to be patient, because if you do, I just might stab you with my pen."

Jack was glad that Sara had regained her sense of humor, at least a little.

"I know it appears that I've been stringing you along, but trust me when I tell you, we are getting close to the end. You may want to consider the possibility that when we get there, things may change. You may change."

"Do you mean that literally, or is that for some dramatic effect?"

"Knowing just what you know now, what do you think?" Jack asked seriously. "I warned you of this before we started our conversation if you remember."

"How then?" Sara asked, more than a little puzzled.

"How, indeed."

"What happened to my mother after she met with Theo?" Sara pressed.

"I'm getting to that, but again, there is some context that needs to be established."

Sara was frustrated, but far less angry.

"What about my dad? If he didn't abandon me and my mom, I want to know what happened to him."

Sara was done with over-politeness. She wanted direct answers to direct questions.

"If I told you he was the very definition of a hero, would that be sufficient?"

"No."

Jack tightened his lips and gave the slightest shake of his head.

"Are you sure you want to hear this?" he said. "It's not a pleasant story."

"Tell me."

Her tone was of someone who was not going to be denied.

"Alright, but keep in mind what I'm about to tell you was unknown to Clara at the time. She didn't know what had happened until many years later. When she told you he left for another life, it was because she really didn't know what happened, or what to tell her daughter. No mother is perfect.

"You may not remember, because of your age, but your father, Don, used to take the train to and from Manhattan five days a week. He was a sergeant with the New York Police Department and worked in the narcotics unit. On this particular day when he was on his way home, he had a most unfortunate encounter.

"He had to take two different trains to get home, and when he got off the first train, he went up to the surface to get a gift for his daughter, A purple stuffed pony."

Sara put the back of her hand to her mouth, as this triggered a deep-seated memory. She remembered begging her father for this toy on several occasions.

"Are you sure you want me to continue?"

Sara didn't speak, just nodded, quickly. Jack relented and went on.

"What he didn't know was that the smell of his wife and daughter permeated his person. The smell was most unique, so unique in fact, it caught the attention of the wrong individuals."

"Who?" Sara asked.

"A female vampire and her evil twin brother."

"The same-"

"Yes. Your dad never made it to the second train. He took him to a nearby apartment and... interrogated him. I'm using that word to spare you the horrific details of what he went through," Jack said, hoping Sara wouldn't ask the question.

She did.

"He was tortured, wasn't he?" she asked.

"He was."

"Why?" Sara asked, almost in a whisper.

"If by fate, luck, or just a strange coincidence, he forgot his wallet at work. When they couldn't find his ID, they asked him several times where he lived and who he lived with. When he didn't tell them, he went through hell. All he knew was that these two deranged individuals meant his family harm. He would be damned if he was going to lead him to the two people he loved most in this world. Quintas went too far and killed your father before he gave up a single piece of useful information. Like I said, he was a true hero, and one of the bravest humans I had ever heard about. To endure what he did, for as long as he did, is nothing short of superhuman."

The tears dropped steadily as Jack stopped talking. Sara said nothing for a few minutes, and Jack let her collect herself. Sometimes a brief silence is more important than any words.

Sara had lived her entire life believing her father was a bastard who left her and her mom for purely selfish reasons. When the truth is the exact opposite, there will be a guilt that cuts like a razor.

"I'm sorry. I know as well as anyone that hearing the truth doesn't always give us the closure we hope for. Sometimes there's an emptiness that can never be filled."

Sara wiped her face with her shirt. The mascara stained her fresh dry-cleaned jacket, but she didn't care.

"Thank you for telling me. I still think it's better than not knowing," she said.

To give herself a break from the personal, Sara changed the topic completely.

"Do you know what happened to Spencer?"

Though it was a question, she worded with the confidence of someone who knew they were asking the right person.

"Yes," Jack said bluntly.

"So, you don't deny having something to do with his disappearance?"

"For the record, that's not what I said. Second, that son-of-a-bitch is evil to the core. You have no idea as to the extent of his treachery. Let's just leave it at that for now, we have more important things to discuss."

"Do we?"

"Unless you are content with the information you have and have no wish to see where this road ends."

Sara was all in now, consequences be damned. She was going to get every answer she could, come hell or high water.

"Please, go on."

"Clara went on to tell me the extraordinary circumstances of how she was turned, which was a direct result of trying to see her daughter. It was a miracle she lived, and you weren't compromised in the process. That's when she made the decision that it would be better if she didn't know where you were. If they ever captured her, she could never tell them anything, even if they hurt her. She entrusted Theo to make all the arrangements to get you and Emily off the grid as much as possible."

"Why didn't she get me later, when it was safe to do so?"

"The fact that the enemy knew her face, but not yours, meant you would always be at risk with her. It was an impossible choice to make, but her love for you made it easy. You would come first, always."

Sara nodded, again, fighting more tears. She waved her hand in a fashion to let Jack know to get back to the story.

82

The next day, there was a knock on my door before daybreak. It was a time when you assume there wouldn't be good news waiting for you on the other side.

I threw some clothes on, prepared for the worst, and answered the door. It was Theo, and he put my fears to rest right away.

"Let's go for a ride," he said.

Theo's car was parked in front of the building and still running. We got in and drove off.

"I thought it best if we talk in my car. I know there's no chance of any unwanted ears listening in. How's Clara?" he asked.

"Good. I still can't believe she's been alive this entire time."

"I want to apologize. It must seem like I'm keeping one secret after

another from you, and to a certain degree I am, but I hope you can understand my reasons."

I nodded. "I understand, really. Where are we going?"

"Nowhere in particular," Theo said. "I just think it's time we had a real
talk."

I swelled with anticipation, knowing that whatever he was going to say
was important. I was starting to see the method as to Theo's acclimation
process, as it pertained to me and my new world. He rushed nothing, and
though it could be frustrating at times, I knew he had my best interest in
mind.

"Tell me what's been on your mind," Theo said.

There was plenty, but one topic came to mind right away.

"When Bili turned me, I could tell that it caused her some emotional
anguish. She never said why."

I suspected the answer was a complicated one that would prompt more
questions. I was right on both accounts.

"Your skills in deduction and reasoning are well developed," Theo said
with an appreciative glance. "To answer your question, it's because of a
promise I made to your mother. A promise I wasn't able to keep."

"Promise?"

"Yes. I told Patricia that I would keep watch over you and do everything in my power to keep you from becoming like me."

"Why?"

"She was afraid that-"

"I would be damned to hell?" I finished.

"Something like that, yes."

That sounded like my mom. She had taken me to church most
Sundays, but I never thought she was overly religious, or a strict practi-
tioner of any singular faith.

"Patricia had some concerns that any rational mother would have,
regarding their only child. Since there is no suitable argument for such an
opinion, I could only concede her point, as I have always pondered the
same question myself. I guess time will tell, as with all things."

"Theo?" I said, hesitantly. "Why would my mom have that kind of
conversation with you?"

When Theo didn't answer, I looked over to see him peering into the
rearview mirror. His expression was troubling.

I checked the rearview mirror on the passenger door the best I could, using no overt body movements. I saw a large black four-door vehicle. It wasn't doing anything obvious, but there was something troubling about it.

"Send Claude a text. Tell him we have a tail, give him our location, speed, and that we are heading toward the pub. Make sure pub is in all caps." Theo said as he drove in the same casual manner that he had been.

I sent the text within seconds and then started formulating all possible options. I know Theo was doing the same. We drove silently and watched the vehicle follow us through several turns in succession. There was no doubt now, it was in casual pursuit.

After approximately eight minutes, Theo turned off the busier city road and onto a two-lane highway with far less traffic. The vehicle was still behind us, trying to maintain some distance, when Theo forced the issue by slowing down. The vehicle would have to either catch up and pass, or risk looking conspicuous. Both would be telling as to their intentions.

The black vehicle got closer just as I saw a single headlight closing in from behind the mysterious vehicle.

Claude.

Their car was much larger than the Cadillac we were in, and Claude was on his cycle. As I pondered how we were going to get the vehicle to pull over, or bring it to a stop at all, Claude made his move. He picked up speed on his cycle, stood up on the seat, and when he got close enough, he jumped onto the trunk. The amazing part of that stunt was how he stayed put when he landed. He punched holes in the rear window with each of his fists and grabbed two of the subjects in the back seat. It was one of the most amazing things I had ever witnessed in person. I would have given anything to see the faces of those in the car.

Claude was about to pull them from the car when I heard a loud gunshot. Claude flew backward and onto the cement highway.

Theo tried to sideswipe the car off the road, but it was too heavy, and we bounced off the vehicle like it was a brick wall. That's when they accelerated like they had just robbed a bank. We could have given chase, but we didn't know the extent of Claude's injuries or if he was still alive. We turned around and went to check on him.

Claude took a bullet to the chest, but luckily it wasn't a direct hit to the heart. He was fine within minutes and more than a little pissed.

There were a few cars that drove past during our little spectacle, and from the looks on their faces, I'm sure they didn't know what to make of it. If they reported what they saw, they would sound crazy. More times than not, when someone does witness the unbelievable, they keep it to themselves. No sane person wants to sound crazy.

We drove Claude back to his cycle. He was pleased to find it in one piece and still operational.

"I'm starting to get aggravated," Claude said.

"Were you able to see anything?" Theo asked.

"There were four of them and I only recognized one. They're still recruiting."

Before Theo could respond, his phone rang. As soon as he hit the accept button, I knew there was a problem.

"We're on the way."

No one missed a beat. Claude got on his motorcycle and was off before we got the car out of park.

Clara had seen someone crossing Theo's backyard by sheer luck. She knew that whoever it was, they weren't there to sell cookies. Clara kept the line open as we drove so we would know what was happening in real time. She scrambled from window to window, trying to see how many there were. That's when we heard a loud and disturbing noise. There was an explosion.

"They're in the house and coming for me. I'm gonna have to fight," Clara said.

"No! Get to the basement Clara, I have a safe room. Get in there and hit the red button! Claude will be there soon," Theo yelled as he gave the Cadillac everything it had.

There were muffled sounds like she was running and then we heard several intruders in the home. The phone must have dropped, as the sounds of confrontation echoed throughout the car. She didn't make it to the basement.

"Clara!"

The deafening sound of the call going dead caused my heart to skip. My gut was on fire and fury flushed over me. I was ready for a fight and prayed that they were still in the house when we got there.

It only took six minutes to get to Theo's house but when we arrived, no one was in sight. I couldn't believe the carnage left behind either. The entire front door area was demolished, leaving a gaping hole big enough to drive a small car through.

We ran inside, and the first thing I saw was the phone on the stairs in several pieces. There was damage to the walls in the same area, suggesting the fight took place in that spot.

Just as we were getting a grip on what happened, Claude entered the house. He arrived first and did a lap around the perimeter, trying to pick up any scent in case they left on foot. They didn't. When he saw what we saw, he left in a rush. Theo told me that if anyone could find her, it would be Claude. We would not be a help to him now and should focus on other aspects.

"The car was a ruse," Theo said confidently.

It made perfect sense. It was just enough to keep us occupied and out of the way while they executed their assault on the house.

"How did they know Clara was here? And why would they go through all this trouble to get her?" I asked.

"The first part is the most perplexing, but the second is easy. They want her for the same reason they want you. Come on, let's get back to the city. I don't like Bili being there alone with everything that's going on."

We took one of Theo's other cars and made our way back to Ann Arbor. I was hoping for the answer to my previously unanswered question, but now we had other things to worry about. I also sensed that he didn't really want to go into it now, so I held my tongue.

When we got back, Theo asked me to stay around the building and close to Bili, just in case. A second attack so close to the last would be unlikely, but nothing had been completely predictable.

I hardly slept that night thinking the worst regarding Clara. I could only hope they wanted to keep her alive, but even if they did, for how long? The ante just went up.

83

One afternoon, I was walking back from picking up lunch when I got a call from Deaglan. I told him I was only three blocks away and gave him the intersection. He said he would be there in thirty seconds. He was.

He pulled up to the curb driving an older model, and very rusty, conversion van. The seventies would have loved this van.

"Get in, and not a word about this piece of shit vehicle, understand?"

Something was happening, and the look on Deaglan's face was an even mixture of what I can only describe as excitement, hope, and oh shit. Bili was in the passenger seat, and I jumped on the rear bench.

"Where are we going, and who are we meeting?" I asked.

I watched Deaglan smirk in the rearview mirror.

"You aren't going to believe it lad," Deaglan said.

Theo had the burned cabin rebuilt as a memorial for his friends. It was much nicer and extremely secure with sensors and cameras everywhere.

We got there just before dusk, and I saw several cars parked haphazardly around the grounds.

"Well, the bloody place isn't on fire, so that's a good start," Deaglan said.

Bili and I looked at each other at the same time with the same expression. Normally such a comment would have been offensive as hell, especially to Bili and me, who saw it firsthand. But if I was being honest with myself, I was thinking the same exact thing, as was Bili.

"I guess your little speech in London worked," Deaglan said. "The entire royal bleedin' family showed up and a few others to boot."

"Does Theo need us to keep watch on the exterior while the meeting is going on?" I asked Bili.

"No. Theo has that covered. Plus, I think a few are waiting to see you. I know one is for sure," she said, sharing a quick look with Deaglan.

We entered the cabin to find at least fifteen individuals engaged in several conversations simultaneously, many of them heated in their fervor. I saw Ted in the back, sitting next to a familiar face. Tanzy. She smiled when we caught eyes.

"Oh, look. The king of America finally showed up," a sarcastic voice said from across the room.

I turned around and saw my friend from England. He was obviously still holding a grudge.

That little comment started more arguments, and some of them were close to physical altercations. Claude and the sarcastic vampire were inching closer to one another as the exchanges became harsher. This was a ticking time bomb.

Theo hammered his fist down on the table, sending splintered pieces into the air. He wanted everyone's attention. He got it.

"We are headed for genocide!" Theo said, looking down at the table, before raising his stare to those around him. He lowered his voice, making sure it would remain quiet as he continued. "I don't know if any of you have been keeping up with current events, but there have been well over three hundred deaths between the clans. Those are just the ones we are aware of. Lies have spread like the plague throughout America and Europe, and I challenge anyone here to tell me who's behind it."

Theo looked behind him, gesturing to his big friend.

"Claude and I have been hunting down one lead after another, and we still have no solid answers."

"Shame you let Parrus go," the big vampire said, directing his look from Theo to Claude. "I'm sure she would have had a few answers."

Claude was at his wit's end.

"Say one more word," Claude said calmly.

I don't know what would have happened if he had, but luckily Bodicea stood up and stepped between them before he uttered that word.

"What Liam is trying to say," Bodicea began, giving the big vampire a gentle nudge backward with the back of her hand. "Is that we all know if the Truzic twins are involved, it's a problem we all share. Theo is right, not only is the death toll rising, but the risks to all of us cannot be ignored."

Bodicea turned her attention to Theo.

"You have our full cooperation and help until the matter is resolved."

"Thank you," Theo said. "If anyone does not feel comfortable moving forward with us, I understand, but you must leave now."

Everyone looked around the room gauging the response, verbal or otherwise. I took the silence as a positive.

"Good. We believe that whoever is behind this campaign is in the States and probably not far from here. The logistics have too many moving parts to suggest otherwise."

"What do we do about it?" Tanzy asked.

Claude walked up to the table next to Theo and addressed the group.

"What we do about it," Claude began, making eye contact with his friend Tanzy, "is we bridge the informational gap."

"Okay, I'm not exactly sure what that means, but how do we do that?" said an unfamiliar voice from the back of the room.

"We shake every bloody tree we find until that one piece of fruit falls," Deaglan said, adding to the conversation.

"And when it does, we make a well-coordinated effort to eliminate the problem," Theo said as he looked over the group. "We don't know if this is one person, or several working in concert, but whoever is involved will pay a toll. Some very good people died on this very spot trying to help."

Theo was saddened at the thought of his friends, and his face showed it.

"Some were friends of mine also," Bodicea added as she walked next to Theo and put her hand on his shoulder. "Andrew and Allison were like family."

Theo nodded absently.

"We split up in groups, run down every small piece of information we currently have, and then report anything we find to the others. This is all we have to go on right now, but it's something," Claude said as he handed out several pieces of paper.

The meeting dissolved, and most left right after getting their instructions.

Bili was still standing next to me when Tanzy approached and gave me a very welcoming hug. There was a subtleness in the way her body touched mine that spoke to me. The gentle dragging of her fingers on my back, to the way her cheek grazed mine as she pulled away. On top of that, she smelled wonderful. There was something there.

"I didn't know you were a king," Tanzy said, teasing me.

Bili bumped my shoulder and gave me a knowing smirk before walking away. She went to Claude and Theo, who were still talking to Bodicea.

"I see you met my friend."

"I did indeed. Always nice to meet a new wolf, especially when they're so cute," Tanzy said, referring to Ted.

I looked at Ted, who smiled. No red ears, no flushed face, and no sign of uncomfortableness. How far we've come.

"She saw how out of place I looked and made me sit with her," Ted said.

"Thanks. That was nice."

Tanzy turned to greet Deaglan, who had just walked up next to me.

"Hello, Deaglan, how was the drive?" Tanzy asked with a smirk.

"Funny," Deaglan said, as he looked at me. "Our friend here thought it was hilarious when she dropped off that hunk of rust for me to drive. If I was capable of getting tetanus, I'm sure I would have."

I looked at Tanzy with a conspiratorial look.

"It was kinda funny."

"No tracker on that van, darling," Tanzy said, using her fake English accent.

"We have to be going, and I'll be driving you to your new lodgings, in said van," Deaglan said. "So, say goodnight. You too Teddy boy, Jack has other business."

"Goodnight. See you later?" Tanzy said.

I gave a quick nod and a smile, which she returned.

The tingle was back.

Deaglan drove Tanzy and Ted back to Ann Arbor, and Bili and I stayed. Theo and Claude wanted to go over a few things in private after everyone else left. Though we appreciated our new allies, trust was something that needed to be earned. Especially when it came to certain information.

84

A few days had gone by and thankfully rather uneventful. If Clara hadn't been in the hands of the enemy, which was very worrisome, life would have almost seemed normal. There was still the odd lead here and there, but we had much more down time.

Ted had sold his house and bought a condo in the same building as Bili and me. I think Theo may have suggested it would make him feel better having all three of us in close proximity. The fact that Theo was paying Ted a handsome wage for his accounting skills also could have played a role.

One afternoon, I got a call from Ted, who said Bili had just invited him to lunch, and if I didn't know, I was going also.

We walked to the restaurant, which was really a bar with good food.

We were able to get a table, which was fortunate because I don't think Ted would have fit into one of their booths.

Bili wasted no time before she introduced Ted to the fine art of sarcasm. Though I could tell she was breaking him in slowly, I don't think he was used to this kind of subtle verbal assault.

"You know, I think I am going to find Ben and turn him as quickly as possible to give you someone to talk to," Ted said, trying to look as genuine as possible.

"I wish you were serious," she said. "He might be the only one of you three with the proper wit."

I thought Bili was going to bombard Ted with more abuse, but instead she looked at me and started telling me a story as if we were alone.

"I had just been turned, as Theo told you, but what he didn't tell you, was that he left right after. Theo told me I could travel with him, and if I chose that option, he would wait for me in the next town for three days. If I chose to go on my own, I was free to do that as well. He left me enough gold coins to last me an entire year and told me to take some time and think about it, carefully.

"I did just that and stayed put for the time being. Landell had been gone overnight and had no idea that I had even left the room. When he arrived back at the Inn and found me missing, he was furious. He raised hell with the owner of the establishment, or anyone he suspected of helping me. He went to the pub next door to get drunk and that's where he inadvertently found me. I was sitting at a table having a glass of wine and talking to a nice young man, who was a local farmer. Landell was confused, as I was nicely dressed, didn't have a mark on me, and showed no signs of fearing him. He intimidated the farmer into leaving by threatening to whip him and burn his land. The farmer left in a hurry, and then he turned his attention to me. I could see the crazy in his eyes, and for some reason I couldn't understand at the time, it made me extremely happy. Being happy, I smiled a wonderfully pleasant grin and asked a question. "How are you, dear?"

I could picture this in my head perfectly. I just wish this was in the age of video surveillance. Ted kept quiet as well, knowing he was hearing a personal tale.

"He attempted to regain control, as he always did, by grabbing my arm above the elbow and squeezing as hard as he could. It must have felt different than usual because he switched his grip to my wrist. His face was a mix of wrath and confusion when he saw I wasn't in any pain. I was able to change his expression again when I grabbed *his* arm and squeezed. I heard the bone snap in my hand. I had such a feeling of euphoria, I almost felt guilty. He started shaking in fear, like any coward, but not near as much as when I grabbed him by the hair and dragged him out of the pub like a helpless child. The other men in the pub laughed at him as I did this, which added to my pleasure."

A grin spread across my face as she spoke. I was loving every word.

"I dragged him straight to our room, where I had a few things in place for just such an occasion. That's pretty much it."

"What?" I said. "Come on, that was hardly a proper ending to a great story."

"Let's just say he got to experience firsthand what it was like to be me. I crammed several years of payback into that one night. I'm sure I could have stretched it out for weeks and had some fun with it, but I was on a deadline."

"I'm glad he got his," I said, leaning back in my chair. "You're a crap storyteller by the way, just so you know."

She sneered and then flicked my ear.

"Ouch. Guess that will teach me. What do you think, pal?"

Ted was looking toward a couple that had just come in and sat at the bar.

"You okay, buddy?"

"Yeah, I think I'm gonna grab another beer. You guys ready for one?"

We both declined, and I watched Ted go up to the bar and sit next to the guy. Bili and I could both sense an issue was at hand, but since the guy at the bar was human, our concerns were minimal, so we watched and waited.

85

"You don't mind if I sit here, do you?" Ted asked.

The man looked like he was about to protest until he saw the size of Ted.

"Free country."

"It is. Funny you should say that, because in a free country you can do all kinds of things," Ted said, and then he looked around the man to the girl he was with. "You know what? If I wanted to, I could pick out the smallest and weakest person in here, start a fight with him, and kick his ass in front of everyone."

The girl gave Ted a terrible look.

"You could if you were a complete asshole," she said, offended by the statement.

"Exactly!" Ted said, as he pointed at the girl. "Only a complete asshole would do such a thing, right?"

The man started to act a little uneasy while at the same time attempting to regain some semblance of control.

"Why don't you sit somewhere else?"

Ted completely ignored him, acting as if he wasn't there, still speaking with the girl.

"You know what would be worse? If I was a girl on a date with a guy like that, and I didn't know it. That would also be terrible, don't you think?"

The girl was angry, but now she was looking at her date. The stare was long and made the guy uncomfortable.

"Listen, buddy. It's time-"

"It's time alright," Ted said, now giving his full attention to the man. "It's time you tell this young lady your true nature."

"What?" The nervousness was now evident in his voice, and Ted could sense it.

"What is he talking about, Thomas?"

"I-," he started to say, but Ted cut him off.

"Let me answer that. Not long ago, a nerdy young man went to a bar with a few friends, not unlike this one. He was nervous in such places, but he pushed the boundaries of his comfort zone in an effort to have some fun. He went to the bathroom and when he came out, he unintentionally bumped into Thomas here. The young man was sorry, of course, and immediately apologized, but that didn't matter. Thomas thought the best course of action was to throw a beer in his face, punch him unconscious, and send him to the hospital. All because the young man had the audacity to simply bump into good ole Thomas."

That statement sparked a memory in Thomas that was visible to Ted.

"Now you remember, don't you?"

Ted looked over at the girl again. "Of course, this nerdy young man was much smaller and weaker than Thomas, which is probably why Thomas felt the need to show off. No chance of getting hurt himself, isn't that right?"

The girl was now mad at Thomas. "Is this true?"

"The lady asked you a question."

When Thomas didn't respond right away, obviously thinking about what to say, Ted became deadpan serious and lowered his voice.

"You have one chance. If you tell a lie right now and deny anything I just said, I'm going to drag you out of his bar and beat you until you're smart. We both know how long that beating will last."

Thomas hung his head and started nodding.

"I did what he said," Thomas said. "He must be your younger brother or something, right? I hope you can tell him I'm sorry. I am an asshole."

Ted patted Thomas on the shoulders.

"Admitting it is half the battle."

Ted stood up and looked over at the girl with a pleasant smile on his face. "Sorry to interrupt. Good day, miss."

Ted walked back to our table and sat down as if nothing happened. I looked at my friend with a newfound respect. Some people who come into power, no matter how much or what kind, wouldn't hesitate to use that power. The way Ted handled this person was pure class.

86

fter Theo sent Wolfgang everything he requested, he had been working diligently trying to find anything related. Theo and I were at the shop together when he received a call from Wolfgang. He had some new intelligence, and it was time sensitive.

Theo and I jumped in his car and sped off. We had only been on the road for twenty minutes when I had a sense of where we were going. After another five, I was certain.

"Are we going to Lucinda and Miah's home?"

"Yes, and I hope we don't find what I am looking for."

After Theo said those words, I recalled the first day I met Miah at the warehouse, along with all of Theo's other friends. All of them ended up being killed for helping us. It was something I had felt terrible about.

Theo parked the car near the main road, which was a good distance from the house. We got out and made our way there on foot. We were downwind, so unless someone was looking for us, making it to the house undetected wouldn't be a problem.

As we got closer, I could see the gravel driveway through the trees. I instantly thought of how we found Steve on that horrible afternoon. I started to get upset, which caused my blood to heat up.

"I'm going into the home through the front door," Theo said, and then he gave me one simple instruction.

"Anyone comes out the back, you stop them. Understood?"

I got his meaning loud and clear.

I nodded, and as soon as Theo saw my acknowledgement, he picked up the pace. By that, I mean he was at the front door in a blink. I sprinted to the back, making sure I was in position.

I heard Theo go through the front door, and I was sure he didn't take the time to unlock it, or even open it. The sound made it clear that a door was no longer there. It was within a second or two that a window in the back exploded in what sounded like the same manner as the front. The person making the exit was not Theo, and I did as I was told. I tackled the subject, and the fight was on. He struggled like hell to get away, but I was able to overpower him and get into a position of dominance. When the person stopped fighting, I saw who it was.

"What the hell?" The him was a her.

"What the hell, indeed," Theo said as he was now next to me.

Miah was lying on her back under my weight. Fear was written all over her face, and rightfully so.

"I didn't have a choice," she said.

87

We took Miah back in the house to have a little chat with her. Theo had her sitting down with both of us standing on either side, not only assuring she couldn't escape, but making sure she understood the situation.

She had been, what Theo thought, a dear friend of his for centuries. This was as upsetting as it was infuriating to Theo. He trusted this person fully, only to be betrayed.

"Speak!" Theo snapped.

Miah knew better than to lie, or even stall, as Theo was not in the mood.

Miah was in tears before she got a word out, but when she did, it was a bombshell.

"It was the Witch. It's her, it's all her."

Theo and I looked at each other with the same thought.

"Explain?" Theo said, directing his attention back to Miah.

"She told me all I had to do to clear my debt with her was to go to the meeting and record a conversation with Rieger."

"What conversation?"

"The Witch had a set of questions she wanted me to ask, and if I could accomplish this, I was in the clear. It turned out to be a complete ruse, and what she really wanted was the exact location of the meeting. The recorder had to be a GPS device of some kind," she said through crying sobs. "I'm sorry Theo, I-"

"No! I don't want to hear sorry," Theo said. "What you've done is beyond forgiveness."

As I stood there, an obvious question needed to be asked.

"Why are you still alive?" I asked.

Miah broke down and cried even harder.

"My beautiful Lucinda. I killed her, but she saved me," she said, covering her face with both hands.

The guilt was eating Miah alive, but I didn't care, and neither did Theo. Good people were dead because of her. She wasn't getting any sympathy from us.

"Answer the question."

"The Witch called me just before the meeting and told me the deal was off, and I had to wait here at the house to be contacted. She knew I would be desperate to be free of my debt, and when I pressed the issue, she acted as if she was doing me a favor by allowing Lucinda to record the conversation instead of me. I was hesitant, of course, but Lucinda insisted."

"You were the bait," Theo said. "The Witch leaked just enough information to get Steve to come to your home, so her men could kill him."

Miah nodded in confirmation.

"That doesn't make any sense," I said. "He would have just died in the fire with the others, right?"

"No," Theo said. "I called Steve and told him to keep working on leads and we would fill him in after the meeting. Somehow the Witch knew this."

I couldn't believe it. The person responsible for everything was the same person we went to for help.

A thought occurred to Theo.

"Why did she allow you to live?"

"She lied to me, Theo," Miah cried. "I don't know how she did it, but she did. I never would have agreed, and you know that."

"Answer me!"

"It's a game to her. I'm just another backup plan of a backup plan. She knew I couldn't go to you, or ask for help, after the fire, so I became harmless. I'm just her expendable pawn, that's all," she said, shaking her head, disgusted with herself.

Miah was telling the truth. I found the information about the Witch being able to successfully lie to a vampire very interesting. If she was capable of that, what else was possible?

"You should have come to me first," Theo said. "You *are* responsible for Lucinda's death. And Steve, Andrew, Allison, and the others as well. I hope you can live with yourself. Have a nice life, Miah."

Theo turned his back on her and started walking.

"Let's go, Jack," Theo said.

Theo's mercy only added to Miah's guilt. I almost felt sorry for her as I heard her scream and cry in anguish as we headed to the car.

We had the key piece of information we had been searching for this entire time. Now that we had it, could we do something with it? Taking on the Witch wouldn't be easy. She had a virtual army of security guards, as well as untold resources at her disposal. This would be the final challenge. Not dying in the process was going to be tricky.

When we got in the car, I checked my phone and saw that I had a missed call from Bili. When I listened to the voice message, my heart sank.

88

Bili had called the number after she reached the Detroit City limits, and they gave her the final directions. The closer she got to her location, she noticed she was no longer getting a signal on her cell phone. She just figured she was in a dead zone because of the large buildings. She wasn't.

The luxury high-rise apartment building was in the heart of downtown. Bili used the code to enter the underground parking area where the elevator took her directly to the third floor.

Once the doors opened, she saw what can only be described as over-the-top opulence. The gold artifacts on the shelves and walls alone made the apartment seem more like a museum than a living space. Bili was admiring a beautiful gold headpiece when she heard the footsteps.

"You know your business, I see. That piece was hard to come by," Cynthia said.

"I'm sure it was. I think the Syrian government is still looking for it."

Cynthia smiled. "They are indeed. Do you see anything else you like?"

When Bili looked at Cynthia, it was obvious she wasn't talking about art any longer.

"Maybe. What is it I can do for you?"

Cynthia smiled as she walked closer to Bili, removing her suit jacket as she did so.

"Did you bring it?"

Bili pulled the leather rope and charm from her pocket and handed it to her.

"Ahh, la lune se leva," Cynthia said.

Bili was looking at the Witch closely.

"The moon rose?" Bili asked. Her French wasn't as good as it used to be.

The Witch nodded.

"You have no idea what this is, do you?" Cynthia said, eyeing Bili's response carefully.

"I'm guessing a house sigil of some kind. How did you know Jack had this?"

"I know lots of things," she said. "And you're right, but it's much more than that, much more."

Bili had had a surge of guilt for going through my things to find the charm. She let me know she took it when she called, but she was on a time crunch and couldn't wait for me to call her back. It also seemed like an easy way to be rid of her debt to the Witch. After what she was told by Theo and Claude, she considered herself lucky to get the debt cleared this easily. She felt certain I wouldn't have cared, especially if it helped our cause.

"It was made for a queen, although the king at the time had no idea. The queen in question was the oldest known wolf in recorded history. It was that queen that produced the first anomaly. So, the legend says."

Bili was surprised the Witch was sharing this kind of information. She also felt confident the pendant wasn't worth that much, or else Theo would have told her about it. He treated it like any old, semi-precious piece of jewelry.

"Does this complete my favor to you?"

"Almost dear, I would like you to help me understand a few things. Sit down, please," Cynthia said, gesturing to the large sofa in the next room.

Bili sat down and Cynthia sat next to her; not too close, but close enough.

"Like what?"

"You could do so much better my dear. I know you are loyal to Theo, but have you ever considered being your own boss? Running your own company, built by your very hands."

The Witch saw that she struck a nerve with Bili. Before she could answer, she got up and walked to the window.

"Come with me."

Bili got up and stood next to Cynthia. It was a wonderful view of the city and the Detroit River.

"What are we looking at?" Bili asked.

"Your future. I could use a smart, motivated, powerful female to run certain aspects of my business. You would be wealthy beyond your wildest dreams, and you would only have one person to report to."

"You?"

Cynthia gave her a nod and a smile.

"And what would you have me do?" Bili asked in curiosity.

"I have many business ventures, a good portion here in Detroit. The city is on the rise, and I'm taking full advantage. I need a resilient personality to get things done, and I believe you are such a person."

Bili couldn't sense any lies or deception from Cynthia, which relaxed her. She was flattered and even took a little pride in the fact she was being sought after by a major player in their world. Before Theo, there were only negative interactions with those close to her. Theo had been her safety net since she met him, and the thought of standing on her own was appealing.

"That's quite an offer."

The Witch moved closer to Bili and used her finger to brush her hair back over her ear. Bili stared her in the eye, silent, as she did this. When she kissed Bili, it was not unpleasant, and the Witch could sense it as well.

Bili grabbed the Witch's hand and held it gently. "Thank you, really. It's an amazing offer, but I'm happy where I'm at," Bili said sincerely.

Disappointment was written all over Cynthia's body language, almost too dramatically.

"Shame," Cynthia said, dropping Bili's hand. "I guess, I will just have to collect the rest of my favor and let you be on your way."

Bili sensed a drastic shift in the Witch's demeanor that made her nervous. She knew she had to get out of there, and quick.

"What do you want?"

Cynthia walked toward her kitchen and grabbed an open bottle of wine from the counter. She poured herself a glass, took a sip, and then set it back down.

"I want you to find Clara's daughter, Theo will know where she is, and I want you to kill her. It may take some convincing but I'm sure you'll figure it out," she said as simply as if she had just asked Bili to go shopping for her.

Bili couldn't believe what she had just heard. There was no trace of guilt, remorse, or apprehension of any kind in her tone or body language. This alone was troubling.

"I can't do that," Bili said. She was steadfast in both her answer and her sense of morality. Bili now knew what was really happening. A debt to the Witch is never paid in full.

Cynthia returned her gaze, and though her tone was still a pleasant one, her look was anything but.

"No? My dear, I would have thought Claude would have explained this to you. You will do as you are asked or I will have you, and all those close to you, killed."

89

called Bili several times, but her phone went right to voicemail. I called Ted when I couldn't reach Bili and he answered right away. I put the phone on speaker so Theo could hear the conversation.

"Hey pal, where's Bili? Exactly?" I asked.

"She said she had to meet someone in Detroit. I asked to go with her, but she said she had to go alone."

I looked at Theo and saw the same worried look that I'm sure I was wearing.

"Did she say where she was meeting this person?" Theo asked quickly.

If my reaction wasn't enough, the urgency in Theo's voice made the situation crystal clear.

"No. She didn't know herself. She said she would get an address when she was inside the Detroit City limit. She said that she owed this person a favor. Is something wrong?" Ted asked.

"Yes," I said. "She's meeting the Witch, and the *Witch* is the problem. She started this war from top to bottom."

I could see Theo thinking hard and fast. We had to come up with something, and quick.

"What car did she take?" Theo asked.

"The Cadillac."

Theo pulled over, right where we were.

"Is that good?" Ted asked.

"We have trackers on all of Theo's cars," I explained.

Theo pulled out his laptop from the backseat and went to work. After a minute or so, he slammed the top down in aggravation.

"The car, and her phone, are not transmitting a signal. This is not good."

This was beyond not good. If the Witch found out that we knew about her, she might kill Bili right away.

"What else did she say? Anything at all that could help us find her?" Theo asked.

"She said she hoped to be back within an hour. That's it, nothing else."

I saw Theo's eyes, calculating numerous probabilities in a span of seconds.

"We need to get in touch with everyone, and I mean now," Theo said. "The Witch would most likely be in a large urban building away from her home. I'm guessing Detroit is the most probable, but we can't rule out some of the larger adjacent cities, like Dearborn, Warren, and even Sterling Heights. It could have been a ruse to have Bili drive to Detroit, only to be given an address further away," Theo said, thinking aloud.

"How well guarded is her place going to be?"

"Probably second to the U.S. Reserve," he said.

"Shit."

Theo nodded in agreement as he put the car in drive and made all haste. We met Claude and Deaglan at Theo's Detroit storage facility. Theo had already come up with a plan of action for each of the groups before we arrived. Every second was important.

Bodicea's group was sent to the east side as well as the Grosse Pointe area, while we stayed in Downtown Detroit. Claude thought we should send two from the group to check the other suburban areas as well. Tanzy and Ted stepped up and volunteered. If they found anything, they were to sit tight and wait for us.

Claude, Theo, Deaglan, and I were in one of the work vans as we looked for any sign of the Witch. We didn't have much to go on, but we had to try something. Theo was frantically searching the internet for anything linked to the Witch while we drove around the city looking for visual clues. Claude believed Cynthia would have guards, inside and out, giving us the opportunity to spot an immortal acting as security.

I was silently praying that Deaglan's Irish luck would come through this one last time. Believe it or not, within the hour, it did. There was just one problem, and it was a big one.

90

Bili was desperately thinking of a way to better her situation. She was sure that if she just fled the apartment, it would only delay a certain death sentence. Theo and Claude made it perfectly clear that this woman was not one to trifle with.

"Why do you want this woman dead?" Bili asked, stalling for time.

"Because," the Witch said flippantly.

It was at that moment that something occurred to Bili. It was the only thing that made sense.

"You have Clara, but she doesn't know where her daughter is, or you couldn't get her to talk," Bili said.

"I was right to pick you," she said appreciatively. "You really should reconsider my offer."

Bili was in a real-life chess game, with real lives at stake. Every answer could potentially be life altering, or just life ending.

"I guess I can kill the bitch. No skin off my back, I don't even know her," Bili said as calmly as she could.

"You're lying to me, young lady."

What? How?

"I know what you are thinking, she's a wolf, she can't detect lies. Oh, but I can sweetie, and probably better than you."

The Witch was smiling a terribly sinister smile, and Bili began to think of options. Last resort kind of options. Cynthia could also sense this.

"The building is surrounded and staffed on every floor, but if you want to run, you are free to try honey."

Bili turned to look at Cynthia but kept quiet for the moment. Cynthia walked close to Bili again, but with a different motive. She ran her hand through Bili's hair, gently at first before grabbing a handful, tightly.

"I had high hopes for you, I really did, but alas, you are destined to remain a sheep in the house of the wolf."

When Cynthia said those words, Bili's eyes widened. That's when she knew. It wasn't just Clara. There was no other logical explanation.

"It was you?" Bili said.

Cynthia removed her hand from Bili's hair and gave her a mock look of concern.

"What was dear?"

"Everything. You sent the letter to Rieger. You released the information about Jack. It was you who hired that psycho, Parrus."

The smile on Cynthia's face widened.

"Yahtzee!" Cynthia yelled. "I always loved that game."

This woman was responsible for countless deaths and there wasn't a remorseful cell in her entire body. This made Bili angry.

"Why?" Bili asked.

"The why is the easiest part my little lamb, I'm the only one who can. I'm afraid we have become too populated for our good. I can't go a week without tripping over one or two immortals these days. Nothing like a good war to thin the herds, wouldn't you agree? The fewer the better, trust me on this."

"Why do you want Jack so badly?"

This was a question Bili wanted to know, but at the same time, the more she could keep Cynthia talking, the better.

"As far as Jack is concerned, once I get the secret to his blood, the sky is truly the limit to what I can accomplish. At first, I thought I needed him alive, but my geneticist assures me that is not the case, hence my change in strategy. DNA is the future, and I can't have anyone as powerful as me just walking about. It's bad business."

"He's far more powerful than you," Bili said smugly.

Cynthia walked back to the kitchen and took another long sip of wine, unfazed by Bili's comment, or at least acting that way.

"I think the word you meant to say is *was*."

"You are one crazy bitch, aren't you?"

"Eccentric. What upsets you the most, dear? The fact that it was Parrus who told you Theo is his father, or the fact that he isn't yours."

That stung Bili, and deep.

"Go to hell."

"Take a hard, honest look at your miserable life. No partner, no real friends of consequence, and even if Jack were to live, which, sadly, he won't, he and Theo would have left you anyway. No one cares about you, just like your husband before, and your family before that. No one has ever given the slightest damn about you. That's what makes you, well, you."

Bili was shaking with anger, as those words cut through her like a sword. She did everything in her power to stop the tears, but it was a lost cause. Cynthia took pleasure in every drop as she pushed one button after another.

"I know what you are going to say, Theo cares, I know he does, he told me so." Cynthia said, putting her hand to her chest, using the stereotypical damsel in distress, look. "Let me assure you, he does not. You have been nothing but a burden on him since you met. He had a moment of weakness when he turned you, and because he is a man of honor, he kept you around. He was never one to shirk a responsibility, no matter how miserable it made him."

When Bili couldn't detect the lies, her heart broke into a thousand pieces. The last thing she wanted was to give her satisfaction, but she had lost control of her emotions and her temper.

Bili charged Cynthia and grabbed her by the throat, wanting nothing more than to kill her right there.

She squeezed with everything she had, but when Cynthia grabbed her arms, Bili knew she was no match for her.

"Poor thing. Always hoping for the impossible," she said as she twisted Bili's arms from her neck one at a time.

Bili looked on in dismay as the Witch brought up a quick knee, breaking one of her arms in a horrible fashion. There was nothing Bili could do to stop it either. She then grabbed Bili by her throat, forcing her to her knees. Tears streamed down Bili's cheeks as Cynthia looked down at her with pity.

"You are a disappointment, aren't you? Do you ever get tired of hearing that, or have you become immune to it?"

Cynthia kicked Bili in the head, knocking her unconscious, just as two wolves from her security detail came out and took custody of Bili.

"Lock her in the vault," Cynthia ordered.

As they dragged her away, the Witch gave an ironic wave.

"Enjoy the company."

91

T heo was furiously thinking about the best course of action, annoyed at his own lack of tangible progress. We were going in circles, looking for any sign that would lead us to the Witch. Claude's theory was not panning out as we had hoped. We were looking for a single strand of hay in an entire hayfield. It was an impossible task without some solid information.

The ring of Deaglan's cell phone interrupted the dead silence. It was the Eighties pop song, "Rock Me Amadeus."

We all looked at Deaglan with the same incredulousness. If the situation hadn't been so dire, I may have laughed at his choice of ringtone for his friend, Wolfgang.

He ignored our stares, apparently excited about the incoming call.

"It's about bloody time, mate. We are in a bit of a bind here."

After a brief conversation, which I could barely hear for some reason, Deaglan disconnected the call with a blank expression.

"Well?" Theo asked.

"It's a good news, bad news sort of thing," Deaglan began. "Wolfgang was able to discern that Cynthia owns a large high-rise building off Woodward, not far from here. It was layered by several shell companies, one of which he knew to be hers."

"The bad?" Theo asked.

"We have to see for ourselves, but it may be impenetrable from the outside. The lower two levels were previously a federal bank and built accordingly."

We drove by the building, and Wolfgang's concerns were verified. There wasn't even a window until the third floor, and the one entrance was sure to be heavily guarded. It also explained why no one was guarding the outside. No need. We went by this building no less than three times in the last hour.

"We have to try something," I said, becoming impatient.

"We won't do Bili any good if we are dead before we reach her, lad," Deaglan said.

Claude, who had been quiet the entire time, spoke.

"We might have one option left."

We all looked at Claude with the same intense interest.

"What?" I asked simply.

"I was hoping it wouldn't come to this, but we don't have much choice now. I can think of only one person who may be able to get us inside," Claude said, looking at Theo first and then me.

"What are you talking about?" Theo asked.

When I saw Claude's face, I knew.

"Kristov," I said.

Just saying his name out loud caused my body to burn hot.

Deaglan, not fully aware of our history, was excited about the news.

"Great, what can he do for us?"

"Go straight to hell, that's what." I said, trying my best not to raise my voice in anger.

Theo looked at me with concern, but Deaglan was just surprised by my anger. Theo, who was thinking solely about Bili, and he was right to do so, knew what had to be done.

"Call him right now and see if he is even willing," Theo said.

The thought of asking him for help was sickening.

Claude got out of the car to make the call.

Theo put his hand on my shoulder. "If he can help us get her back alive, we have to talk to him, agreed?" Theo said.

I was seething, but I nodded, knowing he was right. I had to put the personal aside. I would do anything to get Bili home safely. I owed her my life.

Claude got back in the car after about ten minutes.

"Well? Deaglan asked.

"He's in Detroit." Claude said.

"Luck of the Irish," Deaglan said, smiling.

Claude, again, directed his attention to me.

"He agreed to help, but under one condition. He wants to talk to you first."

I didn't answer right away. Time seemed to stop for the moment, as I had to focus to control myself. I was burning up inside.

"Jack?" Theo said, prodding a response.

The question wasn't whether I could talk to him; it was more a question of can I do it without killing him. I honestly wasn't sure how I was going to react when the time came. The last time I saw him, I was blinded by rage.

"I'll talk to him."

We drove to the rear alley of the old Tiger Stadium, which was off Michigan Avenue, not too far from Cynthia's building. It was late, which was good, limiting the foot traffic in the area. This meeting turning sideways was not improbable.

Claude said he was only about fifteen minutes away at most.

We had no way, due to the time constraints, of doing any kind of counter strategy. If Kristov was setting us up, he would have an advantage over us. It was a risk, but one we were going to take.

Deaglan and Claude did their best to sweep the area before I went in, but it was a half measure at best. The only reason Claude thought Kristov was worth contacting was that he had obtained information that he might have fallen out of favor with the enemy. We could very well be his last and only chip he had to play.

A smaller vehicle pulled into the alley in front of us and stopped. The lights went out, and a lone figure got out and stood next to the car, not moving.

It was him.

"Focus, Jack," Theo said. "She would do it for any one of us."

I did just that. I was thinking only of her when I got out and started walking toward Kristov. The closer I got, the harder this exercise became. My hands began to sweat from my body heat.

I barely recognized Kristov when I got close enough to see him clearly. He was dressed like a farmer in my eyes, with a long beard and a shaved head.

I stopped about ten feet from him and stood silently. I thought to myself, *please do not say anything that will piss me off*. It was all I could do to keep from charging him.

What took place next shocks me to this very day.

92

Bili woke up in the sterile and lifeless room. The walls were smooth but made of heavily fortified brick. The door had no handle or knob of any kind on the inside, and it seeded flush with the wall. There was one dim light in the ceiling, at least twenty feet high, that illuminated the center of the room where Bili found herself. It was something out of a nightmare.

Bili stood up and shook her arm that was broken, glad to see it was straight and good as new. Someone had set it for her, or she would have had to re-break it herself. She walked to the door and felt around the edges, examining every aspect of it. It was just at that moment when she realized she wasn't alone.

"You can knock, but I don't think anyone is going to answer," a familiar voice said from the dark corner of the room.

Though it was dark, Bili knew who it was. She walked over to the same area, plopped down on the floor next to this person, and leaned back against the wall.

"The fact that I'm glad to see you says how screwed I think we really are."

93

"I didn't think you would do it," Kristov said.

The tone in his voice was surprising and unexpected. This was not the same arrogant bastard I remembered from the Piece of History or Mr. Hendricks' home. That being said, I had no less animosity toward him because of it.

"What do you want?" I asked sharply.

"I want to live in the 1300s when life was easier, but I will settle for just living."

"Take off and live in some third world country. You could be a king."

Kristov stared, gauging me.

"I know you're thinking about killing me right now, but your hatred is misdirected. Well, partially," he said, looking down for a split second, and then back up.

"Let me guess, it wasn't you?"

"No, no, it was me, but not how, and definitely not why, you think," Kristov said. "I didn't have a choice."

Before I even had the time to give him the look or state the obvious, he was talking.

"Everyone has a choice, Kris," he said, mocking my potential response. "You're wrong; not with her. It's do, or you're dead!"

I started to get tunnel vision and my entire body burned. It took everything I had to steady myself.

"Why should any of this matter?"

"Because, you know I'm telling the truth."

"So, what?" I snapped.

"Don't you get it? Everything that has happened; your mother, Viktoria, this entire conflict, is because that crazy bitch made it happen!" Kristov said, pointing in the direction of Cynthia's building downtown. "I didn't want to kill them. I had to or I'm in the ground. And she still tasked me with another job. It never ends. If we don't kill her, Bilinda is as good as dead, or worse; she'll be her slave forever."

I could tell he wasn't lying. The thought of Bili being back in a torturous situation because of me was as bad as it gets. He had my attention.

"What does she want?"

He shook his head with a look of a teacher losing patience with a child.

"Power. She's the oldest and richest of us for a reason. She has been systematically killing elders, from both clans, for over a millennium. Once she gets your DNA, that's it, we are all done."

He was telling the truth.

"What the hell does she want with my DNA?"

"She believes it holds the secret to your strength and power, and if you think she will let you live once she gets it, well…"

"How do you know this?"

"Let's say I've made some terrible life choices and been forced to work for that psycho far too long. Plus, I got crazy twin number two drunk one night, and he couldn't stop bragging about his role in all of this. The rest wasn't hard to put together."

The longer I listened to him, the more it made perfect sense.

"So, what the hell can you offer?"

Kristov smiled for the first time.

"Two things," he said, holding up two fingers. "A way in, and vengeance."

94

K ristov went to the main door of Cynthia's building and hit the buzzer. The intercom beeped and a male voice spoke.

"What do you want?"

Kristov reached into the satchel he was carrying and pulled something out. He held it up to the CCTV camera and waved it back and forth making it clear as to what he had.

The door clicked and he went in. The elevator was open and waiting for him to step inside. Without touching anything, the elevator door closed and began to move. When it stopped, and the door opened again, there were three wolves waiting for him; one of which Kristov knew well.

"Jesus Christ, Garrett? When did you join the Witch brigade?"

"Nice to see you too, Kris," he said as he put Kristov up against the wall, not gently either, searching him from head to toe.

Kristov continued as they searched him.

"Last time I saw you, we were in a French brothel, what, about two hundred years ago?"

"How else was I going to meet your sister?" the guard said.

"That place was too nice for my sister," Kristov countered.

After Garrett finished searching Kristov, he spun him around. When he did, the Witch was there in front of him.

"Let's see it."

Kristov pulled the bloody hand from his satchel and held it up for the Witch to see and smell.

"How did you manage this my dear Kris?" Cynthia asked with delight in her voice.

"It was difficult, but I did what you asked. Am I free from all debts?"

"I don't see Theo's hand. And where is the rest of Claude's body?" she asked, looking closely at Kristov.

"In the car downstairs," Kristov said, choosing his words very carefully. "I didn't think you wanted me dragging his carcass into your home, but..."

Kristov started to move back toward the elevator, but she stopped him.

"Not you," Cynthia said. She looked at Garrett and nodded toward the elevator.

Garrett made his way down the elevator, and Cynthia just stared at Kristov, waiting patiently for confirmation from one of her trusted men.

"I thought you had lost your grit. I was sure I was gonna have to kill you," she said. "I will take your debt down to one last favor if this checks out. I'm feeling generous."

"You know I always deliver," Kristov said, trying to keep her attention from the CCTV monitor. "Franklin was never one to handle the pressure of this kind of work."

Kristov felt a small wave of relief when he saw the elevator on its way back up. The door opened slowly, revealing Garrett standing in front. As soon as it was all the way open, Garrett fell face first. Before his lifeless body hit the ground, Kristov tossed Claude's hand in the air, which Claude caught and reattached, as he and I came off the elevator.

More guards appeared, and they all had weapons in hand. They leveled them at us and let loose. Kristov and Claude got in front of me and acted as a shield as we charged toward the Witch, who had retreated to the far wall. Both Claude and Kristov took several shots to the body before I was able to burst through them and grab her. She was astonished at the speed with which I was able to get behind her. I had my arm around her neck like a vise in a blink.

"Tell them to drop the weapons and get in the elevator, or I remove your head from your shoulders. Now!"

I squeezed and tugged on Cynthia's neck, just to show her what I was capable of. She relented.

"Do it," she directed.

There were four of them and they complied. They walked to the elevator slowly, almost anticipating another order from their boss. None came.

"All the guns," Kristov barked.

Three of the four removed weapons from their waste bands and threw them on the floor before stepping into the elevator. The door closed and we watched the floor indicator to make sure it went to the lower level.

I couldn't believe it had worked. Just as I thought we were about to continue with the rest of the plan, the Witch uttered a sentence I will never forget.

"Oh, dear. Looks like someone has a boo-boo," she said mockingly as she looked at Claude.

Claude had stood after the quick assault but had fallen back down. He tried to get up again but couldn't. That's when I saw the dark red stain in the center of his chest. He must have taken ten or twelve direct hits to his heart from the high caliber weapon.

I instinctively let go of the Witch without thinking to help Claude.

"No!" Kristov yelled as he tried to grab her as she sprinted toward the window. He dove at her legs, but she was airborne and crashing through the window before he got close. There was nothing he could do.

I ran to Claude's side trying to stop the bleeding. It was at that moment the elevator door opened, and Deaglan and Theo entered the flat. Their job was to take care of the guards at the bottom and then come back up to assist.

Theo saw me, the hole in the window, and Claude on the floor. He knew exactly what had happened.

"Deaglan, find Bili," Theo said.

Deaglan did just that as Theo knelt next to his friend.

Claude coughed up a sizeable amount of blood as Theo tried to help him sit up. The damage to his heart was beyond repair, even for an elder. How he was still alive was a minor miracle itself. His heart was in shreds.

"Sorry," Claude said, just above a whisper. "I let her get away."

"Don't worry about that," Theo said. "You can heal from this my friend, concentrate."

Claude put his hand on Theo's arm as he struggled to take a breath. He gave Theo a soft pat on the hand and the slightest of nods that spoke volumes to Theo. His eyes flickered one last time before closing for good. His body relaxed and went limp.

"Claude," Theo said, shaking his friend, trying to wake him. "Claude!"

I couldn't believe it. If anyone was indestructible, it was Claude. This was not supposed to happen. Theo stifled an angry roar, deciding to place a comforting hand on his friend's head as he said his last goodbye. I could almost see a shimmer of furious heat coming from Theo's person.

It was at that moment when Deaglan appeared from the back, Bili close behind.

I was so relieved to see her alive. I stood up, about to approach her, when I saw an expression on her face I couldn't decipher. It made me stop in my tracks.

Bili looked off to the side where she had just come from. She was looking at something I couldn't yet see. A second later, I saw another person enter the room, and I thought I was hallucinating.

Viktoria.

95

stood frozen when I saw her, which was only a few seconds, but felt like an eternity. Once Viktoria saw me, she ran and grabbed me in a tight embrace.

We hugged each other tight. The swirl of emotions was hard to deal with at that moment, as we didn't have time. We had to get out of there, and fast. The Witch was gone, but by no means out of the picture.

"We got to go," Deaglan said, as delicately as he could, given the situation.

"Jack, get the elevator," Theo said, as he picked Claude up in his arms and started walking.

We all got in the elevator together, including Kristov, which was a surprise to Bili, who was not in the best of moods as it was.

"What's this asshole doing here?" Bili said, obviously referring to Kristov.

"Saving your ass little girl," Kristov said as the elevator doors closed. "Consider us even."

Theo and I loaded Claude's body in the van, and as soon as he was in place, Kristov approached Theo.

"With that bitch on the loose, we are all dead, you know that, right?" Kristov said.

Theo didn't respond and walked away from him.

Kristov persisted.

"Do you hear me, Theodorus?"

Theo stopped and turned to face him. He had a blank stare, but fury in his heart.

"Wrong. She's dead," Theo said. "If you want to run, run. But we are going to end this, and soon."

Kristov shook his head but said nothing. He struggled with what to do, but in the end, he got into his car and left. He was no longer a concern for us. I even lost some of my unmitigated hatred for him. Not all of it, but he was right about the Witch. She was the sole cause of every senseless death.

The rest of us got in the van and headed back home. The silence was deafening. The sound of humming tires on the road only added to the already gloomy atmosphere.

When we got back, Theo told us to sit tight in our apartments, while he and Deaglan took care of Claude. With the Witch on the loose, we had to be extra vigilant. She would not be happy about what happened, and probably looking for revenge sooner rather than later.

Bili went to her place, and I took Viki to mine. As soon as we got inside, Viki asked if she could use the shower. I don't think the Witch was too accommodating when it came to hygienic needs.

I went to my closet and got her a pair of sweatpants and the smallest T-shirt I owned and set them out for her on my bed.

When she finished, she sat on my couch.

"Will you sit with me, please?" she asked.

I got up from the chair and did as she asked. I felt nervous, like the first time we were alone together in her flat. As I looked into her eyes, an overwhelming feeling of guilt washed over me.

"I'm so sorry I left you. If I hadn't gone after Franklin..."

I couldn't finish.

"It's not your fault. There's nothing you could've done. The Witch gets what the Witch wants."

Viki reached over, grabbed my hand, and held it. There wasn't an ounce of blame in her eyes or body language.

"I was sure you were dead," I said.

"I probably would have been, eventually."

"Why did the Witch want you?" I asked, trying to make sense of the situation.

"You may be the only thing she fears in this world, and I was going to be her last line of defense until they killed you. Then there would be no need for me. So, thanks for not dying."

Viki was doing everything to ease my guilt. It was more than I deserved, but it only made me love her more.

"Glad to help," I said, forcing a smile. "How do you know that's what the Witch had planned."

"It's amazing what people will tell you when they are confident they're going to kill you."

"I can't tell you how happy I am you're alive. And here," I said earnestly.

"You can if you want."

Her voice was just above a whisper now.

"I'm glad you're alive, Viki. And very glad you're here."

I put my hand on the side of her cheek, and she immediately pressed her hand against mine as she leaned into it. She closed her eyes for a second, and when she opened them, I kissed her. It was a short kiss, followed by another long hug. We couldn't get close enough to suit me. Though she was right in front of me, I was terrified of losing her again. I would do anything to make sure that never happened.

96

Theo had called for another meeting at his home the following morning. With Clara still missing, the Witch on the loose, and Claude being killed, our group was in a vulnerable state. We had to do something, and soon.

It seemed like every meeting would result in something catastrophic shortly thereafter. I really hoped this one didn't follow suit.

Viktoria and I got ready, grabbed what we needed, and loaded up in Theo's Caddy. Bili and Ted left earlier and were already there. Bodicea and her clan were there as well. Theo insisted they all stay in his guest house.

We just got on the road when my phone began to vibrate. When I pulled it out of my pocket, I saw who was calling.

I cannot overstate this fact enough. Had I not answered that call, my life, and several others close to me, could have turned out dramatically different.

But I did answer.

97

Ben waited as long as he could before reaching a point where he thought about calling the authorities. I hadn't shown up for our meeting a while back, and now Ted was nowhere to be found. Throw in the fact that neither of us were answering our phones and none of our other friends had seen or heard from us in some time. Ben felt sure something was wrong and he wasn't going to wait around and do nothing.

He decided to make two more stops, and if neither of them panned out, he was going to the police. He went to the Piece of History first, only to find it closed and locked up tight. He even knocked on the rear door just in case I was working in the back.

He made the short walk to Ted's old house, not knowing he had moved out. Though Ted had sold it already, it was still unoccupied and vacant.

When Ben got to the house, he found the rear door unlocked, so he let himself in. He really began to worry when he saw the place was bare bones. The only thing in the house was a coat rack the real-estate company put in there for potential buyers to use.

Ben pulled out his phone and called Ted, which went right to voice-mail. He searched through his contacts, found mine, and decided to call me one last time.

He pressed the button.

98

"Shit," I said, shaking my head when I saw who was calling.

Viki gave me a questioning look, so I answered her before she asked.

"A friend of mine. I've been avoiding him, but now I feel if I don't talk to him, he's going to do something irrational, putting himself in more danger than he already has. Long story, but you get the picture."

"How much does he know?"

"Almost nothing, but just enough to get himself in trouble."

Viki smiled, nodding.

"I remember those days. Of course, that was several hundred years ago. It was much easier to avoid old friends before phones, computers, or the telegraph," she said.

"I bet," I said with a chuckle. "Excuse me."

I hit the accept button.

"Hey, Ben, I'm sorry-"

I stopped talking abruptly and listened.

Viki looked on with concern as I held the phone to my ear.

I handed Viki my phone, put both hands on the steering wheel, and turned the car around on a dime. The tires screamed for mercy as I punched it, giving it everything it had. Thank goodness I was in Theo's Caddy, as it moved when you wanted it to.

"Problem?" Viki said calmly while putting on her seatbelt at the same time.

"Yep. Mind calling Theo for me? Tell him we are on the way to my old house. One confirmed, but maybe more."

Luckily, we hadn't been on the road that long and weren't very far from our destination. I was getting close and thinking about the best workable plan of getting inside with the least amount of warning. I just hoped my friend was still alive.

I made a few more sharp turns, but the closer I got, I slowed down, making sure not to create any sounds that could give away our approach. I pulled over about a block from the house, turned the car off, and looked over at my passenger.

"Listen, I only heard one subject in the house other than Ben, but that doesn't mean that there aren't more," I said, explaining the situation. "I know you are more than capable, but I would feel much better if you waited here until I cleared the house."

"Not happening," she said.

Her tone and eyes were deadpan serious, and I could tell she went into fight mode. The wolf in her was fully engaged and ready for battle. I think my attempt to keep her safe insulted her.

"Okay, let's go." I said, knowing there wasn't time to argue.

We stepped out of the car at the same time and moved along the adjacent houses to hide ourselves until the last second. We stopped one house shy of our target, attempting to make a quick assessment of the logistics.

"Do you know what room they're in?"

"No. I'll go through the back door. Can you go in through the upper window, clear the top floor, meet me at the bottom?"

I was playing the odds that Ben was on the main floor, making sure I encountered the enemy first.

She gave me a quick nod.

"Be careful," she said, giving my arm a gentle squeeze before taking off. I sprinted as well, smashing through the rear door as if it wasn't there.

What I found inside shocked and horrified me.

99

Ben had just hit the button to call me when he was hit from behind, sending him into the wall. The phone flew from his hands and dropped to the floor, but the call connected.

"What the hell!" Ben yelled, trying to get to his feet, unsure of what had just happened.

Before he had time to regain any kind of composure, he was picked up and slammed against the wall, knocking the wind out of him. It was then that he saw his assailant.

"What are you doing in this house?" the large man said.

Ben was scared, but even so, Ben was Ben.

"Dude, you could have asked me that without hitting me, with whatever the hell it was you hit me with. Very uncool," Ben said, rubbing the back of his head.

This irritated the large man, who was holding Ben up off the ground by his jacket like a high school bully picking on an elementary student. He pulled Ben back about a foot, before slamming him back against the wall, crushing the drywall behind him.

This forced Ben to cough uncontrollably as he tried to catch his breath.

"I asked you a question," he said.

"I'm looking for my friends," Ben spit out quickly. "They used to live here."

"Who?"

Ben didn't say anything for a second and then did something incredibly brave, but very unwise. Ben brought up his foot and kicked his attacker in the chest as hard as he could. He was sure he could knock him over, or at least push him back far enough to escape. Wrong.

The large man didn't budge an inch. Ben couldn't believe it. Undeterred, he tried to punch the man in the face. Again, it did nothing but hurt Ben's fist. That's when Ben became paralyzed with fear.

"What in the hell are you?"

The large beast just smiled a terrible smile.

100

burst through the back door and found Ben in the grips of a large wolf. The wolf's back was to me when I came in, but Ben was facing me. His face was covered in blood and both eyes were swollen to the point where he could barely see.

"Hey Jack," Ben said politely. "I was just trying to call you."

Beaten within an inch of his life, and he still had his sense of humor. Seeing him like that enraged me and my whole body flushed hot.

"Drop him now, and I may let you live," I said to the wolf. "And I stress, may."

The long-haired beast turned around slowly, and when I saw his face, it was as if time had stopped, or more accurately, reversed.

"Hello, son."

I was so dumbfounded and confused, I couldn't get any words out. I was transformed back to that scared little kid who was petrified of this monster. I'm sure there is some psychological phenomenon for such an event, and let me tell you, I was experiencing it.

David, who was already big and menacing as a human, had transformed into a wolf of considerable ferocity. I was frozen with fear, and I'm sure my look said as much, which only emboldened David with confidence.

I shook off my initial irrational fear of this man and turned those feelings into a controlled rage. He was no longer the threat he used to be. *I* was the threat.

"I'm not your fucking son," I said through grinding teeth and tight lips. "And I suggest you set down my friend as if he was made of paper-thin porcelain, or I will pull your arms off and beat you to death with them. I mean that literally."

David tilted his head back and laughed. He wasn't scared of me, as I'm sure he still saw me as his perpetual victim.

"I've heard rumors you're some freak half-breed. I think it's horseshit, of course," he said with a shrug, "but why take chances."

As soon as he said this, I knew I had miscalculated something. He was expecting someone, maybe not me, but he was ready.

David dropped Ben, reached inside his jacket, and pulled out one of the largest handguns I had ever seen. Before I could move or find cover, he was unleashing round after round.

I had only taken one to the chest before I was pushed out of the way. When I say pushed, I mean to say I was sent flying into the kitchen with force. If I hadn't hit a support beam, I might have gone clean through the wall.

Viki had shoved me out of the way, and when she did, two things happened in quick succession. One being she took numerous shots to her body, and the second was that the front door flew open, and a second wolf entered the house. I had hoped it was someone from our group. No such luck.

I stood to get back in the fight, and I again took several more rounds to the chest. I fell back to the ground and immediately felt a weight on me. I was lying on the kitchen floor, semi-dazed when I realized that Viki was on top of me. I thought she was injured and just fell on top of me until I tried to move her. She was intentionally covering me while holding herself in place by grabbing a pipe that ran along the kitchen floor with one hand, while the other was tucked under me.

I was injured just enough that I didn't have the strength to push her off.

David and the other wolf walked into the kitchen slowly and stood above Viki and me like a tower of evil. He smiled and shook his head, peering at his partner, who was reloading his gun. He was wearing the same infuriating grin.

"This is my stepson, the indestructible anomaly," David said.

The other wolf snickered.

"I guess you were right. All bullshit."

David laughed harder as I struggled to move. I couldn't believe what Viki was doing.

"You'll have to shoot through me to get him," Viki said, keeping me pinned underneath her.

David and his partner looked at each other and shrugged as they both raised their weapons in unison. That's when I felt the house shake, along with a blur of motion in my peripheral vision.

Theo burst into the room, kicked David's partner out the front door and into the hands of Deaglan. Before David had time to pull the trigger, he was against the wall, gasping for air.

Theo was furious.

"What did I tell you would happen if you ever touched my son again?!" Theo shouted.

David was wheezing and choking on his own blood. Theo had broken the coat rack in half on his way in and shoved it clean through David's chest and into the wall behind him. The only thing keeping him alive was that piece of jagged wood, which Theo pulled out and threw on the floor. David's eyes fluttered before falling shut. His body went limp, and Theo dropped him like a sack of garbage.

Viktoria and I got up as our collective wounds were still healing. It was nothing short of a miracle that neither of us was killed.

"We have to get this place cleaned and get outta here," Theo said quickly. "Don't worry about the blood, grab the body, and let's get going."

Viki and I grabbed David's body and took him out the back door just as Deaglan pulled the Cadillac up and popped the trunk. We dumped him in, and then I made one last check of the house. That's when I saw Ben sitting on the floor in the corner, shaking uncontrollably. I had almost forgotten about him.

I made my way to his side, as Theo and the others had already left.

"I think you better come with me, buddy, what do you think?"

Ben was a mess, but the thought of him going home in his condition, both physically and mentally, didn't seem wise, or moral.

"Am I dreaming," he asked seriously, looking up at me. "I must be, right?"

"Come on, pal."

I grabbed his arm, got him to his feet, and helped him outside. I loaded Ben into the back seat, next to Viki, and we took off.

I don't know if it was the shock or the fact he normally has no filter, but the second he saw Viktoria, his mouth began moving.

"Are you the one who beat up Jack in the coffee shop?" he said through swollen lips.

Viki smiled.

"I am. You should've seen what I did to the drunk who insulted him on our first date," she said lightheartedly, trying to put my friend at ease. "You'll need ice for those eyes right away, or you won't be able to see tomorrow."

I looked back at Ben, who looked at me. He was a mess, and his blank stare told me everything I needed to know. He was still in shock.

We drove Ben back to my place, and he kept quiet for the rest of the ride, which was the most concerning. He was pale, but the color was starting to come back. Deaglan and Viki dropped us off and took care of the body, knowing I would be busy with my human friend.

I walked him upstairs, and we went inside. I could tell he had several injuries, but nothing appeared so bad that I felt he needed the emergency room. I grabbed some ice from the freezer and put together a makeshift ice pack for Ben's face.

"Sit down on the couch, pal," I said as I brought him the ice. "Put this on those eyes."

Ben nodded, still quiet, as he took the ice from me. I could tell he wasn't afraid of me, but he wasn't overly comfortable either. How could you blame him? I couldn't imagine what that scene must have looked like through his human eyes.

"Listen, I know what you're thinking, trust me, I do. It wasn't that long ago I experienced a very similar incident. It was a miracle I didn't die myself."

Ben managed a slight nod, letting me know he was listening. Another good sign.

"You are free to leave if you want, buddy, but my advice would be to hang out here for a while. The building and apartment are very secure, and you'll be safe here until I get back. When I do, I'll explain everything," I said, raising my eyebrows, waiting for a response.

"Can't wait," Ben said.

It wasn't the least bit sarcastic, but it was Ben. He would be alright, he just needed time.

"Do not open the door for anyone but me or Bili, okay?"

I mentioned Bili because he knew her by face. He would not recognize anyone else from the house incident. Not in the state he was in.

He nodded absently.

I felt bad for leaving him like that, but I had no choice. There were things that needed to be done.

I went to meet Theo and the others. We had to come up with some sort of viable plan to find and take care of the Witch before she took care of us.

101

After a quick meeting at Theo's, we came up with the best option to move forward. Wolfgang was still working on a few things to bring the plan together, but we still needed a lucky break.

Per Theo, I took Viki to the Piece of History. She was to stay in the loft apartment until she was needed. Everyone else had a specific assignment, and station, as well. I hadn't really had a chance to talk to Viki about what she did until we got to the store.

"Listen," I began. "What you did today…"

"It was nothing. You would've done the same," she said, downplaying the fact that she saved my life and could have been killed in the process.

"It was not nothing. Why did you do that?"

I didn't have to explain what I was talking about. She was going to sacrifice herself just to give me a chance to live. She could have easily saved herself by leaving the house to get help. I wouldn't have thought any less of her either. When someone does something like that, as Bili did before, it makes you wonder why. It also makes you ask yourself if you're really worth it. If that doesn't make you strive to be a better person, nothing will.

"You know why," she said, not really looking me in the eye. "I love you, Jack. I would have gladly given my life to save yours."

I pulled her close to me and hugged her tight.

She knew I had to go, so she gave me a quick kiss and pushed me toward the door.

"Go. We'll talk later. Please be careful," she said.

I grabbed the door handle but stopped. I turned to look into those beautiful gray eyes.

"I love you too. I always have."

102

I left the store and drove back to Theo's house. Everyone was gone, thankfully, as I wanted some time alone with him. The giant pink elephant in the room needed to be discussed. He let me in, and we took seats in his library. It was the perfect place for this kind of talk.

"Are you really my father?" I asked before he even had time to get comfortable in his chair.

I was in a terrible state when I heard Theo say those words to David, but they burned into my soul.

Theo, who was sitting across from me, put his hands together and rested them on his knees.

"Yes."

"Why didn't you tell me?"

I needed a reason. A reason that made sense to me. Was it him, my mother, or some other dark force that kept this man out of my life?

"I thought I was protecting you. As it turns out, I don't think many of my decisions were correct ones. I should have told you sooner, and for that, I'm truly sorry."

Theo's words were sincere, and I could see the regret in his eyes. I was becoming an expert in the field of regret myself. I nodded, understanding, but this brought up a question that immediately seemed more important than all the others.

"Why did you leave my mother? She could have used you. I could have…"

"I didn't, Jack. She left me. I loved her dearly, and I wanted it to work, but once she knew the truth of me, something in her changed. Her son became her first priority, and rightfully so."

"But I'm *your* son as well." I said, genuinely happy to say that.

Theo nodded and continued quickly.

"That you are, and I couldn't be prouder." He looked down and collected his thoughts briefly. "I felt I owed your mother, so I respected her wishes. My wants and needs had to take a back seat, considering."

"Considering what?"

I could see the pain in Theo's eyes as he continued.

"I had no idea I was fertile, and when your mother told me she was pregnant, no one was more surprised than I. Her not knowing the truth about me, beforehand, was a cause of great concern for me, and, as it turned out, for your mom as well. I had put your mother in a terrible spot, both physically and morally. I hated myself for it."

I tried to imagine what my mother must have been thinking back then, and I don't believe I was capable of it.

"But if you loved each other…"

"We did, but sometimes love is not enough. I did the best I could from the shadows, doing whatever she would allow me. But you're right, you deserved better. I should have been there for you."

"You were there today," I said, now getting emotional.

Theo pulled me up from my chair and into a tight hug. I hugged him back. He is my father, and the one I'd always hoped for. I no longer felt like an adult orphan, roaming the planet alone. I had family, and much more.

I gave him another tight squeeze, and then we separated.

"Go home and get some rest. If anything comes up, I'll call you right away."

I nodded and wiped my eyes again.

"Okay," I said. "Can I ask you one more question?"

"Of course."

"Is it because you are my natural father that I'm the way I am?"

"Yes, I believe so. There is no one like you, son, and probably never will be. You have a unique bloodline that even our greatest historians don't quite understand. We'll talk about it more when all this gets settled. Go on."

103

When I got back to my apartment, I walked in, and Ben was nowhere in sight. I heard the toilet flush and water running in the bathroom. Ben appeared a minute later.

"Want something to help settle the stomach, buddy?" I asked, knowing he had just thrown up.

"I think I'm good now. Third time charm and all," Ben said as he took a seat in my leather chair. Everyone loved to sit in my chair.

I needed to explain a few things to Ben, and that was the problem. Being human, it was going to be much harder for him to comprehend, especially without the proper time. This was a rare situation, and Theo wanted me to work it out the best way I saw fit. That was a lot of trust, and frankly, I would rather he just told me what to do. That's not real life though, and so there I was, not exactly sure what to do, or how to do it.

"The shock is dissipating, allowing your body to think and relax, hence the vomiting. You'll be okay, except for your face, which will probably go back to the way it was," I said.

Ben was able to force a small grin at that.

I walked to the fridge, grabbed a beer, and handed it to him.

"This will help."

I sat down on the couch across from him and watched as he cracked it open and drank until it was empty. He let out a quick burp and then mustered up his first question.

"I saw you get shot, like seven times. I did see that, right? The hot girl too."

Ben was questioning his own sanity, as would anyone in his position.

"Eight," I began. "Listen pal, I'm sorry you got dragged into this, but in it you are. Do you want an answer that will be almost plausible and help you sleep at night, or the painful truth? Frankly, I think you should go with the former, rather than the latter. Another beer?"

"No thanks, I'll probably have a case later, but I think I'd rather have the truth right now. Best policy, right?" he said with a shrug that was followed by a wince of pain.

"Maybe not in this case, but okay," I said. "Here it is in a nutshell. I'm a vampire, recently bitten and turned, but I have an extended family bloodline of werewolves and vampires, both dating back before the birth of Jesus. Questions?"

Ben held his composure pretty well, and I could tell from his body language that he was receptive to the information. So far. If he had completely rejected it, it would have been his mind protecting itself, and thus resulting in a problem for both of us. This was a good sign.

"The warden, the one I met that day in the store, is she one too?"

"Yes. You sure you don't want another beer?"

This made Ben laugh, and it relieved me to see it. He would be fine, if he lived through this war, that is. Those close to me, percentage-wise, were not faring too well.

"What about Ted?"

"He got caught in the middle, just like you actually, and if not for a friend of mine, he would be dead right now. You think I look different?"

"No wonder I couldn't get in touch with you two."

I stood up and grabbed my keys.

"Listen, Ben. There's a lot going on, as I'm sure you can understand from your recent experience, and it needs to be dealt with. You can stay here as long as you like, and I recommend you do. You are free to go of course, like I told you before, but..."

"You have cable, right?"

I smiled and nodded.

"Then my ass will be right here when you get back."

"Good. Beer and food in the fridge. Help yourself."

I turned to leave. I needed to touch base with Ted and Deaglan, and sooner the better.

"Jack," Ben said, stopping me before I reached the door. "Witches aren't real too, are they?"

"Why did you say that?" I asked.

The urgency in my voice was obvious, and Ben picked up on it.

"The monster that kicked the shit out of me. I heard him talking to the other guy before you showed up. He said something about going to see a witch, just thought it was weird."

"Did he mention where the Witch was?"

"Seriously? Witches?"

"Ben, where?!"

Ben thought, searching his frayed memory with a look of defeat.

"Sorry. I'm not sure exactly, but the way he talked about it, I figured the place was right here in Ann Arbor."

It made perfect sense. That seemed just like a move that psycho would make. She could have been right under our noses the entire time.

I was about to leave again when Ben remembered something else. When he told me, a grin overtook my face.

"Ben, you may have just saved countless lives, including ours."

I made two quick phone calls while in the elevator and then headed toward the POH. I didn't make it.

104

The wall of wolves just outside the front doors of the building stopped my movement altogether. On pure reflex, I grabbed the first wolf in front of me by the neck just as the dart hit me in the back. I got lightheaded and blacked out within seconds.

When I woke, I saw Cynthia looking out the window of her makeshift apartment. It was an old office building that had been gutted and retrofitted with the basics. Very luxurious basics, but not what she was accustomed to. It was the perfect place, logistically speaking, to accomplish her goals. She had always been one step ahead, and now I saw why.

The building overlooked Main Street and provided an unobstructed view of the Piece of History. All the windows were heavily tinted. You could look out, but it was impossible to see in. With the right surveillance equipment, all of which she had, both video and audio, you could see and hear everything. It would be very easy to coordinate many tactical advantages from this very spot, which Cynthia, the Witch, did at an expert level. We never had a chance.

I was in the middle of a large open area surrounded by six large wolves. All of them had weapons at the ready.

"Catching you was easier than I thought. I assumed you would have been smarter than the others," she said. "Turns out you're more like your father than I thought."

"Thank you," I said, turning her insult into a compliment.

"He finally told you, did he? Shame, I was hoping to deliver the news myself. I love a surprise reveal, don't you?"

"If done right, yes," I said, looking around the room, evaluating all my options.

She sensed this right away.

"Before you decide to copy my escape plan," she said. "The windows are space-grade, bullet proof Plexiglas, and double thick."

"Thanks for the warning," I said. "That would've been embarrassing."

I was in a terrible position, and I knew it, but seeing the smugness of this woman who had killed so many of my friends and family made me angry.

"I'm curious. You could have captured me like this long ago. Why now?" I added.

I saw Cynthia crack an appreciative smile.

"How else was I going to get a large number of Elders in one place? The fire alone saved me centuries of meticulous planning and millions of dollars," she said as if she was talking about opening a new business. "With the last remaining Elders from Europe in town, I'm confident I'll be the last one before the end of the week. The leaves are changing in Salem, and I don't want to miss it."

"You really think you'll win, don't you?"

"My dear Jack, I've won. When the next phase of my plan is complete, and trust me when I tell you it will be soon, I'll be the most powerful person on the planet. Sorry in advance about killing everyone you hold dear, but my omelet needs some eggs."

She moved a little closer but still kept a fair distance. I know our last confrontation was still fresh in her mind.

"I imagine your little friends will meet at Theo's, as they usually do when there's a problem, to discuss how to find and save you. When the house explodes, caused by a faulty gas line of course, I will have accomplished almost everything I set out to do."

"Almost?"

"Yes. I'm thinking of dabbling in politics. Where else can I cause the most havoc among the humans?"

I could only shake my head in disgust.

"I really do hate the thought of killing you, though," she added.

"Imagine how I feel."

"I'm sure you understand, it's just business."

"I do understand. Just knowing how easily I could kill you has to make you nervous. I could kill you right now, well before your guards got a shot off."

I looked her in the eyes when I said this, gauging her reaction. She saw I wasn't lying, or at least I thought I was telling the truth. She tried to hide it, but I could tell this made her... uncomfortable.

"I don't think I will harm you though, at least not yet," I said.

I could tell from the squint in her eyes that my little comment unnerved her even more. She didn't like the direction the conversation was going. She smiled and then directed her attention to her guard, almost making a show of her next statement.

"Jerome. Is the good doctor here yet?" Cynthia said, looking around me.

The guard looked at his phone.

"Five minutes or less ma'am."

"Ah," I began, knowing that was for my benefit. "Harvest my DNA and become the strongest being alive."

"You sound skeptical."

"Not at all. I believe the science is legitimate and may even be available, it's just you that won't be."

The confidence in the way I said this caused even more doubt in her mind. She also questioned her ability to detect lies. That was troubling to her. My unique status, as it were, raised questions, but she knew more than anyone, I had only begun to discover myself.

"I think I've had enough of Jack's company. Could you take him into the other room and kill him please?" she said, looking at Jerome.

Jerome didn't move a muscle.

The Witch became instantly irate.

"Are you deaf? Now."

Again, nothing. Jerome stood still, staring at the Witch as if he was made of stone.

Then I chimed in.

"Jerome?"

"Yes, sir?" he said promptly.

"Are they on their way?"

"Yes, sir. Should just be a moment," he added.

"Great. How about you boys take a break -- no, make it a vacation. I'll talk to ya when you get back in town and square away the details of our arrangement," I said.

He smiled, gave a simple wave to the other guards with the guns, and all of them left the room together.

I watched them leave and then turned back to see the look on the Witch's face.

"How's that for a surprise reveal? Oh, don't forget about the glass."

The Witch looked dumbfounded. She had never been caught off guard like this in her life. The ruse at the Detroit apartment was a lapse of judgement, but this was well beyond that.

Before she could respond to the events unfolding in front of her, the door behind me opened. My friends, and new acquaintances, filed in one after another, creating a horseshoe around Cynthia.

Theo was the last to enter, shutting the door behind him.

The Witch eyed everyone in the room, wondering how this could have happened to her. And then she saw him.

"You," Cynthia growled, "I should have killed you years ago."

Wolfgang, who was next to Deaglan, took a step forward.

"Yes, I'm sure you wish you had," he said. "You left me a broken shell of myself after you killed my family. I can't tell you how satisfying it is to see you like this."

"You failed to adequately pay your debt to me. They had to pay it for you," she said without an ounce of remorse.

"You don't see the irony, do you?" Wolfgang continued, "Every favor you collected, and every valuable life you murdered, allowed this day to happen."

"This didn't help your cause either," Bili said as she held up a seemingly innocuous piece of paper. "Let me summarize it. I, the Witch bitch, plan to murder everyone but a select few to increase my power. The end."

"And once Wolfgang found your list of employees," Deaglan began. "It wasn't bloody hard to convince them that it was time to move on."

"You made the same mistake all psychotic wannabe dictators make," I said.

"Enlighten me," she said, pulling her intense glare from Deaglan to me.

"You thought fear was better than friendship and loyalty," I said, turning around and gesturing to the surrounding group. "You have never known this, and I can say with a healthy certainty, you never will. You lost."

I thought the Witch would at least try a diplomatic plea to save her life, but she was who she was. She was as evil as they came, and remorse was as foreign to her as compassion.

"I lost? Hmm, I see you are missing a few members of your clan," she said, looking back and forth, as if she was searching for specific individuals.

"Let's see... no Claude, Andrew, Allison, Lucinda, Harold, excuse me," she said, pausing to look at Bili. "I mean, Steve. Then there's the General and his men, which I took particular pride in."

The Witch took a step toward me, covered her face in a wide grin, and stared me dead in the face.

"Oh, and let's not forget the precious little human, your mother, Patr-"

Before my mother's name could fully escape her lips, the Witch's head hit the floor right at her feet. Her still standing body followed, toppling over, hitting the ground awkwardly.

I was now on the other side of the Witch, looking out the window, with just traces of blood clinging to my right hand.

The silence that followed was not from the fact that I killed the Witch, but how I had done it.

The combined years of existence in the room were significant, but no one had ever seen anything like what I had just done.

She made me so furious that my instinctual reaction was laser-focused and deadly. Where a fury like that came from, I didn't know. It was beyond the normal heated rage I would experience when I became angry. I was evolving more than anyone could have imagined.

Viki was the first to approach me. She tore off a piece of curtain from the Witch's fine drapery and used it as a rag to clean the blood from my hand.

"It's over," she said as she wiped my hand clean and threw the dirty cloth on the floor next to Cynthia's body.

I nodded and turned around to leave. The group was still looking on in awe until Theo and Bodicea started giving everyone jobs to do. We searched the place for every bit of intelligence we could find. Wolfgang took the computers and phones for further analysis. Word would spread about what happened here, not only from us, but from the newly freed Witch brigade as well.

Though we felt confident the war would quickly lose steam and end, there were still two problems to be dealt with. The twins.

105

Jack stopped talking, shifting his eyes toward the door. It was as if he had heard a loud noise.

Sara, who didn't hear a thing, looked in the same direction and then back at Jack.

"Something wrong?"

"Yes. I'm afraid we've run out of time."

The confusion on Sara's face was palpable.

"What do you mean? You haven't even told me what happened to my mother. You promised-"

"You don't understand," Jack said, cutting her off. "Get in here."

Jack was now out of his chair, looking out the window. He appeared to be listening more than looking.

"Get in where? What are you talking about?" Sara said, getting more frustrated.

"Sorry Doc, I didn't mean you."

Within seconds, Jack's door burst open and shut just as fast.

Sara turned around, surprised to see the person in front of her.

"Abigail, how did you get in here?" Sara said, getting up from her chair to meet her. "Let's get you back to your room."

"Sara!" Jack snapped, getting the doctor's attention. "Look at me."

Sara stopped and turned around.

"Sara, this is Bili," Jack said, gesturing to their guest.

Sara smirked, looked around the room, sure that a joke was being played on her.

"Sorry for all the dramatics, Doc, but we don't have much time. Sit down," Bili said, walking Sara back to the chair.

The doctor complied.

Knowing that there was no time for a long, drawn-out explanation, Bili cut to the chase, so to speak.

Bili pulled a knife from the rear of her belt.

"Give me your arm," she said, as Jack rolled up his sleeve and stuck his arm out.

"Don't get any on the floor," Jack said calmly.

Sara looked on in horror, seeing what was about to happen.

"Abby, uh, Bili, don't..."

Bili grabbed Jack's wrist, stuck the knife into Jack's forearm near the elbow, and dragged the blade to the base of his hand. As the cut opened, it closed and healed just as fast.

The doctor could only stare in awe.

It's all real.

"Doc, we really are short of time. Are you able to deal with this?"

Sara was stunned, but she kept her wits about her and handled the situation surprisingly well, considering what she had just witnessed.

Sara didn't answer verbally, but nodded, repeatedly.

"Good," Jack said. "Now, listen. There is a largescale incursion about to descend on this town, specifically, this hospital."

"What? Why? I thought you said the war was over?"

Sara couldn't believe she was asking a question that, by its very nature, was an acknowledgement that she believed everything she had been told. She just saw proof, leaving only two possibilities; she was hallucinating, or vampires and werewolves were real.

"The two problems I spoke of. We never found them. We figured they went into hiding, never to be heard from again. That was until Theo received word from Wolfgang, years later, who had continued to monitor the situation. He intercepted numerous disturbing communications, one of which indicated they were close to finding you."

"Why are they coming here?" Sara asked. Worry now replacing disbelief.

"Because of you," Bili said. "Haven't you been paying attention?"

The snide comment brought Sara back to reality and helped her focus.

"Yes, *Bilinda*, I have," Sara said, returning her look, "but why, exactly?"

"With the advancements in DNA, you have become the most sought-after human in the world. No offense, but you're an easy target, relatively speaking," Jack said.

"They want Jack's power, and you may hold the secret. You are their last hope, and somehow your identity and general location were compromised," Bili said.

"And they have just filled in the last piece of the puzzle," Jack added.

Sara's head was spinning with this unbelievable information.

"So, why the ruse? Couldn't you have just told me all of this in a meeting?"

"I thought you were a psychiatrist." Bili said, not quite rolling her eyes, but close. "You just saw undeniable proof, yet you are still unsure what's real."

Sara gave Jack an incredulous look.

"You're right, she is a smart ass," Sara said.

Jack ignored Sara's response but expounded on Bili's.

"Had we come in cold your brain would not have had the time to process, or mentally prepare for you for this reality. Isn't that possible?" Jack said.

Sara's silence was a tacit acknowledgment.

"Not only did we need time to convince you of the truth, but we also had to keep up appearances."

"What do you mean?" Sara asked.

"We needed our bait to act like bait," Bili said, not mincing words.

Sara could only shake her head, still coming to grips with this.

"One more thing, Doc," Jack said.

"What?"

"You have to make a choice, and you have to make it right now."

106

"What choice?"

Jack and Bili leaned a little closer to Sara, attempting to be more sincere and comforting.

"He's offering you the gift of a lifetime," Bili said, raising her eyebrows, hoping Sara could read between the lines.

It only took a second or two before she understood what Bili was talking about.

"Wait... seriously?"

Sara leaned back, took a deep breath, and started shaking her head, as if to clear it.

Is this really happening?

"No, no... no. I don't think I can do that," Sara said, trying to comprehend what was being offered.

It's not an easy thing to contemplate every imaginable, and unimaginable, consequence of such a choice. Let alone to do it in a span of one minute.

Jack looked at Bili, both thinking the same thing.

"It's the hard way then," Jack said. "How close?"

"The first car is almost here," Bili said. "And they're coming from different directions and intervals just as Wolfgang suspected. We'll be lucky to make it out with her like this."

Just then, Bili pulled a cell phone from her pocket and looked at the screen.

"Shit. Another car just entered the parking lot. We are too scattered to mount an adequate defense. We have to find a way out of this hospital without being seen."

"Are any of my staff in danger?" Sara asked, as she stood from the chair.

"Yes, and so are we, move your ass, Doc," Bili said, now looking out the door window.

It was clear, so Bili used a swipe card she had just pulled from her pocket and opened the door.

"How did you get that?" Sara said, stalling her retreat.

"Let's go," Jack said. "We don't have time."

Sara grabbed Jack by the sleeve.

"We have to get Nancy. Get her, or I'm not moving."

Jack shook his head and then looked at Bili.

"I'll get her," Bili said. "Start heading to the rear of the hospital. We'll catch up."

"Please be careful. Not Bili careful, normal careful," Jack said.

Bili took off in a sprint. Sara watched Bili run and then turned to Jack.

"Yes, she's fast. Let's move."

Sara thought about the best route and moved swiftly toward the laundry rooms.

"There might be something this way," she said.

Jack followed as Sara directed him to the last room on the left. She peaked in, found it clear, and swiped her card to get in.

They were checking the large room for another way out when Bili came in, carrying Nancy in her arms.

Sara looked at Nancy, held up her hand and nodded, letting Nancy know it was okay, though it clearly wasn't.

"Shit!" Jack said. "This room has no exit, and the windows are too high to get them through."

A loud scream echoed through the halls of the hospital. Then another.

Jack and Bili got in front of Nancy and Sara.

"What are you doing?" Sara asked.

"We have no choice now. We have to fight. When we are engaged in the fight, you two get out of this room and run north. Someone should be in the area to help you."

"There's a door to a sub-floor behind the large dryers," Nancy said, pointing.

"Where does it lead?" Bili asked.

"To the West annex building in the middle of the parking lot. The tunnel is a good fifty yards or so."

Jack kissed Nancy on the cheek and ran to the door. She didn't know the full extent of the danger they were in, but this was exciting stuff and she loved it.

The panel in the floor had a thick lock on it, causing Nancy's smile to fade.

"I don't have the key," Nancy said.

Jack grabbed the handle and yanked it, sending pieces of steel flying in several directions. Once the door opened, it revealed a ladder going down to a basement.

Nancy's eyes widened.

"You two first," Jack said. "Down you go."

There were more screams, but now they were getting closer.

"Quickly," Bili said urgently, but quietly.

After they were all safely down the ladder, Jack gently closed the hatch door, causing everything to go black. Within seconds, Nancy found the light switch at the bottom.

The lights flickered, and then they came to life.

"You are surprisingly handy to have around," Bili said.

"I know, dear. It's my job."

There were two separate hallways leading in different directions.

"Which way," Jack asked, looking to Nancy for the answer.

Nancy pointed down a long narrow hallway that went to the right.

"At the end of this corridor, we make a left, and there will be an elevator that leads to the garage of the West annex."

Bili's phone vibrated, and she answered it.

"We're in a basement tunnel heading to the annex building out in the parking lot," Bili said into the phone. She listened for another few seconds and then disconnected.

"Theo wants me to get these two out of the area while you guys find that crazy bitch and put her lights out," Bili said to Jack.

Jack nodded and looked at Sara.

"You'll be safe with Bili. I'll meet you guys right after we get this situation handled."

They were now at the elevator door. Jack hit the square button, engaging the red neon light around the edge.

"Good luck, cousin," Sara said, forcing a thin-lipped, worried smile.

Jack returned it in kind.

"You too."

Jack gave Bili a quick nod as the elevator door chimed and opened.

"Jack!" Nancy yelled.

Just as Jack turned, a large vampire was on top of him. Jack got the better of him, grabbed him by the neck, squeezed until he went unconscious, and then snapped his neck.

Jack dropped him to the floor, and only then did he see Parrus, who was directly behind the big vampire pointing a gun. She was already pulling the trigger before Jack could move.

Jack's body buckled as the bullets struck him, one after another, all of them in the chest. Parrus then kicked Jack, sending him flying backwards.

Sara screamed in horror as Jack fell lifelessly to the ground after hitting the wall. She ran to his side as Bili charged Parrus, dodging the first shot and getting the gun from her hand.

As the two fought, Nancy crouched down into a ball with her hands over her head. The damage they were creating was unbelievable.

Parrus grabbed a large iron pipe from a nearby worktable and hit Bili in the back of head. Bili went unconscious and fell limp to the floor.

Sara was shaking Jack endlessly, as Parrus looked on in delight.

"Jack... Jack," Sara said, just above a whisper, shaking him vigorously, trying to rouse him.

"Sorry doctor, but I'm fairly certain your psych degree won't be much use in this situation," Parrus said with joy in her voice.

Sara turned to look at Parrus, and the smugness on her face caused a mild burning in Sara's core like she had never felt before. When she thought of her father, it burned hotter.

Parrus walked past Nancy and wiggled her fingers at her as if she was waving to a small child in a parade. Parrus let her be, knowing her prize was waiting in front of her.

Sara was forced to face the fact that she could die at the hands of beings she never believed existed. Her mind raced as she contemplated any possible solution to her predicament. It was in that split second she realized she only had one option. It was time to find out if she was in a dream world, or not.

Parrus continued to walk forward as Sara knelt next to Jack's body. Using her back to shield what she was doing, Sara stuck her hand in Jack's mouth and brought her knee up with force, striking Jack's chin. Jack's teeth punctured Sara's hand just as Parrus pulled her from the ground. With one hand, Parrus maneuvered Sara's body to face her.

"What a shame I have to kill you, after harvesting your DNA, of course. I would have liked to talk to you about some lingering issues I've been told I have," Parrus said as she dangled Sara in front of her.

Sara had her eyes closed, struggling to free herself from Parrus' grip.

"Nothing to say?" Parrus said, with a condescending tilt of her head. "Probably just as well, as no one is able to hear you. Well, no one who cares."

Just as Parrus finished her sentence, Sara slowly opened her eyes.

Her... icy... gray... eyes.

"What the-"

Before she could finish, Sara grabbed Parrus by her throat while simultaneously breaking the grip with her left. Now it was Parrus who was in the air. Every pent-up emotion she had regarding her mom and dad came to the surface. It was gasoline on a fire.

Sara threw Parrus against the wall as hard as she could, causing Parrus to fall awkwardly to the ground. Sara's attention was briefly diverted to

Nancy, who was running toward her. Nancy ran behind Sara just as Parrus got back up, now holding the metal rod in her hand again.

"This may hurt a little, doctor," Parrus said as she raised the steel bar over her head, about to strike.

Her forward momentum was halted when Bili grabbed her hand and spun her around. At the same time, Sara shot forward, grabbed the metal bar from her hand, and with lightning speed, drove it through Parrus' chest.

Parrus was still conscious as blood dribbled from her mouth. Parrus smiled and spit blood on Sara's white jacket.

"If anything happens to me, my brother will kill you all. And then everyone you ever loved."

Bili watched and waited, but not for very long.

"You mean like this?"

Sara pushed the bar up, and then back down, further tearing Parrus' heart and arteries. She then pulled the bar from Parrus' chest, repositioned it in her hand and shoved it through Parrus' left eye and into the cement wall behind her.

Bili let go, and her body stayed where it was, hanging from the steel bar.

Sara and Bili ran to Jack's side, just as the wounds healed. Sara pulled him up with one hand, shaking her head in relief at his recovery.

"I think you made the right choice," Jack said, before turning toward Nancy. "What do you think?"

"I don't know who you people are, or what is going on, but I hope I can be a part of it," Nancy said.

Sara walked over and gave Nancy a hug.

"You are one strange woman, you know that?"

"This isn't over," Bili said, and then turned to look at Nancy. "Can you stay hidden here until we get back?"

She nodded, "Go get those fuckers."

Jack, Bili, and Sara went up the elevator, taking Parrus' corpse with them. They had one more problem to resolve.

107

Sara opened the door to her home, and Bili, Nancy, and Jack followed her inside. After a few minutes, there was a knock at the door. Sara opened it up to find several more guests. Most of whom she recognized just from Jack's description of them during the story.

"Please, come in," Sara said. "Make yourselves at home."

Theo, Deaglan, Ted, and Viki came in next.

"Hey babe, any luck?" Jack said as he kissed Viki when she came in.

"Crazy number two got away, but we're pretty sure his gang has scattered to the wind. I don't think they were expecting any kind of resistance, let alone what they encountered."

Theo made his way to Sara. "Thanks for letting us use your place. A secluded mountain home seemed preferable to our hotel rooms," he said with a pleasant smile.

"Yeah, I think we would have made quite the scene. And can I say, I'm glad you aren't really a Detective with the State Police. You had me a little nervous."

"Yes, sorry about that. Needed to see the lay of the land, as it were. You've had quite a day, and I must say, you've handled yourself beyond expectation."

Sara gave Theo a long hug. When she let go, she looked over at Jack.

"He does make you feel better, doesn't he?"

"Told ya. Hey, there are a few more of us that could really use the amenities here, is that okay?"

"Of course. More the merrier. Hey everyone, give me anything dirty and/or covered in blood. I might as well get that taken care of right away."

"See, women are always multi-tasking," Bili said, looking at Ted.

"Jack, she's doing it again," Ted said in a mocking childish tone.

"Best behavior kids, we have a newbie trying to adjust."

Jack smiled at Sara as he took off his blood-stained jacket and shirt. "The burn pit would probably be best for these."

"Yep. Don't think I could explain bullet holes and blood to the local sheriff," Sara said sarcastically. "The drink fridge is in the garage if anyone needs anything."

Bili had grabbed some stained clothing from some of the others as well.

"I'll give you a hand. I think we may have a few loads worth," Bili said.

"Thanks. You know, you really do look like an Abigail," Sara said playfully.

"I know. It was my mother's name, so it makes sense, right?

Sara's smile left her as she dropped the clothing in the laundry room. The change in Sara's demeanor when Bili mentioned her mother didn't go unnoticed.

"Just throw the rest in the fire pit in the backyard. I'll take care of it later," Sara said. "Excuse a minute, will you."

Bili watched as Sara went into the bathroom and shut the door.

Sara took a minute to suppress her emotions and took a few deep breaths. She washed her face and hands in the sink, getting every drop of blood off her skin. When she wiped her face with a towel and set it down, she looked in the mirror for the first time since the change. She couldn't believe her eyes.

Oh my.

Sara touched her face, over and over, making sure it was really her. The change in her eye color was drastic, but the subtle changes in her overall appearance made her look even more different. She flexed her hands back and forth, feeling the strength within them. Everything Jack had described about himself during this process was true to her. It was delightfully strange. If only...

Sara heard the door open and more guests coming in. She would deal with her new self later, now she felt the need to get back to the group. She opened the bathroom door and froze in place. She found herself face-to-face with another woman.

"Hello, Pumpkin."

Sara sprung forward without hesitation and grabbed her mother in a tight hug. If there were vampires, maybe there were ghosts too. Clara was real, however, and they squeezed each other tighter and tighter. After a few minutes of joyful tears, Sara released her embrace to look at her mom.

"I was sure Jack was going to tell me you were dead. I can't believe you're here, I can't. I missed you terribly," Sara said, giving Clara another tight hug.

"I'm so proud of you, honey," she said. "I never thought this day would come. Other than when you were born, this is the best day of my life."

Sara could sense what Clara was feeling. Reading the most subtle of clues. It truly was incredible.

"It's not your fault mom, it's not," Sara said, knowing what her mom was thinking. "I would have done the same thing."

Clara smiled, wiped the tears from Sara's cheek, and motioned with her head to come back out to the living room.

"There are a few others I want you to meet."

Sara followed her mom out into the living room, and she suddenly felt as though she was on a stage. Everyone in the room went quiet, as they all knew what an extraordinary event had just taken place. It was a wonderful moment.

There was one more knock on the door, and Sara saw Theo open it, letting in another woman, and two more men. She was striking. Theo kissed her and then walked her to Sara for a proper introduction.

"Sara, this is Bodicea. You may recognize her as well," Theo said with a sly grin.

Sara shook her hand and smiled.

"I do indeed. I saw you in the coffee shop. You all really had me covered. Thank you everyone, for all you've done for me," Sara said, turning to face the group.

Everyone settled in, and after Sara opened a few bottles of wine, the stories started to come out, one by one. Sara listened with her new ears and enjoyed the company of her new friends and family. It was as if she had known these people for years. Jack's story really did help with the acclimation to her new world, though Sara had no ambition to tell him that. She was the doctor, after all.

The madness at the hospital was attributed to a crazy cult, hell bent on getting revenge after their founder died in the hospital. At least that's what the anonymous letter said, taking responsibility for the attack. There were several injuries, and one death that resulted from the incursion. It was a tragedy, to be sure, but it could have been much worse.

After a few hours of catching up with Clara, Sara found Jack in the living room, chatting with Viki and Ted.

"Hey, can I talk to you a moment?"

"Of course, let's go outside," Jack said, knowing that Sara wanted a little privacy.

Sara's backyard butted up against endless forest, leading up an enormous mountain. They walked to the end of her backyard, a good distance from the house.

Jack looked at Sara, knowing just about everything that was going through her mind, as he had been there himself.

"So, I'm guessing things worked out with Viki?"

"I guess you could say that," Jack said. "We've been married for years."

The sun was setting over the mountain, creating beautiful rays of sunshine through the trees.

"What happened to Tanzy?"

"Moved back to London after Viki came back in my life. I felt bad for her. She's a terrific woman, but no Viktoria."

Jack then turned to face his cousin.

"Now ask me what you really want to know."

"What am I?" Sara asked. "I have listened to you, very carefully I might add, and I'm still confused."

"You are you, and nothing less."

Sara cocked her head in such a way that a blind man could see that she was not accepting that for an answer.

Jack relented.

"There *may* be no one on this planet like me," Jack said, pausing briefly. "But I'm certain there's no one like you. You are in uncharted waters. Let's just say, I'm glad we're family."

Sara smiled and gave Jack a big hug.

"I have a family again," she said.

"We both do, and that's the most important thing. Though not as important, there is one other item I didn't have time to mention, for obvious reasons."

Sara stood up a little straighter, unsure where the conversation was going.

"What?"

"Remember the lawyer that contacted you the other day?"

"Yeah. What about him?"

"He is in charge of transferring your inheritance. Twenty million isn't going to make you the richest person in North Carolina, but it's all that Emily had."

Sara blinked a few times before she could think of anything to say. "Excuse me?"

Jack shrugged.

"I know what you're thinking, but don't worry, if you run low, you can always start your own practice," Jack said with a wry smile. "Enough about that, your mother will fill you in on the details. How about we go back in and enjoy the company?"

"That's the best thing I've heard in years."

ABOUT THE AUTHOR

James Herberger is an American novelist, a cold case detective for the prosecutors office in Detroit, and a United States Air Force veteran. In between story ideas he and his wife spend their time watching their son play soccer.

www.ingramcontent.com/pod-product-compliance
Lightning Source LLC
Chambersburg PA
CBHW022235020726
47496CB00004B/917